COVER-UP

COVER-UP

Michele Martinez

An Imprint of HarperCollins*Publishers*

COVER-UP. Copyright © 2007 by Michele Rebecca Martinez Campbell. All rights reserved. Printed in the United States of America. No part of this book may be used or reproduced in any manner whatsoever without written permission except in the case of brief quotations embodied in critical articles and reviews. For information address HarperCollins Publishers, 10 East 53rd Street, New York, NY 10022.

HarperCollins books may be purchased for educational, business, or sales promotional use. For information please write: Special Markets Department, HarperCollins Publishers, 10 East 53rd Street, New York, NY 10022.

FIRST HARPERLUXE EDITION

Library of Congress Cataloging-in-Publication Data

Martinez, Michele, 1962–
  Cover-up / Michele Martinez.—1st ed.
    p.   cm.
  ISBN: 978-0-06-089900-4
  ISBN-10: 0-06-089900-X
  1. Vargas, Melanie (Fictitious character)—Fiction. 2. Public prosecutors—Fiction. 3. Women lawyers—Fiction. 4. Women television journalists—Crimes against—Fiction. 5. Manhattan (New York, N.Y.)—Fiction.   I. Title.

PS3613.A78648C68 2007
813'.6—dc22   2006050199

ISBN: 978-0-06-123314-2 (Luxe)
ISBN-10: 0-06-123314-5

 07 08 09 10 11 ID/RRD 10 9 8 7 6 5 4 3 2 1

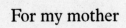
For my mother

ACKNOWLEDGMENTS

I have the amazing good fortune to work with three of the best women in publishing. My agent, Meg Ruley, my editor, Carolyn Marino, and my publicist, Dee Dee DeBartlo, not only contributed hugely to this book, but they make every day of this job fun. I am also grateful to all of the other wonderful people at the Jane Rotrosen Agency (especially Don Cleary, Peggy Gordijn, and Christina Hogrebe) and at HarperCollins (especially Lisa Gallagher, Michael Morrison, Lynn Grady, Liate Stehlik, Jennifer Civiletto, and Wendy Lee) who do so much for me.

I'm lucky to be able to call upon colleagues from my law enforcement days when memory fails or when I need to catch up with changing times. I am indebted to Eric Friedberg, former chief of narcotics in the EDNY

U.S. Attorney's Office, now one of the nation's leading experts on computer crimes; Christopher Falkenberg of Insite Security, formerly a special agent with the U.S. Secret Service; and Special Agent John Kleczkowski of DEA, who's still fighting the good fight. They gave generously of their time and knowledge; any errors or exaggerations are mine alone.

Many thanks to Micah Fink for reading and commenting on an early draft of this book. His insightful comments improved it greatly.

I am grateful to Dean Larry Kramer and the terrific staff at the Stanford Law School Alumni Office for their extraordinary support. Susan Charlton is a happy and successful lawyer in large part because of the three joyous years she spent in Palo Alto.

Love and gratitude to Mom/M and Dad/B for giving me shelter and sustenance when I needed to disappear and write. And of course none of this would be possible without the love and support of my three great guys—my husband, Jeffrey, and my sons, Jack and Will—who have endless patience and enthusiasm for my writing career.

ONE

D on't say I didn't warn you."

FBI Agent Dan O'Reilly looked through his windshield at the large crowd milling on Fifth Avenue. It was eleven o'clock on a rainy Wednesday night in June, but the blazing spotlights from the television news vans made it feel like high noon. His companion in the car, federal prosecutor Melanie Vargas, was surveying the scene with obvious alarm. Here and there, recognizable faces stood out—celebrity reporters from the local news channels.

"You didn't warn me about *this*," Melanie said.

"Famous victim. You've got to expect press."

The NYPD had set up a barricade at the Seventy-ninth Street entrance to Central Park. Inside the gates, a short walk into the Ramble, a tabloid-TV personality lay dead. Suzanne Shepard, the glamorous blond scan-dalmonger, had been viciously raped and stabbed, and Dan and Melanie had come to view the crime scene. But after a tough year, Melanie was fighting serious burnout, and she hardly needed a high-profile case right now. Twenty minutes earlier, she'd been enjoying a romantic evening, getting hot and heavy with Dan on her living-room sofa after taking him to dinner for his birthday. She hadn't been in the market for anything like this. Then his pager started shrieking.

"Press coverage kicks everything up a notch," Melanie said. "More pressure. More scrutiny. I should never have let you drag me out here."

"Admit it. You can't say no to me."

In the semidarkness of the car, Dan smiled. He had a movie-star smile, a football-hero body, and intense blue eyes. He was right. These days, Melanie wasn't refusing him much. Which probably wasn't the smart-est move mere months after she'd divorced her cheat-ing husband, and with a little girl to raise.

"You're full of yourself, O'Reilly," she said.

Dan edged his G-car toward the barricade. Several cameramen walked backward in front of them, film-ing them through the car windows.

"I can't believe this. Look at these guys," Melanie said.

"Didn't you tell me your boss was pissed at you for turning down that terrorism financing case?" Dan asked.

"What choice did I have? It involved overseas travel, and I can't leave Maya."

"Bring in a big murder case," Dan said. "Bernadette'll love you again."

"You know what they say. Big cases, big problems. Little cases, little problems. No cases, no problems."

"You know what else they say. No cases, no job. Trust me, you'll be up on the dais accepting Prosecutor of the Year on this one. Then you'll thank me."

Dan rolled his window down, and they both handed over their credentials to the cop stationed there, who studied them and proceeded to consult with somebody over a walkie-talkie. After a few minutes, he handed the creds back, pulled the barricade aside, and waved them through. Melanie had pushed Maya's stroller through this very gate more times than she could count, but in the reassuring light of day. She wished mightily that she were doing that now. The park looked so different at night. Strange shadows loomed between the arcs of yellow light spilling from the lampposts, and branches flapped in the wet wind. What had happened to the old Melanie? Time was, she would've been eating this up instead of feeling the butterflies.

They drove as far as the Boathouse before the path became too narrow for the G-car to pass. A traffic jam of blue-and-whites and American-made sedans with tinted windows had all stopped at the same place, parked every which way in front of the ornate brick building. Their drivers were nowhere in sight. Slapping a police placard in the front windshield, Dan got out and came around to open Melanie's door.

"At least the service is good," she said, stepping out. He closed the door with a thud, and the sound seemed to echo in the gloom all around them.

"Not as good as what you're gonna get later. I wasn't done with you." Dan winked at her, giving her a jolt right down to her toes.

It was a warm, rainy night, and the sky above them glowed lurid orange with reflected light from the city. They passed through a gate to enter the Ramble, and the manicured park immediately turned wild and overgrown, smelling of wet earth and rotting leaves. The woods closed in on either side, so the footpath was barely wide enough for two people to walk abreast. She couldn't see more than a few feet ahead. The ground was broken and uneven, and Melanie was glad she'd chosen boots with sturdy soles. A sudden scurrying noise in the underbrush made her start.

"You okay?" Dan asked.

"Yeah. Just a squirrel."

"Or a rat. This is Central Park after all."

"Thanks a lot."

"I'd try to take him out with my Glock, but I haven't been to the range lately."

Melanie laughed. "Oh, that gives me a lot of confidence."

The path sloped upward and opened onto a vista that would have been beautiful if it weren't swarming with cops and blazing with strange artificial light. Portable klieg lamps had been set up around the edges of a ravine that dropped off precipitously from the pathway. Beyond the ravine—which measured maybe twenty feet deep by fifty feet wide—an inlet of the Central Park Lake glittered and a spectacular weeping willow swayed in the wet wind. Below, crime-scene detectives in protective white coveralls and face masks were busy photographing, bagging, marking, and sampling, their grim faces washed out to sepia hues by the glare.

Melanie and Dan came to a halt by necessity. Both the path ahead and the steep trail down into the ravine where the detectives worked were blocked off with police barricades.

"There's Brennan," Dan said. He cupped his hands around his mouth. "Yo, Butch! Up here."

A tall, stocky man standing knee-deep in the underbrush in the middle of the ravine looked up. Butch Brennan was the supervisor of the crime-scene team, an old-timer, nearing retirement now, who'd waded through oceans of gore in his day without losing his happy-go-lucky attitude. In fact, the more brutal the crime, the more cheerful Butch got. And Melanie could tell that he was smiling broadly through his face mask now as he gave them a peppy wave.

"He looks way too happy," Melanie said. "I'm going home."

"You can't leave. It's pitch-dark, and there's a killer on the loose."

"Stay there!" Butch yelled. "I'm coming to get youse!"

Melanie shielded her eyes against the glare and watched Butch Brennan clamber up the side of the ravine. He picked his way carefully along a ragged schist outcropping, then doubled back toward them, careful not to disturb anything in the cordoned-off areas.

"Dan, Melanie," Butch said, nodding, breathing heavily as he yanked off a paper face mask. "Glad to see the feds on the case. We need all the help we can get."

"That doesn't sound good," Melanie commented.

"It's not," Butch said. "Whoever did this is a major psycho. Janice Marsh from the D.A.'s office was here before. She saw the body, turned green, and ran off to hurl. Haven't seen her since."

"What's so bad?" Dan asked.

"The victim's hacked all to shit," Butch said, "and the killer carved 'bitch' in her stomach with a hunting knife. I'll tell you, I thought about puking myself, and I've seen everything."

"The D.A.'s office has dibs," Melanie said to Dan. "I should bow out." Melanie was a federal prosecutor, from the U.S. Attorney's Office, whereas the D.A. was state. The two offices were constantly engaged in turf battles. Melanie wasn't just looking for an excuse here. It a situation like this, the politics could get tricky.

"My boss worked out the turf issues already with Manhattan North Homicide," Dan said. "The investigation is joint state-federal. If the Bureau and the NYPD can play nice, I'm sure you can get along with the D.A.'s office."

"Don't leave, really," Butch said. "Janice ain't coming back anytime soon. We need a prosecutor with a strong stomach on this case. I've seen you in action, Melanie. I know you can handle yourself," Butch said.

Given the mood she was in, the fact that the A.D.A. had vomited and fled the scene should've made Melanie run screaming all the way back to her apartment. But Butch Brennan wasn't one to hand out compliments lightly, and his vote of confidence managed to scratch the surface of her attitude. If she said no, she'd risk losing Butch's regard, and that wouldn't feel good.

"If you think so, Butch," she said.

Just then, the wind shifted. A warm mist blew into Melanie's face, coming from the direction of the lake. It carried a whiff of something sharp that cut right through the lush scent of water and woods. A gamy, metallic odor Melanie recognized from crime scenes past, and from a terrible night in her own childhood when violence had invaded her home. Blood.

"I do think so," Butch said. "Let's go have a look."

TWO

In order to view the body, Melanie and Dan were required to don the white jumpsuits, shoe covers, and face masks worn by the crime-scene detectives. The suits were constructed from a space-age slippery microfiber that made Melanie feel like she was embarking on a trip to Mars. As Butch Brennan gave them a rundown of the other forensic evidence on their way down into the ravine, and the brutality of the crime became increasingly evident to her, a feeling that she'd stepped into some sick alternate universe took hold of her.

"Assailant attacked the victim on the path up ahead here. He may have used a stun gun to subdue her, based on a small lesion on the side of her neck, three marks in a triangular formation. Then he stabbed her. There's a shitload of blood. Lucky the rain let up. It didn't wash away," he said, unclipping a heavy rubber flashlight from his tool belt and training its beam on a cordoned-off portion of blacktop. Melanie couldn't see anything but wet black pavement.

"It don't look like much to the naked eye, but it's there," Butch said. "When we sprayed the Luminol, the place lit up like the Fourth of July. We took infrared photos and samples of the victim's blood. We also got what we believe to be samples of the killer's DNA."

"How'd you get that?" Melanie asked.

"The victim was sexually assaulted, and we swabbed. Plus she had long fingernails, and we took scrapings from under 'em. From that, and the defensive wounds on her arms, I'm betting she got her licks in. Our subject's walking around with some nasty scratches and maybe a few contusions into the bargain."

"So you'll submit those DNA samples to the FBI database for comparison?" Melanie asked. As reluctant as she'd been to come out, her brain was kicking in now, working on the puzzle.

"We'll do that. Not to rain on your parade, but just remember you only get a match if your killer was gentleman enough to provide his DNA profile to the FBI in advance. Otherwise there's nothing in the CODIS database to match our sample to," Butch said.

"I understand," Melanie said. "Now, from the spatters, you think she was actually attacked here in the Ramble? Not attacked elsewhere and dumped here?"

"The attack definitely happened here," Butch replied.

"Huh," Melanie said, interested. "What's a woman doing walking around alone in the Ramble at night?"

"Oh," Butch said, "you mean because it's—"

"A major gay cruising location. Suzanne Shepard was a reporter in this town for a long time. You'd think she'd know that. Besides, it was raining. Not a terrific night for a jog in the park."

"The forensics can't tell us why she was here," Butch said. "But maybe they'll tell us a thing or two about why she was killed. To me, looking at the brutality of the crime, it fits with a PCP or meth killing."

"PCP's over, and there's no meth in New York," Dan said, shaking his head.

"That's not true; meth's everywhere now," Melanie said. "DEA's been bringing us a lot of those cases."

"Whatever drug it was," Butch said, "I'm thinking maybe a junkie confronted her, tried to rob her, she resisted, and it went south from there. The uniforms who notified next of kin radioed back that the victim was wearing diamond earrings and a gold Rolex when she left home this morning, which she ain't now."

"Would a junkie rape her, though?" Melanie asked. "The rape strikes me as more consistent with a random sex crime."

"I hear you, but on the other hand, would a rapist rob her?" Butch asked. "This scumbag went through her wallet. We found it next to the body with streaks of talcum powder visible on the leather. The cash was gone, and her driver's license. But the credit cards were still there. That's a little unusual. Most killers who boost a wallet just grab the fucking thing and run."

"Talcum-powder marks. What's that about?" Melanie asked.

"Surgical gloves. They must've been wet from the rain, and the residue transferred. We found powder spots on her clothing, too."

The little hairs on the back of Melanie's neck stood up. "What kind of junkie wears surgical gloves? That sounds like a psycho-serial-killer move. Maybe even somebody experienced, who's committed similar acts before," she said.

"A sexual sadist?" Dan asked. "That would fit with what he carved on her stomach."

"Either way, it sounds like a random killing. I don't like that," Melanie said.

"Random is a lot tougher to crack than something targeted," Dan agreed.

"What do you think, Butch?" Melanie asked.

"From what I've seen, nothing points to the victim knowing her attacker. The stun-gun mark tells me he had a plan to subdue her, so it's not like he was somebody she trusted, who was counting on getting close before he attacked. As for the writing on her stomach, it's hard to say. Could go either way—a robbery, a sex slay. Or even somebody who hated her show, though God knows, that don't narrow it down much," Butch said with a chuckle.

"I never saw that show," Dan said. "*High Crimes*, right?"

"Yeah, what a load of crap," Butch said. "She was always slinging the muck about famous people, digging around in their dirty laundry. But listen to me. I watched it."

"You and a lot of other people," Dan said.

"Hmm, I bet she had a lot of enemies," Melanie said thoughtfully.

"Anyways, getting back to what I was saying," Butch said, "after he stabbed her, he dragged her across this patch of dirt. We got a few footprints, so we're making some casts for you for trial."

Butch directed the flashlight beam down at a section of ground that was studded with rectangular wood frames containing hardening plaster.

"Then he tossed her over the edge of the ravine like a sack of garbage. *Boom.* She lands down there. He goes down after her. It's nice and private down there. We believe the sexual assault took place in the ravine, after the stabbing. And now let's go take a look at what's left."

Melanie nodded, and she and Dan followed Butch wordlessly down into the ravine. The bottom was soft earth covered in ferns and underbrush and bathed in cold white light from the klieg lamps. In the other-worldly glare, Melanie felt like she was sleepwalking. Spacewalking was more like it. As Butch led them toward the body, and the gamy smell grew stronger, she felt numb. She'd been through the crime-scene wringer before on other cases. You'd think it would get easier, but far from it. Lately the job only got harder.

They were right upon the victim now, yet the body was barely visible. The ground sloped down toward the lake, and the victim had landed with her head pointing in that same direction. Her head, torso, and upper legs disappeared into the thick underbrush, obscured by low bushes and dripping ferns. Only her lower legs and feet stuck out, twisted oddly inward. The right leg was completely naked and glowed a dead white punctuated by dark clumps of dried blood. The left leg was partly bare and partly twined in a coiled mess of blood-sopped khaki pants and underwear, its foot still clad in a tan moccasin.

"We photographed the area with the leaves covering her, just like this, which is how we found her. Then we held 'em aside and took pictures of the wounds. After the ME bags her and hauls her off, we'll cut away all the brush and do a final sweep for anything we missed because of the ground cover."

"Okay, good," Melanie forced herself to say. Part of her wanted to run, and part of her knew she needed to stay now and bear witness to this horrible crime. God, human beings were evil.

"He taped her hands and mouth. Plain packing tape like you could buy in any hardware or moving-supply store. We can try to print it, but again, he wore gloves, so my guess is we'll come up empty. I'm gonna show you her face so's you trust my ID, but I'm warning you, it ain't pretty. Ready?"

Melanie nodded mutely, and Butch used his probe to sweep aside the wet ferns that obscured the victim's head.

Suzanne Shepard's mouth, visible through strips of blood-smeared plastic packing tape, was twisted into a grimace of the starkest horror. Her blue eyes were open and vacant, but wide with shock, and the black blood that had sprayed up to dot her face looked like so many flies swarming. She'd died in agony; you could see it in her expression, and yet the cool, beautiful TV star was still recognizable in the gruesome corpse. Seeing a celebrity in the flesh always felt surreal. Melanie's occasional close encounters—Mary Tyler Moore buying a sweater at Bendel's, Kelly Ripa eating ice cream with her kids—had been disorienting just because it was bizarre to realize that television stars existed in real life. But a famous person dead, and brutally, horribly so? Beyond weird.

"It's definitely her," Dan said. He took Melanie's arm to steady her, looking concerned, and she managed a nod to let him know she was okay. Butch was right. She did have a strong stomach. She could handle this, and she liked that about herself. She took a deep breath through her mouth so she could get oxygen without inhaling the stench of blood.

"Here's what we think is a stun-gun mark," Butch said, using his pointer to indicate three tiny burn marks arranged in a triangular pattern on the side of Suzanne Shepard's elegant neck. "Public place, it makes sense he would stun her and gag her to reduce noise."

"How long would a stun gun knock her out for?" Melanie asked.

"It wouldn't knock her out at all," Dan said, shaking his head. "To make somebody lose consciousness, you have to maintain the electrical connection between the stun gun and the skin for several seconds. That's harder than you'd think. Probably he just shocked her enough to get the jump on her."

"Now get a load of this," Butch said. "The main event. This part, I need to be careful, because it's important. We took pictures, but the ME'll want it clean for the autopsy."

Butch knelt down and carefully held aside a low-lying branch that had concealed the woman's torso, then shined his flashlight beam directly on it.

"Jesus!" Dan exclaimed, recoiling.

Melanie gasped and jerked her eyes away, closing them instinctively to shield herself from the monstrous sight. But it stayed with her anyway, vibrating against her eyelids, so after a moment she opened them again, swallowing hard to fight back the sour taste rising in her throat.

A pink cotton sweater was bunched up near the victim's underarms, and a lavender brassiere hung loosely down from her right shoulder. She'd been stabbed many times with tremendous force. Her left breast was half-severed. Gaping slash wounds covered the rest of her upper chest, exposing internal organs that looked like nothing so much as meat at the butcher's counter. But her stomach had been spared, and stood out white and unmarred except for the message the killer had sent.

The letters were carved with unexpected precision: BITCH, in boxy capitals that had been formed by joining together straight-edged cuts that oozed smears of blood.

"Look how neat it is," Butch said. "Like he had all the time in the world. I bet the autopsy's gonna say the knife he used to write on her was different from the murder weapon. Something small and sharp, a box cutter, maybe, or a scalpel. We recovered the murder weapon, and just eyeballing it, it's too fat to make those nice, neat cuts."

Butch let the leaves fall back into place and stood up.

"You got the murder weapon?" Dan asked.

"Yeah," Butch said. "Guy threw it down toward the lake and we found it lying on a rock. Sloppy. Typical resin-handled hunting knife with a ten-inch steel blade. Nothing unusual enough to trace easy. We'll print it and all, but we won't get anything, seeing as he was wearing gloves."

"What about the stun gun?" Dan asked.

"That might be easier to bring back to an individual purchaser than a knife. A lotta guys hunt, but not too many electric-shock people," Butch said wryly.

Somebody called to Butch from above.

"Oh, the footprint casts are set. I gotta go pull 'em up. But you two relax. Stay as long as you want," Butch said, like he was inviting them to sit by the fire.

Dan turned to Melanie, who stood solemn and silent, her eyes glued to Suzanne Shepard's blood-drenched legs protruding from the leaves. They reminded her of the Wicked Witch's legs sticking out from under the house in *The Wizard of Oz,* a sight that had never failed to make her tremble with fear as a child.

"I'm sorry," Dan said. "This one was worse than I expected. You must hate me for bringing you here."

It took her a second to pull her eyes away and meet his gaze. "I hate the killer, not you. Anybody who could do this to another person isn't fit to be called human. I bet it's some jerk who's done this to other women, too."

"That's why I like what I do for a living," he said meaningfully. "We make a difference. We can get him off the streets. You can."

"You're right," Melanie said, sighing deeply. "I'm in."

THREE

Melanie had a special talent for investigating the ugliest crimes—homicides, home invasions, narcotics, gunrunning—that stood in marked contrast to her good diction and fancy education. Indeed, people who met her often thought she seemed too nice or too polite or too feminine to succeed at such a brutal job. But growing up on the block had left her with special insight into how the criminal mind worked and a high tolerance for an environment that sometimes felt like the Wild, Wild West. For months now, she'd been coasting, handling a series of stultifyingly dull bank-fraud cases. The cases rarely went to trial, so she could count on a predictable schedule. They required her to wade through piles of sleep-inducing documents, but she could do that at night in the comfort of her apartment, wearing old sweatpants, after Maya went down to sleep. Doing those cases, Melanie hadn't been within spitting distance of anything violent or gruesome in a long time, and being out here tonight was making her realize that she'd missed the rough stuff more than she'd imagined. She'd been bored out of her mind and hadn't even known it.

When Dan went off in search of his NYPD counterpart, Detective Julian Hay, Melanie stayed behind in the ravine. She wasn't alone. A junior crime-scene detective was stationed nearby, guarding the site so there could be no allegations later that unauthorized personnel had gotten access to the body. His reassuring presence gave Melanie the freedom she needed to stand and look, to think and analyze, to try to figure out what the forensic evidence said about this murder. It took her less than five minutes to come to some important conclusions. A couple of questions leaped out at her regarding the position of Suzanne Shepard's corpse, questions she needed to pursue further by speaking to the deputy ME who'd examined the body.

Melanie found Grace Deng and an orderly on the paved path above the ravine, readying a stretcher and body bag to transport the corpse to their refrigerated van, and introduced herself. Grace had sharp features and a dramatic, angular haircut. They traded pleasantries about cases they'd worked with each other's office and took a moment to exclaim over the brutal and disgusting nature of the crime. Then Melanie cut to the chase.

"I understand you conducted a thorough examination of the body," she said. "A couple of things are bothering me about how and where she was found, but to figure out if I'm right, I need a time-of-death estimate."

"I can give you one, but you understand it's just an estimate, right? I base TOD on average rates of rigor mortis and decomposition applied to this corpse. It's an educated guess at best."

"Understood," Melanie said.

"Okay, I got here shortly after nine-thirty, which put me at the scene about twenty minutes after the police arrived. At that point, the body was still warm and rigor was not established. The neck and jaw had slightly reduced range of motion, which suggested rigor was beginning to progress. But her limbs as well as her fingers and toes were still mobile."

"Mobile, meaning . . . ?"

"I could wiggle them. She hadn't been dead for long. One to two hours, max."

"And this was at nine-thirty?"

"Yes."

"So that would put the time of death no earlier than seven-thirty."

"Don't hold me to it, but yes, that's my hypothesis."

"Thanks, you've been really helpful." They exchanged business cards, and Grace promised to notify Melanie when the autopsy was completed.

Melanie sat down on a nearby bench to make notes about time of death and the weather.

At seven-thirty, the earliest moment at which Suzanne Shepard could have been attacked, Melanie had been doing her makeup and laying out her clothes for her date when rain suddenly spattered against her bedroom window. Melanie knew Dan would be coming up the FDR, which flooded in heavy rain, and she wondered whether he'd hit traffic. It was unusually dark outside for that hour in June, dark enough that she couldn't see out because of the reflected light, so she walked over and leaned against the glass in order to see the street. It was pouring.

What did that tell her? Suzanne Shepard had ventured into the wilds of the Ramble on a dark, rainy night. The Ramble might be situated smack in the middle of Manhattan Island with its two million inhabitants, but it felt like wilderness. Any sane woman would have required a damn good reason to be there. Figuring out what had called Suzanne to that location was a top investigative priority.

But Melanie had spotted an even bigger red flag: the body wasn't visible from the path above. Suzanne Shepard had been thrown into the ravine and covered by the underbrush. At seven-thirty and later, given how dark and rainy it was outside Melanie's eighth-floor window, it had to've been pitch-black down in the ravine. Butch Brennan had told her that the body was discovered by a male citizen who'd called 911. The caller had refused to give his name or stick around till the police arrived. How did he know the body was down there, lying under the dark leaves?

Melanie spotted Dan O'Reilly over near the police barricades where they'd first come in. He was deep in conversation with a tall, handsome African-American guy who wore his hair in long braids.

"Hey, Melanie, meet Detective Julian Hay, my counterpart from Manhattan North Homicide," Dan said as she approached.

Melanie and Julian shook hands.

"My boy Dan here was just telling me about you," Julian said with a sparkly smile. He wore fake gold teeth of the type that street drug dealers called "fronts."

"You guys know each other?" Melanie asked.

"Yeah, we worked cases together before, but I didn't realize it was him till I saw his face because I never knew his real name," Dan said. "This guy is one of the great all-time narcotics undercovers."

"You embarrass me, brother."

"It's the gospel truth. They used to call him Suave Pierre. He does a dead-on West Indian accent. UC'd all the big Jamaican posse investigations in the nineties and cheated the Grim Reaper like a motherfuck."

"That's in the past for me now," Julian said. "I've retired from the front lines. Working normal cases like the resta you mutts."

"Don't knock it, it's a living," Dan said, grinning. "But why'd you retire, man? You were a legend."

Julian held up his left hand and waved it at them. His ring finger sported a thick gold band. "The ball and chain insisted. My odds of walking back through the door at the end of each tour have now improved slightly."

"Only slightly, I hope," Dan said.

"Hell, yeah! I ain't no desk jockey. I'm dying with my boots on."

"Amen to that," Dan said. "You miss it?"

"Like crazy. I still do an occasional hand-to-hand just to keep my wits sharp. Plus that way, they let me keep the hair."

"Look, I hate to break up old-home night," Melanie said, smiling, "but I had a thought."

"What'd I tell ya?" Dan said to Julian.

"Always thinking," Julian said, tapping his temple. "We like that in a prosecutor."

"So here's my brilliant insight," she said. "We need to pull the 911 tape right away. Based on what the deputy ME told me about TOD, and what the weather and light conditions were at that time, I'm guessing our 911 caller witnessed the crime. Either that or he's actually the killer. No other way could he have known there was a body down there in the ditch."

Dan and Julian both stopped smiling. Julian shook his head until his braids swayed, making a soft clicking sound. Then he withdrew a slim silver tape recorder from the pocket of his black leather coat.

"I definitely see what you was saying about this girl, brother. From the get-go, she's on the money."

FOUR

Detective Julian Hay held up the recording device and pushed a button. An ugly crackle of sound emerged, and he adjusted the volume. The call had obviously been placed using a cell phone. All three of them leaned in toward the tape recorder to make out the words through the cacophony of bad sound quality.

"Nine-one-one Dispatch. What is your emergency?" a woman barked.

More static, and what sounded like ragged breathing.

"What is your emergency, please?"

"I'm in Central Park. Something terrible happened." The man spoke through panting breaths. He sounded as if he'd been running like hell and was now about to burst into tears.

"Sir?" the dispatcher prompted after a moment.

"I heard a woman screaming. She was being attacked. I think she's dead. Jesus, she must be dead."

"A woman was attacked?"

"Yes, I saw the whole thing. Just before." His breath caught in a suppressed sob.

"Did you witness this attack, sir?"

"Yes, but it was dark. I saw . . . I saw figures. He had a knife. He was stabbing her. Oh my God, oh my God!"

"Where in Central Park, sir?"

"It happened in the Ramble, near the lake. About five minutes ago."

"And what is your name, sir?"

"What?"

"I'm going to dispatch a cruiser immediately. What is your name?"

A loud click sounded.

"Sir? Hello? . . . Shit, he hung up. Male Caucasian, I think."

Julian clicked off the recorder. "That's it," he said. "Dispatch informs that the call came in at eight forty-six P.M. tonight."

"Placing the murder at approximately eight forty-one, if you believe what the caller said about timing," Dan said.

"The caller sounds like an eyewitness, not the killer," Melanie said.

"I agree. He's scared shitless," Dan agreed.

"Any leads on him?" she asked.

"We got the cell number from the 911 dispatcher. It's a Verizon prefix, but their subpoena compliance department is officially closed till nine A.M. tomorrow," Julian said.

"We can't wait that long. They must have people on staff overnight. Maybe you should send somebody there in person," Melanie said. She was starting to get caught up in the urgency of the situation, forgetting herself and her personal concerns, thinking instead of Suzanne Shepard's stomach, its chilling hieroglyphs, their maker lurking out there somewhere in the bottomless night.

Dan nodded. "I already called my squad. We're sending a guy over to Verizon right now with a subpoena and orders to beat the fucking door down if he has to. The second we have a subscriber name, we're all over the guy."

"Okay, good. Any progress on identifying additional eyewitnesses?" Melanie asked.

"My lieutenant had uniforms fanned out in every direction from the Ramble within twenty minutes of receiving the 911 call," Julian said. "But it's not like when somebody gets whacked in an apartment building and you just go push the neighbors' doorbells.

People don't stay put in Central Park. So far, nobody we talked to saw or heard a thing."

"Are we putting out a call for tips?" Melanie asked. "You know, like on television and radio?"

"Yeah, we're doing Crimestoppers. And the family's offering a reward. Fifty large. That should get people's attention," Julian said.

"Great," Melanie said.

Julian snapped his fingers. "Wait a minute. Television. You just reminded me of something. My lieutenant wants to hold a press conference, the sooner the better. And he wants the U.S. Attorney's Office doing the talking, so that means you. Hold on a second."

Julian cupped his hands and shouted, "Yo, boss!"

A heavyset man wearing a rumpled raincoat and a brown corduroy cap turned and waved brusquely.

"Prosecutor," Julian called, pointing at Melanie.

Lieutenant Jack Deaver immediately marched over and introduced himself. "Somebody needs to give a statement to get the reporters off my back," he insisted. "We set up a perimeter as best we could, but you saw them out there. There hasn't been a murder in the park in three years. They heard about the hunting knife, so now they're calling this guy the Central Park Butcher. Once your perp gets nicknamed, forget about it, the reporters are like dogs smelling meat. They're starting to bypass the barricades, just walkin' right over the fuckin' things."

"Freedom of the press," Melanie said. "You can't keep them out forever."

"They're undermining the crime-scene investigation," Deaver said. "You want these bozos trampling evidence? Or worse yet, finding it before Brennan's boys do, so there's no chain of custody for trial?"

"Park's officially closed, right? Frickin' arrest 'em for trespassing," Dan suggested.

"We can't arrest reporters. Not a good idea," Melanie said with a nervous laugh. This case was potentially explosive, she was possibly stepping on the toes of the D.A.'s office, and her boss didn't even know she was out here.

"Nope, I'm making an executive decision," Deaver proclaimed, "just like they taught me in leadership training. We're holding a press conference. Throw the dogs a bone. It's the only way to corral 'em in one place while we finish up here. Pierre, come with me. We'll tell 'em to set up their cameras, and that Vargas here'll be at the park gate in half an hour to give an update." Deaver strode away, with Julian following.

FIVE

After Lieutenant Deaver left, Melanie turned to Dan in a panic.

"I can't do it," she said. "My boss doesn't know I'm out here. We have a strict press protocol in our office. Even the most routine press releases require supervisor approval."

"So here's a phone. Call your boss and get approval," Dan said, whipping his cell phone out and waving it at her. But Melanie just stared at it, feeling daunted.

"What do you, have fear of success or something? You're about to get on TV. Call her," he said.

"I can't."

"Why not?"

"She's getting married."

"She's getting married Saturday. It's fucking Wednesday. Besides, from what I hear, she's less of a shrew than usual these days. Vito must be keeping her satisfied."

Melanie wrinkled her nose in mock disgust. "What a thought."

"The Melanie Vargas I know is stone-cold ambitious. You'd better do it, sweetheart, or you're gonna be seriously pissed at yourself later. Come on, jump in with both feet. It's the only way."

Dan was right. He was right that Melanie would regret not pursuing this case once she woke up from her torpor. He was also right that her boss, Bernadette DeFelice, chief of the Major Crimes Unit in the New York City U.S. Attorney's Office, had mellowed out lately. The old Bernadette had struck fear in the hearts of her subordinates, Melanie included. But Bernadette was getting married on Saturday night for the first time in her forty-seven years to NYPD lieutenant Vito Albano, the head of the premier narco-terrorism task force in the city and a beloved figure in the law enforcement community. And she actually seemed happy about it, giving the lie to those who swore up and down that she was marrying Vito for his primo drug cases. What the hell, Melanie might as well pull the trigger. If worse came to worst, Bernadette would yell and then order Melanie to go home, which she sort of wanted to do anyway.

"Hand me the phone," she said.

Melanie dialed Bernadette's pager number, and in less than a minute, Dan's phone started vibrating wildly. You might loathe Bernadette, but you had to hand it to her. When it came to her job, she didn't spare herself.

"Hello?" Melanie answered.

"It's one o'clock in the goddamn morning, Melanie. This better be good."

"Turn on your TV," Melanie said.

There was silence on the other end. She'd gotten her boss's attention: Bernadette was doing as Melanie had directed. Melanie prayed hard that the Suzanne Shepard murder was actually on TV or her tactic would immediately backfire and she would never hear the end of it.

After a few minutes, Bernadette came back on the line.

"I'm seeing that a couple of local cable channels and one network affiliate are broadcasting live from Central Park about a stabbing," Bernadette said, her interest clearly piqued. "The Central Park Butcher. Is that what you're calling about?"

"Exactly," she replied.

"What's the case, and what's your connection to it?"

"Suzanne Shepard was stabbed and mutilated tonight in the Ramble. Do you know who she is?"

"Sure. The television personality, right? Celebrity crime reporter?"

"Yes, and listen to this. The killer carved 'bitch' on her stomach with a knife."

"Very dramatic," Bernadette said in a jaded tone. "Enlighten me, girlfriend. What's this got to do with me? Are you suggesting we try to get in on the case?"

"I'm already in. I'm in Central Park. The A.D.A. couldn't handle the blood and guts. She left. I just got done reviewing all the crime-scene evidence. The press wants a statement. The NYPD lieutenant asked me to make it. I called you first to get approval. But, Bernadette, if you feel I'm overstepping, I'll understand completely. Just say the word and I'll go home."

"Are you insane? This is amazing! How the hell'd you swing it?"

"The Bureau is involved in the case, so—"

"O'Reilly tipped you off and you tagged along?"

"Yes."

"And they say you can't teach balls! I admit, I've been having my doubts about you lately, but this is excellent work. You done me proud. Do I have time to get there to do the press conference myself?"

"Maybe. We're doing it at the Seventy-ninth Street gate in about ten minutes."

"Shit, I'm out in Bensonhurst, and I don't have my TV outfit with me. Can you hold them off?"

"No, apparently the reporters are about to storm the barricades and trample evidence if we don't give them something," Melanie said.

"Goddamn Brooklyn! Vito, I told you this was the middle of nowhere. I'm missing a chance to go on TV! Melanie, listen up. I'm sorry, but you're going to have to do this on your own."

"Okay. I can handle it."

"Here's what you do."

"Hold on a minute," Melanie said, and scrambled to dig her notebook and pen from her handbag. She tucked the cell phone against her shoulder and got ready to write.

"Go ahead, Bern," she said.

"Wear dark lipstick and lots of blush or your face washes out," Bernadette declared.

Melanie waited for a moment but there was nothing more forthcoming. "What should I *say*?" she asked.

"Oh. Nothing."

"Nothing?"

"Never say anything to the press. Give them no information, not even the victim's name. Tell them you can't until next of kin is notified."

"NYPD already notified next of kin."

"So what?"

"The press already know the victim's name. I'm not sure who leaked it, but they know."

"You're not listening, Melanie. When you're on the record in front of the cameras, you keep your lips zipped, or else the defendant ends up moving for a change of venue for adverse publicity and you lose. You don't want to be forced to try this case in goddamn Hauppauge or Schenectady, for Chrissakes."

"Okay, but how do I—"

"Get a bunch of the law enforcement guys to stand behind you so it looks like you have a huge team working on this. Cops, agents, whatever. Get the precinct to send over everybody they have, whether they're officially assigned or not. And make sure the cops are ethnically diverse so we don't get accused of racism if it turns out the defendant is black. In fact, if you have a black cop, put him next to you."

"But—"

"This is television, goddammit. What matters is how things look. Do you comprende?"

"Yes," Melanie said, borderline offended. But Bernadette probably would have said that to anybody. She was an equal-opportunity bitch.

"Good. Then you introduce yourself. Say the U.S. Attorney's Office and the FBI are on the case."

"And the D.A.'s office?"

"Forget them. They can do their own goddamn press conference."

"Yes, but the A.D.A. was here earlier and—"

"What's his name?"

"Her name is Janice Marsh."

"Fine. I'll make some calls. Don't give it another thought."

"But what's our jurisdiction? What's the federal crime?"

"We'll figure something out before we indict. Where there's a will, there's a way into federal court. And, Melanie?"

"Yes?"

"Remember the makeup. If I can't be there to lend substance, let's get some mileage out of the fact that you're young and attractive. You look like a prosecutor from a TV show. Our goal is to get the press focused on you instead of some psychotic killer terrorizing the city."

"All right."

"Good luck, girlfriend. And good work."

Melanie hung up. Dan was staring at her.

"Well?" he asked.

"She was happy. Happier than she's been with me in a while."

"What'd I tell ya? Stick with me, kid. We're going places."

SIX

Before the press conference, they convened an impromptu team meeting in an NYPD mobile command center, a fancy name for a trailer outfitted with a bunch of communications equipment that the cops kept parked in a gravel lot near the Central Park precinct. It was cramped and hot inside. As the lone female, Melanie was given the only chair, an old swivel number with a ripped seat. Dan, Julian, Butch, and Lieutenant Deaver, not one of them a small man, crowded around her close enough that she smelled coffee on somebody's breath. By unspoken agreement, Melanie ran the meeting—whether because she'd be doing the talking at the press conference, because she was the prosecutor, or just because she was the one in the chair, she didn't know.

"I plan on saying very little," she explained, "but I still want us on the same page before I go out there. As I understand the forensic evidence, there's a strong possibility this was a random killing. Are we in agreement?"

"Either a robbery gone bad, or some sicko getting his rocks off by hurting women," Butch said.

"Or both," Dan put in.

"Nobody's gonna want to hear that," Deaver pointed out. "Not the commissioner, not the mayor. It says to the public there's a psycho on the loose and we ain't caught him yet. I'm not sayin' lie. I'm just sayin' that don't look good."

"We do have one piece of evidence indicating the victim knew her attacker," Melanie said.

"What evidence?" Butch asked. "Nothing I seen. From the way he stunned her, and the way she fought, this wasn't anybody she trusted."

"I said somebody she knew, not somebody she trusted," Melanie replied. "What was she doing in the Ramble on a rainy night, if she didn't go there on purpose to meet someone?"

"Eight-thirty," Deaver said, nodding. "Good point. I put my trash out right about then. It'd let up from what it was earlier, but it still raining plenty."

"Drizzling at most," Butch said skeptically, shaking his head.

"Whatever. It's enough to strike the reassuring note," Deaver said.

"I'll just say there's a possibility the victim knew her attacker," Melanie said.

"Yeah. Why get the whole city up in arms for no reason?" Deaver said. "Let's do it."

It turned out that facing the cameras with blinding light shining in her eyes, microphones shoved in her face, and reporters screaming questions at deafening volume was just about the most exhilarating thing that Melanie had ever experienced. Almost exhilarating enough to make her forget her burnout and go crazy for her job again. She'd expected to feel dazed and nervous, but the second she got up there, she felt like she'd come home. Armed with Bernadette's advice, Melanie knew exactly what to say. She introduced herself and the key law enforcement personnel working the case. She confirmed the bare fact that a murder had taken place and assured the public that the authorities were hot on the killer's trail. In response to each and every question, she deftly avoided revealing any details while nevertheless managing to satisfy the questioner that he or she was getting an answer. She parried and feinted and explained and even got a few laughs. Melanie could have stood up there jousting with the press all night, but after about twenty minutes, Lieutenant Deaver leaned across her and said they only had time for one more question. He practically had to drag Melanie away from the microphones when that question was done.

"The most dangerous spot in New York—between Vargas and a camera," Lieutenant Deaver joked once they were away from the reporters. But for the first time that night, he smiled, and before he left, he said, "Nice job, Melanie. That oughta hold those piranhas for a while."

Dan and Julian couldn't stop telling her what a natural she'd been, how poised and in control, how articulate. She felt high as a kite on the excitement.

"You've got a television career ahead of you," Julian said.

"Not ahead of her, she's got it now," Dan said. "You're gonna be all over the news."

"And the papers," Julian added. "I can see the morning headlines. 'Melanie Vargas takes on the Central Park Butcher.' "

"See, you're back on the horse. You're like me when it comes to this job. You love the glory."

"I do love it!" she said, and laughed giddily.

Only later would she think, *Pride goeth before a fall.*

SEVEN

It was just past four on Thursday morning, warm, blustery, and still dark out when Dan pulled up on a nondescript side street in midtown. He was dropping Melanie off on his way to Verizon's offices, where he planned to get information about the 911 caller. While the cops searched out eyewitnesses Melanie would attack on other fronts, like trying to figure out why Suzanne Shepard had gone to Central Park last night. She thought it might have something to do with a story, so Dan had brought her to the ugly glass box of a building that housed the Target News Network studios. Melanie reached for the door handle, ready to leap out and race inside the building, which was brightly lit despite the early hour.

Dan caught her by the arm.

"Hold on there, princess. I go out of my way to give you a lift, and you run off without saying good-bye?"

She turned back, startled. She'd been thinking only of the upcoming interview, almost forgetting that it was Dan in the car with her. But when she saw the lust in his eyes, her blood slowed down and grew sluggish in her veins, and her thoughts scattered.

"It's four A.M., and we're working a murder. Are you crazy?" she asked, but she heard the desire in her own voice. She leaned back in her seat, making no further attempt to leave the car.

"When it comes to you, damn right I am. You should know that by now. Watching you up there in front of the cameras. You were something else." He reached out and ran his thumb slowly over her lower lip. Leaning forward, he parted her lips with his tongue and kissed her until she was breathless. God, what this man did to her should be against the law. By the time he pulled away, she barely remembered her own name let alone who she was supposed to interview.

"That's better," he said.

She shook her head to try to clear it. "Better? Now I can't think straight."

"If you don't want to be kissed like that, stop tempting me like you do."

"Maybe I should start saying no," she tossed over her shoulder as she stepped to the curb. Ha, fat chance. The nonchalance was an act, and he knew it as well as she did.

Luckily for Melanie, Seth Parker, the young gun who produced *High Crimes with Suzanne Shepard,* got to his desk early. She'd called ahead, and he had somebody waiting by the elevator to meet her.

"Melanie Vargas?" asked a ponytailed intern type in low-slung jeans and a tight black sweater.

"Yes."

"Ashley LeClerc. I'll be your handler this morning. This way, please."

She led Melanie down a corridor lined with glossy photos of Target News Network's stars. Suzanne Shepard was prominently featured, and Melanie couldn't help stopping before her picture, comparing the face to the one she'd seen staring up with blank eyes from the floor of the ravine a few hours earlier. In the photograph, Suzanne leaned back against a desk, her arms folded over her chest, looking smug and gorgeous and utterly untouchable. For a split second, Melanie understood how somebody could want this woman dead, and it almost made her slap herself. Nobody, not even the rich and the beautiful, deserved such a brutal end.

Ashley stopped at a small room at the end of the hall. A row of chairs faced the door, several of them occupied by people with strangely bronzed skin.

"This is our Green Room. Have a seat, help yourself to some Danish, and I'll go check with makeup to see if they're ready for you."

"Wait a second, there must be some mistake," Melanie said.

"No mistake. We do a live early, early show with a local focus. You're on-air in sixteen minutes."

Tempted as she felt to go on TV again, Melanie knew it was time to get down to the hard work of solving this case.

"I'm not a guest," she said. "I'm here to interview Seth Parker about a criminal matter."

"I know," Ashley squealed. "Suzanne got murdered by the Butcher! Seth's all over it. He wants Cassandra to interview you for *Sunrise Manhattan*. They don't call him the fresh prince of TV news for nothing."

"I'm here to interview *him*, not the other way around. I just gave a press conference. I don't have time to do another."

Ashley's chipper expression turned petulant. "I'll tell him what you said, but he's not gonna be happy," she announced, and flounced off on her high-heeled boots.

A few minutes later, Ashley reappeared. "Follow me," she said flatly.

This time, Melanie was led up a shallow flight of stairs toward a glassed-in cubicle overlooking the brightly lit newsroom set. Everything below was in motion—people, cameras, video cables, flashing images on numerous TV screens. A glamorous brunette in a low-cut dress sat at a desk fussing with her hair, the network logo glowing neon blue behind her.

"I have flyaways. I see them in the monitor. Get Maurice," she ordered.

Ashley opened the glass door and motioned Melanie inside. Opposite the glass wall was an entire bank of televisions screens, each displaying the brunette from a different angle as a slender guy in tight pants sprayed something on her hair. Seth Parker paced the tiny space, his eyes on the monitors, talking into a headset in a flat, affectless voice. He glanced over at them as they entered, holding up a finger to tell them to wait.

"You seem incapable of processing basic information this morning, Howie. I said investment-bank prostitution scandal, then rat infestation on Park Avenue. What's difficult about that? Are those two stories interchangeable to you? . . . Good. In the future, please follow my instructions."

Seth clicked a small switch that hung from his headset by a cord, disconnecting the call, and turned to them. He was thin and pale, with shaggy light brown hair and a wispy soul patch like a smudge of dirt on his chin. In his frayed corduroys and ratty sweater, he looked about fifteen, and he acted like a surfer dude on heavy meds.

"Is this Ms. Vargas?"

"Yes it is, Seth," Ashley said.

"Fine. Refill my coffee. Then go to the Green Room and tell the hip-hop guy we're moving him up five minutes. I've already cued Cassandra."

"Yes, Seth."

"Don't stand there like a retard. Go."

Ashley whirled and rushed out the door.

Seth indicated a leather director's chair opposite his own swivel chair. "Have a seat."

They sat down facing each other, their knees virtually touching in the small space. Before Melanie could say a word, he'd clicked the switch again and resumed talking into the headset in his strange monotone. The interruption gave her a chance to pull her credentials from her handbag.

"No, cut her intro by forty-five seconds. I want time for the kid with stigmata . . . Do it. No back sass, please." He clicked off abruptly and looked at Melanie.

"Mr. Parker," she began, "as I explained over the phone, I'm a prosecutor in the U.S. Attorney's Office. I'm working with the FBI to investigate the murder of Suzanne Shepard, and I need to ask you some questions."

"Ashley tells me you have some kind of problem being interviewed?" he asked, stifling a yawn.

"I'm here to interview *you*. This was a very brutal murder, and the killer's at large, so this is urgent. I need to find out why Suzanne Shepard was in Central Park last night, and I'm thinking maybe it had something to do with a story."

"Yes, of course, I understand. Now, when and where was the body was discovered?"

The question struck her as odd, but then something occurred to her. "Are you taping this conversation, Mr. Parker?"

He wouldn't look her in the eye. "Taping?"

"Lying to me in the course of this interview is a crime. That's why Martha Stewart went to jail, if you recall."

"Are you threatening me?" Seth demanded.

"I'm trying to protect the integrity of my investigation. We have to control what information is made public or else the killer finds out exactly what we know."

"It's my practice as a journalist to record conversations. It avoids disputes later over the accuracy of what's reported on the air."

"You're not reporting this interview on the air. I can't allow it."

"Ms. Vargas, we're all devastated over here. We believe the best way to honor Suzanne's memory is with innovative coverage of her murder. Please don't interfere with our grieving process. I have a very fresh idea, and I'm sure you'll be as excited about it as I am."

"I really don't have time to—"

"We embed a reporter with you, like they did in Iraq. We get inside details of the Central Park Butcher investigation, you get—"

"Mr. Parker—"

"Hear me out. You get complete, one hundred percent access to our files. In return, we get to place a *High Crimes* correspondent on the street with you. I have the perfect man for the job. Duncan Gilmartin, one of our Aussie transplants. He's young, dynamic, handsome, aggressive. He'll shadow your every move—"

"I can't do that," she said firmly.

"Why not?"

"Publicizing all our leads is a sure way to screw up our investigation. Any information we can make public now, we gave out at the press conference. The rest has to be treated as confidential."

"If you won't help me, I don't see why I should help you," Seth said.

Melanie stood up. "If you're unwilling to give me information voluntarily, I'll have to subpoena you to appear before the grand jury. I'll serve the subpoena within the hour, returnable today at nine A.M. at the federal courthouse. Your lawyers can accompany you. Tell them it'll take the entire day. The grand jury is slow. They ask a lot of questions."

They locked eyes briefly, and Seth Parker blinked. He'd been bluffing, and she'd called him on it. He sighed, reached into the top drawer of his desk, and clicked off a tape recorder.

"Sit down. Please," he said. "The Butcher story is big. I can't afford to lose a day to some"—he waved his hand dismissively—"grand jury thing."

Melanie held out her hand. "I need that tape. Otherwise, something tells me I'll be hearing it on the six o'clock news."

Seth popped the cassette out and handed it to Melanie sheepishly.

"I need to know why Suzanne Shepard went to the Ramble last night," she said, resuming her seat. "I'd like to review her calendar, her voice mails and e-mails, that sort of thing."

"I can arrange for all that. Just give me a minute to make some calls."

"Great, thank you."

"But I can do more for you than that. Aren't you interested in getting a list of Suzanne's enemies? Her specialty was digging up the dark secrets of the rich and powerful. Half this town wanted her dead. I'm convinced that she died because of a story."

As much as Melanie would've loved to believe Suzanne Shepard's murder was a revenge killing—since that would make it easier to solve than a random slaying—she wasn't persuaded by Seth Parker's little speech. His ulterior motive was plain to see. If Suzanne had been killed in retaliation for a story, then Target News would get a lot of free publicity and a nice ratings boost.

"I need more than a general statement that Suzanne made people angry," Melanie said. "I need something specific. Like a direct threat. And recent enough to suggest it could be connected to her killing."

Seth leaned back in his chair, tossing his beanbag. "How's this for recent? Just last week, Suzanne got a box of dog shit in the mail, and it had a picture of her inside, cut up into little tiny pieces."

"That could be important," Melanie agreed.

"Our security director can show you the box," Seth said. "He'll be in later this afternoon. He thinks the doggy doo relates to a story Suzanne just ran on the Clyde Williams sex scandal."

Melanie had been taking notes, but she stopped in midscribble and stared at Seth Parker. "Clyde Williams?" she repeated.

"Yes."

"Clyde Williams the city councilman was involved in a sex scandal?"

Clyde Williams was a prominent African-American lawyer and city councilman who'd been positioning himself to run for mayor of New York in the next election. He was handsome and silver-tongued and already had an impressive war chest accrued thanks to his efficient political action committee. He also happened to be the father of Joseph Williams, a shy, intellectual assistant U.S. attorney, and Melanie's best friend in the office.

"I can tell you don't watch Suzanne's show. Clyde had an affair with a young, white intern," Seth said.

"An intern?" Melanie said, horrified.

"Yes. Twenty-one years old. Suzanne was going after the story aggressively, and we thought it had real potential to derail his mayoral bid. What if Clyde killed her? Clyde Williams and the Central Park Butcher, one and the same? The possible future mayor of this city also its most fearsome criminal? God, I love that angle."

"That's the stupidest thing I've ever heard. I know Clyde. His son works in my office. He wouldn't kill anybody," Melanie said.

"The lead prosecutor is personal friends with the suspect? This story gets better every minute. First a sex scandal. Then a murder. Now a cover-up."

"Clyde didn't kill anybody, and I'm not playing favorites. You don't believe any of this yourself, I can tell. It's all just made-up trash."

"I assure you, nothing we've aired so far was made up. Our stories are carefully vetted to make sure they have at least some basis in fact. Suzanne had obtained an amateur video shot with a cell phone at one of those rubber-chicken political dinners. It showed Clyde and his little hottie off in a corner leaning against each other in a very familiar way."

"Leaning against each other? So it's not like you caught them having sex?"

"No. That would've been better, obviously, but the video was pretty damning. If you'd seen it, you'd understand. There's leaning, and then there's leaning."

"Does Williams admit to the affair?"

"They both deny it, but that wasn't a problem for the segment. A self-righteous denial is good television, too."

"Even if Clyde was having an affair, that doesn't mean he'd murder the reporter who broke the story," Melanie protested.

"I can't prove Clyde killed Suzanne. I can't even prove he's behind the dog shit threat. But I've ordered my reporters to investigate his involvement, and you'd better do the same or it won't look too good for the U.S. Attorney's Office. We plan to make the Williams angle the centerpiece of our Butcher coverage."

Thinking of her dear friend Joe, Melanie grimaced. With Target News after him, Clyde Williams was in for a rough ride.

EIGHT

The sun was up over the East River, and doormen were out hosing down the sidewalks in their early morning ritual. Melanie stepped over rivulets of water as she approached the luxury apartment building where Suzanne Shepard had lived with her elderly mother. The officers from the Central Park precinct who'd made the notification hadn't attempted to interview the distraught old lady, so nobody knew yet what details she could provide about the final hours of her daughter's life.

Melanie showed her credentials to the doorman. Hector, the fatherly doorman in Melanie's building, wore shirtsleeves with his uniform pants, but this doorman was dressed in full regalia down to the epaulets and white gloves. After calling to announce her, he directed her to a space-age elevator that whisked her up to the thirty-fourth floor so fast that her ears popped. Suzanne must've been loaded, living in a place like this. The wealth was conspicuous enough that Melanie made a mental note to look into who might've had a financial interest in her death.

As Melanie reached for the buzzer, the apartment door was wrenched open by a boy of twelve or thirteen, barefoot, clad in a T-shirt and plaid pajama bottoms. Underneath long hair and an adolescent complexion, he bore more than a passing resemblance to Suzanne Shepard, and if looks alone hadn't told Melanie who he was, the anguish in his eyes confirmed it beyond all doubt.

"Where's my mom? Can I see her body?" he pleaded.

"Get away from that door, Charlie!"

"My grandmother won't let me see her. Can you convince her? Please! I don't want my mom to be alone," he whispered urgently to Melanie.

A tall, bent woman of at least eighty was making her way across the room toward them, leaning on a metal walker and breathing with some difficulty. She was beautiful, with elaborately arranged white hair and striking features, wearing a blue velvet housecoat.

"Hold on, there, wait one minute!" she called to Melanie in a husky, nicotine-tinged voice. "I'm Lorraine Shepard, Suzanne's mother."

"Gran, I'm going to Mommy!" Charlie cried.

"You are not."

Sobbing, he hung his head. Tears collected and streamed off the tip of his nose. Lorraine Shepard finally reached her grandson, and caressed his shaggy head with a blue-veined, perfectly manicured hand.

"Poor baby, I know, I know, let it out," she said, weariness in her voice. Looking at Melanie over Charlie's head, she asked, "You're the prosecutor?"

"Yes."

"I don't want my grandson seeing the body. He doesn't need to grow up with that memory."

"She's my mother!" Charlie insisted, his shoulders heaving.

"You can't see her anyway, sweetie," Melanie said gently. "The medical examiner has to do a—well, they have to examine her."

"See, Charlie, that's the law talking. You're not allowed to go. What's your name again?" Lorraine Shepard asked Melanie.

"Melanie Vargas. I'm from the U.S. Attorney's Office, and I'm working with the FBI and the NYPD to solve this case."

Mrs. Shepard eyed the jeans and boots Melanie had worn to the crime scene, which were flecked with mud. "Let me see your identification," she said suspiciously.

Melanie pulled out her creds. Mrs. Shepard's reading glasses hung around her neck on a gold chain studded with small diamonds. She settled them on her nose and studied the credentials, holding on to her walker with one hand for balance.

"Vargas. What's that, Mexican?" she asked, handing them back.

"I'm half Puerto Rican," Melanie replied.

"Hmmph. Interesting. How'd you end up an attorney?"

"I went to law school," Melanie answered warily, not sure where this was going.

"Rich parents?"

"Not at all. Quite the opposite."

"Worked hard?"

"Yes, ma'am."

The old lady nodded approvingly. "Good. You'll do."

"Do for what?" Melanie asked, unable to keep her lips from curving into a smile. But Lorraine Shepard gave her an outraged look that froze it right off her face.

"We need smart, hardworking people after this animal. Those idiots who came by before didn't ask me a single question except what jewelry Suzy was wearing when she left the house yesterday."

"Describing the jewelry is important. The killer stole it, so he'll probably try to fence it," Melanie explained.

Lorraine snorted contemptuously. "If you believe this was some mugging gone wrong, you're not as smart as you look. Let's sit down. I have a thing or two to fill you in on. Charlie, go to your room."

"No way. I want to hear."

"I'm not talking to this lady in front of you, young man. She can just leave, then, and they'll never catch the guy. Is that what you want?"

Charlie locked eyes with his grandmother for a few seconds to preserve his pride, then sighed and began to turn away. But he turned back suddenly and fixed Melanie with a pleading gaze.

"You're gonna catch him, right?" he asked.

"I'll do my best," Melanie replied. As Charlie's eyes filled with tears, she had to fight back a sympathetic welling in her own.

"It isn't right. She was my mom!" he said, sniffling.

"Charlie, we'll get him. I promise. It won't bring her back, but at least you'll know that whoever took your mother from you was punished."

Charlie nodded, closing his eyes in pain. "Thank you," he said, and ran from the room.

"I didn't know Suzanne had a son," Melanie commented to Lorraine after the boy had left.

"She kept him out of the public eye. She was a good mother, and it shows."

"Yes, it does. What a sweet kid," Melanie said wistfully. A sweet, orphaned kid, who deserved justice. Families needed closure in situations like this. Seeing Charlie in person brought that home to Melanie.

Lorraine Shepard turned the walker and began moving laboriously across the spacious living room toward an enormous brown suede sofa. The apartment was decorated with understated furnishings in shades of taupe and brown, and modern art that looked important. Shimmering bronze silk drapes skimmed the floor around enormous plate-glass windows, which revealed a breathtaking panorama of the midtown skyline bathed in peachy morning light. From this high up, the city looked fresh and full of promise, as if ugly things like murder couldn't happen here.

Melanie helped Lorraine sit down, took a seat beside her, and pulled out her notebook.

"If you'll bear with me, Mrs. Shepard, I need to ask you some questions."

"I don't stand on ceremony. Call me Lorraine."

"I don't mean to pry, but I need to get a feel for your daughter's personal life. Was she divorced from Charlie's father?"

"She wasn't divorced because Jean Christophe never had the decency to marry her in the first place. Don't get me started on him. Frenchman. Photographer. You get the picture. I stayed with her all these years to help with the boy, since that bum was never around. He lived in Africa for a while, and now he lives in Paris. But as much as I'm no fan of his, I can promise you Jean Christophe had nothing to do with Suzy's murder."

"How do you know?"

"Why would he want Suzy dead? She raised the boy, paid all the bills, and never asked him for a red cent, but she still let him see Charlie whenever he liked. Now he'll be forced to take some responsibility."

"I see. Was Suzanne involved with anybody else? A boyfriend who might've been disgruntled for some reason?"

"Suzanne had no social life. She worked too hard. Hand me that ashtray over there, would you? I need a smoke."

Melanie grabbed a crystal ashtray from a nearby table, and Lorraine lit a Marlboro, glaring at Melanie defiantly.

"At my age, if it kills me, so what?"

"I didn't say a word," Melanie said. "Do you know why your daughter went to Central Park last night?"

Lorraine smiled, exhaling. "See, I knew you had a brain in your head. Now you're getting somewhere. Boyfriends have got nothing to do with this. Suzanne had an appointment with a source last night! She called me around six to say something important had come up and she wouldn't be home for dinner."

"You're sure she meant a source for a story and not just that she was meeting a friend for a drink?"

"What did I just say? You're not listening. Suzanne had no friends. She worked day and night, and other than work, it was just Charlie and me. When she said something important had come up, she meant work."

With Maya to care for and a demanding job, Melanie didn't go out much herself. She was beginning to see Suzanne Shepard in a whole different light.

"Did Suzanne actually say she was meeting this person in Central Park?" Melanie asked.

"Not specifically. But given the timing, it had to be. I can't imagine any other reason she'd go there."

"You said she got this phone call yesterday at work, around six P.M.?"

"That's right," Lorraine said.

Melanie noted down the information. "We'll check her work and cell phones to see if we can identify the incoming call. That's very helpful."

"There's more," Lorraine said, dragging on her cigarette.

"I'm listening," Melanie said.

"We had a robbery here, not this past weekend, but the one before. The three of us were at the beach house. Somebody who works in the building had to be in on it, or the thief never could've gotten in. The security in this building is too tight."

"What did they take?"

"Small things mostly. Easy to carry. A bunch of jewelry, and the cash we leave for the housekeeper to buy the groceries. Maybe a hundred bucks. But what matters is, they went through Suzanne's office, and they took some files. About stories she was working on."

Melanie felt a prickling along her scalp. It was a form of excitement she'd experienced in other cases upon learning something that could help her solve the puzzle. If this was a random slaying, then she was looking for a phantom. The city was big, and full of dark places to hide. Some no-name psycho with a television who'd taken it upon himself to deliver a comeuppance to Suzanne Shepard might escape detection, because there was no pattern to lead her to him. But a man with a motive, she could find.

Melanie started writing faster. "Two weeks from this past weekend, you said?"

"Yup. We don't know which day, because we were gone from Friday night to Sunday afternoon, and we didn't find out about it until we got home."

"Were the police called?"

"Yes. We needed a police report for the insurance."

"Was anybody arrested?"

"Not yet. They say they're working on it, but if you believe that, I got a nice bridge to sell you in Brooklyn."

"Do you remember the detective's name?"

"Pauline something. I got her card in the back bedroom. I'll get it for you before you leave."

"Tell me exactly which files were taken," Melanie said.

"One had to do with a personal trainer at Flex. You know that place?"

"I've heard of it, sure. It's one of the most exclusive gyms in the city."

"This trainer's name is Miles Ortiz. He has a big following among the rich housewife crowd. Suzanne heard from a source of hers who always knows where the bodies're buried that Miles has a criminal record, and that he's selling drugs to 'em."

"Selling drugs to his clients at the gym?"

"Mmm-hmm, and we're talking about women who're married to the most powerful men in the country."

"What kind of drugs?"

"That, I don't know. Suzanne was looking into it, though, and she was starting to make people nervous. There's a woman who lives in this building who had something going with that Ortiz character, and she was giving Suzy funny looks. Thought she was asking too many questions. Kim Savitt is her name. Rich, spoiled little brat."

"She lives in this building?"

"Yes, that's what I'm saying. Maybe an inside job."

Melanie was writing furiously. "You said two files were taken. What was the other one?"

Lorraine hesitated. "This one I told Suzanne to stay away from, just on the idea of don't shit where you eat."

"Excuse me?"

"She was going after somebody close to her, somebody she needed. I was holding her back, telling her not to. She never got very far with the story."

"Who was the target?" Melanie asked.

Lorraine sighed. "I guess it doesn't matter now, huh? It was Dr. Welch."

"Dr. Welch?"

"Benedict Welch? Honey, he's just about the most famous plastic surgeon in this town. He was willing to do what it took to keep Suzy beautiful. Not everybody's so . . . creative like that."

"What do you mean?"

"See, the best products, you can't get here. Uncle Sam won't let us have 'em. A miracle drug may exist overseas, but here the FDA orders a million tests, and if the tiniest thing goes wrong, the drug companies won't touch it with a ten-foot pole."

"Are you saying Dr. Welch was using products that hadn't been approved by the FDA?"

"Did I say that?"

"Like illegal Botox? I read about that. People get paralyzed from it."

"Maybe if you deal with fly-by-night suppliers, but Dr. Welch is careful. Suzanne was a grown-up. Let her make her own decisions about what she needs and what risks she'll take. Her face was her fortune."

And yours, Melanie thought pointedly. "Is that the story Suzanne was working on? The one the stolen file was about?" she asked.

"Why would Suzanne publicize the illegal Botox if she was using it herself? No, she'd found out something else about Welch, something much worse. Bad enough that she felt she needed to find out the truth, even if that meant he wouldn't give her those shots anymore. She said she couldn't tell me the details until she was a hundred percent sure her suspicions were correct. But in the past few days, she was getting close."

NINE

Melanie hadn't slept all night. She was still in the clothes she'd worn to the crime scene. A dull headache pounded behind her eyes, and she had that terrible emptiness in the pit of her stomach that the ugliest cases gave her. The feeling was akin to a bad hangover, and she knew of only one cure. She could use a hot shower and a change of clothes and a strong cup of coffee, sure. But what she really needed was a hug from her daughter.

When she walked into her empty apartment, a whiff of baby smell hit her in the face, that potent blend of Johnson's lotion and the Diaper Genie needing to be emptied that made her long for Maya's funny little face. Her ex-husband, Steve, was scheduled to drop Maya off at eight—ten minutes from now. Melanie would only have half an hour with her daughter, since she needed to head straight to work when the babysitter arrived. If she didn't want to waste her precious Maya time getting ready, she'd better shower fast.

As she was toweling off, the buzzer rang. Melanie pulled on a bathrobe and hurried to peer through the keyhole. Steve looked as gorgeous as ever, with his rugged blond looks and expensive haircut. A big part of Melanie's burnout was lingering shock over her divorce. A child of divorce herself, she'd intended to marry once, for life. But then she'd caught Steve red-handed having an affair right after Maya was born—an affair that had obviously been going on for a long time. He'd wanted to reconcile, and despite the way he'd walked all over her dreams, she'd been tempted to listen—for Maya's sake, for the sake of their history together. But in the end, she just didn't trust the man, and she couldn't stay married to somebody she didn't trust.

Melanie pulled open the door.

"Hey, babe," Steve said.

But now she'd turned her attention to her daughter. Maya was seventeen months old and full of personality. Her dark hair was done up in a lopsided Pebbles ponytail, and she still wore her feetie pajamas. Melanie was used to getting Maya back from Steve in need of a bath and with all her possessions in disarray, so she didn't mind the wardrobe transgressions. But the translucent plastic pacifier moving in and out of Maya's mouth to the rhythm of her suck was another matter altogether.

"What is that *thing* doing in her mouth?"

"Well, hello to you, too," Steve said, looking her up and down, a sexy twinkle in his green eyes. "How was your hot date last night? Did Musclehead get lucky?"

"Steve, do you *read* any of the materials I give you? Why do I even bother?" And she grabbed Maya out of his arms with an indignant sigh.

Melanie always sent Maya to her daddy with not only a carefully packed suitcase but also a full set of typed instructions covering such matters as meals, bath-, nap-, and bedtimes, medicines, favorite stuffed animals and clothing items, et cetera. Permitted pacifier use was the critical topic of the moment, and the instruction sheet had specified BEDTIME ONLY in bold-faced capital letters.

"If I take it away, she cries," Steve said.

"Yes, I know that. Now she'll cry more, and I'll be the bad guy. We have to keep up a united front. You need to support me on this."

Melanie closed her fingers around the pacifier's translucent rim. Beneath it, a fine layer of spit formed a virtual occlusive seal. Melanie started to tug, and Maya's brown eyes widened with terror as she bit down on the thing with all her might. They struggled over it furiously, and if Melanie came up the winner, it was only because she had over a hundred pounds on the girl, not because her will was stronger. Melanie put Maya down, and the child immediately flung herself to the floor kicking and yowling in a full-blown tantrum.

"See what I mean?" Melanie said, her blood pressure skyrocketing.

"She was smiling when I brought her here, baby. You're the one who made her cry."

"Give me her bag and get going before you cause more trouble," Melanie snapped, and Steve wheeled Maya's Dora the Explorer suitcase into the foyer.

"Oh, listen, Mel. I wanted to give you a heads-up. I might have a problem taking her this weekend," he said over Maya's shrieks.

"You remember I'm going to Bernadette's wedding, right?"

"I know, and I feel terrible. But I'm headed to LAX right now on a major deal. The car's waiting downstairs. I'll do everything in my power to be back in time, but I can't promise."

"I told you about this wedding two months ago."

"What can I do? I have to work."

"I have to work, too. This is work for me. It's my boss who's getting married, and she's not gonna be happy if I no-show after I RSVP'd yes."

"So call your mom."

"Call *your* mom. This is your weekend. In fact, it's your first weekend in three weeks because you keep asking me to switch."

"You always say you don't mind."

"I'm usually happy to have extra time with her. But this weekend, I have something important to do."

"Okay, I'll try to reach my mom on my way to the airport. If she can't do it, I'll let you know."

Before Melanie could protest further, Steve pecked her swiftly on the cheek, blew a kiss to the hysterical Maya, and backed out the door at full speed. Melanie sank to the floor beside her howling daughter. She felt like screaming, too. *Ay de Dios,* she hated being divorced. But staying married to the guy would have been worse. He got less responsible with each passing day.

Melanie reached out and drew Maya onto her lap, careful to avoid getting socked by the small flailing fists. "*Tranquila,*" she murmured. "*Cálmate, cálmate. Nena preciosa, cálmate. No llore, m'ija.*"

They'd had a rough winter full of ear infections and colds, and Melanie had learned through trial and error that Spanish soothed her little girl best. Now that Maya had tubes in her ears and, Melanie prayed, the ear infections were a thing of the past, the Spanish still came in handy. Maya's sobs gradually quieted to hiccups. As Melanie hugged her daughter passionately against her chest, she felt her own emptiness ebb away.

The weather was so perfect as Melanie exited the lobby of her building that she thought she'd died and gone to Northern California. Seventy-six degrees with no humidity and lavish sunshine. As she turned the corner onto Park Avenue, dusty pink flowers swayed in a gentle breeze. The gorgeous day and her Maya fix conspired to lift Melanie's spirits to a punchy, sleep-deprived state of near euphoria. She even felt equal to tackling that awful Clyde Williams situation.

Melanie refused to believe the city councilman had anything to do with Suzanne Shepard's murder. Clyde's morals she couldn't speak for, but the guy was too smart and too smooth to do something as crude as killing a reporter over an unflattering story. The information from Suzanne's mother about the robbery at their apartment seemed much more promising. Yet Melanie had an obligation to investigate every lead. If she ignored this one, she'd look like she was playing favorites because Clyde Williams's son was her good friend. The press, in the form of Target News, would be scrutinizing her every move. So really, she had no choice. Melanie had to at least go through the motions on this one.

In the Eighty-sixth Street subway station, as Melanie swiped her MetroCard, a tall, broad-shouldered man at the next turnstile caught her eye. He looked away just as she focused on him, and suddenly she felt like he'd been behind her for blocks. He was wearing a hooded sweatshirt with the hood up, and she couldn't see his face or the color of his hair. The hood struck her as odd on such a warm morning. *Take notice of people in bulky or inappropriate clothing,* the antiterrorism posters in all the subway cars warned; it was right up there with reporting suspicious packages. But Melanie shrugged off the troubling thought as she headed for the platform for the downtown 4 train. Even if the guy had been behind her for a while, so what? Her route down Lexington was the most obvious path to the subway. Coincidence. Nothing to worry about.

It was rush hour, and the subway car was jammed. Melanie held on to a pole, her eyes fixed on an overhead advertisement for computer classes, working through the Clyde Williams problem. If she actually planned to investigate the city councilman, things were bound to get complicated. Her friend Joe would have to be walled off from the investigation, which was standard procedure but awkward nonetheless. And though she knew little about public corruption investigations, Melanie recalled hearing that some sort of special permission was required to investigate elected officials. She'd have to remember to ask Bernadette about that. The darn subway car was so crowded and swaying so badly that she couldn't open her bag to make a note.

Melanie's eyes wandered restlessly around the car as she continued to turn the problem over in her mind. Absorbed in her thoughts, she passed right over the man in the hooded sweatshirt. A fraction of a second later, his presence registered, and Melanie looked back with a start. He stood against the closed doors half a car length down from her, his head turned away, the side of his face obscured by the hood. But there was nothing to be concerned about. He wasn't watching her, definitely not.

Nevertheless, when the train pulled into Forty-second Street, Melanie decided to perform a test. She got out and fought her way down the platform to the next car, leaping inside just as the doors closed. He didn't follow. Even better, there were empty seats in here.

A minute later, as the train lurched through a dark tunnel, the door at the end of the car slid open. Melanie had taken a seat and was jotting reminders of items she needed to discuss with Bernadette. She glanced up to see Hooded Sweatshirt bracing himself against the conductor's booth, his back turned toward her. Had he come in looking for a seat? But there were empty seats, and he was standing. Since she had her notebook out anyway, Melanie decided to write down his description. He was big, around six feet with a muscular build. Caucasian, judging by his hands, but she still hadn't gotten a clear look at his face.

The train approached her stop. Melanie closed her notebook and put it away. She would have to leave the relative safety of the crowded subway car, but she wasn't nervous. This was nothing. One thing she was firm with herself about was not letting the job make her paranoid.

Melanie exited the door closest to the stairs. In her peripheral vision, without looking directly at him, she saw that Hooded Sweatshirt had stepped out of the next one. Her high heels rang out against the tile floor as she walked toward the staircase. He must've been wearing sneakers because even though she knew he was behind her, she couldn't hear him at all, which was somehow creepier than if she could. Telling herself she was being foolish, Melanie nevertheless picked up her pace and almost jogged through the tunnel. Before she knew it she was outside, sprinting across the plaza toward her building. She reached the glass doors and saw the guard at his desk in the lobby, reading the newspaper. A number of people stood at the elevator bank, clutching briefcases and coffee cups.

Melanie did a quick about-face, thinking she'd summon the guard if Hooded Sweatshirt had actually pursued her. But behind her, the plaza where the subway let out was deserted, save for an elderly woman feeding a horde of pigeons in the dappled sunlight.

TEN

There was so much to do that Melanie hardly knew where to begin, so she started with the thing that troubled her most. Before she did anything else—before she checked her e-mail or voice mail or typed a single subpoena—she marched straight to her boss's office to get some guidance on this tricky situation with Clyde Williams.

The chief's suite occupied prime corner real estate at the intersection of the two hallways that housed the Major Crimes Unit. Bernadette's secretary, Shekeya Jenkins, sat at her desk in the small anteroom filling out a form on the computer as she chomped on a bagel. Shekeya was a big woman with braids dyed bright orange and an often poisonous tongue. She'd been Bernadette's secretary for years, taken a heap of abuse, and given back plenty, too. Their dysfunctional relationship provided much entertainment for the junior prosecutors.

"What's good, girl? You famous!" Shekeya greeted Melanie.

"You saw me on TV?"

"Yes, I did. Melanie Vargas taking on the Central Park Butcher. I was jumping up and down in my bedroom screaming at the screen."

"I didn't get to see it. How did I look?"

"Very photogenic." Shekeya lowered her voice and leaned toward Melanie conspiratorially. "The boss is so jealous. She asked me if I thought you looked better than her on TV."

"What did you say?"

"I lied, naturally. Mama didn't raise no foolish children."

Melanie laughed, turning toward Bernadette's door.

"Wait a minute, girl. She's on the phone anyway, and I got a favor to ask you," Shekeya said.

"Anything for you, Shekeya."

"You better find out what it is before you say yes. This one got some downsides."

"Is something wrong?" Melanie asked, concerned.

"No, something's finally right. I'm applying for the paralegal slot that come open in narcotics. They say you need references from three attorneys in the office who know your work, so I was hoping maybe I could count on you for one?"

Melanie's eyes widened. "You mean, leave Bernadette?"

"What is she, my mother, that I can't walk? You have any idea what it's like putting up with that woman in my face all day, every day? I can't wait to see the back of her."

"But, Shekeya, you handle her better than anybody."

"I *can* handle her, but that doesn't mean I like to. It ain't worth what it's doing to my health. Besides, paralegal is a raise, and I got my kids to think about. The extra money could pay for Khadija's braces."

"I hear that." Melanie paused. "Does she know?"

Shekeya glanced at the closed door to Bernadette's inner sanctum and then down at her telephone, where a green light indicated Bernadette was still on the line. "Look, I'ma tell you a secret, so you understand where I'm coming from with this. But you can't breathe a word."

"Of course not."

"The boss wants to be a judge."

"That's no secret, Shekeya. Everybody who's ever met her knows that. But getting appointed to the bench is a one-in-a-million shot."

"Not this time, it ain't. The fix is in. Word is that Judge Cordell is announcing his retirement next week on his eightieth birthday."

"That's not a secret, either. Cordell's slept through every afternoon appearance I've had before him for the past three years. People've been speculating about his retirement since the day I came on duty."

"But it's really happening this time. Seriously, I'm friends with his secretary. And the boss is applying for his seat," Shekeya said.

"Shekeya, you don't just apply to be an Article Three judge. It's a whole big process. You need political connections. And you need, well, less baggage than Bernadette has."

"I'm telling you, Vito got connections, and the boss is talking like this thing is a done deal. She's practically over there measuring for drapes."

The green light on the telephone went off. Melanie glanced at her watch. Time was slipping away, and she needed to end this discussion. "Okay, I believe you. But why leave? Why not go with her?"

"She asked me to go along, and I said yes, on one condition. I don't want to be just a secretary no more. I got my degree in criminal justice administration. I want more action, more responsibility. I want to be her courtroom deputy. And she told me she don't see me in that light, that I'd be rising above my skill level. Now, how'm I supposed to continue working for her after she say something like that?"

Just then, the door to Bernadette's office swung open.

"Speak of the devil," Shekeya said loudly.

"All right," Melanie said under her breath, "I'll do it."

"Are you talking about me?" Bernadette demanded.

"Melanie needs to speak to you," Shekeya said, turning toward Melanie so Bernadette couldn't see, mouthing "thank you" and winking.

"Inside, girlfriend," Bernadette said, jerking her head toward her office.

Melanie took a seat in one of the beige guest chairs. Bernadette's office might be spacious and boast a corner view, but it was still no-frills government issue, with a linoleum floor and a gray metal desk. Bernadette herself was looking rather no-frills this morning. Her face was lined and tired and bare of makeup beneath the exuberant red hair of a much younger woman.

"I'm getting barraged with calls from the media on the Central Park Butcher case," Bernadette said, settling into her swivel chair and picking up her coffee mug. "Fill me in. What've you got so far?"

"Unfortunately, the victim had a lot of enemies, so I have a lot of leads to sort through. One in particular is tricky, and I need some advice," Melanie said.

"Give me the big picture first, then we'll talk details."

"Okay, let's see. The victim received a telephone call at work at approximately six o'clock yesterday from an unknown source, and presumably went to meet that person last night in Central Park. That's the most significant thing I've learned so far. I'll subpoena all the relevant phone records to see if we can identify the originating number for that call. There was a burglary at the victim's apartment approximately ten days ago. The intruder took files on two stories, one about a personal trainer at Flex Gym selling drugs to wealthy clients. The other had something to do with a prominent plastic surgeon. I'll contact the assigned detective and see what I can find out, but that one looks quite promising. Target News is going to send over files on all the stories the victim covered recently. That'll be a lot of boxes, so I'll try to find somebody with a brain to wade through them and see if anything else leaps out."

Bernadette reached into her desk drawer and pulled out a key with a tag attached to it. "Here, I'm assigning you a war room. You can have the files sent there. What's your staffing like?"

"Better than any case I've ever worked. Because the homicide happened in the park, and because the victim was a celebrity, the FBI and the PD are doing a full-court press. I've got Dan O'Reilly and a detective from Manhattan North Homicide as co–case agents, and they have lots of backup. Upward of twenty guys full-time, at least until the weekend. The only caveat is, most of the grunts are tied up canvassing for eyewitnesses, so they're not exactly at my beck and call."

"Who's the detective?"

"Julian Hay. He's a—"

"Suave Pierre? Shit. He's worse than useless."

"What? I thought he was a famous undercover."

Bernadette raised an eyebrow. "You planning to do drug buys on this murder investigation?"

"Not that I'm aware of."

"If you do, great, he'll come through with flying colors. But he doesn't function well outside his area of expertise. Not only won't Pierre do any legwork, he'll distract the other agents with his endless war stories. This kingpin drew down on him, that cartel leader tried to have him whacked. On and on. He's like a celebrity. Your agents will be bringing him lattes when they should be analyzing phone records."

"Thanks for the word of warning. I'll keep an eye on the situation." One thing about Bernadette, she didn't pull her punches. She gave you the straight story, even when it wasn't what you wanted to hear.

"I just spoke to the D.A.'s office," Bernadette said. "They're cross-designating Janice Marsh and detailing her to us for the pendency of the case. She'll report to your office shortly. Give her those files to sort through, or anything else the cops aren't smart or patient enough to do."

Melanie was scribbling away on her notepad, trying to keep up with Bernadette's words. She looked up to find her boss watching her with a pensive expression.

"You've got a big team assembled, girlfriend. That's a luxury, but it's also a responsibility. You'll need to keep them under careful control. You're up for that, right?"

Last night, Melanie would have said no. But since then, she'd viewed Suzanne Shepard's mutilated body, met her grieving son, and started puzzling through the complicated threads of this investigation. Add to that the thrill of the press coverage and the new challenge of supervising a big team, and Melanie wanted this case—badly.

"You bet," she said.

"Good. Any resources you need—experts or travel authorizations or such—just ask and we'll find money in budget. Now, what was it you wanted my advice about?"

"Did you know that Suzanne Shepard just broke a story about a sex scandal involving Clyde Williams and an intern?" Melanie asked.

Bernadette looked startled. "Actually, yes, I did know. Joe's been out for the past few days strategizing with Clyde's brain trust, trying to contain the damage. I have to admit, I didn't make the connection. You don't think—you can't mean—is there any indication Clyde Williams is involved?"

"Personally, I doubt it, but the producer of Suzanne Shepard's show smells a story. Apparently, Suzanne received a threat in the mail right after she aired the segment on Clyde. A box of dog shit containing a picture of her that'd been cut into little pieces. There's no proof that Clyde sent it, but I get the sense Target News is planning to find some."

"Or invent some," Bernadette said, rolling her eyes.

"Even assuming Clyde is innocent, this is still a tricky situation, politically speaking. We can't appear to be going easy on him just because—"

"Just because his son works here! Jeez, you're right." Bernadette dropped her head into her hands and rubbed her eyes.

"It's a conflict of interest, isn't it?"

"It's a pain in my *ass*, is what it is," Bernadette said. She looked up and sighed, her eyes bloodshot. "Not only is Joe one of ours, but Clyde is an elected official. That's a major problem in itself. We can deal with the conflict by walling Joe off from the investigation. But to investigate an elected official, we have to jump through all sorts of hoops."

"I thought I recalled something like that. What are the requirements?"

"Honestly, I haven't done one of these cases in years. Let me make some calls to Main Justice and find out what paperwork they need. As a practical matter, that means you can't start investigating Clyde until I give the green light, understand? Or else we risk running afoul of the protocol."

"It's not like I'm itching to go after him anyway. He's Joe's dad, and I love Joe to death."

"Why do you think they call it a conflict, girl-friend?" Bernadette paused, sipping her coffee and studying Melanie. "Listen, you know I believe in eating what you kill. Melanie Vargas brings in the Central Park Butcher case, Melanie Vargas gets to keep that case until the bitter end. But I have to be able to trust in your impartiality or I can't let you do this one. With all this media scrutiny, the Shepard case will blow up in our faces if it's not handled properly."

Conscious of her boss's eyes on her, Melanie kept her face neutral, but behind it, her thoughts were roiling. The fact was, she hadn't stopped to ask herself how she felt about investigating the father of one of her closest friends.

"Before you answer," Bernadette said, "let me throw one more factor into the mix. You know that when I'm in Cancún, Susan will be acting chief?"

Susan Charlton was Bernadette's deputy, an award-winning prosecutor, brilliant and ferocious.

"Of course," Melanie said. "Everybody expected that."

"Well, that leaves the deputy chief slot vacant for two weeks starting Monday. You know what that position entails?"

"Sure. Supervising junior prosecutors, authorizing new arrests, signing off on indictments and plea bargains. It's a big job."

"Yes, it is." She paused, looking Melanie square in the eyes. "On the way to work today, thinking about the coup you pulled off in landing this case, I was considering naming you acting deputy."

Melanie flushed with pleasure. A deputy chief spot was a cherished dream of hers, and taking a turn as acting deputy made it more likely she'd be considered when a permanent position opened up. Not only did deputy chief pay better—and she could sure use the extra money—but it was the first step on the path to the promised land. Deputy chiefs who were talented and hardworking eventually became unit chiefs like Bernadette. Unit chiefs became chiefs of the Criminal Division. Chiefs of the Criminal Division became magistrate judges, and magistrate judges became bona fide, honest-to-goodness Article Three federal judges with lifetime tenure, the holy grail of the legal profession, the next best thing to the Supreme Court of the United States. A vision of herself in black robes swam before Melanie's eyes.

"Bernadette, I'm honored."

"I didn't say I was appointing you, I said I was considering it. I'm deciding between you and Brad Monahan. As of last night, he was my top choice. As of this morning, you were. The Butcher investigation is a critical factor in my decision. I'm leaving for Cancún Sunday morning. If you handle the case well between now and then, you get the job. If you don't, it goes to Brad. Now, with that in mind, what is your answer to the question of whether you can be impartial in investigating Clyde Williams?"

Moments of truth sneak up on you sometimes. As Bernadette watched her face, Melanie realized she was at an important juncture, one she hadn't been anticipating, where she needed to choose between who she was and who she would become. The choice wasn't just about selfish career advancement, either. This job was hard for a lot of reasons, a major one being the need to put the public welfare ahead of personal concerns. A sadistic killer was on the loose, and Melanie was in the best position to stop him. As weighed against a matter of such magnitude, her burnout and even her close friendship with Joe all looked small. Melanie thought about Suzanne Shepard's mutilated stomach. The fact was, if Clyde Williams was mixed up in that ugly crime, he deserved to go down, no matter whose father he was.

"Growing up ain't never easy, girlfriend," Bernadette said, reading her mind. "What's your answer?"

"I can do it," Melanie declared, nodding resolutely.

ELEVEN

Back in her office, Melanie began her workday as she always did, by checking her e-mail. The subject line read *I'm watching you.* In the quiet of the office, with the memory of the man in the hooded sweatshirt fresh in her mind, the caption got her attention. The message had been sent last night at 1:19 a.m. from an address she didn't recognize, partysover2007@yahoo.com. She clicked on it. It read:

To Melanie Vargas—I saw you on TV and I could tell you have a sexy body under those boring clothes. You can't hide it from me, I always know. I want to see you with the clothes off. How tall are you and how much do you weigh? I don't like women too big. Write back soon. Your secret admirer. P.S. Don't waste your time on that nosy bitch Suzanne Shepard. This Central Park Butcher guy did the world a favor.

Melanie's first reaction was to feel repulsed, as any woman would upon receiving an obscene message. But then the prosecutor in her kicked in, and she started thinking about whether the e-mail could possibly be connected to the Shepard case.

"'Nosy bitch,'" she whispered. "He calls her a bitch."

They had carefully kept all information about the gruesome message carved into the victim's stomach away from the press. As far as Melanie knew, only law enforcement personnel were aware of the mutilation. Holding back signature details of a crime allowed them to truth-test anybody who contacted them claiming to be the killer. She'd been taught that investigative principle, but she'd never seen it in action. Could she be seeing it now?

Melanie did her best to remain calm and think through the events of the past hour or so. This message read *I'm watching you,* and she'd had the distinct impression that the man in the hooded sweatshirt on the subway had been following her. The e-mailer had called Suzanne a bitch. Put those facts together, and suddenly she was leaping to the conclusion that the Central Park Butcher himself had followed her from her apartment onto the subway. But when she thought about it objectively, Melanie didn't believe any of those things. Use of the word "bitch" didn't make this creep the Butcher. The e-mail didn't actually mention the mutilation, which the real killer surely would have. And the e-mailer couldn't possibly have figured out where she lived. Melanie was scrupulously careful about keeping her home address and telephone number unlisted, as much to protect Maya as to protect herself. No stranger who'd seen her on TV should be able to track her down. Besides, the guy in the sweatshirt hadn't even been following her. If he had, when she'd turned around before in the plaza, he would have been behind her. Instead, the place was deserted.

Just as she'd talked herself out of feeling nervous, a loud rap on her office door made Melanie jump. A young woman with a pleasant, doughy face stood in her doorway. She was short and wore a shapeless gray suit.

"Sorry, didn't mean to startle you," the woman said. "I'm Janice Marsh from the D.A.'s office."

"Oh, right. My boss told me you were coming."

Janice walked in and plopped down in Melanie's guest chair. "Are you okay? You look white as a ghost."

"Were you at the crime scene last night?" Melanie asked.

Janice blushed. "I'm sorry I ran out. It was my first murder scene and it was worse than I expected. If you give me second chance, I'll work like a dog on this case, promise."

"No need to apologize. That's not why I was asking. You know the killer carved the word 'bitch' on Suzanne Shepard's stomach, right?"

"Are you kidding, I'll remember that for the rest of my life. Why do you think I hurled?"

"Could you do me a favor and read this obscene e-mail I received?" Melanie asked.

"Sure." Throwing her a curious glance, Janice stepped behind Melanie's desk and leaned over to see the computer. She read the e-mail, then she read it a second time.

"What do you think?" Melanie asked.

Janice straightened up. "You're wondering about the fact that this clown calls her a bitch? Does that mean he's the Butcher?"

"Exactly."

"No way. Every asshole who hates women loves the B-word, right? All this means is that some jerk saw you on TV and decided to harass you. The same thing happened to a woman I work with in the D.A.'s office. She was doing a high-profile case and her picture was in the paper. She started getting obscene phone calls. One of the cops she worked with paid the guy a visit and it stopped."

"That's what I thought, too. I just wanted a second opinion," Melanie said.

"You may have a Web stalker, but I don't think he's the Butcher."

"Too bad, huh? It would make solving the case a lot easier."

As Janice laughed, Melanie's telephone started ringing.

"We got the 911 caller," Dan said when Melanie picked up. She heard static, and a loud siren in the background that was shrieking simultaneously outside her office window.

"You sound close," she said.

"We're right in front of your building. Julian's getting the guy out of the car now, and we're gonna bring him up the secure elevator. You want us to meet you in your office?"

"Why are you bringing him in the secure elevator? Did you arrest him?" she asked.

"The guy's got two nasty-ass scratches on his cheek. You remember the victim had skin under her nails? This could be the Butcher, and he wants to talk."

"I've got a war room," she said, pulling out the key Bernadette had given her and checking the tag. "Six-fourteen-B. Meet me there in five minutes."

TWELVE

Melanie and Janice sat at the conference table, which was oversize for the cramped space. The boxes from Target News had been delivered and were piled on the floor, competing for space with leftover detritus from somebody else's trial. Charts and blowups leaned precariously against the walls and piles of proposed jury instructions were everywhere. But as the door handle turned, Melanie was glad she'd thought to meet this prisoner on neutral ground instead of in her office, where she kept pictures of Maya and other personal possessions. She'd sat across the table from killers before, but this felt different. The gruesome nature of the crime. The man following her on the subway. The disturbing e-mail. This case was starting to make her nervous.

The door opened and Dan and Julian walked in, the handcuffed suspect between them. Melanie saw his face and drew a sharp breath. Two angry scratches slashed across his right cheek, undoubtedly the work of human fingernails. Was this man the Central Park Butcher?

Dan removed a handcuff key from the front pocket of his khaki pants. They were the same pants he'd worn to his birthday dinner last night. It felt like light-years ago.

"Turn around, Dave," Dan said. He had an easy way with prisoners—authoritative, firm, but humane.

"Looks like you get the comfy chair, my friend," Julian said, his gold teeth flashing as he pulled out an old vinyl-and-metal swivel chair that was the only one in the room with arms. The man sat down and Dan handcuffed his right hand to the chair's arm. Dan and Julian both shook hands with Janice, whom they hadn't met before, and took seats on either side of their prisoner.

"Has he been Mirandized?" Melanie asked.

"He said he'd waive his rights, but I'm out of forms for him to sign," Dan replied, holding up his hands.

Melanie went over to the computer terminal that sat on a small side table and printed out a Miranda rights form, which she handed to the prisoner.

"I'm Melanie Vargas from the U.S. Attorney's Office," she said, taking a seat across from him, "and this is Janice Marsh from the D.A.'s office. We're investigating the murder of Suzanne Shepard. What is your name, sir?"

"David M. Harris, Esquire," he said in an educated voice. His unruffled gaze told her nothing. It certainly didn't prove he was innocent. The biggest psychos were capable of taking their own crimes, and law enforcement's interest in them, in stride without breaking a sweat.

"You're a lawyer?" she asked.

"Yes, an associate with the firm of Feinerman, Seidel, Brinkley and Tate."

"I know the Feinerman firm."

"Of course you do. We're the biggest in the city, and the most prestigious," he added with a curt nod.

"You're an associate?"

"Yes, up for partner in fourteen months, so getting arrested right now is not convenient for me. Can we clear up this mistake, please, and get on with the day?"

"Getting murdered last night was not convenient for Suzanne Shepard, either," Melanie retorted. "So I'm sure you understand we need to take our time and get the facts straight. You'll have to bear with us. Please read the form I've placed before you, initial each paragraph separately, and sign at the bottom. Let me know if you have any questions."

"No questions. I'm quite familiar with *Miranda v. Arizona*," he replied coldly. He scanned the page and signed off. Dan took the form, witnessed Harris's signature, and handed it across the table to Melanie.

"Just to fill the two a' youse in," Dan said, nodding at Melanie and Janice as he pulled a spiral notebook from his back pocket and consulted it, "Mr. Harris is the gentleman who phoned 911 from the park last night and reported he'd witnessed a woman stabbed in the Ramble. He subsequently fled the scene despite being told by the dispatcher that a blue-and-white was en route. When we interviewed him this morning at his place of business, he initially denied being the individual who placed the call. Subsequent to that we played the tape, and asked him if we needed to play it for his boss to get a positive voice ID. He stated negative and admitted he'd made the call. We asked him where he got the scratches on his cheeks. He stated—" Dan paused to flip the page—"he stated that he received them while playing with his two-year-old son last night. We said those didn't look like two-year-old-size scratches to us, and requested his home telephone number for verification. One Robin S. Harris answered and identified herself as the subject's wife. Mrs. Harris stated that subject did not return home last night at all because he was, quote, 'pulling an all-nighter on a big case' end quote. Subject has since refused to explain truthfully where he got the scratches, or where he went after the park, but he states he is willing to submit to a DNA test to verify he's not the Butcher." Dan folded up his notebook and put it back in his pocket.

"Ms. Vargas, if I may?" Harris asked.

"Please."

He tried to lean forward conspiratorially, but the handcuffs brought him up short. "Are these shackles really necessary?" he asked, a frown of annoyance flitting across his forehead.

"Those aren't shackles. Shackles are when we put leg irons on and chain them to your handcuffs." *Go ahead, make my day,* her tone said.

But Harris wasn't fazed. "Look, I could have kept my mouth shut and asked for a lawyer. I didn't do that, so show a little courtesy in return. I want to give the DNA sample right away. You'll see that I'm innocent, and then I can get back to the office before I'm missed."

"I can't just test you in five minutes and find out whether you're the killer," Melanie said. "The DNA testing process can take days. In the meantime, we need to figure out what to do with you. Do I file obstruction-of-justice charges? Do you go to jail?"

"Ob-obstruction charges? Why the hell would you do that if I'm being cooperative?" Harris demanded, his voice shaking. He licked his lips nervously. Obstruction charges could lead not only to possible jail time, but to disbarment. That prospect seemed to disturb him more than anything else she'd said so far.

"Agreeing to submit to the DNA test alone is not sufficient cooperation. We need details about what happened last night."

"You actually think I killed some woman in the park last night? That's the most idiotic thing I've ever heard. Why on earth would I do that?"

"You tell us, Mr. Harris. Did you have a grudge against Suzanne Shepard? Did she do a story on you? Was she your lover?" Melanie asked.

"I've never met the woman in my life! I never even watched her brainless show. I certainly didn't *kill* her."

"Then we need another explanation for your actions last night. Why were you at the scene of the crime? Why were you in the park at all on a rainy night? How did you get those scratches on your cheek? Why did you hang up when the 911 dispatcher asked for your name? Why did you run away before the cops arrived? And why did you lie to the agents about placing the call after they tracked you down? If you don't explain yourself, I'm afraid the obvious conclusion is that you did those things because you killed Suzanne Shepard."

Harris's face turned red, and he started breathing faster. "I can't believe this. You're serious."

"Of course we are. Your conduct has given us reason to be."

"I assure you, there is an innocent explanation," he said.

"Okay, fine, I'm listening," Melanie said.

"But I need to know. Are you going to tell my wife?" Harris asked in a voice incongruously small for his powerful frame.

"Tell her why you were in the park?"

"Yes."

"I won't tell her directly. I have no reason to. But neither can I promise to keep your statement confidential. It might get disclosed in court."

"Oh God. . . ." Harris hung his head, screwing his eyes shut and kneading them with the heels of his hands. He almost looked like he was going to cry.

"Hey, Dave, man, let me tell you something," Dan said. "The alternative is getting charged with murder. Then you'll have to tell anyway to get yourself out of jail, and a helluva lot more people are gonna hear about it than just Robin. The whole city's paying attention to this Butcher case. So pull yourself together and give us an answer, or things'll just get worse."

"Okay," Harris said, opening his eyes. "Give me a minute." He took several deep breaths.

"Why were you in the Ramble last night, Mr. Harris?" Melanie repeated.

Harris looked directly at Melanie, avoiding eye contact with Dan and Julian. "I'm not gay. I've just been under a lot of stress lately. This was the first time I ever went there."

He was probably lying, but it didn't really matter for their purposes.

"Your sex life is none of our business," Melanie said, switching to a friendlier tone. "We need to rule you out as a suspect in this murder. If you had some other credible reason for being at the scene of the crime, that's a help."

"I was looking . . . looking for . . . I was looking for companionship, okay? I approached this guy, and he tried to rob me. We were in the middle of negotiating, you know, how much I would pay him, and he jumped me. I lift a lot. I mean, I work out, and I used to be in the military in Israel. I'm in shape. I fought him off, but in the process, he scratched my face. That's how I got these. Swear to God."

"What happened after you fought with him?" Melanie asked.

"I sat on the bench for a little while trying to pull myself together. My face was bleeding, and I had no idea how I'd explain the scratches to my wife. Once I collected myself, I got up and headed east, toward the exit from the Ramble. And that's when I saw it."

"It?"

"*Him.* I saw him before I saw her. He was standing facing me, and he had, like, this harness on his head with what looked like binoculars attached to it. I'll tell you, that freaked me out. Stopped me right in my tracks."

"Night-vision goggles," Dan said.

Melanie felt the same sick chill she had when she heard about the surgical gloves. Those were the tools of a killer who was practiced in his ways, a killer who could strike again at any moment, and someone she'd damn well better get off the street.

"Is that what they were? I knew they were some- thing fucked up." Harris looked sick to his stomach.

"Could it have been the same guy you'd fought with?" Melanie asked.

"No, definitely not. The man I'd fought with was much smaller, and he'd run off in the opposite direction."

"Describe this second man," Melanie ordered.

"Tallish. Six feet, maybe."

"Build?"

"Big. Heavyset."

"White, black, Hispanic?" she asked.

"White, *I think*. But it was dark, and he was wearing something with a hood. Some kind of sweatshirt."

Hooded sweatshirt? The guy on the subway had been wearing a hooded sweatshirt, and come to think of it, the height and build sounded similar, too. Could it be the same person? But no, she was getting paranoid. That guy hadn't even been following her.

Melanie realized she'd tuned out for a minute and that everyone was waiting for her to speak. "What happened next?" she asked.

"I saw a woman kneeling in front of him. She was down on the ground, and her back was toward me. She managed to get partway up on her feet, but I could tell she was struggling. Then I saw him striking at her with something. She started to scream, but I could tell there was something over her mouth because the sound was weird. Oh God, it was . . . the sound. It was different than anything else I've ever heard. It was so . . . horrible. She was shrieking but it wasn't really getting through. It was like this rasping, choking kind of sound. Somehow, that's what made me realize he had a knife. I couldn't see it. But from the noise she was making, I knew he was stabbing her."

They were all silent for a moment, absorbing the horror of the scene.

"Then what happened?" Melanie asked.

"The woman tried to crawl away. He kept stabbing her. Then he kicked her a bunch of times really hard. After that, I didn't see her move again."

"Then what?"

"He dragged her a ways and pushed her off this little cliff. Over the edge, like, to where the ground was lower."

"Into the ravine."

"Right. Then he went down after her, and I ran like hell until I got to the park exit. I called the cops, as you know, then I went back to my office and slept there. I did my civic duty and reported this terrible thing to 911. The reason I didn't stay and wait for the police to arrive was, well, I didn't want anyone to know I'd been cruising. You can understand that, right?"

"You're ex-military, and from the looks of it, you're extremely strong. Why didn't you try to intervene?" Melanie asked.

Harris looked at her like she was crazy. "The man had a knife, and he was in the middle of using it. I was unarmed. He would have killed me. As a father of three, I wasn't about to take a risk like that for a complete stranger."

Melanie gazed back at him evenly, her expression noncommittal. "We need a minute," she said finally, and nodded at Janice and the agents.

"I'll stay here so Mr. Harris doesn't get any smart ideas," Julian said.

Leaving the door ajar on the off chance Harris did decide to make a move, Melanie, Dan, and Janice stepped outside to confer.

"Can we get the DNA sample taken today?" Melanie asked Dan in a low tone.

"The technicians are on beeper. I'll page them and try to get somebody in here. If I can, it's just a swab from his cheek. Only takes a minute. I can't make any promises whether a tech is available, though."

"How long for results once the sample is taken?"

"Normally, it's weeks, but in a case like this, put a rush on it, we'll have an answer in a day or two, assuming there's nothing else big going on that I don't know about."

"Do you believe his story?" she asked.

Janice shook her head. "Too much of a coincidence if you ask me, him being at the scene of the crime *and* getting his face scratched. I think he's lying."

"Dan?" Melanie asked.

"Guys like that are why everybody hates lawyers," Dan said. "I can barely stand the sight of his smug face, but gut reaction, he's telling the truth. Think about how scared he sounded on the 911 tape. He would've had to be one damn good actor to fake that. I think he was out cruising guys and that's why he ran. The scratches bother me, but it's plausible they came from a robbery attempt. Pross gets the jump on the john. Happens all the time in the Ramble. I buy it."

"You're the deciding vote," Janice said, looking at Melanie.

"Obviously, we get the DNA sample done right away," Melanie said. "That's a no-brainer. The real question is what to do with Harris while we're waiting for the results."

Melanie paused, thinking. Arresting Harris on obstruction-of-justice charges might destroy his legal career, and in a different case, she would have cut the guy some slack. But this was a murder case, a particularly brutal and ugly one. What happened if she let Harris walk and it turned out she'd been wrong?

"Just because we don't know of any motive doesn't mean Harris isn't the killer," she continued. "We haven't investigated him yet. He has scratches on his face, and he's the right height and build to be able to inflict the type of damage that our victim suffered. Adding those factors up, I think I have to put him in."

"Lock him up?" Dan asked.

"If I can convince a judge to do it. I can't risk letting a killer out on the street."

THIRTEEN

It was late Thursday afternoon and the arraignment court was buzzing with DEA and Secret Service agents and deputy U.S. marshals, all shepherding prisoners from the day's buy-bust and postal-theft and credit card fraud arrests. The judge was on a break and the bench was empty, but the spectator seats were jammed with Nigerians and Pakistanis and Colombians and people from every corner of the globe who'd come to sign a bond for a cousin or blow a kiss to a lover as he was led away in chains. Melanie slipped into an empty seat at the government's table and nodded to a crew of fresh-faced junior prosecutors from General Crimes who were waiting to handle the minor arraignments. Immediately, somebody tapped her on the shoulder.

"You have the complaint in the Harris case? He just retained me. Bob Adelman."

"Let's talk outside," Melanie said, pushing back her chair.

As they hurried up the aisle together, Melanie had her first small inkling of doubt. Bob Adelman was one of the most successful criminal defense lawyers in New York, and for a reason. He was the real deal. He didn't wear fancy suits or hire publicists like some of the hotshot types. He was just talented. Short and stocky, in his early sixties, with a hound-dog face, Adelman exuded reasonableness. His obviously guilty clients stepped up and took their pleas with minimal fuss. His clients who went to trial did so because the evidence was weak, and they usually walked. Judges loved him, and when prosecutors discovered he was assigned to a case, they often just gave up and followed his lead.

Outside the courtroom, Melanie handed Adelman a copy of the charges, which he quickly scanned.

"You're jumping the gun by filing charges on my guy," Adelman said. "He's a husband and father. Stan Feinerman, the richest lawyer in New York, thinks highly of him and wants to make him a partner. He witnessed the Central Park Butcher murder and he was initially uncooperative. So what? Ten minutes with me, he'll be in your office singing like a little girl. Give me a chance, and I'll bring him around, promise."

"That's not the issue, Bob. He talked, eventually. I'm just not sure I believed him."

Adelman was whippet quick. "Are you saying you suspect him of involvement in the homicide?" he asked.

"I can't rule it out," Melanie said.

"Based on what evidence?"

"I can't discuss that right now."

"Fair enough, but what good does an obstruction charge do you? Boutros is on duty, and she's a stickler. If he was Charles Manson, she wouldn't remand him on charges this thin. Not in a million years."

"I have to try."

"If you really think he's the Butcher, charge him with the homicide. Then you can argue that he's a danger to the community. You'd have a much better chance of keeping him in."

Melanie was silent.

"You don't have the goods, do you?" Adelman said with a knowing smile.

A prosecutor who looked barely old enough to shave poked his head out the courtroom door. "You're Melanie, right?" he asked. "The judge is on the bench. They just called your case."

"Boutros is gonna love this one." Adelman winked at Melanie and turned on his heel, leaving her to follow him into court like a lamb to the slaughter.

David Harris stood before the bench, with two deputy U.S. marshals guarding him. Bob Adelman shook Harris's hand warmly as he whispered instructions, draping his arm around his client's shoulder to show the world what a decent guy David Harris was.

"Defendant waives reading of the complaint?" Judge Boutros snapped, cutting off Adelman's display. Boutros was known as the Iron Lady, both for the color of her hair and her no-nonsense ways. Not a second was wasted in her courtroom. Prosecutors actually competed to clock the fastest Boutros arraignment. The current record was a minute twelve, and the judge looked like she was itching to break it this afternoon.

"We do," Bob Adelman said.

"Agreement as to bail?"

"Before we get to bail, Judge, an application?" Adelman began, and Melanie's palms started to sweat. This guy was an expert at the old adage that the best defense is a good offense, and he was clearly up to something.

With any other lawyer, Judge Boutros would have rolled her eyes, but with Adelman she looked curious. "I'll hear you," she said.

"The defense moves to dismiss the complaint on the grounds of bad faith. Let me tell you what's really happening here, Judge. The government is investigating a brutal homicide that took place in Central Park last night. The case has attracted a lot of press attention, and the government's under pressure to make an arrest. *Any* arrest. My client witnessed the homicide and reported it to the police like a good citizen. Miss Vargas has somehow bootstrapped this into his being the Central Park Butcher, but she doesn't have a shred of proof to back it up. If the government wants to charge murder here, we say bring it on, and we'll beat it fair and square. Instead, they're trying to ruin the reputation of an upstanding citizen with a bogus obstruction charge. This is an outrageous misuse of the criminal justice system, and we ask that the complaint be dismissed with prejudice and Miss Vargas be reprimanded."

"Judge, there's no basis whatso—"

"Quiet, Miss Vargas. I'll hear you when I'm ready."

The judge picked up a piece of paper from her desk and scanned it. Melanie stood there stunned, her chest heaving with fury, her cheeks burning. She'd never had her integrity questioned in open court before.

"I see from the Pretrial Services report that the defendant is an attorney?" Judge Boutros said, looking over the paper at Bob Adelman.

Adelman's eyes were wide and doleful. "Yes, Judge. This obstruction charge could end his career."

"Mr. Adelman, if the allegations in the complaint are true, then his career deserves to end. Obstruction by members of the bar is doubly despicable in my view. But I admit I'm curious about what you hope to gain, Miss Vargas. You can't expect me to remand him on these charges?"

"Yes, Your Honor. The government seeks remand," Melanie said.

"On what possible basis? He's a citizen, correct?"

"Yes, ma'am."

Judge Boutros slapped the page with her free hand. "*How* is this man a flight risk? He's gainfully employed to the tune of nearly two hundred and fifty thousand a year, and owns an apartment on West Seventy-sixth Street where he lives with his wife and three children. He was born and raised in Manhattan and has no known ties outside the United States. *Please*, don't insult my intelligence."

Melanie forced herself to stand up straight, meet the judge's eyes, and speak in a firm voice. She'd take her humiliation like a soldier.

"I'm arguing that he's a danger to the community, Judge, not a flight risk," Melanie said. She felt every eye in the courtroom boring into her back.

"Then you'd better call a witness and make a record about his involvement with the murder, because I don't find one single fact in the complaint that backs you up," Judge Boutros said.

Melanie hesitated. She had no witnesses prepared. She hadn't imagined she'd need any.

"I'm not doing your dirty work for you, Miss Vargas," Judge Boutros said. "Call a witness and make your case, or you risk a finding of bad faith."

If this judge demanded a dog-and-pony show, Melanie had no choice but to deliver. She looked around the courtroom. Dan and Julian had transported Harris to court and now sat on a back bench, waiting to see whether he'd make bail.

"The government calls Special Agent Daniel K. O'Reilly of the Federal Bureau of Investigation."

Dan rose and headed down the aisle. As Melanie marched over to the podium facing the witness stand, her legs were shaky. Never mind David Harris; *Melanie's* career was going down the toilet, in a crowded courtroom no less. Judge Boutros's scowl grew deeper every minute, and Bob Adelman sat at counsel table with a yellow legal pad, ready to tear apart everything she said.

Judge Boutros swore Dan in and turned to Melanie. "Proceed, Miss Vargas."

Melanie cleared her throat and looked down at her legal pad, but of course there was nothing written on it.

"State your full name and spell it for the court reporter," she said, her mind a complete blank. *Think of something, goddammit.*

"Daniel Kevin O'Reilly," Dan replied, and spelled it.

At the sound of his voice, Melanie looked up. Their eyes met across the courtroom. His were blue, the blue of clear skies, of the ocean on a calm day. They seemed to say that she was up to the job.

"How are you employed?" she asked, her voice firm and clear.

"As a special agent with the Federal Bureau of Investigation."

"Where were you at approximately eleven P.M. last night?"

"In Central Park, in the area known as the Ramble."

"Why were you there?"

"I was paged to report to the scene of a homicide."

"Who was the victim of this homicide?"

"One Suzanne Shepard. A TV news reporter."

"As part of your duties at the crime scene, did you view the victim's body?"

"Yes, ma'am."

Melanie knew she needed to tread carefully here or her whole investigation would be laid bare in open court. She didn't plan on giving Bob Adelman free discovery before he was entitled to it, no way, not after he'd ambushed her like that.

She caught Dan's eyes meaningfully. "Agent, I'd like to focus your attention on one particular element of the crime scene, without going into anything else. Can you please describe the state of the victim's fingernails?"

"The fingernails had material under them that appeared to be human skin."

"Did you observe this yourself?"

"No, not personally. This was relayed to me by the head crime-scene detective. By the time I got to the scene, the material had been collected."

"Collected in what manner?"

"By the, uh, the crime-scene detectives taking scrapings."

"What was the purpose of taking the scrapings?"

"For later DNA comparison if a suspect was arrested for the murder."

"Why would the police make such a comparison?"

"Could you—I don't understand the question," he said.

"I'll rephrase it. Whose skin did the crime-scene detectives believe was under the victim's fingernails?"

Adelman stood up. "Objection. Seeks an answer not within the witness's direct knowledge."

Good, Melanie thought. *If he's starting to object, he must be worried.*

"Hearsay is admissible in a bail hearing," Judge Boutros said. "Agent O'Reilly, did the crime-scene detectives tell you whose skin they thought was under the victim's fingernails?"

"Yes, ma'am."

"Overruled. You may answer," the judge said.

"The idea was, the victim fought back," Dan said. "She scratched her attacker. So it would've been the killer's skin."

"That was last night?" Melanie asked.

"Correct."

"If Suzanne Shepard's killer was arrested today, how would you expect him to look?"

"Objection, calls for speculation," Bob Adelman said.

"Overruled. This is plain common sense," Judge Boutros said. She was gazing steadily at David Harris's face, and Melanie's hopes surged. The clear, shiny ointment on Harris's right cheek did nothing to conceal the two angry scratches.

"I would expect his face to be scratched up," Dan replied.

"Directing your attention to earlier today, did you place an individual under arrest for the murder of Suzanne Shepard?"

"Yes."

"Who was that?"

"One David M. Harris."

"Is he present in the courtroom?"

"Yes, ma'am."

"Please identify him and describe him for the record."

Dan pointed. "That's him, seated to the left of Mr. Adelman at the defense table, wearing a gray suit, with light brown hair."

"Please describe for the record the condition of Mr. Harris's face."

"He's got two fresh scratches on his right cheek. Nasty-looking ones."

"Can you describe the facts that led you to arrest Mr. Harris?"

"He had called 911 last night to report the murder, claiming to be an eyewitness. He fled the scene before the police arrived—"

"Wait a minute," Judge Boutros interjected. "If he's the killer, why would he call the police?"

"Mr. Harris called the police, then fled, ma'am," Dan replied. "The killer left the body in a public place anyways, so we figured he wanted her discovered. Sometimes it's about the publicity."

The Judge nodded. "Proceed."

"We then tracked Mr. Harris down through his cell-phone records," Dan continued. "When we found him, he denied placing the call, which we knew wasn't true because it's his cell phone and his voice. We asked him where he got the scratches on his face and he lied about that, too."

"What did he say?" Melanie asked.

"That he got 'em from his kid, but his wife said he never came home last night."

"Did he later give a second explanation for the scratches?"

"Yes. When we said we didn't buy the story about his kid, he stated that somebody tried to rob him in the Park and he sustained the scratches fighting this individual off."

"Did you ask Mr. Harris to provide a DNA sample?"

"Yes, and he agreed. We should have the results in twenty-four to forty-eight hours. If they come back positive, obviously, we'll charge him with the murder instead of just the obstruction of justice."

"No further questions," Melanie said.

She picked up her legal pad and headed back to the government's table. The baby prosecutors were looking at her with admiration. Glancing over her shoulder, she saw that the courthouse grapevine had gone into overdrive, and the courtroom was packed. A possible arrest in the Central Park Butcher case was big news. Bernadette had shown up at some point, and beside her sat the deputy chief of the Criminal Division. In the rows behind them were several reporters whom Melanie recognized from the press conference this morning.

Bob Adelman rose. "Cross, Judge?"

Looking at the clock, Judge Boutros waved her hand irritably. "Sit down, Mr. Adelman. I'm prepared to rule."

"Judge—"

"I've heard enough. The motion to dismiss the complaint on grounds of bad faith is denied. The government had a legitimate public safety concern here—"

"Judge, my client has a good explanation for the scratches—"

"Did you hear me, Mr. Adelman? No cross necessary. As much as I see where the government's coming from, I can't order remand on the facts before me. I'm ready to set bail."

Melanie got to her feet. "Your Honor—"

"For forty-eight hours you can put a tail on him, Miss Vargas. I'm not locking him up on a measly obstruction charge."

"What about electronic monitoring, Judge?" Melanie tried.

"That only makes sense if I order home confinement or severely restrict his movements. I'm not doing that on these facts. Live with it and sit down."

The rest of the hearing passed in a flash, with David Harris agreeing to post the title to his apartment as security for his bail. Afterward, as Melanie headed up the aisle, Bob Adelman caught her by the arm.

"Nice job," he said with a warm smile.

"Bob, you just accused me of bad faith."

"Yeah, and you outmaneuvered me. No hard feelings, okay, kid? You done good." He squeezed her arm, heading off to shake hands with well-wishers in the courtroom. *Gracias por nada,* she thought. Thanks for nothing.

Bernadette and Mark Sonschein, the deputy chief of the Criminal Division, conferred with arms folded and heads together in the first row of spectator seats. Melanie approached them with her heart in her throat. In contrast to his happy name, Mark was grim-faced and sober, with a heavy five o'clock shadow. For some reason, Melanie had always believed he didn't like her, and she felt nervous around him. But Mark and Bernadette both looked up with broad smiles on their faces.

"Nicely done," Mark said.

"You think so?" Melanie asked, confused. "I lost the bail argument. If David Harris is the killer, he's out on the street."

"The *judge* granted bail," Bernadette emphasized. "Whatever happens next, it's not on us."

FOURTEEN

Melanie was concerned with more than just avoiding blame if the Central Park Butcher struck again. She actually wanted to stop him. The FBI and NYPD were focused on surveilling David Harris. But if Harris wasn't the killer, they were simply playing babysitter to her star witness. Melanie half believed Harris's story about the male prostitute, and she thought there was a decent chance that the Butcher was still on the street. She planned to get her butt in gear and start identifying alternative targets.

The Nineteenth Precinct station house was on her way home. She'd called ahead, and the detective who'd been investigating the burglary at Suzanne Shepard's apartment had agreed to stay late so Melanie could meet with her. Detective Pauline Estrada seemed like somebody Melanie might have known back in the day, in grammar school maybe, before she started getting into the advanced placement programs and magnet schools and leaving the block behind. Maybe they would have stayed in touch, or maybe their lives would have diverged, hard to say. Certainly they looked different on paper in the here and now. Pauline couldn't have been much older than Melanie, but based on the pictures on her desk, she had teenage kids. Her hair was bigger than Melanie's, her clothes more revealing, and her accent still resonant of the Bronx. But Melanie recognized a kindred spirit in her, somebody who gave a damn about the job, who cared about making things right. Lorraine Shepard had suggested the cops weren't moving fast enough on the burglary in her apartment, but looking at this woman, Melanie found that difficult to believe.

"I'm glad you reached out to me. I was meaning to call you since I saw the murder in the paper. You want some?" Pauline asked. She stood at a small counter opposite her desk in the open detective's squad area of the Nineteenth Precinct, pouring steaming coffee into a Styrofoam cup.

"Thanks. I'm really fading. I could use it."

It was after seven o'clock, and Melanie's brain was fried after a sleepless night and endless day. She sipped the coffee, which was blessedly strong. The caffeine kicked in immediately, and she could feel her batteries recharging, her energy level ramping up.

"The victim's mother gave me your card. I need to figure out if your burglary has any connection to my murder," Melanie said.

"Yeah, I was wondering the same thing." Pauline shook her head. "Lorraine Shepard. What a piece of work, huh? Watch out for her."

"Why do you say that?" Melanie asked.

"She called my boss on me three times already in two weeks. Why didn't I arrest nobody yet, when am I gonna make a move, yada, yada, yada. I'm lucky, though. My boss is from God. He won't listen to a word against me."

"People have unrealistic expectations. Do you even have a viable suspect?"

"Oh, I do. But that doesn't mean I can prove it."

"I know how that goes," Melanie said.

Melanie sat in a chair beside Pauline's desk. Pauline leafed through a file. When she found what she was looking for, she yanked out the mug shot and slapped it down in front of Melanie. The man in the picture had a striking face. Handsome and cruel, with sharp cheekbones and dark, sunken eyes.

"Miles Ortiz, personal trainer at Flex Gym, and narcotics trafficker," Pauline said.

"Your burglary suspect?" Melanie asked.

"Yep. Found his prints in Suzanne Shepard's apartment. One of the files that got boosted had a whole lotta dirt on him which now won't see the light of day."

"Lorraine told me he was selling drugs to his clients."

"Not was. *Is*."

"He has priors?" Melanie asked, fingering the mug shot.

"Yep, and not for singing too loud in church, neither. Two criminal possessions of a controlled substance and an assault. I'm amazed this guy is walking the streets let alone teaching kickboxing to rich housewives."

"It sounds like you have a lot on him," Melanie said.

"Yes and no. I'm convinced he's the one who broke in and took the files. Took some money and jewelry, too. But the fact that his prints are inside the apartment, unfortunately, he can explain that away."

"You interviewed him already?"

"Yeah, but I'm not taking his word for nothing. I heard it from Suzanne Shepard. Before she died, she corroborated everything he said."

"So what's the explanation? Why was Miles in her apartment?"

"You heard of Drew Savitt?" Pauline asked.

"I've heard of a Kim Savitt. From Lorraine Shepard."

"Right. Kim is Drew's wife. Savitt's a big mogul type. Runs a major real-estate development firm that's buying up all this waterfront property in Jersey and building fancy condos."

"Oh, sure. Now I remember."

"Savitt owns the building where Suzanne Shepard lives. Lived, I mean. He's separated from Kim, and he gave her an apartment there. Here's Kim."

Pauline laid down a picture that looked as if it had been ripped from a glossy magazine. It showed a group of five gorgeous, perfectly groomed women standing together, all in evening wear. The caption said the picture had been taken at a benefit for New York Hospital, and identified the woman in the center as Kim Savitt. She was taller and blonder than the rest, with more lavish cleavage, bigger diamonds, and a whiter smile. *I'd be smiling, too,* Melanie thought.

"It's an ugly situation," Pauline said. "Bitter custody battle over their little girl, lots of lurid allegations. Anyway, long story short, Kim Savitt belongs to Flex Gym, and her trainer is none other than our friend Miles Ortiz."

"Really."

"Mmm-hmm. And, Kim and Suzanne Shepard were friendly. Miles is a frequent visitor to Kim's apartment. In-home training sessions, don't you know.

Kim brought Miles to see Suzanne on a couple of occasions. So that's his cover."

"Suzanne confirmed that?"

"Yes. Like I said, I wouldn't take that lowlife's word for nothing."

"Have you interviewed Kim?" Melanie asked.

"No. I figured she'd just back Miles up and say they visited Suzanne socially."

"I hate to sound cynical, but if Kim's in a custody battle, the last thing she needs is police scrutiny," Melanie pointed out. "Maybe she'd be willing to talk, just to keep a lid on things."

"Good idea. Worth a try, anyway. I'll make a note."

"Where in Suzanne's apartment were Miles's fingerprints found?"

"Two locations. Hold on."

Pauline pulled a fingerprint report from the file. Melanie took it, squinting, trying to locate the conclusion amid long paragraphs of bureaucratese.

"I find these things impossible to read," she confessed.

"I know, right? Here," Pauline said, running her finger along the text. " 'Latent print of value, yada, yada, lifted from right stainless-steel bar stool at kitchen island,' and there's a diagram, okay? Money was taken from that location, so makes sense, right? Now, 'Analysis performed and identification effected with subject's right forefinger.' This is all crap about the whorl patterns, but here we go: 'Latent print of value identified on top right drawer of desk in third bedroom and identification effected with subject's right palm.'"

"Third bedroom? That's Suzanne's office, right?" Melanie asked.

"Yes. All of which means we can put him in the kitchen and at the desk in the back bedroom, both locations from which items were taken during the burglary."

"So he didn't wear gloves," Melanie said.

"Doesn't look like it."

But the Butcher did, Melanie thought, remembering the talcum-powder marks on the wallet. What does that mean?

"Did Suzanne tell you whether Miles went into her office when he came to visit with Kim Savitt?" Melanie asked.

"She said he didn't. Kitchen yes, office no. And even in the kitchen, his last social call was more than a week before the burglary. Their maid comes five days a week, and she always wipes down the bar stools with cleaning fluid, so those prints were fresh."

Melanie paused, thinking. "Could Lorraine Shepard testify about Miles's social visits?" she asked after a moment.

"She was there when they happened, yes."

"And she'd say he never went in the office?"

"She'd say cows have wings if it would get somebody arrested. But yeah, I asked her, and she could testify he wasn't in the office," Pauline said.

Melanie pondered for another moment. "Well, there's probably enough."

"Enough to get a warrant?" Pauline asked.

"Close, but—"

Pauline broke into a huge grin. "*Hallelujah.* Now I see why guys love to take shit federal. I knew we had a case, but I just couldn't make that *cabrón* of an A.D.A. understand."

Melanie couldn't help laughing.

"So I can go ahead and pop Miles now?" Pauline asked.

"I love your enthusiasm, but let's not jump the gun. The burglary charge is pretty weak given his innocent explanation. If we got a warrant, it would only be to keep in our back pocket in case Miles decides to skip. We need to know more before we actually arrest him. Like where he was at the time Suzanne Shepard was murdered, for instance."

"You think he's the Butcher?" Pauline asked.

"I don't know. If he knew she was planning to expose his drug operation, and he's as ruthless as he looks, maybe. But I'm not convinced. Wasn't there a second suspect in the burglary, anyway? A plastic surgeon named Benedict Welch? Lorraine mentioned him."

"Files were stolen relating to Welch, but I never really considered him a suspect. There's nothing that jumps up and bites you like with our boy Miles," Pauline said.

"Why take his files, then? Is there some connection between Dr. Welch and Miles Ortiz?"

"Not that I know of, but I never really checked." Pauline was frowning, but not like she minded being challenged. More like she was annoyed with herself for not covering every base.

"Can I see what you have on Welch? Lorraine said Suzanne was working on a big story on him. Something damaging. She seemed more concerned about Welch than about Ortiz, actually," Melanie said.

"Surgeon. Butcher. Could be. You never know," Pauline agreed.

She pulled out a sheaf of notes held together with a black binder clip and labeled *Benedict Welch, MD* in neat handwriting. The girl was organized, you had to give her that.

"Benedict Welch, M.D., PC," Pauline said. "Fancy office on Park Avenue. High-powered clientele. Shows up in the society columns a lot. Sixty-four YOA. Caucasian male, blond hair, blue eyes. Born and raised in Tulsa,

Oklahoma. Married, no children. Board certified and licensed by the states of Oklahoma and New York in dermatology and plastic surgery. Two complaints on file with the Board of Medical Examiners, both investigated, one ruled without merit and dismissed, the other ruled inconclusive, no finding issued, allowed to lapse." She looked up at Melanie uncertainly.

"What were the complaints for?" Melanie asked.

Pauline shuffled through the pile, pulling a couple of blurry photocopies from the bottom. "The one without merit, for inappropriate physical contact with a patient rendered unconscious due to anesthesia. Not to put too fine a point on it, he groped a lady when she was under. The inconclusive one, for, um, hold on a second. For the same thing. Groping a different lady while she was under. Sorry. I guess I never focused on this. I was so busy with the Miles Ortiz angle."

"Suzanne was raped by her assailant," Melanie pointed out.

"I didn't know that," Pauline said, her eyes widening. "It wasn't in the paper."

They were silent for a moment.

"We should take a closer look at this Dr. Welch and see what we can turn up," Melanie said.

"Jesus. I hope I didn't miss something," Pauline said, looking upset.

FIFTEEN

Melanie called Dan O'Reilly's cell phone as she hurried toward her apartment from the precinct and, when he didn't pick up, left him a voice mail. She told herself she needed to fill him in on what she'd learned today and check whether the surveillance of David Harris had turned up anything of significance. She also needed to schedule a team meeting. All of that was true. But deep down, she knew she'd really called so she could hear his sexy-as-hell voice. And let him know how much seeing him across the courtroom this afternoon had steadied her. And, okay, maybe ask if he wanted to stop by after Maya was asleep, when the next shift of surveillance guys came on duty. She was dead tired, and she imagined he was, too. But all the way home, she was thinking about how good his body felt next to hers in bed at night.

When Dan hadn't called her back by the time she'd let her babysitter go home and given Maya her bath, she tried him again, and got voice mail.

"Hey, it's Melanie . . . Uh, it's about eight-thirty and . . . um, I'm just wondering what's going on with the surveillance. Give me a call."

She was too tired to cook, so she nuked some macaroni and cheese left over from Maya's dinner and ate it at the kitchen table with her daughter sitting in her lap, snuggling and sucking her pacifier, her eyelids growing heavy. Maya's little body was warm and compact in soft cotton jammies. The weight of her calmed Melanie's frayed nerves. By the time Melanie had finished eating, Maya was asleep. Melanie got up gingerly and carried her to her room, putting her nose to her daughter's silky dark locks as she walked, drinking in the fragrance of baby shampoo.

The nursery had white furniture and a wallpaper border of pink bunnies, and already it seemed too babyish for Maya. Melanie lowered the little girl into the crib and stood there marveling at how *long* she was. When had that happened? Time to buy a real bed. *The days are endless, the years fly by.* She'd read that somewhere, and it felt too true. Maya was growing up, and between work and the divorce and everything else, Melanie was missing too much of it. The thought depressed the hell out of her. She had another vision of Charlie Shepard, of his grief this morning, of how his life with his mother had come to such a brutal and unexpected end. What if that happened to her? Would she look back and feel like she'd spent her time in the right places?

"Snap out of it," she whispered, and hurried back to the kitchen, where she cleaned up her dishes and settled down with a pile of photocopies from Pauline Estrada's burglary file.

But the fact that Dan hadn't called her back was nagging at her enough that she couldn't concentrate. He always jumped right on her messages. Maybe something had happened on the case? If so, she needed to know. After pretending to read for a few more minutes, she gave up and went into the foyer to get Julian Hay's card from her handbag. She'd page Julian. Maybe *he* would call her back.

About fifteen minutes later, she was sitting at the table with the phone beside her when it finally rang. She grabbed it, eager to hear Dan's voice.

"Hello?"

"This is Detective Hay. Somebody page me?"

"Julian, it's Melanie Vargas."

"Hey, Melanie. What's happening?"

"Are you still out on the Harris surveillance?"

"No, some guys doing the four-to-midnight tour relieved us a while ago. Everything was quiet. No news.

Harris just went back to his apartment after court and didn't come out. They'll page me if anything unusual happens."

"Okay, good. Where are you now?"

"Home. I was thinking about getting a little shut-eye and coming in real early tomorrow, but if you got something important . . . ?" He trailed off.

Come to think of it, here was an opportunity to put Suave Pierre's special expertise to work. Bernadette had said Detective Hay was useless at the grunt work of regular investigations, but a genius at drug buys. Melanie decided to be a smart supervisor and utilize her staff strategically.

"Actually, there *is* something I need you to do, although it can wait till morning. Turns out there's a drug angle on this case."

"Gimme the skinny, sister. You know that's my specialty."

She filled him in on everything she'd learned about Miles Ortiz. Julian took notes on Miles's birth date, Social Security number, last known address, and the dates of all his arrests.

"So you want to know what he's selling, and who to?" Julian asked.

"That's right. And anything else you can find out. Who supplies Miles? Is he a small-time guy, or does he play with the big boys? Where does he stash? Can you buy from him? If we can arrest him, maybe we can get him to talk, and tell us whatever he knows about the murder."

"No problem. Pierre's on it. I'll have something back to you in no time."

She smiled. "Great. Thanks . . . Oh, and Julian?"

"Yeah?"

She knew she shouldn't, but she couldn't stop herself. "You don't happen to know where Dan O'Reilly is, do you?"

"He went to visit somebody in the hospital. Out on the Island, I think."

"Oh. He didn't mention that."

"That's what he told me. You have a good night now, hear?"

"Yeah. You, too."

She hung up, wondering who was sick and why Dan hadn't said anything to her about it. Two hours later when she got in bed and turned out the light, he still hadn't returned her calls. It took her a torturously long time to fall asleep. Whenever she looked at the clock, her eyes burning with fatigue, she assured herself it was Detective Estrada's coffee keeping her awake, and not that she was in over her head with this guy.

SIXTEEN

It had been more than six years since Dan O'Reilly's wife walked out on him and went to live with a buddy of his from his football days, and he'd done a bang-up job ever since of pretending she didn't exist. He kept so busy that he didn't have time to remember her. Worked his ass off on the job. Hit the gym till his muscles ached. Worked construction on the weekends with his cousin Brian and the guys from Brian's firehouse. So he could avoid any place she might turn up, he'd skipped pretty much every social event he ever got invited to, but what the hell, he wasn't much for parties anyway. Lately, with Melanie in his life, his efforts had really paid off. He didn't have to struggle not to think about Diane anymore. She just wasn't on his mind. He saw a future for himself again, and there was somebody new in it.

Dan found a parking space at the hospital in West Islip and searched out the oncology floor. Two women were on duty at the nurses' station, one middle-aged and heavy, the other young and heavy, both wearing brightly colored scrubs and gobs of makeup.

"What can I do for you, hon?" asked the young one, checking him out.

"I'm looking for Seamus Fields."

"It's after visiting hours. You a relative?"

"Son-in-law," he replied, leaving out the "ex."

"I don't see a ring. You sure you're married?"

Annoyed, Dan flashed his shield instead. "You're sure fast with the questions. Maybe you should join the FBI."

She tossed her head. "No thanks, but if you're single, you can buy me a drink."

Her colleague shot her a glance, snickering.

"What? He's a hottie," the young one shot back.

"I'd like to see my father-in-law while he's still alive, please. From what I understand, that won't be too much longer."

The nurse's eyes softened. "Sorry. We get a little crazy here on the night shift." She checked her roster and gave him the room number. As he walked away, the two of them were giggling behind him.

Dan trudged down a long, brightly lit hallway, feeling like he was going back in time. Seamus Fields was one of the biggest reasons Dan had fallen for his daughter. That, and her angel face and unbelievable body. *Don't think about Diane.* But it was hard not to, since he was about to see her.

Dan and Diane had known each other their whole lives. Their dads were both on the job, both important men, the main difference being that Seamus handled the stress by becoming humane and wise, whereas Frank O'Reilly had shriveled up inside. Dan had adored the big, bluff Irishman and taken every opportunity to spend time at Seamus's house. It didn't hurt that Seamus had a gorgeous daughter, either. Dan and Diane had been born on the same day. When they were eight, Diane told him the shared birthday meant they were destined to get married, and he'd believed her. When they were thirteen, he'd kissed her under the mistletoe at a Christmas party, his first kiss although not hers, as it turned out. When they were sixteen, they did it in a borrowed car on the night of the junior prom, and he was careful not to ask if it was her first time. When they were twenty-one, they got married, and when they were twenty-five, she left without so much as a good-bye while he was dead asleep after a long surveillance.

Diane's second marriage had run its course. Had fallen to shit, was a more accurate way to put it. They'd fought and cheated and bad-mouthed each other to the point where Dan couldn't help hearing about it even though he tried not to. Just recently, Paul had left Diane for some twenty-two-year-old he'd met in a tattoo parlor. Another guy might've felt gratified, might've said what goes around comes around, but that wasn't Dan. The past had too strong a hold on him. In fact, if he hadn't been dating Melanie, he was pretty sure he'd've called Diane up to see if she needed a shoulder to cry on.

Diane's sister Patty was leaning against the wall outside the hospital room scrolling through text messages on her cell phone. She looked up as Dan approached.

"Hey, Danny! Long time no see."

"How you been, Patty? You're looking good."

Dan kissed her on the cheek. Patty was beautiful like her sister. All three of the Fields girls were beautiful, but none of them had managed to pull off happy. Patty had married a firefighter who'd died in the World Trade Center, and her youngest kid was autistic. She had a decent job in human resources at a big company, and she was okay enough financially with the insurance settlements and all, but life had taken its toll. You could see it in her eyes. The oldest sister, Denise, was the black sheep—three kids by two different guys, never married, living at home. That's what happened when you relied on your looks and never developed any other part of yourself. Eventually your looks faded and left you with jack.

"How's he doing?" Dan asked.

"Not good. It won't be long now. He's sleeping, but you can go in. Diane's in there. Mom stepped out to the chapel to light a candle."

The thought of being basically alone with his ex-wife made Dan so nervous that his hands and feet went cold.

"I don't know," he said, taken aback.

"She'll be glad you came. It's more than Paul did. He's in Atlantic City this weekend gambling with his girlfriend, piece a' shit that he is." Patty shook her head in sisterly solidarity.

"I came to see the old man," he felt compelled to say.

"Sure. We know that. So go ahead." She smiled wearily and went back to her phone.

Dan had to stifle a gasp when he saw Seamus lying lifeless in the bed. The guy'd been the size of a Mack truck and looked like he could've stopped a bullet with his massive chest. Now he was shrunk to a pile of bones, his normally pink cheeks sallow and waxy. *Ashes to ashes*, Dan thought. *We're all dust in the end, even him.*

Dan was so shocked by Seamus's appearance that it took him a minute to realize Diane was standing right beside him. He hadn't laid eyes on his ex-wife since all the funerals right after 9/11. Dan's youngest brother, Sean; Patty's husband, Eddie O'Dare; a bunch of cousins, scores of their friends. The Irish in the services took a heavy hit. And making it that much worse was Diane, showing up at the funerals hanging all over her new husband, her white skin glowing against a black dress. Here she was now in the flesh, looking beautiful, but older, and harder somehow. The change was noticeable.

"Danny," she said, her hand going to her throat. "I wasn't expecting you."

"What, like I'm not gonna come? You know I love the old man."

"I'm just surprised. I'm glad to see you."

And she stood on tiptoe and kissed him tenderly on the cheek. She still wore the same perfume, and the smell of it took him back. He'd been wondering if he'd feel anything, and he did. He felt nostalgic and sad, like a lot of years had passed and neither of them had much to show for it. But he did, now. He had Melanie. He'd had a hard time finding his way, all those bleak years without Diane, but once Melanie had come along, he'd finally gotten his bearings.

"How's he doing?" Dan asked.

"They disconnected the life support yesterday. He's been unconscious since then. They didn't think he'd last this long. But he has a morphine drip, so he's not feeling any pain."

"I'm so sorry. He's young, too."

"Seventy-one. Is that young?" she asked.

"In this day and age."

Diane was gazing at him intently. Her eyes were bright blue. If they'd ever had kids, the eye color wouldn't've been in doubt. But it had turned out she couldn't. That had been hard for both of them, and he'd always said it was what drove them apart. She felt guilty about it and acted out. But he knew he was making excuses. Diane had always been fickle, somebody a more careful man wouldn't have put his faith in.

"I could use a cup of coffee. The cafeteria's open twenty-four/seven," she said.

He nodded toward the bed. "I'm here to pay my respects."

"Sure, of course. But when you're done? We're collecting stories for the eulogy. I figure you must have some nice ones about him."

She smiled at him sadly, twirling a strand of her golden hair around her finger the way she had when they were kids. He studied her face. It was beginning to look familiar, less hard around the edges, more like the girl he remembered.

"Okay," he said after a moment.

She nodded. "I'll wait outside. Take your time."

Dan approached the bed. He reached out to grasp the old man's hand, but Seamus had IV's going into both arms, and Dan worried he'd screw something up. Instead he pulled a chair over and sat down beside him. The acrid chemical odor emanating from Seamus's emaciated body smelled like death.

"Seamus, it's Danny O'Reilly. I came to see you. I don't know if you can hear me or not."

Memories came rushing in, and he choked up so bad that he was forced to stop. Seamus had been more of a father to Dan than his old man had.

"So I . . . uh, listen, I know we haven't seen too much of each other the past few years. It's a shame, this thing with me and Diane coming between us. But you've been like a father to me, Seamus. You know how my old man is. I would never talk against him or nothing, but it meant a lot that you stepped up when he maybe, uh, had too much on his plate. You made me feel like I was worth something, like somebody saw the good in me."

He stopped again, fighting for composure. Dan thought he saw Seamus's lips move. He bent down eagerly, putting his ear to the old man's mouth.

"You want to say something?"

There was nothing, barely even a whisper of breath. Still, Dan felt like Seamus had heard him.

He straightened up. "Anyways, I came by to say . . . to thank you for what you did for me over the years. If anybody's right with God, it's you, so I know you're heading upstairs. I'm hoping to wind up there myself someday, and I'll look for you. We'll grab a pint, tell a few war stories." He paused, touching Seamus on his waxen cheek. "Okay, then. I'm not gonna say good-bye."

Outside, Diane and Patty were deep in conversation. They broke off the second they saw him.

"Going to the cafeteria," Diane said to her sister. "You want something?"

But Patty's phone rang, and she waved the question off in her rush to grab the call. Some guy, probably. The Fields girls always had guys dangling on a string. Which reminded him.

"I heard you and Paul split," he said to Diane as they stepped into the elevator. All of a sudden, in the space of the few minutes he'd spent with Seamus, he'd started feeling comfortable around Diane again.

"Yeah. I didn't even see it coming, that asshole," she said. "What are you gonna do, right? You probably think I deserve it. I mean, I wouldn't blame you if you did."

Dan said nothing.

"I screwed up big-time, didn't I?" she said, and gave a nervous little laugh. The elevator reached the basement level and they walked down a short hallway to a cafeteria that reeked of steam tables and cleaning fluid.

"I heard you're dating some Puerto Rican girl with a kid," Diane said, when Dan continued not to reply. "I heard your dad's not too happy about it, either."

She flipped the lever on the coffee urn, filled two Styrofoam cups with light brown coffee, and handed him one.

"Ah, he's full of shit. He never even met her. I won't introduce 'em until he acts more respectful. Besides, I don't live my life by him. You know that."

"Oh, hey, wait a minute. I just remembered something," she said, and went over to the counter where the desserts were. She came back with a piece of carrot cake. They paid and sat down at the nearest table, the only two people in the place besides the Salvadoran woman working the cash register. Diane put the slice of cake down in front of him, smiling.

"Happy birthday. Carrot cake's still your favorite, right?"

He laughed. "Yeah. I guess you can't forget the date. Happy birthday to you, too."

"It was weird, all those years, celebrating our birthday apart. Did you ever feel that?"

Their eyes met. He felt strange, light-headed, like he was falling back in time. "It was your idea," he said finally.

She held his gaze. "You ever think maybe we just got married too young?"

"Honestly, Diane, I never think about it," he lied. Looking away, he took a swig of the coffee and grimaced at its metallic taste.

"Coffee here sucks, huh?" she asked after a moment.

"Yup."

"So what's up with the Spanish chick?"

He took a bite of the cake instead of answering. "Cake's not bad. Better than the coffee, anyway."

"Come on. What's she like?" Diane persisted.

"What do you care?"

"I'm interested. I'm always hearing about you. People love to tell me what you're up to. You know how that is, right?"

He smiled, chewing. "Maybe."

"Thought I'd get it from the horse's mouth. Is that such a crime?"

"All right, let's see. She's smart. Beautiful. She's a prosecutor. We have some cases together. Satisfied?"

"Oh. A lawyer." Diane nodded slowly, like everything made sense now. "Nobody told me that part."

"What did you think, she was a welfare mother or something? She went to Harvard, for Chrissakes."

"Okay, whatever. No need to get defensive." She frowned. There was a vertical crease between her brows that hadn't been there the last time he'd seen her. "I don't see you with somebody from Harvard. That seems wrong for you."

"I'm out of my league, but she puts up with me."

"It's serious?"

"Yeah, it is."

He saw the news hit Diane, saw how she'd been hoping for a different answer.

"What, like headed-for-the-altar serious?" she asked, her tone joking, brittle.

"Maybe," Dan said. Time was weird. He'd been wrapped up with this woman his whole life, then she was gone, and now she was back again, so familiar that he could hardly believe the years between had happened.

"Oh." She swallowed and looked away.

"But who knows? It's too early to say. It's not like we're engaged or anything." Diane had enough going on, between her marriage falling apart and Seamus dying. She didn't need to worry about Dan getting married to someone else.

"Okay." Diane's smile reached her eyes. The lines around them were new also, and they made him feel protective of her.

"Now, about that eulogy," he said, taking another bite of the carrot cake. "Let's talk about the old man."

SEVENTEEN

Friday morning, on her way to an appointment with the head of security for Target News, Melanie made what she thought would be a brief detour to the Frank E. Campbell Funeral Home to pay her respects to Suzanne Shepard. She did it because she thought it was the right thing to do, but her little trip turned out to have some unanticipated benefits.

Frank E. Campbell was Manhattan's prestige funeral parlor, the place where the wealthy and socially prominent took their final bows. It sat, austere and imposing, on a fine Madison Avenue block, within striking distance of the palatial apartment buildings of Fifth and Park Avenues and convenient to the best shopping. The rich and famous didn't even need to call a limo to take them there, although of course they preferred to. Two uniformed officers and a sober-suited funeral director took shelter from the sun under the red awning, checking IDs to make sure that no unauthorized mourners crashed Suzanne Shepard's last personal appearance.

Melanie flashed her credentials and got waved inside, where she stepped into a small elevator with a blonde wearing a tight black dress, four-inch slingback heels, and a black picture hat. Though her perfect smile and generous cleavage weren't on display at the moment, Melanie instantly recognized Kim Savitt from the photo Detective Estrada had shown her yesterday. Kim's overpowering gardenia perfume made Melanie sneeze, which in turn caused Kim to shoot Melanie an annoyed glance. She was talking on a cell phone and apparently finding it difficult to hear.

"What? Say that again . . . Oh, *come on*, Miles. I told you, I can't," Kim said, studying her manicure with a frown, as if it were, to her expert eye, less perfect than it appeared. On her left index finger, she wore a square-cut diamond that reached to her knuckle. Kim seemed utterly oblivious to Melanie's presence in the elevator.

"*Because.* I'm going to Suzanne's viewing, then I have to find something good to wear to Danielle's party at Buddakan tomorrow night. They're expecting photographers from *Avenue* . . . No, just the viewing. The funeral's tomorrow . . . Do whatever you want, but don't expect *me* to talk to you if you show up. All of New York's gonna be there, and I need to be careful. Drew's lawyer is having me watched. He's got some pond-scum PI after me."

The elevator doors opened.

"Gotta run," Kim said. "I'll see you Sunday. Don't call before then; they're watching my phone bills, too. Kiss, kiss."

She snapped her phone shut and met Melanie's eyes briefly, as if by accident, without seeming to actually see her. They both stepped out of the elevator. Trouble in paradise? Could Kim and Miles Ortiz be on the outs, leaving her willing to snitch on him? Melanie had to bite her tongue to stop herself from demanding an interview on the spot. She'd find her opportunity later, but for now it felt like dirty pool to corner the woman at a viewing—although she had to admit Kim Savitt didn't exactly look brokenhearted.

Melanie stayed a few steps behind Kim as they made their way into a large, high-ceilinged room, soothingly lit and filled with the hushed buzz of whispered conversation. The carpet was thick and soft and absorbed the sound. Between the backs of the moneyed and influential, Melanie caught a glimpse of a gleaming mahogany coffin hoisted on a stand at the front of the room. Before it, Lorraine Shepard greeted the mourners like a royal princess receiving guests at court, extending her hand with lofty courtesy, her coiffed head erect. Melanie's eyes flew around the room until she spotted young Charlie seated on a chair near a window, rubbing his face with his hands. Nobody seemed to be paying any attention to him, so Melanie maneuvered through the crowd to his side.

"Charlie?" she said gently, touching his shoulder. "Are you okay?"

He looked up at her, his cheeks wet. Recognition dawned in his eyes. "My mom in a box. It's too weird. How can that be her?"

Charlie's shaggy hair showed fresh teeth marks from a comb. He wore a prep school blazer with a crest and beat-up Top-Siders without socks, so that his too-short khakis left several inches of gangly white ankle exposed. He looked even younger than he had yesterday, and Melanie's heart ached for him.

"You'll see her again someday," Melanie said.

"I wish I believed in that afterlife stuff. Maybe I'd feel better. But the truth is, my mother's dead, I'll never see her again, and my life is ruined." His eyes welled up, and tears streamed down his face. Melanie gave him a Kleenex from her bag.

"Your life isn't ruined," Melanie insisted. "What happened is incredibly sad, but people survive the loss of a parent. I did. My father left me when I was just about your age, after a terrible act of violence."

Charlie wiped his eyes with the Kleenex, looking interested.

"He owned a furniture store in Bushwick," Melanie continued. "He was shot during a robbery. I was there. I saw the whole thing. My father survived, but he was really different afterward. He left us—moved back to Puerto Rico, remarried, had a second family. I've only seen him twice since then. So for me, it's like he died, except . . . I always thought it was my fault somehow. I'm telling you this because I had a terrible time, but I got through it. I have a daughter now, and I love her more than I ever knew I could love anyone. I have a job I love. You just go on, and eventually things get better."

"I know you're trying to help. But don't lie. Your life was never the same again after that, was it?"

"No," she admitted.

"Did they catch him?"

"The man who shot my father? No, but don't let that worry you. The city was different then. Rougher. There was more crime, fewer cops. And besides, my family was poor. We had no connections. Your moth-er's murder is getting the best attention. That may not be *right,* but it's true. We'll find the man who did this. I promise."

"Good. Because it's the only thing I care about. That's what I'm holding on to. The thought of seeing him locked up like some animal in a cage keeps me going. Do you think I'm bad for wanting that?"

Melanie put her hand on the boy's head, as if to protect him. The roughness of his hair made her want a son.

"No. I think you're human."

Seeing Charlie Shepard's grief spurred Melanie on. She expressed her condolences to Lorraine, who seemed more interested in the celebrity chef on line behind Melanie than in hearing about the investigation, anyway. Then she hurried to the doorway, where she'd caught a glimpse of Kim Savitt's dramatic hat making its exit. Manners be damned; Melanie couldn't stand on ceremony if she wanted to get justice for that motherless boy.

By the time Melanie got out to the hallway, the elevator doors were closing. She raced down the stairs, reaching the ground floor in time to see Kim stepping out into the blazing sunlight. Melanie tailed her south for half a block. Kim was heading for an enormous white Escalade idling on a side street. A handsome, dark-skinned driver wearing a business suit and mirrored aviators stepped smartly around the massive vehicle and pulled the rear passenger door open as Kim approached.

Melanie broke into a run. "Mrs. Savitt, wait!"

Kim turned.

"Melanie Vargas. I'm a federal prosecutor investigating the murder of Suzanne Shepard." She flipped open her credentials.

"What's that got to do with me?" Kim snapped.

"You're involved in a relationship with Miles Ortiz. I need to ask you some questions about him. He's a suspect in Suzanne Shepard's murder," Melanie said.

"Jesus." Kim glanced at her driver, then over to the spot where a bunch of photographers congregated in front of the funeral home.

"From what I know of your personal situation, you can't afford bad press," Melanie said.

"Get in." Kim walked up to the driver, placed her hand in his, and used it to hoist herself smoothly into the Escalade, quite a feat in heels and a tight dress. Melanie clambered in after her. Inside, the second row of seats had been replaced with two luxurious leather swivel armchairs that boasted acres of space between them and control panels in each arm that presumably operated the flat screen TV. The air conditioning combined with the tinted windows made the hot city feel suddenly a hundred miles away.

"Hamad, take me to Michael Kors," Kim commanded as the driver took his seat.

Kim removed her big hat and smoothed her lemony-blond hair. Without the hat, she looked less extraordinary, more like a woman with a good body and an average face who'd made herself over at great expense rather than a true beauty. She seemed to be shrewd without being intelligent, and the faintest trace of Jersey lingered in her voice.

The driver stared straight ahead as if he were deaf and blind, but that didn't make it so. The last thing Melanie needed was a leak.

"Ask him to turn on some music," she said quietly. "What I'm about to say, you'd prefer to keep private."

"Hamad, put on your headphones," Kim ordered.

The driver whipped out an iPod. Tinny music emerged from the headphones as he inserted them into his ears.

"Listen, I know you eavesdropped on my conversation in the elevator before," Kim said. "No wonder you think I'm involved with Miles. But that was a different guy. I was talking to Miles *Drentell,* not Miles Ortiz. Miles Ortiz is just my trainer. I barely know him."

"Mrs. Savitt, lying to a federal official in the course of a murder investigation is a crime. You could go to jail for what you just said."

"How dare you accuse me of lying!" Despite her huffy tone, Kim looked frightened.

"I'm not an idiot. Miles Drentell was a character on *thirtysomething*. Besides, in order to prove you're lying, all I have to do is subpoena your cell-phone records. They'll tell me who you were talking to."

"What if I *was* talking to my trainer on the phone? Big deal. You can't do anything to me over that," Kim insisted.

"You have a sexual relationship with Miles Ortiz, and he gives you drugs," Melanie said calmly. "Miles broke into Suzanne Shepard's apartment a week before she was killed. Your husband owns the building. The building has tight security, and under normal circumstances, Miles wouldn't have been able to get in. But because of his relationship with you—well, you begin to see how bad this looks? You could end up implicated not only in a burglary, but in the biggest murder of the year."

Kim hadn't denied a single word Melanie said, but her eyes had grown wider as Melanie spoke.

"I have a daughter," Kim said. "Abigail Rose. She's three. She's my mini-me. I dress her up like a little doll. Drew is trying to take her away from me. Not because he wants her, but because he wants to hurt me. It would be a big problem if I got arrested for anything. Okay? Can you understand?"

"I understand completely. I'm divorced, and I have a little girl, too," Melanie said. And she did understand, enough to feel grateful that her own divorce had been amicable and swift, and that Steve hadn't resorted to any nasty tricks.

"So you won't arrest me?"

"Whether you get arrested or not is up to you, Kim. If you're truthful and cooperative, there won't be any need."

"What are you asking me to do? You're not going to make me talk against Miles, are you?"

"Why? Are you afraid of him?"

"No, but he *is* my friend."

"How would you feel if you knew he was involved in a murder? Would you think of him as a friend then?"

"What men get up to in the business world is none of my concern. My husband develops waterfront real estate in Jersey. You have to bust heads to do that. Nothing shocks me, and I don't judge."

"You may have an incentive to look the other way so you can enjoy your lifestyle without guilt," Melanie said, "but don't expect *me* to. You facilitated a burglary by letting Miles into your building. I'm betting you knew what he was up to. As soon as I can prove it, I'll arrest you."

"You're wrong, I swear. I'll tell you the truth, okay? Miles came over on Saturday when the nanny took Abigail to music class. We did some yoga, that's all. I didn't know anything about him robbing Suzanne's apartment."

Melanie took out her notebook. "You admit Miles came over to your apartment that Saturday?"

"Yes."

"What time?"

"Around two, which is when Abigail has her class at Diller-Quaile."

"Where?"

"Diller-Quaile. It's a music school, an important place to be seen for the pre-K set. Abigail has a class there every Saturday, and I get some 'me' time."

"Was Miles carrying anything when he arrived?"

"He usually carries a Louis Vuitton messenger bag that some client gave him last Christmas. I'm pretty sure he had it with him then. He can fit a lot of stuff inside that thing, so for all I know, he made a stop at Suzanne's on the way to my place. Once he's past the doormen downstairs, Miles can go anywhere he wants. It's not like they patrol the hallways."

"If Miles committed the robbery first, there would have been a long wait between when the doorman called to announce him and when he arrived at your apartment. Is that what you're saying happened?"

Kim didn't answer.

"Well?" Melanie demanded.

"Not that I recall," she conceded.

"What time did he leave?"

"Around six," Kim said, flushing. "I know, you're probably going that's a long yoga workout, right? But I have some back problems. Miles is certified in deep-tissue massage, and he does that for me sometimes. Therapeutically, I mean."

"At any time during the four hours he was in your apartment, did Miles leave?"

"Like leave and come back?"

"Yes."

"Maybe. I fell asleep, and at one point I was in the shower, so I can't be sure." Kim paused, studying Melanie's reaction, then added, "Sleeping and showering are normal for me after a workout. So you see, he could have snuck out and done any old thing, and I wouldn't have known. If Miles robbed Suzanne's apartment, I didn't have a clue. You can't hold me responsible."

Kim was so clearly lying about the nature of her relationship with Miles that Melanie found it difficult to believe she was telling the truth about anything else. But she wrote down everything Kim said anyway.

At least she'd have a record of what the woman's story was, so she could check up on it.

"Where was Miles on Wednesday night when Suzanne was murdered?" Melanie asked.

Kim shrugged. "Not with me."

"Did you speak to him or see him at all on Wednesday?"

"We might've talked on the phone at some point, although I can't remember what about. Nothing important. I was at Bliss all morning getting a facial and waxing, then I picked up Abigail from school and took her to my hairstylist to get her ends trimmed. At night, I went out with some girlfriends."

"What drugs is Miles selling?"

"I don't know anything about any drugs. The strongest thing Miles ever gave me was some echinacea when I had a cold."

"You're lying, Kim."

"I'm in the middle of a custody fight. If I get high once in a while, you can't expect me to admit it. I'd lose my daughter." Kim looked at Melanie pleadingly. She seemed to be telling the truth, and for the first time, Melanie actually felt sorry for her.

"Michael Kors, ma'am," the driver said.

They'd gone down Fifth Avenue, circled around, and ended up in front of a Madison Avenue boutique that was right near where they'd started. They could have walked there faster and saved the gas, but apparently walking in her Jimmy Choos wasn't part of Kim's lifestyle. Melanie's momentary sympathy dried up and blew away.

"I can't force you to talk," Melanie said in a disapproving tone. "But don't think you're immune, Kim. I plan to look into these drug allegations, and if they're substantiated, well, I would feel an obligation to let the family court know you're using drugs."

Kim blanched. "No, please."

"It's not a healthy environment for your daughter."

"I never do anything in front of her! Please, let's talk this over. I want to help. I want us to be on the same team. What can I do to show you that I'm acting in good faith?"

"You could start by telling the truth."

"If I say I'm sleeping with Miles or getting stoned, I lose Abigail. Isn't there something else?"

"Like what?"

"I know I said Miles was my friend, but you're right, if he's the Central Park Butcher, that's not okay. I mean, I would be shocked, but people can fool you. Let me do something, anything, to help you out. Wear a wire. Whatever you want."

Melanie thought for a moment. "There is something you can do. But it involves some risk to yourself."

"What?"

"I need you to make an introduction. To introduce somebody to Miles, to vouch for this person."

"Like a narc?" Kim asked.

"Honestly, Kim, it's better for you if you don't know the details."

EIGHTEEN

The director of security for Target News was a big lug with slicked-back salt-and-pepper hair, a mustache, and a Vegas-style double-breasted suit. Tony Mancuso had an oversize personality that sucked the air out of his tiny office, but he seemed like a straight shooter, an old-time law enforcement guy with no ax to grind. That's why Melanie was so surprised when he told her Clyde Williams, or someone close to him, had probably sent the threatening package to Suzanne Shepard.

"You don't seem like the type to toe the corporate line," Melanie said.

"Look, we both know Seth Parker is looking to take Williams down. I don't give a rip about that. Parker's a twit. His agenda has nothing to do with my findings.

But facts are facts. The package was mailed right after Suzanne broke the Williams scandal."

"Why would a successful politician do something so stupid?"

"Honestly, I don't think it was Williams himself. I think it was somebody around him, somebody with a stake in him winning the election."

"Why do you say that?"

"Because I reviewed the surveillance video from the post office where the package was mailed, and Williams isn't on it."

"You have the surveillance video? I need to see it right away."

"No, I never had it. This U.S. postal inspector I contacted let me review the tape. I'll give you her name if you want it, but it's kind of a waste of time. The tape is inconclusive anyway, because the camera malfunctioned."

"In what way?"

"The date and time stamp was turned off. I know what time the package was mailed, but it would take a video forensics expert to match that up with a specific point on the tape. The one thing I can say, though, is that Clyde Williams isn't in any of the footage I reviewed, and I reviewed a mountain of it."

"Walk me through the timing," Melanie said. "When exactly was the package mailed?"

"The Williams story ran a week ago Wednesday, and the package was mailed Thursday," Tony said. "I think that looks pretty bad. Bad enough to be worth investigating. Seth told me Williams's son is a U.S. attorney. Not for nothing, but if you don't look into this, Seth is gonna make a huge stink. I'm not saying that like a threat. I just thought you should know."

"I *am* looking into it. That's why I'm here. But I still find it hard to believe that Clyde Williams would be so reckless."

"Let me brief you on the evidence. You'll see, it's more convincing than it sounds."

Tony laid out a series of eight-by-ten glossies on the desk in front of Melanie. They showed a white box addressed in block capital letters to Suzanne Shepard, first in progressive stages of being opened, then with its contents laid out on a desktop. Several photographs featured pieces of excrement on a plastic backdrop, and others showed what looked to be torn scraps of colored paper.

"The box was hand-addressed in permanent marker to the location given on the Internet for people who want to contact Suzanne," Tony said. "No return address, as you would expect. It was postmarked from a facility on Roosevelt Avenue in Flushing, Queens, at three seventeen P.M. last Thursday, which was June first. It arrived here the next afternoon and was clocked into our mailroom at approximately four nineteen. We have a whole protocol for X-raying packages, but the X-ray machine was down, so the package wasn't screened until Monday morning."

"You mean, just this past Monday?" Melanie asked.

"Yes."

"And Suzanne was murdered Wednesday night."

"Right. Again, close timing. Monday morning, the screener detected suspicious contents. He called me. I took custody of the package, brought it here to my office, and performed a secure opening. One of my security officers witnessed the procedure and took these pictures."

"Was Suzanne present when you opened the package?"

"No," Tony replied. "We perform the secure opening wearing hazard suits, just in case the contents are dangerous. Then we inform the addressee and ask if they want to inspect it. She didn't want to. I can't blame her."

"But she knew about it?"

"Oh yes. In fact, Suzanne and I had a long talk about whether she should get protection, because I was so convinced the threat was real. I kick myself for not insisting. See, Suzanne had always attracted a large amount of hate mail. People get numb to it after a while. I couldn't make her take this seriously."

"You actually suggested she hire protection? Like a bodyguard?" Melanie asked.

"Yeah. But I didn't push, you know. I wish I had. Maybe this Butcher prick could've been stopped."

"If she got so much hate mail, what made this threat different? I understand the dog excrement is disgusting, but—"

"It wasn't the excrement that worried me, it was the picture," Tony said.

Melanie picked up one of the photographs showing the torn-up pieces of paper and examined it. "What about the picture? I can't tell from this photo. Did it have a message written on it or something?"

"No. The scary thing was that the guy actually took it."

"Took what?"

"The person who mailed the box took this photograph." He plucked up another photo and handed it to Melanie. "Here's a picture of the ripped-up pieces taped back together. You can see, it's a photograph of Suzanne having dinner at an outdoor café near her house. It was taken the night before the box was mailed, literally an hour after the Clyde Williams segment aired."

"An hour?"

"Yes."

"Seth Parker never told me about this," Melanie said. "I assumed the ripped-up picture had been taken from a magazine or something."

"If it had, I wouldn't've been so nervous, and I wouldn't be so convinced now that this threat is connected to her murder. But, you see, we know that whoever sent the box was actually *following* Suzanne."

The hair stood up on the back of Melanie's neck as she remembered the guy on the subway and the strange e-mail she'd gotten. *I'm watching you,* it had said. Melanie was so busy doing her job and so jaded after four years in law enforcement that she hadn't taken those small events very seriously. Wasn't that the mistake Tony Mancuso was describing, the mistake Suzanne Shepard had made that resulted in her death? Melanie decided she would mention the e-mail and the guy in the hooded sweatshirt to Dan and see what he thought.

Her eye fell on one of the photographs lying before her on the desk. "This is a picture of the box before it was opened?" she asked.

"Yes."

Melanie scrutinized it closely. "It's sealed with clear plastic packing tape," she said.

"Does that mean something to you?" Tony asked.

"Suzanne was gagged with very similar tape."

"There you go. Another fact to support my theory."

"I need to have this tape analyzed to see if it matches," Melanie said.

"Everything is off getting fingerprinted by a private lab we use. I can ask them to do a report on the tape also, unless you'd rather—"

"I want the FBI lab to do it."

"Sure, no problem. Frankly, our lab is very professional, but they take a year and a day to do anything. I'll get it back from them and deliver it to the FBI lab for you."

"Thank you."

"You're welcome. So you've seen the evidence. What do you think? Do you agree with me now?" Tony asked.

"I'm still not convinced that Clyde Williams sent this box," Melanie replied, "although I agree the timing is troubling and bears investigating."

"What about the idea that the Butcher sent it?"

"That, I'm starting to believe. We have more work to do to establish the connection with certainty. But this box is going to turn out to be a critical piece of evidence."

NINETEEN

Clyde Williams was on Melanie's mind, and not only because Tony Mancuso had convinced her that the threatening package was connected to Suzanne Shepard's murder. At lunchtime, Melanie ordered in some pizzas and held a small team meeting in the war room. Lieutenant Jack Deaver, Dan O'Reilly, Detective Julian Hay, and Janice Marsh from the D.A.'s office were in attendance. Melanie tried to focus on details of surveillances and witness interviews, but the meeting was dominated by Lieutenant Deaver's complaints about press coverage on the Clyde Williams issue.

"Am I the only one in the room who's getting heat from the brass?" the bluff lieutenant asked. "I got a call from the deputy commissioner just half an hour ago giving me hell over the negative press on the Butcher case."

"What negative press?' Melanie asked.

"Where you been, Vargas?" Deaver said.

"Investigating the crime, not reading the papers," she said.

"It ain't the papers, it's the TV. Listening to Target News, you'd think Clyde Williams was caught with the bloody knife in his hand, and the only reason he ain't locked up is because you're in bed with his kid. Figuratively speaking, I mean. They haven't actually suggested you're bangin' the Williams kid." Deaver paused. "*Yet.*"

"There's nothing I can do," Melanie protested. "A full-scale investigation of an elected official requires clearance from Main Justice. My boss is dealing with Washington, and they're slow as molasses. Once we get the green light, we'll move full speed ahead."

"How much longer are you planning to wait?" Deaver demanded. "The press is making a huge stink. It's getting to the point that I got guys in my own chain of command asking if there's special treatment here."

"That's no good," Melanie said.

"*No.* It's not."

"Look, I'll speak to Bernadette as soon as we're done here. I'll try to get authorization to ask Clyde if he has an alibi, at least. If he does, and we make it public, that should shut up the tabloids."

The minute the meeting ended, Melanie kept her word and headed for Bernadette's office. But when the elevator door opened on the Major Crimes floor, she barreled out so fast that she nearly knocked over her good friend Joe Williams.

Joe looked very much like his famous, handsome father, except smaller in every way. He was short and slight where Clyde was tall and robust. The charismatic, outgoing Clyde dominated any room he was in, while Joe came across as timid, an unsuitable trait in a prosecutor and one that had hindered his career. Joe's best-known courtroom escapade was fainting dead away while getting screamed at by the nasty Judge Warner during his first month on the job. He'd never lived down that moment, nor the widely held—though incorrect—belief that he'd gotten his job through his father's political influence. Joe had been overshadowed by his father his entire life, yet his response had been to become a better person for it—a more dedicated prosecutor, a more committed intellectual, a more loyal friend. Melanie couldn't stand the thought that her efforts might lead to his father's arrest and therefore cause her friend pain.

Startled, Melanie said the first thing that popped into her head. "Joe, I thought you were on trial this week."

"The jury's deliberating already, so I'm on beeper. It was in front of Stanchi, a reverse heroin buy. The evidence is pretty weak, but at least she's pleasant to appear before."

"Definitely," Melanie agreed, catching the elevator door as it began to slide shut. She opened her mouth then closed it again, wanting to say something about the Shepard case but knowing she shouldn't.

Joe's eyes seemed to understand and forgive all. He patted her on the arm as he stepped onto the elevator. "Hey, I know how much pressure you must be under on this Central Park Butcher thing. Don't worry about me. Just do what you have to do."

Which of course only made her feel worse.

TWENTY

Bernadette authorized Melanie to approach Clyde Williams with the limited mission of asking him whether he had an alibi. Because of the sensitive nature of the assignment, Melanie was instructed to bring witnesses.

Clyde Williams's office was located on the first floor of a renovated brownstone off St. Nicholas Avenue in the Hamilton Heights section of Harlem. Melanie, Dan, and Janice cooled their heels in the reception area waiting for Clyde to finish a conference call. The room had hardwood floors and freshly painted white walls hung with public service posters and artwork from the local elementary school. It was dominated by an enormous campaign poster of Clyde from the last election, smiling his toothpaste-commercial smile.

A receptionist and a press aide sat at nearby desks fielding telephone calls.

Melanie leafed through a day-old copy of the *Times* she'd picked up from the coffee table. They'd run a story on the Shepard slaying above the fold on the front page of the Metro section. On the morning after the murder, the *Post* and the *News* had gone with huge front-page headlines, but when it came to the *Times*, front page of the Metro section was considered big coverage for a local crime story.

Janice was busy reviewing old segments of *High Crimes* on an iVideo player. She claimed to have fast-forwarded through sixty episodes in the past twenty-four hours, enough to script the show herself.

Dan looked at his watch. "Guy's a city councilman," he said, catching Melanie's eyes. "You'd think he was the fricking president of the United States the way he's treating us. What's it been, half an hour now?"

The receptionist heard him, and she sent a huffy look sailing in his direction. She probably assumed Dan was some racist Irish cop who didn't like being made to wait by a black man. Melanie, who'd carefully probed Dan's views on such matters over time, knew this wasn't true. Dan thought of himself as a working stiff. He didn't take it well when anyone, of any race, pulled rank or treated him disrespectfully, and he really hated it when somebody slowed the pace of his investigation. The fact was, Melanie was getting pretty annoyed herself.

"How much longer?" Melanie asked the receptionist, an attractive woman in her fifties with a West Indian accent.

"I *really* can't say. He's *talking* to the mayor."

"Ma'am, I understand that, but we're investigating a brutal murder that took place in Central Park Wednesday night. The Central Park Butcher—perhaps you've heard of him? He's at large on the streets of this city. If he strikes again while we're being delayed here, you can imagine how bad that would look for the councilman."

The receptionist appeared to weigh what Melanie said. "I can text him and remind him you're out here."

"I would appreciate that."

As the receptionist turned to her computer, Dan winked at Melanie.

"Hey," she said, "how's your sick friend?"

He looked startled. "What?"

"I was calling around last night to check up on the Harris surveillance. Julian Hay told me you were visiting somebody in the hospital."

"Oh. Yeah. Sorry I didn't have a chance to get back to you."

Their eyes held. He didn't volunteer anything further, and since he didn't, she felt she couldn't ask. "That's okay," she said.

"Hey, I found something!" Janice exclaimed, ripping off her headphones. "Remember you asked me to look for links between David Harris and Suzanne Shepard, to figure out whether he had a reason to want her dead? Well, about two years ago, Suzanne did a segment on a couple of big-name New York City lawyers who were taking fat fees to advise clients on appearing before this business ethics review board that they actually served on. Clear conflict of interest, right?"

"Harris was one of the lawyers?" Melanie asked.

"No, but his boss, Stan Feinerman, was. The segment caused a minor scandal. Feinerman resigned from his position on the ethics board, and Suzanne made a fuss. Here, I'll play it for you."

Janice turned the video player so Dan and Melanie could see. On-screen, Suzanne Shepard was jogging backward in front of the imposing federal courthouse at Foley Square, trying to get a comment from a tall, bent man with a craggy face and silver hair.

"Mr. Feinerman, why did you resign?" Suzanne yelled, shoving a microphone at him.

"No comment," Feinerman said, waving his hands as if to swat her away like a gnat.

"Leave him alone!" yelled the muscular man hurrying along behind Feinerman. The camera focused on his face for a brief moment. It was David Harris.

Janice paused the monitor at looked at them triumphantly.

"That's *it*?" Melanie asked.

Janice shrugged. "It's a connection. Why didn't Harris tell us he'd met Suzanne? And under such adversarial circumstances?"

Dan nodded. "She's got a point. Harris claimed he never met Suzanne, never even watched her show."

"Maybe he forgot?" Melanie asked dubiously.

"Who'd forget something like that?" Dan asked.

"Then he lied. You've got him under surveillance, right?" she asked Dan.

"Every minute. And we should get the DNA results back soon, so if he killed Suzanne Shepard, we'll know."

"Ms. Vargas, Councilman Williams will see your party in his office now," the receptionist said, still eyeing Dan with hostility.

Clyde and an aide, a thin, bookish-looking guy with a pockmarked face and glasses, stood up as they entered the room. Clyde was a big man, tall and solidly built. Melanie couldn't help noticing that he was the right size and body type to be the killer—if you believed David Harris's description—albeit the wrong color.

Clyde came around the desk with both arms raised, and Melanie promptly stuck out her hand out to fend off an embrace. It was tough to put the screws to a suspect who greeted you with a big hug. Clyde, always an expert at taking the temperature of a room, shook her hand with distant politeness as if that's what he'd intended all along.

"Sorry to keep you waiting. We're in the middle of budget negotiations and as usual the mayor and the City Council are at odds."

Introductions were made, and they all sat down at a conference table situated in a bay window overlooking the street. Melanie's seat faced into the room. Every square inch of wall space was covered with memorabilia from Clyde's political career—testimonials, handshake photos with presidents and civil rights figures and movie stars, plaques and certificates and awards. Even in the U.S. Attorney's Office, where people framed every last atta-boy letter that came across their desks, she'd never seen a wall of glory so extensive. It was difficult not to feel intimidated. Melanie cleared her throat, placed her notepad squarely on the desk before her, and looked Clyde in the eye.

"Councilman, as you know, Suzanne Shepard was murdered on Wednesday night," she began.

Clyde drew his brows together and steepled his fingers. "I do know that. What I don't understand, Melanie, is what the *hell* it's got to do with me."

The anger in his tone took her by surprise. This was not going to be a collegial visit with the father of a good friend.

"We're not here to accuse you of anything," she replied. "We need to cover our bases, that's all. We're speaking to a lot of people who—well, frankly, who might've had reason to be angry with the victim. We're talking to you because Suzanne Shepard had just run a very damaging story on you."

"Some reporter smearing Clyde with a pack of lies makes him a murder suspect?" demanded the aide. His name was Rockwell Davis, and Clyde called him Rocky. Davis radiated cold hostility.

"He's not a suspect. We're here to cross his name off the list of people who might have been involved. In order for us to do that, he simply needs to tell us where he was at the time of the attack."

"I'm supposed to start accounting for my movements?" Clyde said.

"Only at the time of the murder," Melanie replied. "That's all we're interested in. We're not trying to burden you. In fact, we have your best interests at heart.

The press is making a big fuss about your connection to our office through Joe. If we could tell them you have an alibi—"

"You *are* burdening me. I find the question completely outrageous and insulting, and I have no intention of answering," Clyde said.

Melanie looked at Clyde in amazement. For all the time she'd spent thinking about how to phrase the question, it had never occurred to her that he might refuse to answer. Her only hope of salvaging the situation was to keep her cool and try to ease his hostility.

"Clyde," she said in a soothing tone, "I'm begging you not to take this personally. I'm only here because questions have been raised in the press. I'll tell you right now, I don't believe you're involved in any murder, but we have to follow procedure. You're not the first person we're asking to provide an alibi, and you won't be the last."

"What do you plan to do with the information if he tells you?" Davis asked.

"First, we'll verify it, and if everything checks out—"

"You see where this is going?" Davis demanded, turning to Clyde with a sneer. "*Verify it.* We give an inch, and next thing we know, they're all up in our business. They'll want your phone records, a list of everybody you talk to, where you went. Domestic spying. Big Brother tactics. Plain and simple."

"You're making that up," Melanie insisted. "I haven't asked for any of that stuff."

"You know what I don't understand?" Clyde said to Melanie. "You already arrested another man for this crime. It's all over the papers. Rocky, hand me today's *Daily News* from over there."

Davis grabbed a newspaper from the chair beside him. Clyde slapped it down in front of Melanie. The front-page headline, over a picture of David Harris and Bob Adelman leaving the courthouse, read, LAWYER NABBED IN TV STAR SLAY.

"Why the hell should I let you question me when you're in court telling a judge somebody else did the deed? You think I'm a patsy?"

"Mr. Harris was an eyewitness to the murder," Melanie explained. "We charged him with obstruction of justice for refusing to cooperate with the FBI. We're investigating him thoroughly, and we think there's a chance he's the killer. We've taken a DNA sample from him, and we're waiting for results. But we're still duty bound to check out other credible leads."

"Clyde is not a credible lead," Davis said. "You're on some kind of fishing expedition here."

"That's not true," Melanie replied, fixing Clyde with a steady gaze. "We're being careful and deliberate. That's why we're asking a broad spectrum of people to provide alibis. We need to hear from you, Councilman, in order to stop the hysteria in the press that says we're giving you a free ride."

Clyde folded his arms across his chest. "That's your problem, now, isn't it? Don't expect any help from me. See, I don't forget who appointed your boss."

"You mean, the U.S. attorney?"

"That's your boss, isn't it?"

"Not my direct boss. There's a bunch of layers of hierarchy between me and him."

"But he's your ultimate boss?"

"Yes."

"And this president appointed him, am I correct?"

"Yes," Melanie said.

"A president who would do anything to stop me from becoming mayor?"

"That may be, but it has nothing to do with why I'm here. I never even speak to the U.S. attorney, and I sincerely doubt that he talks to the president. The president has bigger concerns than one little murder in New York."

"Yeah, like who's gonna be the next mayor of this city!" Davis exclaimed.

Melanie was speechless.

"You bust into my office asking me intrusive questions when you already have another man in custody," Clyde said, shaking his head in disgust. "What else am I supposed to think? This is harassment. It's a conspiracy. It's politically motivated, and it's a blatant attempt to smear me."

"Why would I smear you, Clyde? I support you!"

"If you support me, then you know I had nothing to do with this murder. So take my word for that and leave."

"You of all people should understand the position I'm in," Melanie exclaimed, frustrated. "Your son is a prosecutor in our office. We can't do you special favors or treat you differently than we would anybody else who might've had a motive to go after Suzanne Shepard, or it'll look bad. If you won't answer questions voluntarily, then . . ." She trailed off, thinking about how ugly this could get.

"Then what? You subpoena me? Force me to take the Fifth?"

"I'd have no choice. And taking the Fifth would look pretty bad for a guy running for mayor, wouldn't it?" she asked.

Clyde folded his arms across his chest and glared at her. "Not if he's the victim of ugly smear tactics. You want to get into a pissing match with me in the media, I promise you, I'll win."

"I *don't* want that. The only thing I want is to catch this killer."

"I need you to leave now. Rocky, show them out."

They stepped from the brownstone into bright sunshine. The scent of warm soil and lilac wafted toward them from a community garden down the block, and children's laughter rang out from a nearby playground. Dan's car was parked down the street, and as they headed for it, their moods could not have been more at odds with the glory of the day.

"What a fiasco," Dan said. "Could you believe that horseshit about how we're persecuting him because the U.S. attorney works for the president and the president hates Clyde?"

"Everybody's got a conspiracy theory these days," Melanie said.

"He's guilty as sin," Janice, who'd been silent during the interview, said with surprising vitriol.

"You think so?" Melanie asked. Yesterday, Janice had been convinced David Harris was the killer. Melanie was beginning to question the girl's judgment.

"He told us he's planning to take the Fifth! Why would he do that if he wasn't involved with the murder?" Janice asked.

"For political reasons," Melanie said. "Maybe we stumbled into some game Clyde is playing with the press. I'm more concerned about Rockwell Davis. I got the distinct feeling he was turning Clyde against us."

"He's a troublemaker, big-time," Dan agreed.

"What do we know about him?" Melanie asked.

"Not enough. Nothing, really," Dan said.

"You should've asked them both for DNA samples," Janice said.

"I wasn't authorized to," Melanie said. "Besides, they'd never agree. If we get to that point, we'll need a court order. Hell, we'll need straitjackets."

"Here's what I don't get," Dan said. "If Clyde gave us his alibi, we'd pack up and go home. Leave him alone. So why not give it to us? He's hiding something about where he was that night."

Melanie was getting tired of defending Clyde Williams. Besides, in her heart of hearts, she was beginning to wonder about him herself.

"To hell with the paperwork," she told Dan. "Start looking at them. Find out whatever you can."

TWENTY ONE

Forty-two hours had passed since Suzanne Shepard's murder. The Central Park Butcher was still at large, as the TV news kept reminding the public. And Melanie was languishing in yet another waiting room, feeling no closer to an answer.

Dr. Benedict Welch, the plastic surgeon whose file had been stolen from Suzanne Shepard's apartment, maintained an office on Park Avenue in the Sixties, the toniest part, right where all the socialites lived. The reception area was decorated to resemble an English country manor. Melanie sat in a chintz wingback chair beside Detective Pauline Estrada waiting for an audience with the beauty guru. All around them, glamour girls of a certain age perused *Town & Country* and gossiped. They sported identical blond highlights and plastic faces with collagened fish lips, and were dressed to the nines in little suits or slacks and cashmere twinsets with high heels and sparkly jewelry. Not exactly how Melanie would have put herself together for a visit to the doctor. But in New York, she'd noticed, the women with the least to do were always the most dressed up.

"She's on something, and I'm not talking multivitamins. The last time I saw her, she walked right by me as if we'd never even met," one of them was saying to another within Melanie's earshot.

"That's just how she is."

"She wasn't snubbing me. I'm telling you, it's drugs."

"Well, everybody's on something these days. Takes the edge off."

At the window where Melanie had checked in earlier, the redheaded nurse, whose name was Gigi, was pointing at her. A tall man with a thick head of yellowy blond hair looked in Melanie's direction and nodded. He wore a white lab coat. As he came toward her several women blushed and tittered like tweens who'd just spotted a member of their favorite boy band.

"She's new," one of them said loudly, eyeing Melanie with resentment.

Benedict Welch stopped before Melanie. "Miss Vargas?" he asked.

"Yes."

She made as if to stand up, but he held her in place with a caressing hand on her shoulder.

"No, baby. Sit for a moment and let me look at you."

And he perched on the arm of her chair, staring down into her face, too close for Melanie's comfort. He looked as artificial as any woman in the room, with skin deeply tanned yet smooth as a child's, and eyes of such an intense violet blue that the color could not possibly be natural. His eyes had a strange, glassy quality, too, as if he'd been writing himself a few prescriptions.

"Doctor," she said, "weren't you told that we're here—"

"Quiet. Let me appreciate you." He brushed his fingers across Melanie's lips, and she recoiled. His fingers were long and thin, and his touch oddly light, like an insect's.

"Please don't touch me like that," Melanie said. Pauline was looking at Welch with intense interest. Here he was, lending credence to everything they'd read in those complaints to the medical board.

"I'm mesmerized by these Latin lips, but my interest is purely medical," Welch said, in a soft, hypnotic voice. "Besides, a doctor always touches his patients. It's normal, and necessary, and very much a part of the intimacy we'll develop as we work together. You'll get used to my touch. Your mouth is just luscious, and you haven't had any collagen, have you? But I do see the start of worry lines. You came to the right place, sweetie. A little pinchie and they'll go bye-bye. Shall we?" He stood up.

Either Gigi had misinformed him about the purpose of their visit, or he was putting on a show for his patients. Melanie nodded at Pauline.

"Detective Estrada is working on this case also," she said, loudly enough for other patients to hear.

From Welch's strained smile, Melanie saw that he'd known all along.

"Of course," he said coldly. "This way."

He led them through a door and down a hallway lined with treatment rooms, into an office decorated with leather club chairs and a big mahogany desk. Welch sat behind the desk and gestured for them to take seats.

"Just to be sure we're on the same page regarding the purpose of this visit," Melanie began, "I'm with the U.S. Attorney's Office and Detective Estrada is NYPD. We're investigating the murder of Suzanne Shepard. We're also interested in a burglary that took place at her apartment shortly before her murder, and we need to ask you a few questions."

"Of course. I want to help. Whatever I can tell you without breaching doctor-patient confidentiality rules," Welch said.

"We're not interested in Suzanne's beauty treatments. We're here to talk about you, and your relationship with her," Melanie said.

"Anything I can do. I adored Suzanne, and from what I've read in the papers, this was a terrible crime."

"Yes, it was. We're following up with anybody who might have had a motive to harm her. Were you aware that Suzanne Shepard was researching a story on you, Dr. Welch?" Melanie asked.

"No, but I can't say I'm surprised. As the person who took care of her looks, I was very important in her life. Favorable publicity is something I'm fond of, and Suzanne knew that. She was probably planning a story as a way to thank me. Patients give me gifts all the time."

"And you accept them?"

"If the gift is valuable, I declare it on my tax return. All the formalities are observed, so no room to play gotcha there." His smile was about as genuine as a three-dollar bill.

"In this case, the gift would not have been valuable. The story was negative. Scandalous, in fact."

Melanie watched his face closely for a reaction. Lorraine Shepard hadn't a clue what was in the stolen file folder, or what the terrible secret was that Suzanne had discovered about Benedict Welch. Melanie was fishing, hoping for a little information here, but unfortunately Welch wasn't biting.

"If you're looking for people who wanted to hurt Suzanne, you've come to the wrong place," he said. "Suzanne was one of my favorite patients, and the affection was mutual. She would never say anything negative about me."

"Suzanne's apartment was broken into two weeks ago, Doctor, and a file containing information about you was stolen. Why would somebody take a file that only said nice things?"

"I don't have the slightest idea. I never knew such a file existed, and I didn't know anybody took it. Maybe it was a mistake. I'm sure the taxpayers can count on you to find out."

He met Melanie's gaze evenly, as if he didn't have a thing to hide.

"You know a Miles Ortiz?" Pauline Estrada asked suddenly.

Welch's head snapped around. "No."

"No?" Pauline asked, surprised.

"I gave the answer. The answer is no. I don't know anybody by that name."

Pauline drew from her bag the file on the Shepard burglary that Melanie had looked through yesterday at the precinct. She pulled some papers out and handed them across the desk to him. Melanie could see the cover page of a telephone bill.

"This is your office telephone number, correct?" Pauline asked.

"Yes."

"A cell phone subscribed to by Mr. Ortiz called that number seventeen separate times in the past month," Pauline said.

"People call. That doesn't mean I speak to them. For all I know, he's Gigi's latest boyfriend. She goes through several a week, it seems."

Pauline took the telephone bill back.

"Do you live alone?" she asked.

"No. I'm married. I live with my wife, Gloria. She's a former patient of mine. See?" He turned a gilded frame that sat on his desk around to face them. The woman in the photograph could have been any one of the Botoxed socialites from the waiting room. She looked rich and skeletally thin, and a lot older than Welch himself did—which set Melanie to thinking.

"This is your home telephone number?" Pauline asked, showing him another phone bill.

"Yes, it is."

"Mr. Ortiz called your home number eleven times in the past month. Is he your wife's boyfriend, too?"

"You know, I've been very patient with you people. But the tone of these questions is beginning to get objectionable, and I'd really like you to leave now."

"I apologize, Dr. Welch," Melanie interjected. "You've been very accommodating. One more question, sir, and I promise, we'll get out of your hair. Where were you on Wednesday night at around eight forty?"

Melanie was half expecting Welch to blow up and order them from the room, but instead he leaned back in his chair, fighting to suppress a smile that played around the corners of his lips.

"That's easy enough," he said. "I was at a dinner meeting with several fellow board members of All the Pretty Children. It's a charitable organization that provides free plastic surgery to third-world kids with harelips and other congenital deformities. I do a lot of work for them. At eight forty, we were at Café Boulud talking about writing grants for next year's budget. I'm happy to give you the names of my companions. They're all most reputable people."

Ooh, I wanted to punch him in the mouth so bad. Wipe that nasty smile right off his face," Pauline Estrada said as they hit the pavement on Park Avenue.

Melanie glanced at Pauline, who laughed. "Just kidding. Figure of speech."

"Right." Melanie had heard enough cops say things like that to have some serious doubts about how they behaved when she wasn't around. Even cops like Pauline, who wore lipstick and had kids at home.

Melanie was planning to grab a cab back to her office, but she started walking south toward the precinct, falling into step beside the detective. It was late afternoon and gorgeous out. Flowers in front of the fancy buildings danced in the sunlight, their scent obscuring the exhaust fumes from passing cars, and the warm air felt like velvet on her skin. A group of construction workers heading north as they headed south pulled one-eighties to stare at them.

"You ladies free?" one of them called.

"No, we're very expensive," Pauline retorted, eliciting a friendly series of whoops and hollers.

"C'mon. Welch was lying. He's a total asshole," Pauline said to Melanie as they continued walking.

"Of course he is. Believe me, he creeps me out bigtime. Did you see how he touched me?"

"I did see, the perv."

"Remember those complaints to the medical board?" Melanie said. "Now that I've met Welch, I'm positive he groped those patients. I'm just surprised he waited until they were unconscious. Think about the fact that Suzanne Shepard was raped, and then think about the man we just met. I know it sounds far-fetched to accuse a prominent doctor of murdering one of his patients. But I get such a strong vibe from Welch that he's capable of rape."

"For me, it's all about the phone records," Pauline said. "When I got them this morning, and I saw we could connect Welch to Miles Ortiz, I said, that's it, that's the answer. The two of 'em had something going on together, something involving drugs. Suzanne found out. She was gonna blow it sky-high, so they whacked her. And Welch got his rocks off by raping her first."

"Could be," Melanie said, thinking out loud. "Welch certainly got agitated once you started asking about Miles."

"Yeah, that's when he asked us to leave," Pauline said.

"And did you see his eyes? He's on something, I just know it."

"I thought so, too."

"He's hiding something important. The only thing that gives me pause is that he claims he has an alibi. Why would he tell us he went out to dinner if he knows it won't check out?" Melanie asked.

"Maybe he got our boy Miles to do the dirty work," Pauline said. "They were in it together, but Miles was the one who pulled off the murder. And the burglary, too, which is why we found Miles's fingerprints in Suzanne's apartment instead of Welch's."

"We need to learn more about Welch, Pauline. Let me ask you something. How old did he look to you?"

"Welch? I don't know. Thirty-five. Forty, maybe."

"How old did you tell me he was, based on that profile you worked up?"

"*Oh.*" Pauline's brows drew together, and she stopped in midstride, pulling her folder from her bag and plopping it down on top of a metal box holding fliers for the Learning Annex. She rifled through frantically until she found what she was looking for, and looked up at Melanie in shock. "Oh my God! Sixty-four."

"Where did you get that information?"

"From the Medical Licensing Board."

"That man was not sixty-four," Melanie insisted.

"He's a plastic surgeon, though. Do you think—?"

"Did you see those women in the waiting room? His patients?"

"Yes."

"They get the full benefit of his skills. How old did they look?"

Pauline nodded. "Old."

"Welch may be a plastic surgeon, but he's not Dorian Gray. He can't reverse the effects of nature. I think the age you have for him is wrong."

"It can't be. I got it from a bunch of different sources. Medical school and licensing records, driver's license, his Web site. Everything matches up."

"Welch has his own Web site?"

"Yeah, for making appointments, but mostly for flaunting himself. He's got mad pictures posted on it of himself with all the beautiful people. In one of 'em, he's standing on a beach wearing white pants and a blazer, barefoot, holding a martini. I almost barfed. But the point is, every single item of paperwork puts the guy as sixty-four."

"Paper doesn't always tell the whole story," Melanie said. "Something's not right. Did you tell me yesterday Welch was from Oklahoma?"

"Yeah, Tulsa."

"That's where he went to medical school and was licensed to practice medicine?" Melanie asked.

"Yes."

"Ever been there?"

Pauline made a face. "With the wind rushing down the plains? No thanks, not my style, *chica*."

"You're very skilled at digging up information, Pauline, but this task may require the personal touch. If you're game, I can find money in the budget for a plane ticket."

"You know me, I'm game for anything. What the hell, I'll check my closet. I got an old pair of red cowboy boots hiding in there somewhere that might look good when I'm riding a horse," Pauline said with a twinkle in her eye.

TWENTY TWO

Back at her desk, Melanie was feeling the pressure. It was close of business on Friday afternoon, and she had too many leads. In a case like this, where the victim had a lot of enemies, a shotgun approach was often necessary at the beginning. You followed up every last tip just far enough to rule it out. The problem was, this wasn't the beginning anymore. The weekend was about to hit, meaning offices and labs would close and the PD would cut staffing to save on overtime. Melanie's job was about to get harder at a moment when she'd made little discernible progress in narrowing her focus. She was checking her voice mail and e-mail simultaneously to save time when the caption of an e-mail gave her a nasty shock. Her pen pal partysover2007 had written to her again.

The e-mail read, *I'm still out here.* The phone fell from its place at Melanie's shoulder into her lap as her eyes moved over his words.

Hey, Melanie Vargas [the creep had written], *you forget about me? I didn't forget you. If you keep ignoring my messages, I'm gonna be really ticked off when we meet in person and it won't be fun and games for you. I saw you again today and you didn't even know it. I saw your legs behind David Harris coming out of court in that picture in the* Daily News. *Your legs look just right. Firm, not too skinny. I'm gonna like them under me.*

"Jesus," she said under her breath. She looked over her shoulder, half expecting to see a guy in a leather face mask standing behind her with a bloody knife. It was late on a Friday, but thankfully there were other prosecutors in the hallway. She heard somebody laughing. Everything was okay. Nobody could get to her here. But still, she'd better stop shrugging this off and do something, before the creep decided to make himself known. Whether he was actually the Butcher or just some average Joe with a penchant for weird pranks, Melanie had no desire to meet him in person.

She plucked the receiver from where it had fallen in her lap. Her voice mails had been playing on while she read the latest installment from her Web stalker, and she heard the reassuring sound of Dan's recorded voice

in midmessage. He'd called while she was out interviewing Welch to tell her that Suzanne Shepard's telephone records had come in.

". . . looking for a call around six o'clock Wednesday
that could've lured Suzanne out for a meet in Central
Park," Dan's recorded voice was saying. "I think I found
it. Five forty-eight P.M., originating from a pay phone in
Flushing. If that sounds right, throw me a beep, and I'll
send somebody to do lifts off the pay phone. Unlikely
we'll get anything, but you never know."

Wait a second. Flushing. What else had Melanie
heard about Flushing today? Wasn't that where the
threatening package had been mailed from? She flipped
through her notebook hastily looking for the notes from
her interview with Tony Mancuso, glad for the distraction from that disgusting e-mail. Yes, there it was in
black-and-white. The package had been sent from a
post office on Roosevelt Avenue in Flushing. Melanie
dialed Dan's cell to tell him that, but all she got was his
voice mail.

"Hey, it's me," she said. "I got your message about
that call in Suzanne's phone records. It sounds right.
You should definitely take lifts off the pay phone,
because something else important happened in Flushing." She gave him the details on the threatening package. "I need your advice on a couple of weird e-mails

I've gotten. I was hoping you could take a look at them and tell me if they're worth investigating. So call me, or just come over. Bye."

Melanie hung up and stared at the wall for a long moment to avoid looking at her computer screen. But then she got impatient with herself. There was too much going on to let this jerk slow her down. She minimized the e-mail into a tiny blip.

Melanie resumed listening to her voice mails. A call had come in not ten minutes earlier from Susan Charlton, Bernadette's deputy chief and one of Melanie's favorite colleagues, and it was troubling enough in its own right to take her mind off the cyberstalker.

"Mel, it's Susan. Witchie-poo left for the day and she won't be back in the office until after her honeymoon. A problem came up on your murder investigation. I'm acting chief, so that puts me in charge of discussing it with you. Stop by as soon as you get this message."

Susan Charlton was on the telephone. As Melanie dropped heavily into a guest chair, fatigue overwhelming her, Susan met her eyes and held up an index finger.

Baseball caps from every agency in law enforcement bristled from all four walls of Susan's office. The entire alphabet soup of the federal justice system—FBI,

DEA, ATF, ICE, IRS, NYPD, hanging from nails in neat rows. There must've been a hundred hats. Agents who didn't know Susan called her "Miss Alternative Lifestyle" behind her back, but any guy who'd ever worked a case with her eventually brought his offering and vied to have it placed in a spot of honor on her wall.

Susan's freckled face was so vivid pink with exertion that it clashed with her flaming carrot hair, which clashed with the red Stanford Law baseball cap she wore. Susan was captain of the U.S. Attorney's Office coed softball team. The fact that she was in shorts and her uniform T-shirt reminded Melanie that today had been the grudge rematch against their big rivals, the U.S. Marshals Service.

Melanie wondered why her own life didn't leave room for something as sane as playing on the office softball team. Susan had no children. She and her partner, Lisa Friedman, an antipoverty lawyer, had been talking about adopting for ages but hadn't done anything concrete about it. Yet Melanie suspected that even if Susan were a mom, she'd find time to win her trials, play sports, volunteer at her church, and hit the pub after work to gather intelligence from the cops. Susan was simultaneously well adjusted and crazy, cutthroat competitive and widely liked. If Melanie had to name one quality that equipped Susan for all her success, she would've chosen this: Susan had no angst. She didn't worry. And she never, ever second-guessed herself once she'd made a decision. Unfortunately, these were the ways in which she differed most from Melanie.

Susan hung up and looked at her.

"D'you win?" Melanie asked.

"Whupped their bee-hinds, girl," Susan exulted, taking a swig from a bottle of Poland Spring water on her desk and smiling broadly. "It was a beautiful thing. They're so friggin' full of themselves."

"Score?"

"Six–three. A clear victory. Watch, none of my prisoners'll get transported to court next week, but I don't care. We're celebrating at Grady's tonight if . . . oh, but what am I saying? You're too busy."

"I listened to your message. What's up?" Melanie asked.

"I got a call from the front office," Susan said, referring to the big walnut-paneled suite that housed the U.S. attorney and his first assistant.

"That can't be good," Melanie said.

"They're concerned about the press activity in your case. Are you aware that Target News is doing twenty-four/seven live coverage on the Butcher?"

"I heard they were making a stink. That's their style," Melanie said.

"With all that dead air to fill, they're spouting a lot of dreck, as you can imagine, and some of it upset the higher-ups. Take a look."

Susan picked up a remote and clicked, and a television sitting on a wheeled cart beside her desk sprang to life. She rewound to an image of Lorraine Shepard clad in the exquisite black Chanel jacket and pearls she'd been wearing this morning, standing outside the Frank E. Campbell Funeral Home.

"I loved her with all my heart," Lorraine said as tears welled picturesquely in her big blue eyes. "My only daughter. And to think that cronyism is standing in the way of arresting her killer. The people of this city should demand answers. It was my daughter this time, but that animal is out there. Next time it could be yours."

"Lorraine Shepard gets her fifteen minutes of fame," Melanie said with disgust. "This woman has a habit of second-guessing investigations."

"Good to know. But keep watching," Susan said.

The camera cut to file footage of Clyde Williams walking down the steps of City Hall, flashing his toothsome smile as he waved to a crowd of well-wishers.

"Allegations of cronyism and special treatment swirl around this man," the correspondent's resonant, Australian-accented voice said, "City Councilman Clyde Williams, the subject of a scathing exposé aired on *High Crimes* just last week by the brave and relentless and now very *dead* Ms. Shepard. Williams is currently the front-runner for the Democratic mayoral nomination, but his prospects have been seriously undermined by allegations first reported by Target News that he had an affair with this woman"—the image changed to a high-school-yearbook photo of a pretty blond girl—"gorgeous, *young* Emily King, intern in Williams's office, a mere twenty years old, sophomore at Princeton University and daughter of a wealthy Connecticut footwear magnate."

"Footwear magnate. I love that," Susan said, chuckling. She'd been leaning back with her feet up on her desk, but now she sat forward and paused the video. "Okay, it's this next part that has the front office, well, concerned. Listen and tell me what you think," she said, pushing play again.

"Despite questions about the obvious motive Williams or his supporters might have had to harm Suzanne Shepard," the voice-over continued, "no action has been taken against him in the days since the brutal crime was committed. Target News has uncovered an alarming explanation for this otherwise unthinkable oversight in the person of Williams's son"—here the screen flashed to footage of Clyde and Joe shaking hands side by side on a receiving line, both in tuxedos, looking a lot alike— "Joseph Franklin Williams, a prosecutor in the very same office as Melanie Vargas"—and here, footage from Melanie's press conference—"the young, inexperienced prosecutor handling the Shepard murder investigation."

"Inexperienced!" Melanie exclaimed.

"Shh," Susan said, holding up one hand and pointing at the screen with the other.

"Target News has learned that Vargas is not only acquainted with but in fact good mates with the younger Williams, and on close personal terms with both Clyde Williams and his wife, Cherise, because of that relationship," the voice-over continued. The screen faded in to focus on a big blond man with a chiseled face standing outside the building in which Melanie and Susan now sat.

"With the Butcher of Central Park still at large, what do the parties involved have to *say* about this disturbing conflict of interest? Can it be possible that one of our brightest politicians has knowledge of, or even involvement in, one of our most *horrific* crimes? Councilman Williams plans to address the allegations at a press conference later tonight, which we will bring to you live. The U.S. Attorney's Office, for the moment, remains *suspiciously* silent. Duncan Gilmartin, Target News, outside the U.S. Attorney's Office, waiting for some answers. Cassandra, back to you in the studio."

Susan clicked and the screen went blank.

"I can tell you exactly why they're doing this," Melanie insisted. "Seth Parker, the producer at Target News, wanted me to embed this guy Gilmartin with the investigative team, and I refused."

"Embed, like in Iraq?"

"Yes."

"That's a new one. We don't do that."

"That's what I told him. Now he's punishing me for turning them down. And obviously, they're looking for a ratings bounce."

"I believe you, but that doesn't change the fact that the front office is upset. Nobody told them this Williams thing was out there, and they don't like surprises."

"Bernadette was in the loop. I went to her earlier today and asked her to speed up the paperwork at Main Justice so we could go after Clyde and address the allegations of favoritism. I specifically told her that the NYPD was upset with the press coverage. Shouldn't she have been the one to say something to the front office? It's hardly like I play racquetball with the U.S. attorney every morning."

Susan looked thoughtful. "Hmm, there's an angle. You know Witchie-poo's on their shit list, right?"

"Seriously?"

"Why do you think she's so keen to get out of here?"

"I thought she was itching to get on the bench," Melanie said.

"She's itching to jump before she gets pushed. Bernadette's turf battles have come back to bite her. Turns out her enemies are better connected in the front office than she is. If we hand them Witchie-poo on a platter, we could save your butt on this one, Mel. Being Bernadette's good German isn't necessarily a smart strategy for you right now in any event."

"I'm not her good German," Melanie said, her cheeks burning. "I don't follow her blindly. But she is my boss, and I respect chain of command."

"I'm just saying it's time for you to raise your profile with the higher-ups. You know, look independent, differentiate yourself from Bernadette. Letting them know she was the one who dropped the ball on this Williams thing would go a long way toward achieving that."

"I'm not selling her out."

"I admire your loyalty, but get real. If Bernadette lets you take the fall, isn't she selling *you* out?"

"What kind of fall are we talking about here?" Melanie asked.

"For starters, after the higher-ups saw this"—Susan gestured at the TV—"they wanted to pull you off the Shepard case."

Melanie was stricken, and it showed on her face.

"I talked them out of it," Susan said. "I bought you some time to do damage control. At least a day."

"A day?"

"Hey, it's better than nothing. A lot can happen in a day on an investigation like this. Who knows, you could have the Butcher locked up by tomorrow."

"Susan, this is really stupid. The Clyde Williams thing is a distraction manufactured by the media. He didn't kill anybody."

"People can surprise you," Susan said with a shrug. "But Clyde's guilt or innocence isn't the point. The front office knows Target News is a bunch of tabloid crap. The content of the story didn't upset them as much as the fact that they got blindsided. They need controversy fronted to them ahead of time, before they see it live at six."

"I understand."

"Good, then we're on the same page. Here's the plan. I go to them with the Bernadette explanation, then we—"

"No. I'm not down with that."

"I don't know why you're so devoted to her," Susan said, exasperated. "She'd feed you to the lions in a heartbeat if it suited her purpose."

"Maybe you're right, but Bernadette's done a lot for me. Besides, she's getting married tomorrow."

"Yeah, poor Vito."

Melanie and Susan looked at each other, at an impasse.

"May I speak frankly?" Susan asked finally.

"Of course."

"I have an ulterior motive here that you should know about. I plan to be chief of this unit once Bernadette's gone, which may be sooner than anybody expects. And I want you as my deputy. That ain't gonna happen if we don't fix this little dustup."

"I'm flattered. But why would you want me for deputy instead of Brad Monahan? You guys are such good friends."

"I love the Bradalator, but I don't trust him to watch my back. He'd be too busy scheming to get my job. *You*, on the other hand, would be an awesome deputy, and as you've just demonstrated, you'd be loyal to a fault. So what do you say?"

"I'm still not tattling on Bernadette."

"I'll try my best to find a way around it, scout's honor, but you've got to give me some latitude to work here. There's something else you need to focus on if you want to redeem yourself with the front office."

"What's that?"

"Like the man said, Clyde Williams is holding a news conference tonight after his big fund-raiser. On the steps of the Met, surrounded by his glitterati contributors no less. You need to find out what he's going to say, so we're not caught off guard again."

"How am I supposed to do that?"

"You could try asking him."

"He threw me out my ear just a few hours ago."

"I trust you to overcome whatever hard feelings might exist and get Clyde to spill his guts."

"What about the ethical implications? Clyde is a suspect. How can I beg him for a favor like that?"

"In this job, we work for the greater good. We're public servants, not blind technocrats. You do what needs to be done in the big picture, regardless of what the fine print says. Are we in agreement?"

Melanie shook her head, marveling. "You're a force of nature, Susan."

"I'm not sure whether that's a compliment," Susan said with a laugh, "but I'll take it as a yes."

TWENTY THIRD

As Melanie walked down the hall toward her office, anxiety took hold of her. She could handle running a huge case with a thousand scattered leads. And she could handle having a sicko creep Web-stalking her. But the office politics really threw her for a loop. Susan could say what she wanted about fixing this dustup, but with the front office breathing down Melanie's neck, she was starting to worry about getting fired.

She opened the door to find Dan seated behind her desk, talking on her telephone. Their eyes met, and he smiled. God, that smile, those eyes. Suddenly she was back in one of the most intense moments of her life—the first time she'd ever seen him, when she'd returned to her office just like now and discovered a gorgeous stranger sitting in her chair. Her marriage had been on the verge of collapse, and she'd seen the echo of her own need in Dan's eyes. In that very instant, Melanie fell hard, even though she had every reason not to.

She watched him for a moment. Then, seemingly of its own accord, her hand reached out, closed the door, and turned the lock.

"Yeah, she just walked in," Dan said, holding her gaze as he spoke.

He'd noticed that Melanie had locked the door. He raised an eyebrow at her and she raised one right back, provocatively. She had no idea what had come over her, but whatever it was seemed to have a will of its own, and she was in no mood to argue with it.

Dan was staring at her. "Uh, Julian, can you hold off on giving me that report on Ortiz? I have to take care of something over here first . . . Okay, okay, if it's that important. Go ahead."

Dan pointed at the phone and shrugged helplessly. Melanie walked around behind the desk and sank her fingers into his thick dark hair, pulling his head back. He shook his head no, but she leaned down and kissed him anyway, slowly and lingeringly, in careful silence, until she got a reaction. Within seconds, they were licking and biting and breathing hard. She straddled him on the chair, and he tucked the phone against his neck and ran his hands up under her skirt, making her shiver. She loved the way he tasted, the clean way his skin smelled. So many things in her life were insane right now, but Dan made her feel good.

She pulled away. She was wearing a tailored wrap dress and high-heeled pumps. With the telephone receiver on his shoulder, Dan eased her back against the desk and carefully undid the cord that held her dress closed. She shrugged the dress from her shoulders and let it fall into a heap on the floor. His eyes glittered as they raked over her body. Melanie could hear Detective Hay's voice squawking on the other end of the line.

"I didn't catch that," Dan said sideways into the telephone, his voice hoarse.

Melanie grasped Dan's hands and drew him to his feet. He was tall and massive as a brick house. She reached for his belt buckle.

"You're crazy," he whispered, but he didn't tell her to stop. Quite the contrary. He fumbled at his waistband for his gun, almost dropping it, catching it again, and setting it down on top of her desk with a thud. He helped her get his pants down, using his feet to get out of his shoes and yank the pants off, but keeping his Jockeys on. He was hard as a rock.

"I'm still here. Must be a bad connection," Dan said into the phone.

He was getting impatient now. As he spoke he unhooked Melanie's bra, yanked it from her shoulders, and tossed it aside. She leaned back against the desk, arched her back, and gave herself up to his hands, which were kneading her breasts and exploring her flesh all the way from her throat down to her underpants, which he was beginning to work off her hips. He bent forward and kissed her neck and started sucking her nipples, and she shuddered.

"Hang up," she whispered, her legs so weak she could barely stand.

But he shook his head, and she could tell he was getting off on the situation, the idea that this was all happening in her office, in the middle of a phone call.

"You're twisted, O'Reilly," she whispered.

Dan leaned sideways, looking at her complicated telephone. "*Me?* Where's the goddamn mute button?" he said under his breath.

She muted the telephone. Dan held the receiver in one hand, and he placed the other lightly over her mouth.

"People in the hall can still hear," he warned.

"You gonna let that stop you?" She raked her teeth up and down his fingers, staring at him with challenge in her eyes.

"Agh, Jesus, what are you doing to me? I'm climbing the walls here."

He slammed the phone down and spun her around, grasping the back of her neck and bending her over the desk, so her back was to him. He yanked her panties down to her ankles, pulled his own underwear off, and put his hot mouth against her ear.

"Is this what you want?" he demanded.

"Yes."

"Tell me. I need to hear you say it."

"C'mon, fuck me."

He entered her from behind with one hard push, thrusting in and out until she was breathless and panting. She gripped the edge of the desk till her knuckles went white, squeezing her eyes shut, every nerve in her body alive and vibrating.

"Yes. Keep going," she said, gasping.

She must've been too loud because he put his hand over her mouth again and shushed her tenderly. But she could tell Dan was having as much trouble as she was staying quiet. He had great stamina, almost too great. After a while, she started worrying that someone was sure to knock on the door, they'd been at it so long.

Then, suddenly, he clutched her by the shoulders, bucking and twisting, gave a stifled gasp, and collapsed against her.

They stayed that way for a minute, not moving. Then Melanie's phone rang. Dan laughed and pulled out of her, grabbing his underwear from the floor. She was naked except for her high heels when she picked up the phone.

"Melanie Vargas," she said, and cleared her throat.

"Melanie, it's Julian. Is Dan there? We got cut off."

"Sure. Just a second."

As Dan resumed his phone call, they both found their clothes and hurriedly got dressed. His hair was damp with sweat; he ran his fingers through it. Melanie took her handbag from the bottom drawer of her desk and fixed her makeup. She went to the ladies' room, came back, and Dan was still on the phone. Finally, he hung up.

They looked at each other.

"What the hell was that?" he said. Melanie couldn't tell whether he was amazed or upset, so she just shrugged.

"*That* was the best sex I ever had. In my life," he said.

"I can't believe we did it *here*," she said.

Coming down from the high of the sex, Melanie was beginning to feel deflated and upset with herself. How could she have gone and instigated something so risky, so foolish, so plain unprofessional, and at a moment when the front office was mad at her, no less?

But Dan felt otherwise.

"Believe it, sweetheart," he said, laughing joyously. "You're incredible. No wonder I'm out of my mind over you."

TWENTY FOUR

I have some big news," Dan said.

They had adjusted their clothing, opened Melanie's office door, and sat down. They were sitting and talking as calmly as any prosecutor and agent discussing evidence in a case, as if the wild tumult of ten minutes earlier had never happened. Melanie felt relieved, like she'd stepped onto solid ground after being lost at sea.

"You found out who's sending the e-mails?" she guessed.

"What e-mails?"

"Didn't you get my message?"

Dan pulled out his phone and looked at it. "Oh. Sorry, I've been on the damn thing the whole time."

"You've been hard to reach lately."

Dan looked back at her without answering.

"Never mind," she said. "Tell me your news first, then I'll explain."

"David Harris is free and clear. The DNA profile developed from the skin found under Suzanne's fingernails doesn't match the sample he gave. We already pulled the surveillance detail off him."

"Quick turnaround time on the DNA test," she commented.

"Yeah, even I can't believe how fast they did it, and I was the one hounding 'em. We still don't have the results back from the CODIS database comparison, and we sent that sample over almost a full day earlier."

"When will we get that?"

"I was told by close of business today, but it hasn't come through. I have no idea what's taking so long. All's they have to do is push a button on a computer."

"Can you call them again?"

"I tried. Nobody picked up. I'm afraid we're gonna have to wait till Monday morning now."

"If Harris is innocent, that means the real Butcher is still out there, and we need to find him. *Fast*," Melanie said.

"I know that. But it's not like the results on Harris come as a surprise. You didn't really think he did it, did you?"

"Not really."

"To me, his story always had the ring of truth. I mean, what married guy is gonna put himself in the Ramble looking to blow another guy if it isn't true? Even to beat a murder rap?"

"We should offer Harris protection," Melanie said. "If he's not the Butcher, then he's my star witness."

"You're right."

Her phone rang. "Hold on a second," she said, picking it up.

Melanie listened to the sound coming over the wire. It took her a minute to figure out what she was hearing.

"What's the matter? Something wrong?" Dan asked, seeing the look on her face.

"That's so weird. It's—it's *me*."

"What?"

She pressed the speakerphone button. The sound of Melanie's own voice filled the room, answering a question at the news conference she'd given in the early morning hours after Suzanne Shepard's murder.

"What the hell is that?" Dan said.

"It's me. At the news conference. Somebody must have recorded it off the TV."

"Is anybody on the line?" Dan asked.

"Hello? Hello?" Melanie said into the speaker.

The only reply was audible breathing, followed by a moan.

"What the fuck!" Dan leaped to his feet and came charging around the desk. "Who's there?" he yelled into the speaker.

The line abruptly went dead.

Melanie looked up at him with frightened eyes. "I wonder if that's the same guy who's e-mailing me."

"Tell me about these e-mails right now," Dan demanded.

She took a deep breath. "I've gotten two so far. Both moderately obscene in content. The first one was the morning after the murder. The guy said he'd seen me on TV, which is what makes me think this phone call might be from him. Janice and I decided he was just some creep, that it was nothing to worry about. But he sent another one earlier today, and he makes it sound like he's following me. That one got me nervous."

"Any reason to think this asshole is connected to the murder?"

"In the first e-mail, he called Suzanne Shepard a bitch and said the Butcher did the world a favor, but that wasn't enough to raise a red flag for me. I figured the actual killer would have said something more specific about the crime."

"Show me the e-mails, now."

Dan was scowling. It occurred to Melanie that getting him involved might not have been the smartest move. Dan had a tendency to become overprotective and lose his cool when her safety was at stake. Too late now. Under his thunderous gaze, Melanie printed out the two e-mails and handed them to him.

"Why is it you invariably fail to tell me shit like this in a timely fashion?" he demanded when he'd finished reading.

"I left you a message that you didn't bother to listen to, remember? Why is it you haven't been answering your phone lately?"

"Don't change the subject. You left that message an hour ago, but you got the first e-mail a day and a half ago."

"We're not talking about me, and I don't want to fight. Just tell me what you think of the e-mails."

Dan's face flushed with fury. "What do I think? I think I'm gonna find this prick and pummel him to a bloody fucking pulp without due process of law."

"Be serious."

"I'm very serious. Break every bone in his goddamn body and leave him bleeding in the gutter."

"But do you think he's dangerous?"

"I think he's a dead man."

"Okay, I get the point."

"Fucking psycho. The guy was jerking off on the phone just now, you know."

She swallowed hard. "We can't be sure of that."

"Oh yeah? What do *you* think he was doing?"

Melanie didn't answer.

"I'm gonna put him in the ground," Dan said.

"You don't mean that."

But he stormed out of her office, slamming the door behind him.

"You wonder why I don't tell you this stuff," she muttered to the still-vibrating door.

TWENTY FIVE

It was seven o'clock on Friday night, and Melanie was running late, although that wasn't why she took a taxi instead of the subway to her favorite neighborhood pasta joint. With the memory of the strange phone call fresh in her mind, and a sense of unease left over from her encounter with the man in the hooded sweatshirt, Melanie felt more comfortable in the private cocoon of a cab. She didn't want to overreact to a couple of crank e-mails and a heavy-breathing call, but neither could she disregard them.

Inside, the place was crowded, and deliciously redolent of garlic and tomato sauce. The harried hostess directed Melanie toward the back of the restaurant, where little Maya sat in a high chair chomping on a huge piece of Italian bread as Melanie's good friend and former college roommate, Sophie Cho, cut up some ravioli for her.

Maya's eyes lit up as Melanie approached. "Mama!" she cried, lifting her arms with delight.

"*Hola, niña pequeña.* Mommy missed you all day." Melanie leaned down and covered Maya's face with little kisses that made her giggle.

"Careful, she's quite sticky," Sophie said.

"Did she eat the meatballs?" Melanie asked, slipping into an empty chair. She had to talk loudly to be heard over the din in the restaurant.

"They're mostly on the floor, but she's crazy about my spinach ravioli."

"Maybe she'll grow up to be a vegetarian like her aunt Sophie."

"I'd like to think I'm having some influence. I ordered your food about fifteen minutes ago, so it should be here any minute."

"Thank you, and thank you so much for picking Maya up from my apartment. Sandy hasn't been feeling well enough to work past six these days."

Sandy Robinson, who'd been babysitting for Maya for over a year and doing a splendid job of it, was seven months pregnant.

"What is she planning to do when her baby comes?" Sophie asked.

"She's planning to *quit*. I have to start interviewing, I just haven't been able to face it yet. The thought of learning to trust a new person with this little girl—ugh. Makes me wish I could afford to quit, too, and just stay home with her." Melanie surprised herself by tearing up for a moment, her chin quivering. She took a deep breath and a sip of water.

"Don't worry. You'll find someone good," Sophie said, and patted her hand.

"You're so reassuring, Soph. I love that about you."

"I'm just being realistic. You've always had good people, because you're careful about who you hire. Sandy's wonderful, and even that, what was her name, Eloise?"

"Elsie."

"Elsie was good, too," Sophie said.

"She was good with Maya. Me, she hated," Melanie said. "But enough about my babysitter problems. You know what I want to hear. How was your date with Ray-Ray?"

Melanie had set Sophie up with a DEA agent named Raymond Wong, but she hadn't had the chance yet to find out how it had gone. Ray-Ray was a deeply decent guy, but ex-military and tightly wound, which Melanie thought might suit him well to Sophie, who was high-strung, extremely bright, and obsessed with her flourishing career as an architect. Either they'd hit it off or they'd hate each other, but either way it was worth a shot. Like Ray-Ray, Sophie was so buried in work that she didn't have time for a social life, yet she longed to be a mother, as shown by the hours she devoted to babysitting Maya. Melanie was convinced that Sophie had trouble meeting men only because she made no effort. She was reserved to the point of being cold. And while a pretty appearance might have made up for that, Sophie wasn't beautiful in the conventional sense. She had lovely skin and eyes, but she was short and chubby, pulled her hair back any old way, and wore a hipster-architect uniform of black pants, black T-shirt, and black Nikes every single day. Melanie had decided to give fate a shove and help Sophie find a man who would appreciate her.

"The date was nice," Sophie said in a neutral tone.

"That could mean anything from 'I hated him but I can't say so because he's your friend' to 'we're engaged.'"

Sophie laughed. "In between. I understand why you fixed us up. We have a lot in common. Similar backgrounds and values. We met for coffee last Sunday and went for a stroll afterward. He was intelligent and polite. I'd go out with him again. I couldn't tell whether he felt the same way. He said he would call, and he hasn't yet. So there you have it." She finished with a shrug.

The waitress arrived with Melanie's fettuccine.

"Enough about my so-called love life," Sophie said. "Let's talk about yours. How are things with Dan?"

"Great, although sometimes I think I'm just . . . I don't know, mixed up about him," Melanie said, flashing on the intense sex they'd had in her office. *Wow.* She felt her cheeks get hot, and wondered if Sophie noticed her blushing. She had to fight off a powerful urge to sneak outside and call Dan up to see if they could do it again. She twirled fettuccine around her fork and shoved it in her mouth.

In the depths of her handbag, Melanie's cell phone rang, and she dug for it frantically. The display showed an incoming call from Julian Hay's cell phone.

"Oops, sorry, work," she said to Sophie as she flipped the phone open. "Hello?"

"Melanie, Julian. I only have a second. I need to know. You want I should go ahead and buy this dude, or what?"

"You mean Miles?"

"Who else, boss?"

"You're in a position to buy from him already? I'm amazed!"

"Yeah. Turns out he's moving crystal meth, and he's like begging to sell me some."

Now, *this* was the reason to have Julian Hay on a case. He might be a slacker when it came to matters that didn't interest him, but there was no better narcotics undercover than Suave Pierre.

"Crystal meth? He'd be looking at real jail time," Melanie said.

"Like the Big Bad Wolf says, the better to flip you with, my dear," Julian said.

"If Ortiz flips on Welch, we'll be cooking with gas. Pierre, you're a genius."

"One step at a time, sister. I'm calling only because I need a prosecutor's authorization to requisition the buy money before I start negotiations. Give me the Benjamins and I'll see what I can do."

"You're authorized. Sign my name on the dotted line."

"Now you're talking, sister. My aim is to put your boy in bracelets in the next twenty-four. Fingers crossed," he said, and hung up.

Melanie put her phone away and looked back at Sophie. "Where were we?"

"You were telling me that things are mixed up with you and Dan. I've been waiting for this." Sophie shook her head sadly.

"What's that supposed to mean?"

"Just that I've always thought this was a rebound relationship for you, Melanie. Not destined to last."

"That's not what I meant."

"Oh, come on. You got involved with Dan right after learning of Steve's affair. You were distraught over your marriage, afraid of being alone, and an attractive man fell head over heels for you, so you rushed into a relationship. I'm not blaming you. But what do you two have in common for the long haul? He's a very nice person, and great *looking*, but he's not your equal intellectually or emotionally. You share no interests beyond work. He's a blue-collar suburban guy. You're an uptown girl. He—"

"Stop right now. Be quiet!"

Reading Melanie's expression, Sophie looked startled. "I'm sorry. I didn't mean to upset you. I thought I was only saying things you already knew."

"I don't know anything of the kind. I'm madly in love with this guy."

Sophie sipped her Diet Coke, looking chastened. "Well, that doesn't mean you can't question it."

"I can't. I don't. I'm way too into him to question anything right now."

"That's not good."

Melanie sighed. "Maybe not. But it's the truth."

"I would never say this if I didn't love you and Maya so much, but is this really the right moment to be in such a passionate, all-consuming relationship? What about her?"

Melanie's eyes lingered on Maya, who was busily feeding ravioli to her doll, chattering away in half English, half baby.

"I do worry about the time I spend on Dan," Melanie said, "and how much room he takes up in my heart. Sometimes I think I should focus on nothing but her, at least until she's older. But am I not entitled to have a man in my life? Dan's *it* for me, Soph. I don't want anybody else, and I can't imagine feeling this way again. Am I supposed to let him go because he came along too soon?"

"Do you ever think the strength of your feelings might come from the fact that you met him at such a vulnerable moment? In a crisis, we don't always make the best decisions."

"That sounds like something you read in a magazine. Smart women, stupid choices. I'm not a self-help stereotype."

"Maybe you just don't want to hear what I have to say," Sophie said gently. "But fine, on a more practical level, then, does Dan accept Maya?"

"He adores her. You should see him down on the floor with her, playing with her dollies, rolling her around."

"No, but . . . This is sensitive, but how does he feel about dating a woman with a child? Do you think he would marry you, or is this bound to be a temporary thing?"

"I just got divorced."

"So he hasn't asked?"

"Of course not," Melanie snapped, her tone defensive. "It's much too soon."

Dan hadn't introduced her to his family, either. It wasn't too early for that, and Melanie was beginning to find the omission worrisome. But she had her pride, and she wouldn't voice her fears to Sophie, given the tone of this conversation.

"But he loves you, right?"

"I think he does. He'll say he's crazy about me, or that he can't live without me. He doesn't actually say, 'I love you,' but that's not his style."

Sophie frowned. "He's never told you he loves you?"

"Will you *stop*? I'm happy with Dan. More than happy, I'm besotted. I express one little iota of doubt, and suddenly you're on this rampage of negativity. I don't want to hear it."

"I just worry that you'll get hurt, Melanie. A man changes once the chase is over, once you're under his thumb. He loses interest."

"Fine, so I'm making a huge mistake," Melanie said, exasperated. "It's my life. Butt out." *Not to mention that* you're *hardly the queen of relationships,* she thought.

Melanie's phone started ringing again. She was glad for the excuse to end the conversation, which was more troubling than she cared to admit. Dan had been difficult to reach over the past few days, and a nagging little voice in her head was starting to ask if something was going on. What if he was seeing somebody else? He wouldn't do that, would he? What if he broke up with her? Steve had shattered her plans, but Dan could break her heart, and she knew it.

"Sorry about all the calls," she said to Sophie as she flipped open her phone. "Work is crazy right now."

Tony Mancuso from Target News security was on the phone.

"Sorry to bother you," he said, "but I have some news I thought you'd want to hear immediately."

"What is it?"

"I brought the box of dog shit to the FBI guys this afternoon, and they examined it right away. They don't have the fingerprint analysis complete yet, but listen to this. The packing tape used to seal up the box?"

"Yes?"

"It matches the tape used to gag Suzanne. Matches exactly. Not just the same brand, but there's a flaw in the weave that matches up so perfectly, they think it was contiguous pieces ripped off the roll. Melanie, the Butcher definitely sent this box."

TWENTY SIX

David Harris was on the telephone with his wife, and the call was not going well.

"But I didn't have to tell you!" he said, exasperated, dropping his head into his hands. "Don't you see, Robin, I could have just lied. You would never have found out. I told you the truth because I love you, honey, and I want to make things right."

"You think I'm an idiot? Of course I would've found out, and I'm not the only one! You'll be testifying about this abomination in open court. The whole world will know. My parents. All the moms from play group. The teachers at Jake's school." And she started to wail.

"Robin, I didn't even do anything. I told you, nothing happened. It was just something I was thinking about. A fantasy."

"Sex with a prostitute is your fantasy? How do you think that makes me feel?" she screamed.

Dave felt a migraine coming on, a bad one. In confessing to Robin, he'd left out the gay part, which was just too hard to explain. He kneaded his forehead with his fingertips and directed himself to remain calm.

"And you do it in the *park*?" Robin yelled. "You can't even be discreet and call some high-class hooker so people don't find out? That is *sick*."

"I feel terrible that I hurt you, honey. I swear to you, nothing like this will ever happen again. I'll go to therapy. I'll get to the bottom of this. It was the stress. You can't imagine the pressure I'm under, with the partnership decision so close. We'll come out better than ever, promise . . . Robin?"

But she was sobbing hysterically on the other end of the phone.

"I have an idea. Robin? Robin, are you listening? Sweetie? Listen to me."

"Don't call me sweetie!" she cried. "What am I supposed to do now? I have the kids. I haven't worked in ten years! How am I supposed to support them?"

"I'll support us, like I always have. Don't talk that way, please. We can work this out. I know you're upset about what people will think. How about this? We buy a house in Scarsdale. A big house with a backyard for the kids. We can even renovate if you want. New kitchen, baths, the works. You'll make friends who've never heard about out troubles."

"Scarsdale's . . . not . . . far enough!" Robin said, sputtering through her sobs. "Everybody in Scarsdale knows people in the city. They'll find out!"

"Bedford, then. We can get enough land for a pool."

"Bedford?" She quieted, hiccuping and snuffling.

"Sure."

"You always said you wouldn't commute that far."

"I'd make that sacrifice if it would help you get past this. I know you love it in the country. We'll get a dog, have a separate laundry room instead of that stacking thing stuck in the closet. Live like human beings."

Robin coughed and blew her nose loudly. "But, Dave, Bedford is expensive."

"Doesn't matter. With prices in the city what they are, we'll clear a mint on the apartment. And I'm still gonna make partner. I can get old man Feinerman back in my camp if I just ace this Simpson litigation. I know I can. What do you say, Rob?"

She was silent.

"Robin? Are you there?"

"Are you *sure* nothing happened? I need to go over that part again."

Robin had eventually agreed to let him stay in the apartment that night if he slept on the couch in the den. Dave consulted his watch. It was about nine o'clock, on the early side to leave his desk. Putting in face time was critical to making partner at Feinerman, to the point that certain senior partners were known to call around late at night in the months leading up to the decision, professing to ask for research on some minor point when in fact they were checking whether you were still at your post. Dave was scrupulous about not getting caught out like that. But what the hell. He'd just witnessed a brutal murder and his marriage was on the rocks. He could knock off early for once.

Dave speed-dialed the internal extension that patched him through to Tri-State Limo.

"Tri-State Limousine Service. How may I help you, Mr. Harris?"

"Ready now at the office."

"Destination?"

"Home."

"Very good, sir. You want your regular driver?"

"Yes, I want Stanislaus. How long?"

"Let me check. Hold on please."

Dave waited on hold. He drummed his fingers on his desk impatiently, studying the photograph that sat in a silver frame next to his telephone. Dave, Robin, and the kids, taken by a professional photographer last summer in Westhampton. They were seated on an appropriately beachy rock, wearing matching outfits of khaki pants and white dress shirts, looking prosperous and content. Like a family should.

The dispatcher came back on the line.

"Good news, Mr. Harris. Stanislaus is actually downstairs outside your building. He just returned from his previous call."

"Car 130 as usual?"

"That's correct. He'll display the number in the window."

"Thank you."

"Have a good night, Mr. Harris."

Outside, it took a second before Dave spotted the town car with the big red number 130 in the window. Stanislaus hadn't parked in his usual spot. Instead of idling directly in front of the building with all the other black sedans from Tri-State that awaited the departures of other lawyers from the Feinerman firm, Stanislaus had for some reason parked halfway down the block on the opposite side of the street. Dave waved at him testily, but getting no response, gave up with a sigh and trotted across the street, dodging traffic.

"What's the idea, parking all the way over here?" he said as he slid into the roomy leather backseat and slammed the door with a thunk. The smoked-glass barrier between the front and back seats was raised. Apparently Stanislaus hadn't heard Dave, because instead of responding, he pressed the button that locked all the doors and pulled out into the stream of traffic so fast that Dave rocked backward into the seat.

"Take it easy, Stan!" Even his driver was stressed out tonight.

The *Wall Street Journal* was folded neatly in the seat-back pocket in front of Dave, just as he liked. He turned on the small reading light above his door, took the newspaper out, and snapped it open, enjoying the smell of fresh newsprint. But as he scanned the bullet points in the "What's News" section, his head started to throb again. Wherever he turned, this nightmare dogged him. *David M. Harris, Esq., a litigation associate at Feinerman, Seidel, Brinkley and Tate, testified today . . .* the news brief began. He flung the paper aside furiously, his breath catching in his throat. This was not how he'd planned to make his first appearance on the front page of the *Journal.*

Dave sank back into the cushy seat and rubbed his temples, closing his eyes and resting for a few minutes. Eventually, he took a few deep breaths and looked out the window.

As he registered his surroundings, Dave's heart gave a jagged thump. They were nowhere near where they were supposed to be. Instead of heading uptown via the Westside Highway, toward his apartment, they were somewhere in the no-man's-land leading to the Holland Tunnel, heading for New Jersey. *What the . . .* He opened his mouth to yell at Stanislaus, but shut it again as all the signposts finally clicked into place. He felt like throwing up. What an idiot he'd been, caught up in his meaningless personal problems. He'd forgotten to stay alert to his environment. How could he have been so stupid? He was an eyewitness to a brutal murder. His name and photograph had been in every newspaper. Had been on the evening news, for God's sake. Of course the Butcher wanted him dead. What had happened to his survival skills, honed like a knife's edge in the desert so many years ago? He'd gotten soft and lazy, and now he'd pay the price.

It was true what they said: Dave's life flashed before him. A beautiful day in Jerusalem with his best friend when he was nineteen, holding his father's hand as he died, the birth of his first son. *No,* he thought, *I will not leave my children fatherless.*

Dave snatched up the newspaper from the seat and pretended to read, his heart pounding. He knew how to do this. He could cope. He could fight. He could escape. Using the paper as a screen, he unfastened his seat belt and leaned sideways to peek at the driver up front. Silently, Dave berated himself. How could he have failed to notice? This man was blatantly, obviously not the diminutive Stanislaus. He was taller and bigger altogether, robust and thick-necked. He was an impostor, armed and dangerous, surely intending to shoot Dave in cold blood and leave him to die like a dog in the street. Additional visual reconnaissance supported that awful conclusion: the driver's hands on the steering wheel were encased in rubber gloves. Dave's scalp crawled at the sight.

They were doing about forty, and the street was deserted. They were five blocks from the tunnel. Dave was running out of time fast. He didn't want to leap out inside the tunnel, and he would have a decidedly poorer chance of survival once they reached the other side and the dumping grounds of the Meadowlands. If it was empty here, it was desolate there. Now was the time to make his move. Realizing that, Dave panicked, his eyes darting around wildly. He had to struggle to control his breathing so as not to alert the driver.

Still holding the newspaper in front of him for cover, Dave tried the door lock. It wouldn't budge. He tried the window. Same result. The automatic locking mechanisms must be equipped with those childproof features, like they had on their minivan, where the backseat controls could be disabled completely. His best option was going to be kicking out the window and escaping though it. Dave studied the window. It was tinted, but otherwise appeared to be made from standard automotive glass. A well-placed, vigorous kick would shatter it. He was wearing his Johnston & Murphy wing tips, which had hard, sharp heels. They would do the trick. What he needed now was a diversion. A loud noise perhaps. Something to confuse the driver for several seconds, or as many as he could manage anyway, to allow Dave to make his escape before getting shot to death. He contemplated what he'd brought with him in his pockets and his briefcase and weighed the possibilities.

They were heading straight for the tunnel entrance. Still camouflaged behind the *Journal*, Dave drew his cell phone from his pocket. Calling for help was useless: he was flat out of time. But his phone came with a variety of ring tones, including one that sounded like a police siren. His hands shook violently as he scrolled through the menu searching for that one. He ramped the volume up as high as it would go and selected TEST.

The shrill blast of a wailing siren filled the car. Dave reeled back onto his shoulders, raising his legs and kicking with all of his substantial strength. Just as the window shattered and he felt the rushing air on his face, he heard an explosion. Chunks of rough glass showered down on top of him. He'd propelled himself forward and up, going for the window. He heard a second explosion and felt a burning in his back. His breath had been knocked out of him; he'd been kicked or punched or . . . Robin! Everything went black.

TWENTY SEVEN

The facade of the Metropolitan Museum of Art had recently undergone a cleaning that had left it draped in a material resembling cheesecloth for nearly two years, but the end result was breathtaking. Melanie paused at the bottom of the sweeping limestone steps that led to the main entrance of the museum, her eyes drawn upward to take in the magnificent sight. On this sultry Friday night, with spotlights trained on it, the Met glittered like a white diamond set against a purple velvet sky. Three enormous banners in jewel tones of red, blue, and green graced the facade, trumpeting the latest blockbuster exhibits. The gigantic structure stood sentry at the eastern edge of Central Park, and the scent of flowers and green leaves floated out to Melanie on the warm summer breeze. It would be easy enough to forget to look over her shoulder to-night, or to lose sight of the fact that she was here on serious business.

Clyde Williams's fund-raiser was going on inside. When Susan Charlton had instructed Melanie to inter-cept Clyde and find out what he intended to say at his press conference, they had both been relatively confi-dent of Clyde's innocence. But Melanie had since learned that the killer had gagged Suzanne Shepard with the same packing tape used to seal the box of dog excre-ment. This established an undeniable nexus between the box and the murder. The box had contained a photo-graph of Suzanne taken an hour after the segment about Clyde had aired, and it had been mailed the following day. Circumstantial, Melanie told herself. Perhaps only coincidence. Yet the inference was there to be drawn. There was at least some chance that Clyde Williams, the father of one of her best friends and many voters' hope for the future of this city, had if not actually committed murder at least arranged for it to happen. Or that some-body close to him had. And not just any murder, but a horrific, ugly, brutal murder, the gruesome results of which Melanie herself had witnessed two nights ago, less than a ten-minute walk from where she now stood.

Immediately inside the main entrance, velvet ropes channeled Melanie toward a long table used for searching bags. Several guards in blue blazers were stationed there. One of them, a tall Indian man, gestured at her warningly, saying something, but his words floated up and dissipated into the vast empty space between the terrazzo floor and the three formidable marble domes that topped the Great Hall.

"I'm sorry?" Melanie said.

"The museum is closed, ma'am."

"I'm here for the Clyde Williams fund-raiser at the Temple of Dendur."

"In that case, I need to see your invitation and picture ID," the guard said, holding out his hand.

"I forgot my invitation, but here's a photo ID." Melanie handed him her creds, crossing her fingers that they would impress sufficiently to do the trick.

"If you don't have an invitation, you'll have to wait while I check the guest list," he said, and walked away with her credentials.

Damn, they were sticklers here. Sure, they were guarding world treasures, but did she look like an art thief?

Melanie pulled out her cell phone, toying with the idea of calling Joe Williams, whose cell number she had in her directory. Surely Joe was inside and could come out and vouch for her. But she hesitated, thinking how awkward that would be in light of her mission.

Yes, there was the part about asking Clyde what he planned to tell the media. But first, Melanie intended to inform Clyde about the packing tape, on the off chance that the news might shock him into confessing. If there was anything to confess.

Before she could make up her mind, Melanie spotted the guard walking back toward her, frowning. Almost simultaneously she saw a familiar, slight figure crossing the cavernous hall. Chance had decided for her.

"Joe!" she called, waving. He saw her and hurried over.

"Melanie. I had no idea you were planning on coming tonight. Everything all right?"

Joe searched Melanie's face, and a great deal of information passed between them silently. He understood she was there for reasons that would upset him if he were fully informed about them. She wished she could tell him what they were, but she couldn't. He realized that she was only doing her job, and he wouldn't stand in her way.

"This young lady is a friend of our family," Joe said to the guard.

"She's a *crasher*," the guard retorted.

"If her name's not on the list, then there's been an oversight. She can come in. I'll escort her back to the Temple," Joe replied.

The guard thrust Melanie's credentials at her, obviously annoyed that his authority had been trumped. Melanie and Joe took off for the Egyptian wing, their shoes ringing out on the hard marble floors.

"Once we're out of range of that guard, you can go in on your own. I've got to find Rocky Davis so he can set up for the press conference. You know how to get to the Temple, right?" Joe asked.

"Sure."

They paused in front of a set of ruined walls built from colossal marble blocks many thousands of years old, and Joe turned to Melanie.

"I'll let you go on from here, but there's something I need to say first," he said.

"Sure."

"Melanie, I haven't interfered in your investigation. I've been silent because it's technically the right thing to do, but what's technically right can be wrong in your heart. I get the feeling that you're here because you've got new information, information that reflects badly on my father."

As Melanie opened her mouth to reply, Joe held up his hand.

"I'm not asking you to disclose any evidence. And when I'm done, you can report me if you feel you must. But hear me out."

"Go ahead, Joe. I'm listening."

"My father admittedly has some bad qualities. He's arrogant and full of himself. He's manipulative, as many successful politicians are. I'm even willing to buy that he's a bit of a womanizer and hasn't always been faithful to my mother. But what he's *not* is a rapist and a killer."

Melanie nodded solemnly.

"He's just *not*," Joe repeated. "I swear to you. So please, examine your evidence carefully before you accuse him of any crime. Examine your conscience. Otherwise you'll risk damaging the reputation of an innocent man, possibly with very serious consequences for his career."

Joe's eyes were haunted as he turned and walked away. Speaking out had clearly cost him a great deal.

Watching her friend disappear into the next gallery, Melanie was at a loss. Joe had as good as invited her to rat him out for trying to influence her investigation, but she wouldn't. He was one of the most ethical people she knew, and his words rang true: the technical rules didn't always jibe with what was morally right. She'd have done as much herself for somebody she loved and believed in. The problem wasn't that Joe had tried to sway her, but that he'd succeeded, at least partly. His plea had taken the wind out of her rush to judgment, and now the doubts were pouring in. What evidence did she have against Clyde Williams, really, beyond the mere coincidence of timing? A politician of Clyde's skill and finesse wouldn't resort to brutish murder to silence an enemy, even an enemy with a bully pulpit as powerful as Suzanne's. Clyde's reputation mattered to his career, and his career mattered to the future of the city. Melanie might be under pressure to get a killer off the streets, but that didn't justify anything less than the greatest caution in investigating this important man.

But wait a minute. Had Clyde put Joe up to making his emotional appeal? Was she allowing herself to be manipulated? It was like she'd told Dan the other night when she'd hesitated about going to the crime scene— big cases, big problems. And big confusion. As she stood at the entrance to the Temple of Dendur, surveying the lavish scene, Melanie felt less certain than ever that she could solve this case.

TWENTY EIGHT

Even under normal conditions the Temple of Dendur was a sight to behold, its ancient stones bathed in sparkly light and set against a vast, slanting wall of crystalline glass. But decked out for a party, it was drop-dead gorgeous. A reflecting pool shimmered before the indoor plaza where the millennia-old structure had been reassembled, meant to evoke the Temple's original location beside the Nile. Tonight, the pool was decorated with potted reeds and grasses that swayed in the breeze from the air-conditioning. The spaces between the Temple columns were filled with enormous arrangements of palm fronds and lilies. Altogether, the scene bore an uncanny resemblance to the Nile on a dazzling Egyptian afternoon.

The crowd sipping cocktails on the marble plaza was just as glamorous as the location. Melanie recognized many famous faces—media people, politicians, even the stray movie star or two—interspersed with those who were lesser known but, to a person, beautiful and richly attired.

Unsure of her purpose and feeling intimidated, Melanie hesitated on the outskirts of the party. The buzz of laughter and conversation washed over her, and a waiter walked up carrying a silver tray.

"Champagne, miss?" he asked.

Thinking she'd look less conspicuous with a glass in her hand, Melanie accepted. The champagne was pink. Holding it up to the light, she watched tiny bubbles race to the top of the fluted glass. The color suggested it would taste cloyingly sweet, but when she sipped, the champagne had a dry, delicate bouquet. Oh, to be rich. Maybe she should quit this crazy job and go to work for some sweatshop law firm that would pay her a ton of money. But then she thought of David Harris, how miserable he seemed, how shoved into an ill-fitting mold, and realized that wasn't an option for her.

The crowd parted, and—as if conjured by Melanie's fleeting thought of David Harris—his lawyer, Bob

Adelman, stood before her amid a group of powerful-looking people.

"Bob!" Melanie said, startled.

"Hi, Melanie. What are you doing here? Isn't there a rule against you people contributing money to political campaigns?"

"There is," she said. "I'm here on business, not as a contributor." Then, fearing he'd guess that she was here to investigate Clyde Williams, Melanie quickly changed the subject. "Didn't you get my voice mail about your client's DNA results?" she asked.

"Yes, I did, and I was thrilled. Hey, Lester, don't you love it when you stand up in court spouting off about how a guy's innocent and it actually turns out to be true?"

A man in a fancy suit turned around. He had a memorable face—strong nose, heavy black eyebrows, and shoulder-length, snow-white hair. Talk about famous. Bob Adelman might be revered within the New York legal community, but Lester Poe was as celebrated as lawyers got—nationally known, a cultural icon, a legend even. For decades, he'd defended the highest-profile and hottest-button criminal cases. He was a counselor to celebrities and royalty as well as to prisoners of conscience, and a fixture on all the talking-head TV news programs.

"I only represent the guilty, Bob. Less stressful that way. Now, who is this lovely creature, and where have you been hiding her?" he asked, grasping Melanie's hand in both of his.

"Melanie Vargas from the U.S. Attorney's Office. Pleased to meet you, Mr. Poe," she said, amazed to be speaking to somebody of Poe's renown.

"Are they making prosecutors younger, Bob, or are we just getting older?"

"Both!" Adelman said, laughing.

"They're certainly making them better-looking."

"Melanie's trying to harass me about business while I'm drinking, Les."

"Hopefully that means she's not here to fork over her hard-earned cash to Clyde's campaign. The bastard has a big enough war chest already. Take my advice, dear. Keep the pittance they pay you and go buy yourself something pretty."

"I could do that. Or I could buy food," Melanie said, smiling.

Poe raised his glass. "Here's to the government underpaying its lawyers. May they all see the wisdom of joining the defense bar."

"Hear, hear," Adelman said.

"When you get tired of the noble-suffering routine, Melanie, give me a shout. I can always use a smart young lawyer. And easy on the eyes doesn't hurt, either. Oh, I see Katie Couric. I owe her a phone call. Do you have a card?" Poe asked.

Melanie took a business card from her wallet and handed it to him. He put it in silver card case and withdrew one of his own, pausing to write something on the back. "The number I'm giving you is my private line, so you don't have to go through a secretary. Give me a call. We'll talk about your future," he said, and walked away.

"Am I dreaming, or did Lester Poe just offer me a job?" Melanie asked.

"Actually, I think he was hitting on you. But with Lester, it's always a fine line."

Melanie laughed.

"On a more serious note, I did indeed get your message about David."

"I'm so glad I found you. The surveillance team was pulled off hours ago. I don't like leaving Harris out there uncovered. Say the word and I'll get protection assigned to him right away."

"Thanks for your concern, but we're not interested in your help under present circumstances."

"Why not? The killer is at large, and they don't call him the Butcher for nothing. He knows your client is a witness. It was in all the papers."

"My client is not a witness. He has no intention of testifying for the government as long as the obstruction charges stand."

"Are you kidding me?"

"Why would I kid about that? Dave doesn't want to cooperate with you while you're intent on a course of action that will destroy his legal career. Makes sense to me. Drop the charges and I'm sure I can get him to reconsider."

"But if he testifies, he'll get credit at sentencing and do zero jail time."

"He won't do time anyway, not in a million years. We both know that. The only thing he's interested in from you is a complete dismissal. And fast, before it screws up his partnership chances."

"He *did* obstruct justice," Melanie said.

"So what? People do all sorts of things and never get charged. That's why they call it prosecutorial discretion, kid."

"If the government makes the charges disappear, Harris loses credibility as a witness in the eyes of the jury. Sweetheart deals don't sit well," Melanie said.

"That's your problem, not his," Adelman insisted. "I'm sure you're a talented enough trial lawyer to make a jury comfortable with that situation."

"But what about the protection we can offer your client?"

"Why does he need the government for that? Dave leads a very sheltered life. Doorman building, car service home, the whole nine yards. If he feels he needs something more, this town doesn't lack for top-shelf protection services."

"I'm sorry Harris feels that way. But dismissal isn't warranted here."

"We obviously don't see eye to eye. When you're ready to do business, give me a call. Until then, enjoy the party."

Adelman turned and strode away.

TWENTY NINE

Melanie made a complete circuit of the Temple grounds, working up her nerve to approach Clyde Williams. Clyde stood in a prominent spot on the plaza surrounded by an ever-shifting horde of well-wishers and glad-handers. Melanie sampled the hors d'oeuvres along the way. She had to; they were too tempting. Tuna tartare with dilled crème fraîche, puff pastry filled with wild mushrooms, rare roast beef with wasabi cream on pumpernickel toast points. The food was delicious, but her excursion was nothing more than a stall for time, and she knew it.

Melanie could no longer justify her presence at the party if she wasn't going to do her job, so she climbed up onto the plaza and attached herself to the outer edge of the crowd that orbited Clyde. She began working her way inward until she could overhear the conversation—which was better described as a monologue, really, given that Clyde was the only person talking. Everybody else seemed to be there merely to laugh appreciatively at the proper intervals.

"Back in '79, President Carter had called up and asked me to lead a task force on urban renewal," Clyde was saying. "We were looking for a public face, somebody glamorous for the press to latch on to. Even then, we understood PR. Well, one night I was out at CBGB for an aide's birthday. The club of the moment, what Lotus is now. What Studio 54 used to be. But hardly my sort of crowd. There were, there were—"

At that moment, Clyde's restless eyes settled on Melanie, and he lost his place in his speech. Rockwell Davis was standing beside him. When Davis noticed his boss's stumble, his glance sought out the point where Clyde's eyes had fixed. As he caught sight of Melanie, Davis's expression changed dramatically, and he slipped from his boss's side, melting into the crowd.

"It was a punk crowd," Clyde said, recovering, "with a dangerous vibe, not my scene at all. But suddenly across the room I spot Debbie Harry. This was in Blondie's heyday. She was a huge star and hot, mmmph, like you would not believe. About five minutes later, she sends somebody over with a note asking me to meet her in the bathroom. Being a single brother at the time, and club bathrooms being what they were in those days, naturally I had some exotic things on my mind. Here I am thinking me and Blondie—"

Rockwell Davis suddenly materialized at Melanie's elbow, giving her a start. He leaned down and whispered fiercely, "Who let *you* in?"

"I need to speak to Clyde right away. Something big has come up. I'm sure he'd rather hear it from me than on the eleven o'clock news."

"He can't talk to you now. Whatever you have to say, you can say to me. And outside."

Davis's fingers closed around her arm with viselike strength. Melanie locked eyes with him.

"Hustle me out of here against my will and not only will I make a huge scene, but you'll face charges," she said through gritted teeth.

People were turning to look, and Davis saw that. Clyde was watching them out of the corner of his eye, and he raised his voice, racing to the punch line to distract his curious guests.

"And then Debbie said, 'Why, Mr. Williams, that's not what President Carter told me!' "

The crowd broke into waves of laughter. Rockwell Davis dropped her elbow, but the way he loomed over her was pure intimidation.

"The only road to Clyde is through me. Your choice. We step outside or you leave."

"Back off, I said."

Melanie stood her ground, and Davis took a step backward. There was ruthlessness in his ascetic, pock-marked face. Clyde might be too smart and too smooth to commit murder in pursuit of his political goals, but was Davis? Melanie had asked Dan to look into Davis's alibi as well as Clyde Williams's, but with everything else going on in the investigation, she hadn't had time to follow up. Could she be looking at the Butcher of Central Park?

"Come with me. We'll talk privately," Davis said under his breath.

He turned and headed for the exit that led out into the Egyptian galleries. Melanie considered the possibility that she'd be walking into a trap if she followed. Granted, she was now powerfully curious about Rockwell Davis, but that was no reason to get sloppy. She checked the reception on her cell phone and noted the locations of guards surrounding the Temple entrance. She wouldn't sacrifice her safety, but she had to follow him. She couldn't resist the prospect of learning more about Davis.

Melanie stepped into a long gallery that displayed mummies and sarcophagi and sculptures of emaciated cats with blank eyes. The place was full of dead people, empty of live ones, and eerily silent in contrast with the buzz of talk at the party. Melanie's footsteps echoed back at her as she walked halfway down its length looking for Rockwell Davis, who seemed to have disappeared. She was far away from the guards, but still within screaming distance. Melanie paused before two identical statues flanking an entrance to a secondary gallery. They were strange beasts carved from blackest stone, with the head of a lion and the body of a woman.

SEKHMET. THIS GODDESS REPRESENTS THE FORCE OF VIOLENCE AND UNEXPECTED DISASTER, read the plaque.

Great.

"In here," a voice, insinuating and cold, said from behind the statues.

Melanie's senses were on high alert. She found Davis standing before a glass case that held a display of three painted coffins suspended by wires. They levitated weirdly, one on top of the other, several feet apart.

"Why the theatrics?" she asked.

"No theatrics. I'm just looking for privacy. There's press around. I saw that piece of trash Gilmartin before. God knows how he got in."

"I need to talk to Clyde," Melanie said.

"You told me that already. I'm indulging your request by meeting with you myself. You should be grateful for that, given what happened at our meeting earlier today. You can tell me your news, and if I think it's important, I'll convey it to the councilman."

"You're calling the shots around here, aren't you?" Melanie asked.

"I don't have time to discuss the dynamics of our organization with you. Say what you got to say, or I'm going back inside."

She noticed he hadn't denied her accusation.

"We have evidence that Suzanne Shepard received a threat the day after she broadcast the segment on Clyde's affair with Emily King—" Melanie began.

"*Alleged* affair. We deny it."

"Alleged. Whatever. That's not my concern. The point is, we've now linked this threat definitively to the murder. I'd be willing to preview the evidence for Clyde and give him a chance to prove that he wasn't the one who made the threat. But in return, I need some information."

"What kind of information?"

"A heads-up on what he's planning to say at the press conference later."

Davis laughed. "Am I hearing right? You'll *allow* us to give you some information if we pay for it by giving you some other information? What kind of suckers do you take us for?"

"I don't understand why this has to be such an adversarial discussion," Melanie said.

"Maybe because you're trying to hang a murder on my man that he didn't commit."

"I'm not trying to hang anything on anybody. I'm looking for the truth."

"You say that," Davis said, snorting derisively. "But in reality you're looking for a conviction and some sweet press. Who you have to screw over to get to that, you don't care."

"You're wrong, Rockwell."

"You want to know what Clyde's gonna say at the press conference? He's gonna say you're harassing us. And the more you mouth off, the louder he's gonna say it. He's going to accuse you by name of trashing his reputation in order to throw this election to his opponent. You coming here to try to sabotage our fundraiser just gives him more ammunition."

"Sabotage? I'm beginning to think you're seriously paranoid."

"Think whatever you want, sister. But if I was you, I'd watch my back." Davis pushed by her roughly and was gone.

Was that a threat? By telling Melanie to watch her back, was Davis signifying an intent to get violent, to go to the mattresses? Filtered through his icy anger, the words had seemed deadly enough. Melanie decided that on balance, this encounter had been quite productive. Not only could she give the front office a heads-up on the scathing press she was about to receive, but she had a viable new suspect, one she hadn't focused on carefully enough before.

But as she turned to leave, the unmistakable sound of a footfall in the long gallery froze Melanie in place. Somebody was out there, just beyond the twin statues of Sekhmet. The steps sounded like a man's, and they were coming in her direction. Had Davis returned to make good on his threat?

Melanie ducked around behind the case holding the three coffins and peered through the glass, prepared to make a run for it if she saw him. But it wasn't Davis. He'd been wearing a dark suit, and this guy had on a blue blazer with brass buttons. She couldn't see his face, but he was big and blond. Big and blond, big and blond. What was she remembering? Male, big, and heavyset, probably white, David Harris had told them about the man he'd seen in the Ramble. But no, this didn't add up. Killers didn't buy their clothes at Brooks Brothers, not in her experience. She was just about to emerge from behind the glass case when he spoke.

"I know you're in there," he said.

And he reached into his pocket and pulled something out. Melanie saw the bright glint of metal. A gun, a knife? She backed up fast and slammed into a huge marble sarcophagus. Her head connected with the stone and she grunted in pain. She looked around for an exit, but the gallery came to a dead end. The only way out was back between the statues, right past her pursuer.

"You can run, but you can't hide," he called out, and this time Melanie listened to his voice. It was deep and resonant, with a heavy Australian accent.

She stepped around the case, so mad she could have spit.

"What the hell are you doing, Gilmartin?"

"I'm working on a breaking story, Vargas." He pushed a button on the small silver tape recorder he carried. "Duncan Gilmartin reporting from the Clyde Williams benefit at the Metropolitan Museum, speaking with Assistant U.S. Attorney Melanie Vargas."

"Put that thing away!" she snapped.

"I'm giving you a chance to respond to the allegations," he said. "I'd take it if I were you, or things might get unpleasant."

"What allegations?"

"The allegations of a cover-up. The allegations that Clyde Williams will go scot-free despite all the evidence pointing to his involvement."

"Don't you people worry about libel laws?"

"Oh, we study them carefully, looking for loopholes. Truth is a defense. It's true Suzanne Shepard was murdered after she aired a segment on Clyde Williams. It's true that you're friends with the Williams family. What I make of that truth is protected speech."

"Go to Clyde's press conference. You'll see what good friends we are."

There were no limits to what this guy would do to advance his career. As Melanie looked at Gilmartin in disgust, something clicked. Something in his height and build, in the way he carried himself.

"Wait a minute, you followed me onto the subway the other day, didn't you?" she said.

"I do what it takes to get the story, Miss Vargas."

"Stay the hell away from me."

Melanie turned and hurried toward the exit, pleased with herself for finding Gilmartin out, for refusing to let him get over on her. Then she realized that his tape recorder had been on the entire time. So much for outmaneuvering the tabloid press. She'd be hearing her bold words played back to her on the eleven o'clock news.

THIRTY

Melanie slept like the dead, and didn't wake until eight o'clock on Saturday morning when she heard Maya chirping from her crib in the next room.

"Mama mama mama mama mama!"

She rushed into the nursery to find all of Maya's stuffed animals on the floor and the little girl standing up holding on to the crib rail.

"How long have you been awake, *pobrecita*?" Melanie asked. "I'm so sorry. Mommy was really tired."

"Toast!" Maya said.

"I'll bet you're hungry. Did you throw these poor babies down? Don't do that, Maya. It makes them sad."

Melanie bent over and started picking the animals up and tossing them back into the crib. Down the hall, the telephone shrieked, so she lifted Maya up and deposited her on the floor.

"Hold on, sweetie. I'll change you in a sec," she said, sprinting back to her room to catch the phone before the machine picked up. Melanie worried with each step that it was Susan calling to tell her she was fired. Susan had been very reassuring last night as they watched the eleven o'clock news together over the phone from their respective apartments. And in truth, not only had Clyde Williams's press conference been better than Melanie had feared, but Duncan Gilmartin had restrained himself from playing the tape of her telling him to go to hell. Maybe he hadn't liked the prospect of getting taken down a peg on national TV.

She swiped the phone from its cradle just in time. "Hello?"

"Melanie. Julian."

"Julian," she said, relieved. "What's going on?"

"Good news. I popped your boy Miles Ortiz with enough product to put him away for a good long stretch."

"How much?"

"Sixty grams of crystal meth."

"Whoa. That's a ten-year mandatory minimum."

"He knows that. And now the man would like to talk."

"Fantastic work. We need to hold a proffer session right away. Make sure you have him execute a Waiver of Speedy Arraignment first so we don't have to take him to court today." If Miles got arraigned in open court, his arrest would become public knowledge, and he'd no longer be useful to do undercover work for them.

"I'm not down with paperwork, sister," Julian said. "Not my style. When you get here, you get him to sign whatever you want. I paged O'Reilly, and he'd like to participate in the debriefing, too."

The mention of Dan's name reminded her that she'd tried his cell phone three separate times last night to fill him in on what had happened at the museum, but with no success. She'd ended up leaving a curt message on his voice mail about how inconvenient it was not to be able to reach him, and he still hadn't called back. Sitting awake last night in the chair in her bedroom with the phone in her hand, staring out at the sky, Melanie should have been worrying about the case or about her career. But instead she was in a panic over Dan's mysterious disappearing act. If he'd been a different man—if he'd been Steve, certainly—Dan's sudden change in behavior would be enough to convince her he was seeing someone else. That was the reason men made themselves un-reachable, wasn't it—to sneak off with other women? Given Melanie's personal history, her mind naturally went there. But this was Dan O'Reilly, she told herself. He was incapable of infidelity.

As hard as she tried to believe that, Dan's phone had kept on ringing. Finally, Melanie had dragged herself into bed and fallen into a dreamless sleep, blank and deep, hiding from her life.

"Where do you want us to meet you?" Julian asked, snapping her back to the present.

Before she could answer, Maya came toddling into the room, and another unpleasant truth dawned on Melanie. It was Saturday. Her babysitter didn't work today. Steve was in L.A., and she hadn't heard a peep out of him, and Sophie had more than done her duty by watching Maya while Melanie went to the fund-raiser last night. Melanie had an important suspect to debrief and her boss's wedding to attend. But in order to do those things, she needed to find somebody to watch her daughter.

She picked Maya up and kissed the top of her dark head.

"I'll see you at my office in an hour," she told Julian.

An hour later, Melanie struggled out of a taxi in front of her office with Maya on her hip, her dress for the wedding draped over her arm, and a diaper bag full of toys, snacks, and videos hanging off her shoulder.

Melanie's mother, Carol, would take Maya starting at three o'clock and keep her overnight. Carol helped out when she could, but she had a job and an active social life to work around. For the hours between now and then, Melanie had come up empty-handed. Steve hadn't returned from his business trip or made any arrangements for Maya's care despite the fact that this was his weekend. Sophie Cho was working on a rush project all weekend herself. And Melanie's glamorous sister, Linda, was on assignment in Miami for her job as an entertainment reporter with a Spanish TV network. That left Melanie with two options. Either she could bring Maya into the debriefing with Miles Ortiz, who was a thug, a meth dealer, and possibly a killer. Or she could leave her seventeen-month-old alone in a separate room where she couldn't see her, with only a Barney video for company, at a moment when some psycho creep might or might not be stalking Melanie.

Signing in at the guard's desk in the lobby, she saw that Shekeya Jenkins had come in an hour before. Beneath Shekeya's signature, two other names were printed in childish letters—Khadija and Rashida, Shekeya's little girls, who were seven and five. Melanie stopped on the Major Crimes floor on her way to the war room, and poked her head in to the chief's suite to commiserate. Shekeya was at her computer. Her daughters sat on the floor nearby with their coloring books.

"Hey, girl. You brought reinforcements, too, I see," Shekeya said, smiling at the sight of Maya.

Khadija, the older child, jumped up and ran over to Melanie.

"Can I hold the baby?" she pleaded. Melanie set Maya down. She immediately began giggling and running around in circles, which made Shekeya's girls crack up.

"They're getting so big," Melanie said.

"I haven't brought 'em into work in a while, so you haven't seen 'em."

"You're working overtime?" Melanie asked.

"Actually, I'm filling out the application for the paralegal position. I waited till today so there wouldn't be any chance of the boss showing up to look over my shoulder."

"She's getting her hair and makeup done, right?" Melanie asked.

"Mmm-hmm. I have the place to myself. By the way, thank you for the letter of recommendation. I know how busy you are, but you still found time to do it."

"No problem."

"What are you here for?" Shekeya asked.

"Proffer session."

"You're not bringing Little Miss Thang to meet your bad guy, are you?" Shekeya asked disapprovingly.

"I don't have a choice. I got caught with no babysitting."

"I hear you. Kwame's working today, and my sister's putting on a potluck at her church. That's why I brought these two in. But leave Miss Thang here. We'll watch her for you."

"Seriously?"

"Sure. My girls love babies. Especially pretty ones with hair they can fix. You'll make their day. Don't be surprised if you get her back with a new hairstyle, though."

THIRTY ONE

Melanie sat in the war room on the sixth floor facing Miles Ortiz across the table. His eyes were glittery and sharp as ice picks. The left one was decorated with a jailhouse tattoo that looked like a stitched cut, as if Miles had just been sliced with a beer bottle in a bar fight. The pricey personal trainer dressed in pure gangsta-thug style—diamond studs in both ears, a nylon do-rag tied over his black hair, and a wifebeater T-shirt showing off lean, muscled arms. For the bored housewives of the Upper East Side, there was nothing sexier than violence.

Dan and Julian sat on either side of Miles. They'd been in place already when Melanie had arrived at the war room, putting to rest her faint hope of seeing Dan alone. She had plenty to ask him about. The status of his investigation into her Web stalker. Where Rockwell Davis and Clyde Williams had been at the time of Suzanne Shepard's murder. And of course, why he'd ignored her phone calls again last night. But this debriefing was just too pressing. Her questions would have to wait.

Melanie slid a piece of paper across the table.

"You speak and read English?" she asked.

"Yes, ma'am," Miles said. His voice was a hoarse growl.

"This is a Waiver of Speedy Arraignment form. Saturday arraignments happen only in the mornings. We can either bring you before the judge right now, in which case your arrest becomes known and your value as a cooperator diminishes accordingly, or else you can sign this and wait until Monday morning, when we'll try to arrange for a closed-courtroom arraignment. There are no Sunday arraignments, so if you want to do the debriefing, you'll have to spend tonight and tomorrow night in jail before seeing a judge. Are you comfortable with that?"

"It true what Pierre say, I'm looking at a ten-to-life?" Ortiz asked.

Despite his chilling appearance, Miles's demeanor was matter-of-fact and intelligent. As a seasoned narcotics trafficker, he handled his arrest in a businesslike manner—exploring his options, unbowed but not whining.

"The quantity of methamphetamine you attempted to sell to Detective Hay carries a mandatory minimum sentence of ten years," Melanie said.

"But I can get out from under the minimum if I talk?"

"If you cooperate, I can ask the judge to reduce your sentence. Otherwise, he's required to sentence you to ten years. But cooperation isn't just talking. For somebody in your position, with a significant criminal record, arrested selling a large quantity of a drugs, you need to make cases and testify."

"Make cases. You mean wear a wire?"

"Do something that helps us arrest other violators. What that is depends on you, on what information you're privy to. The whole point of talking today is to figure out what you can do, and whether it's worthwhile for us to proceed."

"But if I don't go to court, I don't get no lawyer?"

"If you want a lawyer, I can call somebody in right now to advise you on the cooperation process. That's not a problem."

"That would be good. I don't need to go to court, but I want a lawyer to talk to before I decide."

"Is there somebody in particular you'd like me to call?"

"Legal Aid is good with me. They always done right by me before."

"Fine. I'll make some calls," Melanie said.

"If we just sitting around, any chance I could get a coupla Egg McMuffins?" Ortiz asked Julian.

Within half an hour, Jerry Siler from Legal Aid showed up to confer with Miles while Melanie, Dan, and Julian waited outside the war-room door. Jerry was an old-timer, a stoner, affable, burnt-out, cynical—all of which made him wonderfully easy to work with. Short and slight with graying hair, he wore red high-tops with his shabby suit and gave the impression of someone who wasn't paying attention, which was far from the truth. Jerry got better results for his clients than virtually any other lawyer in Legal Aid. He'd been around the block a few times too many, and it showed in his face, but he knew his job inside out. After fifteen minutes or so, he called them back into the room. Jerry sat beside Miles now. The two of them had taken to each other with no fuss, like the professionals they both were.

"We're good," Jerry said, lacing his fingers behind his head and contemplating the ceiling. "Miles has some information I think you'll be happy with. We need to execute a proffer agreement first to protect him in the event the cooperation doesn't go forward."

"I've got one right here," Melanie said.

They all signed the agreement.

Dan flipped open a notebook to make a record of what Miles said in case he decided to recant later. Miles's right hand was cuffed to the chair, and he was using his left to polish off one of the Egg McMuffins that Julian had ordered for him.

"Okay, let's get started," Melanie said.

Melanie had planned to begin by discussing last night's methamphetamine bust and Miles's other drug activities, which she believed would be fairly painless topics for him. Once she had his confidence, she'd circle around to his relationship with Dr. Benedict Welch, the burglary of Suzanne Shepard's apartment, and other more sensitive subjects, including the murder itself. But her strategizing turned out to be unnecessary. Dr. Welch figured more prominently in Miles's criminal activities than Melanie had ever suspected, and Miles gave him up without batting an eye.

"The meth Pierre took off of me, it locally produced," he said meaningfully.

"You mean, not imported?" Melanie asked.

"Correct," Ortiz said.

This was, in fact, unusual. The vast majority of methamphetamine consumed in the United States was imported from Mexico, where a robust trade in precursor chemicals like pseudoephedrine allowed it to be produced in enormous quantities. Pseudoephedrine had once been readily available as a decongestant in the United States until exploding methamphetamine addiction had convinced most states to regulate it. Pseudo, as it was affectionately known in the trade, was now kept behind the pharmacist's counter and even required a doctor's prescription in some places. Anybody wanting to make meth in their garage would find this necessary ingredient hard to come by. Domestic meth labs got a lot of press, but they were a tiny slice of the voracious meth market, just little mom-and-pop shops, for exactly this reason.

"So what are we looking at?" Melanie asked. "A lab in somebody's bathtub?"

"Naw. Big-time."

"What's that mean, Miles?"

"A whole warehouse. If and when we get to yes, I'll give you the 411 where it located at."

"What kind of quantity are they producing?" Melanie asked.

"Between twenty and fifty keys a week, depending," Miles replied.

Dan glanced up from his notes and their eyes met. Melanie had to look away, or those baby blues would suck her to a place she couldn't afford to go right now.

"You're kidding me," Dan said. "Fifty kilos? That's just not possible."

Miles looked unfazed. "I'm telling the truth. Whether you believe me or not, I don't give a shit."

"What's the street price of meth these days?" Melanie asked.

"About fifteen thousand a key on average," Julian replied.

Melanie's phone had a calculator function, and she did the math. "So this organization is pulling down somewhere between three hundred thousand and seven hundred and fifty thousand dollars a week in sales?"

"Sounds about right," Ortiz said.

"Not bad," Julian said.

"Where are they getting their pseudoephedrine? Doesn't it take a huge amount of pseudo to produce a kilo of meth?" Melanie asked.

"Yeah," Dan said. "That's why I'm finding this so hard to believe."

"It takes over seventeen thousand pills to make a kilo," Julian said. "Seventeen thousand two hundred and eighty to be exact."

"My man know his drugs," Miles said, smiling.

Miles didn't seem the least bit angry at Julian for arresting him, although he'd apparently called Kim Savitt every name in the book when the cuffs went on.

Julian was that rare cop who had an effortless rapport with his informants. They were too happy hanging with him to want to blame him for their reversals of fortune, which naturally enhanced his success at undercover work.

"Answer the question," Julian said, looking Miles in the eye.

"Where I got the pseudo?" Miles repeated.

"Yeah," Julian said.

"We got a connect who can get however much we want."

Melanie's ears pricked up. She felt something big coming.

"Why is it that your supplier can get so much pseudoephedrine?" she asked, her eyes glued to Ortiz's face.

"Because," Miles replied, "he a doctor."

THIRTY TWO

Miles Ortiz had met Dr. Benedict Welch eight months earlier in a perfect example of Manhattan networking. It'd happened at a "separation shower" thrown for Kim Savitt by her girlfriends the night after she'd moved out of the five-story town house she'd shared with her mogul husband, Drew, and into her luxurious bachelorette apartment. The shower gifts tended toward La Perla lingerie and the latest designer meds displayed in carefully selected, jewel-encrusted pill cases. Miles attended in his capacity as Kim's personal trainer and one of her many lovers of the moment. Dr. Welch was there as her plastic surgeon, and because he always got invited to everything. Welch had heard all the rumors about Miles; beyond hearing, he'd listened. He knew every flavor of drug Miles dispensed and every detail of his criminal record. Far from shying away from the man because of this, Welch had crossed a crowded room to seek him out.

Miles had been hovering awkwardly beside a table laden with caviar, sushi, and salmon in aspic. He felt out of place. The room was packed with gorgeous, rail-thin women getting smashed on Grey Goose martinis who wouldn't dream of coming near the food table because they never ate in public. Miles would've been right at home if called upon to train them, fuck them, or sell them drugs, but he didn't have a clue how to make jaded small talk with them over cocktails. He was quite alone when the good doctor approached.

Welch began by sampling an unagi roll. When he'd swallowed it, he turned to Miles nonchalantly, as if he were simply a random stranger standing within earshot.

"The eel is a bit dry, don't you think?" Welch asked.

"What?"

"Did you try the sushi?"

"I can't eat that shit. What the fuck is in it anyway?"

Welch laughed as if Miles had made a clever joke. "Touché."

Welch smeared a blini with some black caviar, topped it with a dollop of sour cream, and shoved it into his mouth, contemplating Ortiz the whole time with the watchful gaze of a cat.

"So you're the famous Miles Ortiz, are you?" he said eventually.

"What are you, a faggot?"

"No, although you're not the first person to mistake me for one. As a well-dressed man with good manners, well . . ." He gave a worldly little shrug.

"Why you talking to me, then?"

"This is a party. Aren't you here to talk to people?"

"Not to you I'm not."

With his sunken dark eyes and ripped muscles, Miles looked utterly menacing, but Welch neither flinched nor retreated.

"The thing is, I understand from my dear friend Kim that you have a sideline beyond your employment with Flex Gym."

"Huh?"

"I hear you sell drugs."

"You a narc?"

"Not at all. I'm a doctor and a businessman, and I have a proposition that I think will interest you."

So it was Welch who approached you? Not the other way around?" Melanie asked Ortiz.

"That's right. I did a stretch in Rikers a few years back that wasn't no fun. My best shorty got shivved right before my eyes, died in my arms. After that, I clean up my act, throwed out my gang beads, and got my personal-trainer certification through this reentry assistance program the city got. You people should make more programs like that; they help put guys like me on their feet. Anyways, when Dr. Ben come to me, I was out of the life, just pitching small-time shit to my ladies at the gym. Club drugs, tranquilizers, maybe some reefer now and then, nothing that's gonna bring la DEA down on my head. Flying below the radar, you feel me?"

"Give us the details on the offer Welch made to you that night," Melanie said.

"He tell me he got girls at every pharmaceutical company in the U.S. willing to give him as much pseudo as he want for the right price."

"Girls?"

"Like, sales associates. They all pretty girls be selling to the doctors. Ex-cheerleaders and such. Anyway, Ben realize what a gold mine he sitting on, how many Washingtons within his reach, but he ain't got the connects to make it happen. That's where I come in. He tell me, think of it like you an entrepreneur getting offered a partnership in a dot-com start-up. Don't miss the boat."

"And you went for it?"

"Fuck, yeah. I ain't no loser," Miles said, flaring his nostrils.

"So what'd you do?"

"I'm from Marcy Projects. I got my peoples there."

"You contacted individuals you knew to be in the drug trade," she translated.

"Exactly."

"Like who? We need names," Melanie said.

Miles hesitated and looked over at Siler, who'd been busy folding a discarded Egg McMuffin wrapper into an origami bird. Siler looked up, instantly grasping the situation.

"It never feels good to rat out your homies, Miles," he said. "But the government won't accept half-assed cooperation. If you don't have the stomach for it, quit now and we can still get you arraigned today. The statements you've made here can't be used against you because of the proffer agreement."

"But my man Pierre got me on tape selling him sixty grams of meth."

"Then your choices are simple," Siler said. "Answer every question they ask, or step up and do your time."

"I don't mind the inside, but ten years?" Miles said.

"They got you by the balls, man, I can't disagree," Siler said. "So how do you want to play it?"

Miles shook his head. "I don't know. Some a' these dudes I been with from a shorty. I don't think I can."

Melanie wasn't about to let this witness slip away over the names of a few meth dealers in Marcy Projects. She wasn't here to make a drug case; the meth bust was just her leverage over Miles. What she needed was evidence on the murder.

"Miles, if this part is difficult for you, it can wait. We will eventually need those names, but there are other topics I'd just as soon cover first."

They had to keep their eyes on the prize. If Welch and Ortiz had been mixed up in major narcotics trafficking, if that was the deep, dark secret Suzanne Shepard had unearthed about them, then it was looking more and more likely that one or both of them had a motive to kill.

"Getting back to Welch," Melanie said, "does he use? His eyes looked funny to me when I met him."

"Yeah, uh-huh," Miles said nonchalantly.

"What drugs?"

"Little of this, little of that. But with the ice, he got a real habit. Like, he can't be without it."

"With the methamphetamine, you mean?"

"Yes."

"New topic, okay?" she said.

"Sure thing," Miles said.

Siler leaned back in his chair and resumed work on his origami. Dan picked up his pen.

"I hear you knew a woman named Suzanne Shepard," Melanie said.

"Whoa, time-out. This comes out of left field," Siler said, springing to life.

"I need to explore this area with him, Jerry."

"This is the woman who was murdered in Central Park a few nights back. By the guy they're calling the Butcher, right?"

"Yes, it is," she said.

"My client's in here charged with a narcotics offense. That's all I've discussed with him, and all he's prepared to discuss with you. If you're trying to put him with a murder, or even knowledge of a murder, we've got a problem."

"I—" Miles began, but Siler clapped a hand over his client's mouth.

"Shut up and let me do the talking here," Siler said. "I assume from what you just said that you have evidence that my client knew this victim?"

"That's correct."

"What evidence?" Siler asked.

"I can't go into it with you."

The second you told a suspect what you knew, you were setting the parameters for what he'd confess to. Melanie had learned that the hard way on other cases. If Ortiz knew what Melanie had on him, he'd admit to exactly that much and not one iota more. But if he didn't know, he'd be much more likely to tell her something approximating the truth about his involvement in Suzanne Shepard's death.

"Do you have any evidence he was involved in the murder?" Siler asked.

"I have some evidence tending to suggest that, but now that he's in custody, we can find out definitively. All he has to do is submit to a DNA swab."

"You can get that whether we consent or not."

"Yes, I can, and I intend to. But if he's really innocent, let him submit voluntarily. Keeps things friendly," Melanie said.

Siler looked troubled. "The swab isn't a problem, but I need some time to speak to him. I can't just let him start yapping about a murder without knowing what he plans to say."

"Fair enough," Melanie said, nodding.

Julian rehandcuffed Miles behind his back, and he, Dan, and Melanie stepped out into the hallway again, shutting the door. Melanie used the time to check in with Shekeya, who reported that her girls were having a tea party with Maya as guest of honor.

After a few minutes, Siler opened the door and beckoned them inside.

"We're making progress," he said. "My client is prepared to proffer on his involvement in the burglary of Suzanne Shepard's apartment at the behest of this Dr. Welch. But he insists he had nothing to do with the murder."

"Is he willing to submit a DNA sample for testing?" Melanie asked.

"Not only willing, enthusiastic," Jerry said. "He's confident the test will show he's innocent."

"All right, we'll make arrangements to get the technicians over here. In the meantime, let's hear what he has to say," Melanie said.

They all resumed their seats. Siler nodded at Ortiz.

"Here's how the burglary go down," Ortiz began in his gruff voice. "We up and running on this meth operation. I get a small percentage and my man Ben get a handsome chunk of change outta every batch. Sales is good. Everything going nice and smooth. Then one day about three weeks ago, Ben come to me and say we got a problem. I say, 'What?' He say, somebody sniffing around, asking too many questions, and I need you should do something about it."

"Did he tell you who was sniffing around?"

"He tell me straight up it Suzanne Shepard. I know exactly who she is because my friend Kim be friends with her. I met her a coupla times."

"What did Dr. Welch want you to do?"

"First thing he want is, I should find out how much Suzanne know."

"How did he want you to do that? Ask her?"

"No. He tell me she gots lots of information written down in files that she keeps in her house."

"He wanted you to break into her apartment?"

"Right."

"Why didn't he do it himself? He's the one who knew what to look for," Melanie said.

"The man don't like to get his hands dirty, you feel me? Ben know I'm hooking up with Kim. He know Kim live in that same building, and her husband own it, so he want me to have Kim help get me into Suzanne's apartment. He don't want no involvement. He don't want me mentioning his name. None of that."

"Did Kim Savitt actually agree to help you burglarize Suzanne's apartment?" Melanie asked.

Miles sighed and looked over at his lawyer.

"Any chance we can finesse this point?" Siler asked.

Melanie looked at Miles pointedly. "For purposes of today's interview, yes, but if Kim Savitt is involved, she doesn't walk. You'll need to give her up, because I'm not letting her off the hook."

Custody battle or no, how much slack could Melanie cut the woman? Kim was a drug user. She consorted with serious criminals. And now it looked like she'd conspired to commit a burglary and lied to the feds about it.

"Look, the bitch ratted me out," he said, "but I won't tell on no woman."

"Take the weekend to get comfortable with the idea, Miles, but it's not negotiable. For now, let's move on. With or without Kim's assistance, you knew you were entering Suzanne Shepard's apartment illegally?"

"For sure. I ain't playing with you. I know this is a B and E on my record, straight up. I stole shit, too."

"You mean you took more than just the files Welch asked for?"

"Yes, ma'am."

"What did you take?"

Miles proceeded to recount the burglarized items so precisely that he might have been reading from the police report Lorraine Shepard had filed. He was being scrupulously truthful.

"What did you do with the proceeds of the robbery?" Melanie asked.

"The money I spent. The jewelry I sold to a fence I know and then I spent what he gave me for it."

"Did you share the proceeds with Benedict Welch?"

"Hell, no. He just tell me take the files. The other stuff was my idea, my work, so it belong to me."

"Okay, let's focus on the files now. Exactly what did you take?" Melanie asked.

"One folder with Ben's name on it. Another folder with my name on it. Got 'em off a desk in the back bedroom of Suzanne's place, right in plain sight."

"That's what Dr. Welch had told you to take?"

"He say, take anything about him."

"About him? About Welch himself? Not about you, or the methamphetamine?"

"Naw. He say about him. It was only once I got in there that I saw a file with my name on it. Naturally I took that, too."

"Did you open the files after you found them?"

"Yes, I did. Once I made it back to my crib, I read 'em cover to cover."

"And did it appear that Suzanne Shepard was onto your methamphetamine operation?"

"No."

"*No?* She didn't know about the meth?"

"That's what so weird. She ain't know nothing about it, not as far as I could tell from the files."

"So what was in the files, then?"

"In mine, it was like, what clients I'm hooking up with, and a rumor Suzanne heard that I was selling Ecstasy last year at a party. Bitch be paying attention, looking for dirt on me."

A flash of anger in Ortiz's eyes when he said that made Melanie study him more closely. It was hard to read people sometimes. She generally bought what

Miles was saying. That Welch was the instigator. That Miles was small-time. That he didn't have the motive or even the imagination to have murdered Suzanne. Yet Melanie couldn't help wondering whether she was getting suckered. It would hardly be the first time a cooperator had lied.

"What did you do with the information in the file about you?" she asked.

"Burned it."

Melanie looked Miles dead in the eye. "Burning the notes didn't change what Suzanne knew. She could still have made trouble for you."

Jerry Siler, who'd been using a pen cap to clean his fingernails, stopped and zeroed in on Miles's face, listening attentively. But Miles kept his cool.

"If you asking whether I killed her, I didn't," Miles said. "Test my DNA and you'll see. Why would I? Just because she knew I hooked up with a few clients or sold a couple tabs of X? Big deal. That can't hurt me."

Miles was so matter-of-fact that Melanie couldn't help believing him. "What about Dr. Welch?" she asked Miles. "If Suzanne didn't know about the meth operation, then what did she have on him?"

"His file was interesting," Ortiz said. "It was a bunch of articles and court transcripts and shit from way back, about a murder. Some girl got raped and stabbed. The strange thing was, the stuff wasn't about him. Didn't talk about him at all."

"The articles didn't mention Benedict Welch?" Melanie asked.

"No. They caught the guy that did the murder, and it wasn't Welch. Whoever it was got locked up."

"What was the killer's name?"

Miles shrugged. "I don't remember."

"What about the girl? The victim? What was her name?"

"I don't remember that either. Just some girl. A stripper."

"Well, try. This is important," Melanie said, glancing at Dan and confirming that he was getting all this information down.

"Uh, lemme see. Her name was maybe April. Or Sheri. Something girlie."

"April or Sheri?" Melanie repeated. "That's the best you can do?"

"I said, I can't remember. Maybe it'll come to me."

"How long ago did you say this happened?" Melanie asked.

"Like twelve, fifteen years, something like that."

"Here in New York?"

"No. In California. In L.A. That part I remember."

"What did you do with the file on Welch after you read it?"

"I gave it to him."

"Did he say anything about it?"

"He say, good work."

"No, I mean did he say anything about the newspaper articles or the transcripts? Did he explain what connection he had to that murder?"

"No."

"Did you ask?"

Miles snorted. "Why I'm gonna mess in his business like that? As far as he concern, I never look inside the file, so he not gonna start explaining some shit about some old murder. Either it ain't got nothing to do with him, or if it do, he don't want me to know."

"Did he look at the file while you were there?"

"Yeah, he checked to make sure I got what he wanted," Miles said.

"And? Did he seem surprised about what was in there?"

"No. He seemed like that was what he was expecting. He looked through it and he nodded, like."

"Did he say anything at all about the files, or what was in them?" Melanie asked.

"He just say one thing. He say, Miles, if anybody ask you, none of this ever happened."

THIRTY THREE

After the proffer session, Melanie left the agents and the defense attorney waiting with Miles Ortiz for the DNA technicians to arrive, and went back her office to get organized. There was a big team meeting scheduled for late that afternoon, and she planned to report on her new favorite suspect. Dr. Benedict Welch was a major player in a serious narcotics conspiracy, and he also might be linked to the rape and murder of a stripper in Los Angeles over a decade earlier. Okay, she had to admit that part was pure speculation. But what else could those newspaper articles that Miles had stolen from Suzanne Shepard's apartment mean? Welch hadn't expressed any surprise when he'd examined the contents of Suzanne's file on him in front of Miles. That told Melanie that he'd expected all along to find out Suzanne was investigating that old crime. He must have had a guilty conscience. She would have to figure out some way to track down those articles despite the scanty information Miles had provided.

For the first time, Melanie was starting to feel like the investigation was on track. With her other suspects—David Harris, Clyde Williams, and even Rockwell Davis and Miles Ortiz—she'd harbored doubts about whether they were capable of rape and murder. But she didn't feel that way about Welch, who'd struck her from the start as a classic sex offender. Her suspicions about Welch had seemed to rest on shaky foundations, based on her own personal repulsion at the way he'd touched her. Yes, the complaints she'd seen suggested he'd fondled his patients when they were unconscious. But those allegations hadn't been substantiated, and didn't prove he was a cold-blooded killer. But if she could link him to another sex slaying—well, that would be a different story. Then she'd believe that Welch not only had a motive to kill Suzanne Shepard, but the proclivity as well. Melanie wouldn't forget about her other leads, but she decided to move this one to the top of the list.

The red light on her phone was flashing insistently, reminding her of the disturbing phone call from yesterday, the one where her news conference had been played back at her, set to a sound track of heavy breath-

THIRTY FIVE

Melanie— [the e-mail began], *Show some respect and write back or it'll go hard for you when we meet. You're wearing black pants and a black sweater today. The sweater is nice and tight and shows off your tits. What kind of noises do you make when you're scared? It won't be long now. Don't believe me? Think I'm playing? You saw what I did to Harris last night. He didn't see it coming. You won't either.*

She was alone in her office when she read the message. The team meeting was scheduled to begin in fifteen minutes, and the hallway was full of cops. Just to be sure, Melanie got up and walked over to the door. Lieutenant Deaver stood not twenty feet from her, conferring with two large detectives. The sight of their guns calmed her down. No way could this psycho get to her here.

Melanie went back to her computer and read the message again. She realized that up till now, despite her own better judgment, she'd nursed a faint hope that her stalker wasn't involved in the crimes she was investigating. That he was just some loser who got off on scaring women. Well, that hope had just died a painful death. He had to go and tell her he'd shot Harris.

Wait a minute, should she believe him? Or was this a con? The David Harris shooting had been all over the news today.

But no. Wishful thinking again.

Melanie's mind was a muddle. Soon it would be time to go to the meeting, and she couldn't decide what to do. Maybe she should print his message out and show it to everybody. Or maybe she should write back to the creep and try to get more information out of him. She could try to confirm that he actually was the killer, and not just some wannabe attention seeker. That would be a coup—walking into the conference room with an e-mail from the Central Park Butcher describing some overlooked detail of the crime.

Melanie's eyes fell on Maya's picture, and she lost a couple of moments to a reverie about her daughter, intensely relieved that the little girl was on her way to safety at Melanie's mother's apartment. After hearing about the way David Harris had been watched and stalked, Melanie had taken precautions, insisting that Dan drive Maya to Forest Hills himself, alone, without Melanie in the car. Dan was trained in countersurveillance driving, and he knew how to make sure he wasn't being followed.

But Dan hadn't come back yet, and he hadn't called.

Melanie had just picked up the phone to dial Dan's cell when a sharp rap sounded on her office door. She looked up, her heart pounding. But it was only Susan Charlton. Standing beside her was Mark Sonschein, the deputy chief of the Criminal Division, the one Melanie found so intimidating.

"I come bearing tidings from the front office," Mark said.

"It's really not a good time," she said.

"I know you're about to start a meeting," he replied, "but this can't wait. It's about the Shepard case."

Mark and Susan both wore grim expressions. Behind Mark's back, Susan caught Melanie's eye and mouthed, "Sorry." Something bad was coming. Melanie put the phone down.

"I'm taking over as lead prosecutor," Mark said. "You should not take this as a vote of no confidence.

You can continue to work the case as my second seat. With the two new murders—"

"One new murder if you're referring to the limo driver. David Harris will recover," Melanie said. Her voice was flat. She felt numb more than angry. Too many difficult things in a short period of time.

"One new murder is one too many," Mark said. "The point is, the press is going apeshit. The Butcher case is the biggest investigation in the office right now by far, and it's too much for you to handle alone. That is not a criticism of you or your work."

"I'm not alone. Janice Marsh from the D.A.'s office is assigned to help me. She would have been at the meeting today, but she had to go to a wedding in Cape May."

"A.D.A.s have no work ethic," Mark said. "You just proved my point. Who goes to a wedding in the middle of a murder investigation? You need somebody federal. Somebody proven and senior. If I blame anyone for the lack of progress, I blame Bernadette for leaving you poorly supervised."

Of course, Bernadette herself was getting married in a couple of hours, and Melanie intended to be there. Minutes ago, she would have been spitting mad at Mark for speaking to her like this. But now her thoughts were taken up with a more pressing concerns.

"No point in arguing," Mark insisted, though Melanie wasn't putting up much of a fight. "The decision's been made. I'll attend the team meeting with you and introduce myself to the troops. I still need you to run it, since I'm not up to speed on the facts. You're okay with that?"

"I guess so. Yes."

"Glad to hear it. Well, I'm looking forward to working with you."

Melanie didn't reply. Mark looked flustered.

"Uh, well, all right, then. I'll . . . see you in there." He flashed her a big phony smile and backed out the door.

"Don't feel bad, Mel," Susan said when he was gone. "This really isn't about you. It's about a million things other than you, in fact. Mark's shouldering two private school tuitions and he needs some good press to help him get a law-firm job. Bernadette's at war with the front office, and putting Mark on the case is a way for them to slap her. The press is on a rampage, so the higher-ups want somebody with an impressive title doing the news conferences instead of a line assistant like you. I could go on and on."

Melanie stared back at Susan in stony silence. If she could've mustered a drop of real indignation over this turn of events, she might have directed some of it at the woman standing before her. Susan was a political animal. Who knew what she'd said about this decision behind closed doors? As much as Melanie liked and admired Susan, she never fully trusted her.

"Are you okay?" Susan asked.

"I have a lot going on right now," Melanie said.

"I understand. All the stress. And this can't be welcome news."

"It's not."

"One more thing and I'll get out of your hair. You should know that this isn't Mark's fault. The higher-ups asked him to step in. If he comes across as a dick, it's because he honestly feels bad about cherry-picking your investigation but he lacks the social skills to communicate that to you. Underneath his pompous exterior, he's a good guy, really. And a fine prosecutor."

"If you say so," Melanie said.

"I do. Give him a chance. Try to make friends."

"All right."

"At the end of the day, I know you two will hit it off. You'll catch the bad guy together, and he'll reward you. I'm sure of it. Then we'll get what we've been after. Me as chief, and you as deputy."

Susan smiled at Melanie brightly, and then turned and left.

"If I'm still alive," Melanie said under her breath.

Melanie considered her predicament and decided there was only one thing for it. She needed to deliver up this stalker creep with his head on a platter and prove he was actually the Butcher. Then she could kill two birds with one stone. One, revive her career. Two, save her life.

She turned back to her computer and clicked reply.

Why should I believe you when everything you say comes straight from the TV news? You're a big liar. If you were the real killer, you'd tell me something I don't already know, she typed.

Melanie clicked send. While she waited for an answer she'd call Dan.

"Hey," he said, picking up on the first ring.

"Everything go okay?' she asked.

"Dropped the cutie off. No sign of trouble."

"Did you fill my mom in on what's going on?" she asked.

"Yeah. Nice lady. She's worried about you."

"I'm worried about Maya."

"She's safe where she is now. It's a secure building, and your mother's on a high floor. I told her not to go out or let any strangers in."

"You think that's enough?" Melanie asked.

"I do. Let's not lose perspective. We don't have any proof that the guy who e-mailed you is the same one who shot Harris or killed Suzanne Shepard."

"*Not yet*," she agreed, looking at her computer screen, which didn't show anything new.

"He could just be some pathetic jerk with time on his hands."

"Have you had any luck tracing the e-mails?" she asked.

"Agh, long story," Dan said with obvious frustration. "I'll give a full report at the team meeting. The bottom line is no. I have some leads on where to look, but nothing solid. He's been using public access terminals. I sent guys to stake out the two places he used. But A, he's probably too smart to use the same terminals again. And B, we don't actually know what the prick looks like."

"He's careful. It's going to take a creative strategy to find him."

Dan went quiet for a moment. "When you start saying stuff like that, I get very nervous," he said finally.

Melanie looked back at the computer screen and drew a sharp breath. She had a new e-mail. It was from *him*.

"You there?" Dan said.

"Yeah. How far away are you?" she asked.

"Ten, fifteen minutes, depending on traffic. I might be a little late for the meeting."

"Do me a favor, keep your phone on."

"I will," he said. "Promise me you're not planning anything crazy?"

But she'd already hung up. Melanie opened the e-mail.

Something you don't know, you uppity whore? How's this? The best way to shut up a whiny bitch is with a stun gun blast to the neck. Should I use it on you? I don't think so. I want you awake, feeling things. You'll be begging me to kill you.

Reading his words, Melanie felt cold and nauseous, but her brain still functioned. She remembered that the stun-gun lesion on Suzanne Shepard's neck hadn't been reported in the media. It hadn't even been confirmed by their forensics people yet. But it was definitely real. He was telling her something true. Melanie knew that because she'd seen the mark with her own eyes, that night in the Ramble when she'd viewed his handiwork. There was no question in her mind now that this was the killer talking. This was the Butcher. She knew what he was capable of. She'd seen what he'd done to Suzanne. And he was saying he planned to do the same things to her.

THIRTY SIX

Melanie might be reckless, but she wasn't stupid. Once she was convinced she had the killer online, she called in the big guns.

When he heard the news, Mark Sonschein rushed to her office, bringing along his boss, Sam Estes, who was the chief of the Criminal Division. Sam had been on his way out the door to a meeting in Washington with the deputy attorney general, and the fact that he'd taken time out to confer with her brought home to Melanie the gravity of her situation. These guys *were* the front office. When people talked about the higher-ups, when they worried about what the chain of command would think, this was who they meant. And now they were sitting here with Melanie talking strategy. She realized this was because she was in danger, not because she was a force to be reckoned with in the office. Yet she couldn't help feeling gratified at how impressed Sam and Mark seemed by her bravado.

"We should view this as an opportunity," Estes said. He was blond, bearded, and thickset, with a reputation for being a big-picture guy, an idea man, while the thin, intense Sonschein specialized in nitty-gritty details. "How do we use the e-mail connection to capture the killer while keeping Melanie safe? Has any effort been made to trace the e-mails?"

"The FBI already determined that this guy is using public access terminals," Melanie said. "Different ones for each communication. Even if we run down an e-mail as soon as it comes in, he'll be gone by the time we get people over there."

"What about the e-mail address?" Sam asked. "Partysover2007@yahoo.com? Have we investigated who holds that account?"

"That's the first thing the FBI did," Melanie replied. "Yahoo's a free service. They don't require address verification to send a bill. The name and address used were false. We did learn that the account was opened only thirteen days ago, for what it's worth."

"Does the e-mail address itself mean anything to either of you?" Sam asked.

"Party's over?" Mark said. "It sounds like he plans to put an end to somebody's fun."

"Yeah. Like mine," Melanie said.

The guys laughed, but she didn't.

"Hmm, well . . . is there some way to get him to tell us his location?" Sam continued. "I mean, here we sit, three of the most skilled questioners in America. We should be able to come up with a clever way of asking."

"What question could we ask that he wouldn't see through?" Melanie asked.

"He'd have to be an idiot to fall for that," Mark said. "Besides, we'd risk scaring him off. Whatever message we send has to be carefully crafted to keep the lines of communication open."

"Maybe we should consider an e-mail wiretap," Sam said.

"Wiretaps tell us the content of his communications, not where he's e-mailing from," Mark said. "We already know what he's saying, since he's writing to Melanie."

"Wait a minute, I think that's an interesting idea," Melanie said. "What if the killer's writing to other people, too? If we find out who he's communicating with, what he's saying to them, maybe we can identify him that way."

"Like if he's writing to his aunt Flo in Peoria, we track down Aunt Flo," Sam said.

"That won't work," Mark insisted. "You'd be asking to intercept innocent people's communications. What about Aunt Flo's privacy rights? No judge would sign off on such a request."

"We limit our request to communications that reference the killer's identity or location," Melanie said.

"Who knows, it just might fly," Sam said.

Mark frowned. "How long is Main Justice taking to turn around an authorization on an e-mail wire these days?"

"If we're lucky, a few days," Melanie said. "With an unusual request like this, maybe closer to a week." She sighed. "You're right, I'm dead by then."

"No moping now," Sam said. He gave Melanie's shoulders a jaunty squeeze, like she was a prizefighter and he was her trainer. "We're the feds. The bad guys never beat us. Mark here managed to outwit an entire Colombian cartel, and he's not half as smart as you are, Melanie."

"Actually, Sam, I do consider myself half as smart as Melanie," Mark said, deadpan.

"You were threatened by the Colombians?" she asked.

"Yeah, good story," Mark said. "About five years back, we were up on a wire on this big cocaine cartel, and the agents called me up all excited because they'd intercepted a call about a murder plot. Our targets were negotiating for some C-4 to make a car bomb. So the agents bring me the transcript, and I'm sitting there reading along. The bad guys start talking about this Honda Civic they want to blow up. They give the plate number, and lo and behold, it's *my* car."

"What happened to the Colombians?" Melanie asked.

"Thirty to life, the scumbags, and it was better than they deserved," he said.

"No, I mean how did you catch them?" she said.

"Oh, we set up a sting. We used my car as bait. Lured them out."

They all looked at one another.

"I know what you're thinking, Melanie, but in this case, the bait wouldn't be a car," Mark said. "The bait would be *you*."

"It's the obvious next step, isn't it?" she asked.

"Put you out there with a panic button to push when the Butcher shows up?" Sam said. "No way. You could be killed. This office isn't losing any assistants on my watch."

"That's a job for agents, not prosecutors," Mark said.

"Gentlemen, I'm divorced and I have a daughter to raise," Melanie said. "I'm not looking to take foolish risks. But this lunatic is after me anyway, and I want him caught. Can't we come up with something more controlled? A scenario where we lure him to a specific place, and I have protection?"

"You can have protection without doing a sting," Mark said. "I'm calling in the Marshal's Service the second we're done here."

"It's *my* safety at stake, and I'd rather be proactive than sit around and wait for the ax to fall," Melanie insisted.

"Look, I respect that," Sam said.

"Me, too," Mark said, "but we'd also understand if you were reluctant to take this kind of chance. In fact, we'd think you were smart."

"You're missing the point," she said. "I'm already in danger. I've been in danger for a while now. The Butcher fixated on me after seeing me talking about him on TV, the morning after Suzanne Shepard's murder, but we just didn't realize it. He hasn't gone away, and he's not going to."

"You're right," Sam said. "By e-mailing him, what you accomplished was outing the threat. Now we know your cyberstalker *is* the Butcher. And we know the Butcher is serious about attacking you."

"We also know what he's capable of. That's why I want to get out in front of the problem," Melanie said.

Sam turned to Mark. "If that's how Melanie feels, maybe it's worth you talking to the FBI about a sting."

"Can't hurt," Mark agreed. "I'll find out what they think and what the logistics would be. Who's the supervisor of the squad that's working this case, Melanie?"

"Mike Fagin."

"Don't call him," Sam said. "I know the guy, he's got shit for brains. Who's the case agent?"

A noise at the door made them all look over. The case agent was standing there, and he did *not* look happy.

"I heard you're e-mailing with the Butcher," Dan said, glaring at Melanie, ignoring the powerful men who stood beside her. "Are you out of your fucking mind?"

THIRTY SEVEN

Half an hour later, Melanie took her seat at the head of the long table in the windowless conference room down the hall and called the team meeting to order. She'd succeeded in convincing Dan that luring the Butcher into the open was a better option than sitting by and waiting for him to find her. Dan had already set somebody from the tech squad to work on tracing the last e-mail, the one in which the Web stalker had confirmed that he was indeed the Central Park Butcher. Now, as the lead FBI agent on the case, Dan had primary responsibility for formulating an ops plan. Many of the cops and agents who'd showed up for the meeting had been sent home, so that the only personnel remaining were those with direct contributions to this critical phase of their investigation. They planned to play the sting operation close to the vest and watch out for leaks.

"As I see it, we have three priorities," Melanie said. "We need a strategy for how to lure the Butcher out from under his rock. We need a meeting place that the FBI deems suitable for a surveillance and capture operation. And we need to pull together our evidence on the Butcher's physical description so we know who we're looking for."

"I can help with that last part," piped up a petite woman with a poodle perm sitting midway down the table. "Terri Landry, United States postal inspector. I'm in charge of investigating the threatening package Suzanne Shepard received."

"You took over from Target News security?" Melanie asked.

"That's right. We have jurisdiction under the threat by mail statute. Okay, quick background. Suzanne Shepard received a box of dog excrement in the mail two days before her murder. The box also contained a ripped-up Polaroid taken by somebody who was following her. Yesterday, we were able to confirm that the Butcher himself sent the package. The lab reported that the package was sealed with the same tape used to gag Suzanne Shepard during the attack. Contiguous pieces from the same roll."

"Wasn't there was a surveillance camera in the post office where the package was mailed from?" Melanie asked.

"Yes, and we've reviewed the tape," Terri said. "Unfortunately, the date and time stamp were screwed up, so we weren't able to reconstruct the time frame down to the exact minute. But I can show you photos of six males with large builds who were in that post office at approximately the time the package was mailed. The camera was at an angle and the image quality isn't terrific, but it's the best we've got. Here goes."

A projector and screen had been set up, and Terri shut off the lights. One after the other, grainy black-and-white stills of men standing in line at the post office flashed on the screen. The men's faces were blurry, but the hairs on Melanie's neck still bristled as each image appeared. One of these men was the Central Park Butcher, and he wanted to kill her. But which one? The muscular guy with the bandanna and leather jacket? The strange one with the weird mustache? The strung-out-looking guy with greasy hair? It could be any of them.

"Stop," somebody called out. "Go back to that last one."

Terri clicked back to the previous image, which showed a large, moon-faced man in his thirties or forties with close-cropped light hair. He was wearing jeans and a T-shirt that said WE DELIVER FRESH FOOD FAST.

"Well?" Terri Landry asked.

"I don't recognize the guy, but I recognize the shirt," the agent said.

"Your name?" Melanie asked.

"Special Agent Tim Crockett, FBI. I'm from Dan O'Reilly's squad."

"Delivery guys all over town wear that shirt," Mark Sonschein observed. He was sitting at the foot of the long table, opposite from Melanie. "It's from that chain soup place."

"I feel like I saw it recently, while I was on the job," Crockett said.

"Go through your surveillance notes," Dan suggested. "See if you come up with anything concrete."

"Will do," Crockett said.

"In the meantime, let's mark that picture for special attention," Melanie said. "We'll show it to David Harris when he regains consciousness. Can we compare it to mug shots of known sex offenders?" Melanie asked.

"The Bureau can do that by computer," Dan said. "We have special software that scans the photos in, sorts 'em by basic facial characteristics, and compares 'em to mug shots. Unfortunately, you probably need better images to work with than what we got here. But we'll give it a shot anyway, see what we get."

"Is this really all we have on the killer's physical description and identity after so many days of investigation?" Mark Sonschein asked.

"Only three days," Dan said, annoyed.

"We've ruled out a bunch of our early suspects," Melanie explained. "We have one guy left who seems really fishy, but even he has a valid alibi."

She gave Mark a brief rundown of what they'd learned about Dr. Benedict Welch, including the fact that he was living under a false identity, had orchestrated the burglary of Suzanne Shepard's apartment, was involved in a big meth operation and might be connected to the murder of a stripper in Los Angeles years earlier.

"As soon as David Harris is conscious, I plan to show him Welch's photograph," Melanie said. "I'll also show him the photos from the post office surveillance video. Hopefully he'll be able to recognize the Butcher, either from the night of the murder or from when he was kidnapped last night."

"What about the newspaper articles your cooperator saw, about the old murder? That sounded like a hot lead," Mark said.

"We don't have much to go on," Melanie said. "I can assign somebody to do an online search for all murders of strippers that occurred in the Los Angeles area between twelve and fifteen years ago. But we don't have a victim's name, or the name of the man who was convicted."

"Do it anyway," Mark said. "Any results you get can be shown to your cooperator. Who knows, maybe something rings a bell."

"Okay."

As they turned back to discussing the sting plan, Dan got a call on his cell phone from the FBI tech squad. They'd managed to trace the most recent e-mail to a computer in a public library in the East Thirties.

"What's he doing there? I thought we had him pinned down to Queens," Melanie said.

"There's a Little India in that part of Murray Hill. Maybe he's going out for Indian food," somebody suggested. A couple of people laughed nervously.

"He's getting smart, is what he's doing," Dan said. "He figures he needs to change up in order to avoid detection."

"He *is* smart," Melanie said. "So how do we come up with a hook that he'll fall for?"

Dan, Lieutenant Deaver, and some of the other agents began batting around ideas for meet locations. They wanted somewhere well lit, with clear lines of sight, not too many civilians around, but enough cover so that a surveillance team could set up without attracting attention. The problem was, everyplace they suggested seemed certain to arouse the Butcher's suspicions. When they started talking about the piers in Brooklyn, Melanie had had enough.

"You're doing a good job of convincing me this whole idea won't work," she said. "What am I supposed to say to the guy? 'Meet me at the piers at midnight. I'll come alone.' He'd have to be brain-dead to agree to that."

"She's got a point," Sonschein said.

"We need to be subtle if we want him to take the bait," she said. "We should propose a place he expects me to go anyway, like my office or the courthouse. And I should just let it slip that I'm planning to be there, like it's an accident. That's our only hope."

"I don't like it. Office, courthouse. Both those places got too many civilians," Deaver said.

"Not on Saturday night they don't," Melanie replied.

Saturday night. Melanie wistfully pictured the party dress that was hanging on the back of her office door. Bernadette's wedding ceremony began in less than two hours. But what could she do? Her boss would just have to understand that when the most vicious killer in recent New York City history was after you, it was hard to take time out for a wedding.

———

The reply that Melanie ultimately sent to the Butcher was as subtle as she could make it, which unfortunately wasn't terribly so. If she buried the message too deep, she'd risk having him miss it altogether. But that was a difficult balance to strike, and Melanie worried that her plan would backfire. Her only other option, however, was to do nothing and let the Butcher pick his moment to strike. She found that one plain unacceptable.

You don't scare me, she wrote to partysover2007 as a roomful of cops and prosecutors looked over her shoulder, offering advice on wording. *I'm safe in my office on the sixth floor of the U.S. Attorney's Office. We have bulletproof windows and doors. You can't get to me here, you creep.*

"It's enough of a provocation that he just might go for it," she said as she clicked send. But there was doubt in her voice.

The sixth floor held only war rooms and debriefing rooms and was seemingly deserted on this Saturday afternoon, but the FBI did a security sweep for good measure anyway. Melanie took up position in an office that faced the public plaza, although it was unlikely that the Butcher would be able to see in from the street six stories below, at least until darkness fell, which wasn't for several hours yet. The offices on either side of the one where Melanie sat were filled with cops. The FBI arranged to replace the guard in the lobby with one of their own. The lobby was well lit, and the sham guard was instructed to take conspicuous ten-minute breaks at predictable intervals and forget to lock the glass door to the street. A number of cops and agents were stationed in undercover vehicles at strategic points around the plaza.

Now all they needed was for the Butcher to take the bait.

After an hour alone in the decoy office during which she kept calm by Googling her own name and catching up on press coverage of the Butcher case, Melanie really started to get antsy. She dialed Dan's cell phone. Through the shoddily constructed government wall, she heard it ring in the next room.

"What's up?" Dan asked. "Did he respond? We're monitoring your e-mail over here and we don't see anything yet."

"No. I'm just getting impatient."

"Then you could never be a cop. A lot of what I do is this. Sit someplace all night staring at nothing until my ass falls asleep."

"I feel bad about missing Bernadette's wedding."

"You never know, we might still make it," Dan said. "I got my suit downstairs in the car."

"I have my dress in my office."

"Yeah? What are you wearing?"

"The black halter with flowers."

"Mmm, I like that on you."

"Careful now. The guys'll hear what you're saying."

"They know we're going out," Dan said, "and they're all jealous."

"Hey, pal, you better not be—"

But Melanie's reply was swallowed up in her gasp as her eyes caught the computer screen.

"Oh my God. He wrote back."

"Yeah, we just got it in here, too," Dan said.

She opened the e-mail, and it was as bad as her worst fears.

I knew you would pull something stupid, you bitch. You think I can't smell a setup? You think I don't know what floor your office is on? You just made a huge mistake. I was planning to hurt you before, but now it's gonna be so much worse.

THIRTY EIGHT

The upside of having her plan to catch the Butcher fall flat on its face was that Melanie got to go to her boss's wedding. The tech squad went to work tracing the new e-mail, and Mark Sonschein made arrangements for the U.S. Marshal's Service to begin providing round-the-clock security for Melanie starting first thing in the morning. In the meantime, she'd be with Dan. Dan always carried his Glock nine-millimeter, and besides, they were going to a party full of cops who would be armed to the teeth, even while off duty. For added security, Dan instructed Agent Tim Crockett to take up position outside the church.

Bernadette was getting married in a magnificent Gothic edifice on a picturesque, brownstone-lined block in Brooklyn Heights. Dan and Melanie, decked out in their party clothes, pulled up in front of the church mere minutes before the ceremony was to begin. The New York City law enforcement community had turned out in full force, so not only was every parking space taken, but every legally parked car was blocked by double- and triple-parked ones, each with a police placard in its window.

"This looks bad. Should I run in and get us seats while you find a spot? You can watch me from the car to make sure it's safe," Melanie said.

"Not on your life, princess. I'm not missing the I-dos. I love weddings. If you're lucky, I'll start blubbering like a little kid and you'll have something to blackmail me with."

Dan threw the car into reverse and backed down the street at top speed. Then, taking advantage of a small gap between the parked cars at the corner, he threaded the needle, driving up onto the sidewalk with tires screeching.

"That defensive driving course comes in handy," he said, cutting the engine and grinning. His smile took her breath away.

They leaped from the air-conditioned car into sticky heat. During the course of the afternoon, the weather had turned sultry in a way that felt permanent. The few hours of glorious summer New Yorkers were granted each year had ended, and they'd have dog days from now to September. As they dashed toward the church hand in hand, Melanie felt like she was running through warm water, and was grateful for her bare halter dress and high-heeled sandals. Halfway up the steps, she was gasping for breath and laughing when Dan abruptly turned and caught her by the waist.

"Hey," he said.

"What?"

"C'mere."

He pulled her tight against his chest, which felt hard as steel. In the glow from the setting sun, his blue eyes looked bottomless. She wanted to fall in and drown. They kissed for a long moment, and she forgot all the bad and scary things in life. All around her the sounds of the city hushed so that the only thing she heard was the beating of their hearts.

"Mmm," she murmured.

Inside, the organist struck up "The Wedding March."

"Let's go. We're missing it," Dan said, and grabbed her hand, pulling her the rest of the way up the stairs.

The ushers had already disappeared. Melanie and Dan ducked into a back pew just ahead of the wedding party. The church was jam-packed and eighty degrees inside. All around the soaring space, papers fluttered as guests fanned themselves with hats, invitations, newspapers, anything they could find. Dan took her hand, and they turned to watch bridesmaids and groomsmen step in time down the aisle. Bernadette appeared on the arm of her frail father. She wore a true fairy-princess dress—pearl-encrusted bodice, enormous tulle skirt—and a long, trailing veil, and the incongruity of the costume on her calculating, tyrannical boss seemed to Melanie like the pure triumph of hope over cynicism.

As he'd promised, Dan's eyes glittered with real tears. He raised Melanie's hand to his lips and kissed it tenderly. With a price on her head, everything became clear. So there were ups and downs. So this relationship was intense and stormy. So be it. She wanted to be at his side.

THIRTY NINE

In New York, the line between the cops and the bad guys can be paper-thin, as befits people living cheek by jowl in the same colorful neighborhoods. The catering hall in Bensonhurst where the Albano-DeFelice reception was being held was straight out of a wise-guy movie, and so were a lot of the guests. Christmas lights twinkled in June. Naked nymphs danced in the wall murals, squirting wine from leather pouches into one another's mouths. Men in pastel satin tuxes imitated them, feeding champagne to their big-haired, big-bosomed companions.

A ten-piece orchestra played as Melanie and Dan wound their way across the teeming dance floor to their table. They were seated with others from the Major Crimes Unit, next to a table full of judges and their clerks. Melanie slid into a seat beside Susan Charlton, who'd brought her girlfriend, Lisa. Susan wore a practical navy-blue business suit and Lisa a tank top and sequined peasant skirt. On the other side of Melanie, Shekeya Jenkins and her husband, Kwame, who worked for the MTA, were tucking into plates groaning with enormous piles of antipasti. Shekeya, who looked like a celebration in hot-pink satin, waved her fork enthusiastically.

"The shrimp is out of this world, girl. You got to get some before it's all gone."

Melanie glanced over to an adjoining table with cops and agents from Vito Albano's Elite Narcotics Task Force. She spotted DEA Agent Raymond Wong, the guy she'd set her friend Sophie up with, sitting there among his colleagues. She waved at Ray-Ray, but he didn't notice, so wrapped up was he in a conversation with the perky, athletic-looking blonde sitting next to him, who wore a red dress. As Melanie watched, Ray-Ray leaned in and smooched Detective Bridget Mulqueen full on the mouth.

She turned to Dan. "Hey, is something up with Bridget and Ray-Ray?"

"They're here together?" Dan asked, following the line of her gaze. "What do you know? They were sorta going out for a while, but I heard she dumped him."

"I set him up with Sophie Cho."

"Your friend Sophie?"

"Yeah, just last week. I had no idea he was dating Bridget. He never mentioned it."

"Dating is an overstatement. He follows her around like a dog. Sometimes she lets him, mostly she just kicks him. But he's a goner. I wouldn't hold out much hope for your friend."

"I thought Ray-Ray hated Bridget."

"There's a thin line between love and hate," Dan said, and then laughed at himself. "Listen to me, the philosopher. Like I have a fucking clue."

"You do okay," Melanie said.

From across the table, Joe Williams gave Melanie a look so withering that it shocked her. Her stomach sank. Regarding the whole Clyde matter so far, Joe had been more than understanding, and now Clyde was cleared. Joe didn't know that yet, but why would he suddenly get so angry? Had something changed? Joe was alone as usual, the seat beside him empty. In all the years she'd known him, Melanie had never seen Joe with a date. She made up her mind to go sit next to him and find out what was wrong, but then the band segued into a romantic song.

"Come on," Dan said, grabbing her hand.

"We just sat down."

"It's a slow dance," he said.

The lust in his eyes worked on her like a narcotic. "Okay," she said.

On the dance floor, Dan put his powerful hands on her hips. Their eyes locked together and their bodies melded from the waist down. His hands caressed ever so slowly from her bare back to her derriere and up again.

"I can't stop thinking about the sex we had in your office," he said, his voice husky and low, so only she could hear. "I can't get the image out of my mind. You, bent over, looking back at me with those hot eyes. Aagh, let's do that again."

She rested her head against his broad chest, closed her eyes, and sighed. "Okay . . . but not in my office."

"How about my car? Or better yet, the stairwell over there? Standing up against the wall. You like it like that."

She opened her eyes and stared at him. "Now?"

"Don't expect me to wait until I get you home. You're way too sexy in that dress. Your ass looks amazing. I was walking behind you the whole way, drooling."

"Dan, I've got a psychotic killer stalking me."

"So what? He's not in the stairwell."

"How do you know?"

"I'll check it out first," he said.

She laughed. "Seriously, we can't do that again."

"Can't do what?"

"Have sex like that. Where we can get caught by people I work with. It's unprofessional. I mean, it could jeopardize my career."

His face fell. "Don't say that! I've been fantasizing about it nonstop ever since."

"I'm sorry, but that's how I feel."

"Why not? People already know we're going out."

"Going out is one thing. Knocking boots on my desk could get me in trouble."

"*I'm* in trouble. Have been from the day we met. Jump in, the water's fine."

She laughed.

"Come on," he coaxed, leaning down to whisper in her ear. The soft buzzing made her melt all over again. "If we're careful, we won't get caught. That's half the fun, the challenge of the thing. Don't you want to have crazy memories to look back on when we're sitting in our rockers on the front porch fifty years from now?"

"I never thought of you as so reckless," she said, struck by his reference to the future. Fifty years from now. He'd talked of marriage when they first met, but not recently. Was that only because Melanie seemed like she wasn't ready? She wasn't ready, yet when he'd stopped mentioning it, she'd begun to worry.

"Look who's talking. You locked the door and jumped me," Dan said.

"You're right. It was all my fault."

"That wild streak. I can't get enough of it. And what a contrast with how sweet you seem on the surface."

The song ended. She shook her head, "Let's sit down."

"Fine, but I'm not giving up. A little vino, and maybe you'll change your mind. A guy can always hope, anyway," he said, smiling at her dreamily.

When they returned to the table, Joe Williams was gone. Shekeya said he'd gone to the men's room, but when he didn't return after a while, Melanie got worried. She thought about calling his cell phone, but she wasn't sure what to say. What if Joe's absence had nothing to do with her? She'd just be harping on a sore subject. Then dinner was served. Melanie had prime rib and lots of red wine. Everybody seemed to be in a great mood. Susan danced with Judge Fox, who'd been threatening to sanction her the day before, and came back pink-cheeked, telling everybody what a charmer he was. Dan and Kwame got into a rousing argument about the Knicks that ended with them laughing uproariously and slapping each other on the back. By the time the best man, a hefty lieutenant with white hair whom Melanie recognized from somewhere or other, tapped on a wineglass to make the toast, she'd utterly forgotten that the Central Park Butcher was stalking her, or that one of her best friends had walked out on the wedding because he was so pissed about how she'd handled her investigation into his father's activities. As Bernadette and Vito crammed fluffy white cake into each other's face, Melanie cheered and hooted with the rest of the crowd as if she didn't have a care in the world.

When the newlyweds stepped onto the floor for their first dance, most of Melanie's table got up to join in. Melanie and Dan stayed behind, their fingers intertwined. She leaned toward him and they kissed, their tongues exploring, teasing. Before she knew it, she was thinking about that stairwell.

"Let's go home," she said, sliding her hands up his muscular thighs.

Just then, Dan's phone buzzed in his jacket pocket. He pulled it out and held it up to read the display, which glowed a vibrant blue green in the romantically lit room. Melanie glanced at it, absorbing without intending to.

"Hold on, I have to take this," he said, and despite the dim light, she saw his face flush red.

The number had come up as DIANE CELL. It took a minute for Melanie to get her mind around what her eyes had just seen. If his ex-wife's cell-phone number was registering that way on his caller ID, it must be programmed into his phone. Yet Dan had assured her he never had contact with Diane.

"What's up? Any news?" Dan said. She couldn't help noticing that his tone betrayed no surprise at the call. To the contrary, he sounded as if he'd been expecting it.

"Aw, jeez, I am so sorry . . . God, I loved that guy. We knew it was coming, but that doesn't make it easier . . . I can't right now, I'm at a wedding right . . . Yeah, yeah, with Melanie," Dan said, glancing up at her as he spoke her name.

Seeing the stunned expression on Melanie's face brought Dan up short.

"Listen, Diane, I'm gonna have to call you back . . . No, I really have to go. Tell your mom to count on me for a pallbearer, okay? Bye."

He hung up and thrust the phone back into his pocket. Within seconds, it started vibrating again insistently, but he didn't answer.

"Your phone's ringing," Melanie said hollowly.

"It can wait. You look upset."

She shook her head, at a loss for words. Upset? Melanie felt like she'd been kicked in the stomach. She felt like somebody had taken the world and tilted it sideways until she didn't know where she was. Not to be the only woman in Dan's life? Then she didn't recognize herself.

"That was my ex-wife," Dan said.

"I figured. I thought you said you never talked to her." Her voice came out lower than normal, quiet, unlike herself.

"I just . . . well, I hadn't, not for a long time. But come to find out, her dad was dying of cancer. She just called, uh, just now, actually, to tell me he passed. I think I told you once, Seamus was like a father to me growing up because my old man didn't give two shits. Seamus really stepped up and did right by me. So I been going by the last couple of nights, to pay my respects."

"The sick friend you were visiting in the hospital was your ex-wife's father?" *When I couldn't get you on the phone? When you didn't return my calls? When I didn't know where you were?*

Dan was watching Melanie's face intently. "Yeah. Uh-huh."

"When you visited, *she* was there, too?"

"Sure. Yeah, of course. Not only Diane, but her whole family."

"You never mentioned any of that. You never told me."

"I meant to. But you know, we've been so busy with the case and all."

Melanie looked down at her hands dumbly. Dan's last remark had been her cue to shrug the incident off. To say she understood and that this wasn't a big deal. But she didn't, and it was. Early in their relationship, Dan had been so jealous of Steve that Melanie had taken to reporting on all her contacts with her ex-husband, just to make Dan feel secure. She thought of this as their "full-disclosure policy" and she'd always assumed Dan was following it, too. But obviously, he hadn't felt obliged to. How could she have been so trusting?

"So you *do* talk to your ex-wife?" Melanie asked. Her words were coming out slow and strangled, like she was underwater.

"Only in the past couple of days. But don't worry, sweetheart, nothing's going on. We just hung out at the hospital a little bit. I bought her dinner the other night, but that was only—"

"You bought her dinner?" she repeated, trying to comprehend the enormity of that revelation to her own heart. She couldn't remember the last time Dan had bought her dinner. Her last birthday—many months ago now? Their dates generally consisted of Dan coming over after Maya was asleep. Which wasn't his fault, really. Maybe if she didn't have Maya he would take her out to restaurants more. Not that she would ever wish not to have Maya. But as things stood, they tended to order in Chinese or pizza and take turns paying.

"Just in this diner across the street from the hospital," Dan was saying. "I felt sorry for her, with her dad dying right after her husband left. But it wasn't a big deal."

"Her husband left her?" This kept getting worse. Diane was available, and hurting, and Dan was comforting her. Suddenly all the food and wine Melanie had consumed weren't sitting well in her stomach.

"Yeah, I guess I forgot to mention that part. He left her for some chick who works in a tattoo parlor. Not that Diane doesn't deserve it, seeing how she left me for him and all, but still, it's hard not to feel for her. You know, you should meet Diane. I think you would like her. I mean, she's an untrustworthy bitch, but otherwise, she's a lot of fun." He forced a laugh.

Melanie stared at him, dumbstruck. Then, because she couldn't think of anything else to do, she stood up and grabbed her handbag.

"Where you going?" he asked, concerned.

"I don't feel very well. I think I'll go home now."

"Okay, I'll drive you."

"No. No, you stay. I think I'd rather just take a cab."

"A cab? You can't do that."

Melanie took a few steps backward. Dan stood up and clutched at her arm, but she yanked it away. She was trying not to cry.

"Sweetheart, you're overreacting," he said gently.

"Dan," she said, struggling to keep her voice calm, "I inform you every time Steve calls, every time he e-mails, for God's sake. And you don't mention this? Not one word?"

"I just did. I told you about it."

"Because she called you right in front of me!"

"I told you that I bought her dinner," he said. Dan's voice was getting shaky, and he was starting to look upset. "I didn't have to say anything about that."

"Right, you could have deliberately concealed it from me. Let's award you ten points for honesty," she said bitterly.

"You're taking this the wrong way."

"Your ex-wife just separated from her husband. She's crying on your shoulder, and you don't mention a word about it until you're caught in the act. What's the *right* way to take that?"

"What I'm trying to say is, nothing was going on. Nothing physical. She wasn't crying on my shoulder physically. She was just doing it, like, metaphorically."

"Metaphorically? You sure about that? That's a big word for you."

His eyes widened with hurt. As Dan hesitated, Melanie turned and ran for the exit.

"Get back here!" Dan called after her. "We're not done!"

Despite his longer stride, she was smaller and lighter and maneuvered through the dense crowd more nimbly than he did. She beat him to the street and hailed a passing taxi, but the driver didn't see her, thank God. Because the next second she had the sense to stop and reflect on what she was doing. The sickest killer she'd encountered in her entire career was out there somewhere, lurking in the dark night. And as much as she wanted to get him, it seemed he wanted to get her more. Dan was right. She shouldn't take a cab.

She spotted the unmarked car parked across the street and ran for it, banging on the passenger-side glass. Agent Tim Crockett rolled down the window.

"Everything okay?" he asked, concerned.

"I need a ride home. Now."

Melanie jumped in and slammed the door. Dan plunged through the catering hall door just in time to see them speed away.

FORTY

In front of her building, Melanie told Agent Crock-ett that it wasn't necessary for him to come inside as long as he watched to make sure she made it to the lobby safely. She'd managed to hold herself together on the ride home, but the strain of her fight with Dan was beginning to tell. She needed to be alone. If she broke down and cried, she didn't want some guy she barely knew from Dan's squad witnessing her pathetic scene.

"I live in a doorman building," she explained. "It's pretty secure. I'll take down your cell number and call if anything seems out of place."

"I'll remain stationed here until U.S. Marshal's Service relieves me."

"Thank you. Just so you know, my protection detail isn't showing up until morning."

"No problem, ma'am."

Melanie dashed from the door of the unmarked car into her building. In the lobby, she was greeted by Hector, her portly, fatherly Puerto Rican doorman. The sight of him made her think twice about having Agent Crockett come in. Melanie loved Hector to death, but the most vigilant guy on the planet he was not. He was too fond of his newspaper and of chatting with delivery people to keep an unrelenting watch. He made her building feel like a home, but a clever intruder would get past him with little trouble.

"Hey, Melanie, a man was here looking for you," Hector said.

"Did he give a name?" Melanie asked, anxiety clutching at her chest. Had the Butcher figured out where she lived? She wouldn't be able to stay in her apartment.

"No, he didn't say."

"What did he want?"

"To see you, *chica*. He asked was you home, but he gave me a bad vibe. So I sent him away and didn't tell him nothing about you."

"What kind of bad vibe?"

"Pushy. Mean."

"What did he look like?"

Hector, who was short, held a hand up over his head. "Big, tall guy with blond hair."

"You told him I live here?"

"I didn't have to tell him. He already knew."

"Right, of course. I'm sorry."

"Something wrong, *mi'ja*?" Hector asked.

"Maybe. How long ago was this?"

"Over an hour, and he hasn't come back. Listen, I know from the papers that you're working on that Central Park Butcher case. I read your name in the *Daily News*. I want to say on behalf of Puerto Rican people everywhere, you make us proud. And you can count on me to keep the door secure."

"You're the best, Hector. I *do* count on you," Melanie said. She gave him a peck on the cheek, but she pulled out her phone and dialed Agent Crockett all the same.

Agent Crockett came into the lobby immediately, and together he and Melanie debriefed Hector about the visitor. The fact was, if the Butcher had paid a call on Melanie at home, not only was that a security issue, it was also a potential break in the case. They decided to show Hector the photos of the men standing in line at the post office on the day the threatening package was mailed. Agent Crockett had the photos in his car, and he fetched them and lined them up on Hector's bellman stand. The doorman studied the photos diligently.

"These pictures. So blurry," Hector said, shaking his head. "I'm sorry, but I don't recognize nobody. I don't think it's that the pictures is bad, either. I think the guy isn't in here."

"You're sure?" Melanie asked.

Hector looked over the row of photos one more time.

"Yeah, I'm sure of it. He's not here," Hector said, nodding more decisively.

Melanie patted him on the shoulder. "Good work. That tells us a lot."

She and Agent Crockett got in the elevator.

"What exactly does it tell us that your doorman can't pick anybody out of the photo lineup?" Crockett asked.

"Hector might seem goofy, but he remembers faces," Melanie said. "So either it wasn't the Butcher who visited me or we don't actually have the Butcher's picture among those surveillance shots from the post office. I don't know about you, but I'm pulling for the former."

When they got to her floor, Agent Crockett unholstered his gun and did a security sweep. He checked the back stairwell where the trash chute was located. Then he put his ear against the door to Melanie's apartment for a long moment and just listened. Hearing only silence, he nodded to her, and she turned her key in the lock. He flipped the light switch in the foyer, setting the place ablaze with light.

"Stay here," he whispered.

He came back after a few minutes and reported that everything looked normal.

"What should I do?" Melanie asked. "Should I sleep here tonight? Should we call in forensics guys to dust the lobby door for prints?"

"Your call, ma'am. You're the prosecutor."

Crockett wasn't much help in the ideas department. Melanie caught herself on the verge of calling Dan for advice, but then the memory of their argument hit her with the force of a punch.

"Give me a minute to think," she said.

Melanie settled Agent Crockett in the living room and went to get her gun. She'd had the foresight to purchase one—or really, the hindsight—after surviving a harrowing episode on another case. Every once in a while, she'd catch a ride to the range upstate with some DEA or FBI guy and practice firing. Melanie was actually a decent shot, though of course there was a world of difference between hitting a paper target and going to the mat with somebody in a gunfight. Still, having the gun made her feel better at moments like this.

The metal gun safe was hidden at the back of a high shelf in her bedroom closet. She felt around for it blindly, dislodging several unopened packages of panty hose and sending them raining down on her head. She pulled out the matte-black pistol. The Beretta seemed to exude a brilliant light—trust the Italians to make even an instrument of death look sexy. Melanie kept the gun unloaded and stored her ammunition at the top of a cabinet in the kitchen in another locked metal box. All the manuals on gun safety said to do this if you had children in the house. Well, Maya wasn't home tonight, thankfully. She was safe with Melanie's mother. Besides, the gun wouldn't be much help against an intruder if its bullets were on the other side of the apartment.

She had to go to the kitchen to get the bullets. The light was blinking on the answering machine on the counter. Melanie played the message as she loaded the gun.

"Melanie Vargas, Duncan Gilmartin of Target News. I've now obtained your home address and telephone number, so you can't hide from me. As you may have heard, I paid you a visit tonight. I will not rest until I get the real story. What is your reaction to Mr. Sonschein revealing at the press conference that Clyde Williams was *trysting* with Emily King at the time of the Shepard murder? Did you tell him to go public with Clyde's alibi? What do you say to the speculation that the Emily King affair is being used as a *smoke screen* to distract the public from Williams's involvement in the murder? And what's your comment on Clyde's decision to drop out of the mayoral race? You might as well call back, because I won't give up."

So *that* was why Joe had been so upset at the wedding.

And, more urgently, that's who had paid her a visit. Duncan Gilmartin was a tall, blond male. It was Gilmartin who'd been here, not the Butcher. At least, she hoped it was him. One way to find out. Melanie went over to the intercom and buzzed down to the doorman's station.

"Front desk," Hector answered.

"Hector, it's Melanie in 8-B."

"He ain't showed his face again, *m'ija,* and I didn't leave my post, not even to use the lav."

"Let me ask you something. This man, did he have an accent?"

"Yeah, he did. English or something."

"Could it have been Australian?"

"Australian?"

"Like Crocodile Dundee."

"Oh yeah. It was just like that."

"Thanks, Hector."

"Don't worry about a thing. I got your back."

Melanie told Agent Crockett the news, then sent him down to his car with a bag of microwaved popcorn and a can of Diet Coke. She brushed her teeth, tucked the Beretta in to sleep beside her on the nightstand, got her cell phone out in case she needed to call for help, and huddled under the covers.

She'd planned to have a good cry, but she just couldn't. She felt too numb and empty inside. Instead, she stared at the ceiling in the dark for what felt like hours, and fell asleep wondering where her life was going.

FORTY ONE

Melanie opened her eyes to dazzling sunlight and a shrieking telephone. Her cell was going nuts right beside her head, half hidden under the pillow.

"Hello?" she mumbled. Her brain was foggy from lack of sleep. Something terrible clawed at the edge of her consciousness, then broke over her like a wave.

Dan!

"Miss Vargas? Hello? Are you there?"

Her throat burned with tears, but she wouldn't let herself cry. "Who's this?" she managed, her voice barely audible.

"Peter Terrozzi from the U.S. Marshal's Service. I'm assigned to protect you this morning. I'm standing down in the lobby, ma'am. Your doorman buzzed you several times on the intercom but got no response."

Melanie held the cell away from her ear for a moment and looked at it. Other things were falling into place now. The e-mails from yesterday. The Butcher.

"How did you get my cell-phone number?" she asked.

"From my office, ma'am, which presumably got it from your office."

"I need a minute, Deputy. Stay where you are, okay? I have to make a phone call."

"Uh . . . okay," he said, sounding confused.

Under present circumstances, Melanie couldn't just let some stranger into her apartment because he claimed to be her protection detail. Mark Sonschein was the one who'd made the arrangements with the U.S. Marshal's Service. She got out her office directory and paged him. By the time he called back, she'd made a much-needed pot of coffee, and she was standing at the kitchen counter in her nightgown, drinking some, her gun set down next to the milk carton.

"Sonschein here. Somebody page me?"

"Mark, Melanie Vargas."

"I was just about to call you."

"My protection detail is down in the lobby. I need to confirm his name and get a physical description before I let him in."

"Smart move, but you'll have to call the Marshal's Service. They didn't tell me who they planned to send."

"Oh, so why were you—"

"Calling? Because I just heard from the FBI. We got a big break, and I need you to come into the office right away to follow up on it. Turns out you were on the right track, Melanie. More than anybody knew. The Bureau traced the final e-mail the Butcher sent you last night. You know, the one where he told us to pound sand, that he wasn't falling for the ruse?"

"Yes?"

"The e-mail was sent from the office of Dr. Benedict Welch."

Melanie grabbed her bathrobe from the bedroom and ran to answer the buzzer. She tried to put her gun into the pocket, but something was in the way. Reaching in, she pulled out a pair of lace panties. The other night, in between Dan's birthday celebration and getting called out to the crime scene, they'd done it on Melanie's living room couch. Somehow the panties had ended up in her bathrobe pocket. She looked down at the wispy fabric in her hand as if she was seeing an artifact from another century. Would she ever have sex with Dan again?

She shoved the panties back where she'd found them, put the gun in her other pocket, and peered through the peephole. The man she saw matched the description she'd just been given over the phone by the U.S. Marshal's Service: short, muscular, balding. He did not match the description of the Central Park Butcher, to the extent they had one. While this should have reassured her, it didn't. According to what David Harris had told them, the Butcher was a considerably larger man than the one who now stood outside her door.

"Deputy Terrozzi?"

"Yes, ma'am. You can call me Pete. I was starting to think I was at the wrong door."

"No. I'm here. Can I see your shield, please?"

He held his shield up in front of the peephole. It looked official enough. She undid all three locks and opened the door. Terrozzi was no taller than Melanie and wide as he was high, with biceps and thighs thick as hams. His head was shaved, and from the pattern of the dark stubble it was plain to see this was done to camouflage encroaching baldness. His pleasant smile marked him as a nice guy who worked out a lot rather than a fearsome pit bull of a cop. If this was her protection against the psycho who'd mutilated Suzanne Shepard and shot David Harris in the back, Melanie couldn't help worrying that he wouldn't be equal to the task.

"Rough night?" he asked, smiling as he took in her bed head and swollen eyes.

"I was nervous. I didn't sleep well. I don't know whether you were briefed, but the man who threatened me is extremely dangerous."

"Sure, but you were in good hands. The agent who just left struck me as extremely competent."

"You met Tim Crockett outside?"

"Crockett? No. He said his name was Dan O'Reilly."

Melanie stared at him in stunned silence.

"May I come in?" Terrozzi asked finally.

"Oh. Sure."

Melanie held the door open. She told Terrozzi where to find the coffee, and turned away to go shower and dress.

"Uh, Miss Vargas?" he said.

"Yes?"

"What's that in your pocket?"

She looked down. A blush started on her cheeks because she thought he was asking about the panties, but his gaze was fixed on the handle of the Beretta protruding from her bathrobe pocket.

"That's my gun," she said.

"Uh-uh." He held out his hand. "Hand it over."

"Excuse me?"

"Are you qualified with that thing?"

"I go to the range," Melanie said indignantly.

"What, like once a month?"

She shrugged. It was less than that, actually. A lot less.

"I can't protect you if I'm worried about you whipping out a pistol and plugging me one by mistake," Terrozzi said.

Melanie hesitated. She believed this guy was indeed her protection detail; she just didn't trust him to protect her. She toyed with the idea of keeping the gun and getting rid of Terrozzi instead.

"That's not me talking," he said, seeing her hesitation. "It's U.S. Marshal's Service protocol. 'The protectee should remain unarmed unless the protectee is duly qualified and authorized to carry a firearm.' From what my supervisor told me, which was based on what your supervisor, Mr. Sonschein, told him, you're not authorized to carry a firearm as part of your duties. Am I right?"

The weight of all those supervisors was too much for Melanie to fight. Reluctantly, she handed Terrozzi the gun.

"But I want it back whenever you're not with me," she insisted.

"I'll always be with you. From what I understand, I'm stuck to you like glue till the Butcher's caught. We're gonna become *very* good friends."

Time to solve the damn case, Melanie thought.

FORTY TWO

Melanie and Mark Sonschein sat in his office, strategizing their next move.

"We have PC to search Welch's office, because that's where the Butcher sent the e-mail from," Melanie said. "But we don't have an eyewitness who can finger Welch and say he sent the e-mail himself. Without that, Welch can argue somebody else got access to his office computer and did the deed. Bottom line, we don't have enough to arrest him for murder."

"One fallback position would be to get the search warrant for now, and hope that a search of his office turns up proof of the murder," Mark said.

"And if it doesn't? Welch is still on the street. You've seen the crime-scene photos from the Shepard murder."

"Yes, and I've read those sickening e-mails he sent you. I want the Butcher locked up as badly as you do. Isn't there something else we can arrest him for?"

"Conspiring to burglarize Suzanne Shepard's apartment," Melanie said. "But my proof is weak. I have the testimony of one cooperator with no corroboration. Miles Ortiz. He's got a sheet as long as your arm, and he looks the part, too. I don't see putting him up against a supposedly reputable doctor. Not with Boutros on duty."

"She's still on?" Mark asked, frowning.

"Until tomorrow morning. We could wait." Judge-shopping was an honored tradition in their office.

"Who's on duty if we wait?"

Melanie flipped through the court calendar she had Scotch-taped to the inside of her official U.S. Government Planner. "Warner. Even worse."

"Hmm." Mark steepled his fingers and thought. "Reputable doctor. But he's not, right? Didn't you say Welch is a fraud?"

"Yes, but practicing medicine without a license? We can't get him remanded on that," Melanie asked.

"I'm not suggesting we arrest him for practicing medicine without a license. I'm saying maybe the atmospherics make it easier to convince a judge . . ." He trailed off.

"What, to issue a warrant for murder when we don't have the proof to back it up? I don't think so. Not Boutros. And the detective who was researching Welch's background is on a plane on her way back from Tulsa. I won't even have proof of the false name in my hands until late tonight or tomorrow morning."

They were both silent for a minute.

"Did you find out anything more about that old murder case in California, the one your cooperator said was discussed in the file he stole?" Mark asked.

"We came up with twenty-seven known murders of strippers in the relevant time period," Melanie said. "We'll have Ortiz look through them and see if he can pick out the right one, but it's a long shot. Besides, somebody else was convicted for the murder that Ortiz saw in the file, so we're not even sure what the connection is."

"What a mess," Mark said.

They were silent again.

"You know what I think we should do?" Melanie asked.

"What?"

"Set up a drug buy. Ortiz puts Welch in a major methamphetamine conspiracy. If Welch were to deliver drugs, not only could we get him remanded, but I bet we could get warrants for his apartment as well as his office."

Mark nodded. "That's by far the best idea I've heard. Do it."

You gonna lock Welch up, no problem," Miles Ortiz said. "I know the man. Show him the green, and he come running."

Melanie had authorized Detective Julian Hay to requisition twenty thousand dollars in marked buy money. It sat in an open metal briefcase on Melanie's desk, bundled with rubber bands and arranged in neat stacks. Miles lifted up his Flex Gym T-shirt, exposing coffee-colored skin and rippling abs. Julian's face was set in deep concentration as he taped a recording device securely to Miles's lower back. Julian knew about the e-mail, and knew that Benedict Welch was suspected of being the killer they were calling the Central Park Butcher. But there was no need to tell Miles that.

"He's really gonna do this out in the open in a restaurant?" Julian asked dubiously, tearing another piece of black electrical tape from the roll.

"He ain't got no fear," Miles said. "Never been caught before, never tasted the inside. He get his kicks selling drugs in front of people's eyes and they don't know what's happening."

"Brazen," Melanie said. "The restaurant he picked is a real Upper East Side haunt. Ladies who lunch. Or brunch, I should say. It's Sunday."

Miles fingered a cigarette and tucked it behind his ear like a pencil.

"Good to go," Julian said, straightening up. "Let's move."

Melanie and Julian accompanied Miles uptown. They planned to sit in Julian's undercover vehicle and listen to the buy unfold over the wire. Melanie would decide when they had enough evidence to make an arrest. The car was a late-model black Lincoln Navigator with custom rims and ultradark tints. It had been seized from a Brooklyn kingpin whose current address was twenty-three-hour lockdown at FCI-Florence. The Navigator was a perfect ride for a drug buy on Queens Boulevard, but it stuck out among the more discreet vehicles of the Upper East Side, so Julian dropped Miles down the block from the meet location and found an inconspicuous parking spot on a side street where they still had a decent view.

The location Welch had chosen was a posh sidewalk café with marble-topped tables set up outside a Madison Avenue bistro. Miles sat down alone at a table to wait for Welch to arrive. Julian tuned his two-way radio to the right frequency and tested to make sure he was picking up Miles as well as the other agents, who were stationed in the surrounding blocks awaiting the arrest signal. When he was done with that task, he took some test shots with the large digital camera that hung around his neck.

Within minutes, a white Escalade pulled up beside the Navigator and parked them in, looking every bit as glitzy as they did.

"Shit, they're blocking my view," Julian said, lowering his camera.

"That's Kim Savitt's car," Melanie said. She hunkered down in her seat, until she remembered they had dark tinted windows. Kim would never spot her.

"Kim Savitt's *here*?" Julian asked.

"Yeah, but why, I haven't a clue. Maybe she gave Welch a ride?"

"I never met her. When she hooked me up with Miles, I spoke to her over the phone. I hear she's something to see."

The driver came around and opened Kim's door, holding out his hand. A slender, tanned arm reached out. Long, bare legs ending in strappy sandals stepped to the pavement, followed by a lithe torso and big chest, wrapped up in the most casually chic little cotton minidress. Acres of blond hair completed the effect.

"Whoa," Julian said. The exclamation sounded involuntary.

"Who invited her?" Melanie demanded.

"I don't know, but I'm not complaining. Damn, I love my job." And he lifted his camera and snapped a picture.

"Miss Hottie could queer our deal, Julian. Miles hasn't seen her since he found out she set him up. He'll go ballistic. Hand me that radio, quick."

The Escalade pulled away, revealing Kim in the process of crossing the street toward Miles. She saw him and stopped dead in the middle of Madison Avenue. Even from this distance, Melanie could tell that Miles looked stricken. A bus was bearing down on Kim. She sprinted out of the way, heading toward the café, her yellow hair streaming behind her.

"Hurry, before Kim gets to the table," Melanie snapped.

Julian picked up a transmitter attached by a spiral cord to the radio and thrust it into Melanie's hand.

"Push this and talk," Julian said.

"Miles, it's Melanie. Do you read me?"

"Yeah." Miles spoke without moving his lips. If you didn't know he was talking into a tiny transmitter hidden in his shirt, you never would have guessed.

"You see Kim coming, right? Act like nothing is wrong. If you confront her, she'll know you've been arrested, and it could blow the whole buy. Do you understand?"

"The fucking bitch. I'm gonna fucking crush her."

"Miles, this is important. You're looking at ten to life. You need this deal to go through or you'll end up rotting in jail. Do what I say," Melanie insisted.

The radio crackled. "Detective Jarmin, over. I got the eyeball. We got Benedict Welch on set. He's crossing Seventy-fourth, heading south on the west side of Madison. Subject is on foot, pulling a large black roller suitcase."

Julian motioned for Melanie to hand him the mike. "Roger that," he said. "Subject is approaching. Maintain radio silence until you hear the arrest signal."

Across the street, Kim was leaning down and kissing Miles on the mouth. His hand rested nonchalantly on her ass, like nothing bad had happened between them.

"Atta boy, Miles," Melanie whispered.

"What up, baby?" Miles said to Kim.

"You're not mad, are you?" Kim asked. She sat down across from him.

"Mad about what?"

"Uh . . . just that I haven't called you."

"You said you wasn't gonna call, remember? Did you come here to see me? I'm supposed to be meetin' Dr. Ben. We got business."

"Ben told me to meet him here. He never said you were coming, though. I'm surprised to see you."

"I bet you are," Miles said, a note of bitterness creeping into his tone.

Kim looked at him appraisingly. "I wonder what Ben was thinking, not mentioning it," she said.

"Ask him. Here he comes now."

As Welch approached, Julian's camera clicked repeatedly. Kim signaled a waiter and demanded a bottle of Pellegrino and some menus immediately. Welch sauntered into the sidewalk café pulling the roller bag after him. He did some fancy footwork to maneuver the bulky suitcase between the tables and up to the one where Miles and Kim sat. The waiter glanced at the suitcase with an annoyed look. Welch rapped Miles on the back hard enough to send a loud whooshing sound over the air, which hurt Melanie's ears.

"Hello, Miles. And beautiful Kim. Don't get up." Welch sat down between the two of them, his bleached yellow hair competing with Kim's in dazzling display. After hearing Pauline Estrada's report from Tulsa, Melanie had decided that Welch must have dyed his hair blond and started wearing those weird violet-blue contact lenses in order to better match the physical characteristics of the real Benedict Welch. Now that she knew he was the Butcher, it made sense that he needed a false identity, a place to hide out between crimes.

"So Miles and I were sitting here wondering why you invited us to lunch without telling the other," Kim said.

"What's the problem? You like each other, don't you? You certainly give that impression," Welch said.

"I don't want to discuss business in front of a lady," Miles said.

"We don't keep secrets from Kim," Welch said, unfazed. "We're among friends. Now, why don't we order some lunch?"

Back in the car, Julian turned to Melanie. "I know why Welch brought Kim," he said.

"Why?"

"She's his insurance policy. Welch is hinked up. He's suspicious of Miles for some reason, and he thinks he'll be safer with Kim around."

"I'll bet you're right. He's in for a shock. I'm sure Miles would love nothing better at this moment than to bring the cops down on Kim's head," Melanie said.

"And the press," Julian said.

They went back to watching. Welch was reading the menu. Miles was glowering at Welch. Kim was looking back and forth between the two of them, frowning.

Julian took a few pictures of the assembled group. Just when things were starting to drag, and Melanie was seeing why agents always complained that surveillances were boring, Miles got to his feet in a pretty good imitation of fury. Welch looked up from his menu, alarmed.

"What is it?"

"You're stalling!" Miles said.

"No, I'm not. I'm hungry."

"I didn't come here to socialize. I got my people waiting for this delivery. You got the pills. I got the money. So let's do the deal."

"Will you be quiet? Someone will overhear." Welch scanned the restaurant nervously.

"Why you set the hand-to-hand up here, then? I could've just as easy come to your office."

"What is going on?" Kim demanded. "If you guys are doing what I think you're doing, I'm leaving."

"Kim, if you walk out, you will draw even more attention to yourself," Welch said.

"I don't appreciate being put in the middle like this. If Drew finds out I was in on some drug deal, he'll crucify me in court."

"Oh, I forgot. You're all about keeping *your* money. God forbid somebody else should make some," Welch said.

"I don't care what you do, but don't mix *me* up in your shit," she said, standing up.

"Sit down." Welch grabbed her arm and jerked her back to her seat.

"Hey, watch it!" Kim exclaimed, rubbing her arm.

"Shut up, both a' you," Miles interjected in a calming tone. "Let's make the trade and get this over with, so Kim can rest easy." He leaned over, sinking temporarily from view, and came back up with the silver metal briefcase that held the money. As Miles placed the briefcase on the table in plain sight, Julian furiously snapped photographs.

"Count it," Miles commanded. "It's all there. Now I need to see the product."

"I can't count the money here," Welch said, glancing over his shoulder. "Too risky. And I'm not letting you count the pills. You couldn't possibly, anyway. There are thousands of them."

"This is so fucked up," Kim said, dropping her head into her hands. "I can't believe you clowns are putting me in this position."

"Shut up," Welch commanded. "Miles, what happened to the trust? We've never counted money or product in public before. I'm telling you, this is not smart." He was talking in a low voice, but urgently enough that the wire picked him up loud and clear.

"I was told to check the merchandise. There was a problem last time," Miles said.

"What problem? You never mentioned any problem before."

"I don't know. But if my shorties from the Houses say to check, I'm gonna check. Or else I walk away with the money right now and this shit is off. *Permanently.*"

Welch stared at Miles with a slackened jaw, then blinked. "The suitcase is beside you," he said, sighing. "Tip it over, and you'll be able to open it without having everything spill out. Just please, try not to let people see."

Miles did as Welch directed. Julian snapped photos of him bending over, opening the suitcase, and examining the contents. Kim stood up abruptly and backed away like she'd never met either of them in her life. She turned and broke into a trot. Miles raised his hand high in the air and gave the previously agreed-upon signal. Melanie nodded at Julian.

"We got a positive visual on the drugs. Move in for the arrest," Julian barked into the mike.

He jumped from the Navigator and hit the ground running. Suddenly the block was swarming with well-built guys wearing jackets that screamed "NYPD" and "FBI" in big white capital letters.

"Police! Don't move!" somebody shouted.

"You're under arrest! You're under arrest!" some-body else yelled.

Welch was facedown on the sidewalk being hand-cuffed. Miles Ortiz had been hustled away and was no longer in sight. Kim Savitt raced down Madison Ave-nue faster than Melanie had ever seen anybody run in high heels. A tall agent sprinted after her, his legs pumping, and grabbed her around the waist, lifting her into the air kicking and flailing. After a brief struggle, the agent handcuffed Kim, his walkie-talkie picking up her curses and screams and carrying them over the airwaves to Melanie, who could hear them anyway from a block away, they were so loud.

"Let me go! You fucking asshole! You're hurting me! Do you know who I am? My lawyer's gonna squash you like a cockroach."

Melanie would make sure that Kim Savitt was re-leased. *Eventually.* Kim had had no prior knowledge of the drug deal and had beat feet after she learned about it, so there was no probable cause to charge her with a crime. Nevertheless, getting hauled down to Central Booking and cut loose at the last minute before she was processed might be good for Kim. Might give her some time to think, to reevaluate her lifestyle and make bet-ter choices about how, and with whom, she spent her time. She ought to. She had a little girl to raise.

Melanie got out of the car and went over to where Julian had Benedict Welch spread-eagled against a wall. Julian patted Welch down while other detectives retrieved the cases full of pseudoephedrine and cash and filled out evidence tags.

"Let me see his identification," Melanie said as Julian withdrew a Gucci wallet from the breast pocket of Welch's tweed blazer.

Melanie systematically went through the wallet. Every piece of identification in it—driver's license, credit cards, medical board identification card, memberships to a golf club and to various museums, a Blockbuster video card—was in the name Benedict Harold Welch.

Welch turned around. His eyes glinted savagely at Melanie through the unnatural violet lenses. She stared back at him with an expression of revulsion. In her mind's eye, she was seeing Suzanne Shepard's brutalized corpse, the left breast severed and hanging loose, the ugly word carved into her stomach. And she was reading those disgusting e-mails he'd written to her. He'd be locked away now, unable to harm her. She'd won.

"What's your name?" she demanded.

"You know my name," he replied, clearly taken aback.

"I know it's not Benedict Welch. The press calls you the Butcher, but I'm going to find out what your real name is."

He looked scared, which gratified her greatly. Hell, he was the one who'd taken this personal, so shoot her if she enjoyed seeing him squirm. Melanie nodded at Julian, who shoved Welch from behind toward the police cruiser that had pulled up beside them, its door yawning open to receive the prisoner.

FORTY THREE

The man who went by the name Benedict Welch was now in the MCC facing serious narcotics charges. But methamphetamine distribution was nothing compared to the heinous crime Melanie was convinced he'd committed. She planned to nail him for real, to prove he was the Central Park Butcher, to lock him in a dark place until the end of his days. And she planned to do it by tomorrow morning. She had to: that's when the Butcher's bail hearing was set for. She refused to let this man hit the street.

The evidence was already strong enough that Melanie managed to get search warrants for Welch's home and office out of Magistrate Judge Helen Boutros with little difficulty—and over the phone on a Sunday, no less. Trailed by Deputy U.S. Marshal Peter Terrozzi—who refused to leave her side no matter how much she begged him to or how loudly she reassured him that the Butcher was already in custody—Melanie went to Welch's office. She'd left several messages for Dan O'Reilly asking him to meet her there to conduct the search.

But neither one of the agents who awaited her on the chintz chairs of the reception area was Dan. They stood up in unison, virtual carbon copies of each other, young and brawny and squeaky-clean with short brown hair, part of the constant stream of new recruits flowing into the Bureau since 9/11.

The slightly taller, slightly older-looking one spoke first.

"Ma'am, Agent Ryan Waterman from the Bureau. My partner, Agent Brandon Mills. My supervisor informs me you need agents to execute a couple of search warrants."

"Are you guys assigned to this case?" Meaning, *Who the hell are you?*

"As of now we are."

"Where's Agent O'Reilly?"

"Ma'am, following up another lead and unavailable to work this search."

Was Dan avoiding her? But he'd left her a couple of voice mails since last night asking her to call, so he obviously wanted to talk to her. She hadn't returned either of them.

"What about Agent Crockett, or any of the agents who attended the meeting yesterday?"

"It's Sunday, ma'am, and we're new. Low men on the totem pole."

"Do either of you know anything about the Butcher case?"

"No, ma'am, but we are warm bodies with two eyes and two hands. We can execute a search warrant."

"Have you done searches before?"

"Numerous mock searches at Quantico," Agent Waterman said.

"I assisted a real search two weeks ago," Agent Mills added, his chest puffing out.

"Well, it seems I have no choice. I'll take you, but you do everything I say, understood?"

The agents glanced at each other uneasily. They might be newbies, but they'd already managed to pick up the agents' code that made it a point of honor to give prosecutors, especially female ones, a hard time.

"Whatever. Just get in here," she said.

They followed her back to Welch's office with the leather club chairs and big mahogany desk. She reminded them to photograph and diagram the place before they searched it.

"Standard procedure, ma'am," Agent Waterman said, though he'd been standing there the second before looking like he didn't have a clue. The "ma'am" thing was starting to bug her, too. It made her feel old.

"Fine. Just checking," she said.

Melanie fell into one of the cushy leather chairs and took a load off. Her eyes were burning and her head pounding; she could use a few minutes to catch her breath. When the agents were done diagramming and photographing, she gave them a copy of the warrant that listed the items they were allowed to search for. Melanie wasn't supposed to touch anything herself; she was present only as a legal adviser. Judging from appearances, these two needed one.

Both agents pulled on rubber gloves. A long credenza sat beneath the far windows beyond Welch's desk. It was covered with files. Ryan walked over to it and lifted the top one.

"Should I read every page of every file, ma'am?"

"Call me Melanie. No, in fact, if a folder contains medical records, you shouldn't read it at all. Medical records are privileged. But if you find something else, let me know."

Every file on the credenza contained medical records, so the search went quickly. The same was true of every file in the four cabinets lining the adjoining wall. But when the agents got to Welch's desk, things got interesting.

"All three drawers on the right-hand side of the desk are locked," Ryan announced.

Melanie, whose head had been drooping onto her chest in the comfortable depths of the chair, perked up instantly. It was a basic tenet of her profession that the presence of a lock usually indicated something worth hiding. And something worth hiding was generally worth finding.

"The warrant allows you to search locked areas," she said. "Do what you have to do to open the drawers. Obviously, try to keep the property damage to a minimum."

Ryan opened a duffel bag and pulled out a tool case, taking from it a tiny screwdriver. He jimmied the top lock easily. Melanie saw his eyebrows shoot up as he reached in with rubber-encased hands.

Brandon moved in, blocking Melanie's view. "Yes!" he crowed, pumping his fists as if he'd just scored a touchdown.

"What have you got?" Melanie asked.

"Sparkle," Ryan said. "Jenny Crank. Redneck heroin. Hillbilly crack."

"Huh?"

Brandon laughed. "Ryan means methamphetamine. You know how the Eskimos have fifty different words for snow? Well, the Bureau dug up Ryan working narcotics in Milwaukee. Meth's the only drug they got out there in East Blowhole, unless you count sniffing gas. He has a million names for it."

Ryan snorted. "Stop making fun of things you don't understand and grab me a few of them plastic evidence bags and the heat sealer."

Melanie came around the desk and watched as Ryan laid out a hefty haul of glassine envelopes on the fancy leather desk blotter. Each glassine held a small amount of a substance that had the consistency and appearance of sea salt.

"Look how transparent it is," Ryan said lovingly. "This is highly pure and very expensive meth. I counted. We've got fifty-seven doses here, more than half a G-pack. You want me to field-test one before I seal 'em all up for transport?"

"Definitely," Melanie said. "Welch is getting arraigned tomorrow morning. His lawyer is sure to spend the whole bail hearing talking about what a reputable member of the medical community Welch is. I'd love to fire back with the dangerous narcotics he keeps hidden in his office drawer, but I need to confirm this is really meth first."

"No problem. One field test, coming up."

Melanie watched Ryan break the seal on a fresh field-test kit labeled with the chemical name for meth.

Slowly and carefully, he assembled his tools and pipet-ted a tiny amount of crystal from one of the glassines into a test tube. He squirted in a clear solution from a plastic bottle, swirled the mixture around, and set it to stand in a tray.

"This'll take a minute to react," Ryan said.

"I know Welch had a meth habit," Melanie said as they waited. "But this is a lot of drugs. Do you think he was selling as well as using?"

"He was doing both," Ryan said.

"How do you know?"

"I know these drugs are for personal use because there's a pipe in the drawer, see?" Ryan reached in a gloved hand and pulled out a glass pipe with a visible layer of gunk in the bottom.

"It's got obvious residue," he continued, "so we know the pipe was used, if not by him, then presum-ably by someone else in his presence since he kept it locked in his desk. The reason I say the baggies were also meant for sale is that no icehead could smoke this much crank within sell-by date without going belly-up. Drugs go bad just like food. Any discerning junkie is gonna care how many days out of the lab his product is, and he won't pay top dollar for anything older than a week. With shit this pure, I'd say if you're doing two or three bags a day, that's a pretty intense habit. Any more, and you're incapacitated and can't hold down a regular job. More than that, you're dead. So what's here is way too much for one man to use, at least if he wants it fresh."

"I wonder if Welch was selling to patients," Melanie said, her mind racing. "But a really bad personal meth habit. That makes sense, too, you know? I mean, if Welch is the Butcher."

"What do you mean?" Ryan asked.

"The murder we're investigating was very brutal. That's why the press came up with the nickname 'Butcher.' The victim was raped and stabbed so many times that one of her breasts was severed. The killer carved 'bitch' on her stomach with a scalpel. The crime was so ugly that I'd almost have trouble believing Welch committed it, despite how creepy I find him. Unless he was high on meth."

"The Scooby snacks mess with your head big-time," Ryan said, nodding. He picked up the test tube. The liquid inside had turned cobalt blue. "And we have a yes! The substance has field-tested positive for the presence of methamphetamine, and I'm prepared to swear to that in court."

Ryan and Brandon went to work cleaning up the field test, sealing the glassine envelopes and the pipe into clear plastic evidence pouches and filling out the labels.

"This is great evidence for our narcotics charges," Melanie said. "But what I'm really looking for is evidence about the murder. I have the Butcher e-mailing from this office, but I also have three well-known plastic surgeons claiming Welch was with them in a fancy restaurant at the time of the crime. I refuse to believe Welch is innocent. Maybe the doctors are lying or maybe he had an accomplice. Either way, I need a trump card, something powerful enough to give the lie to his alibi."

Ryan picked up the small screwdriver he'd used to jimmy the top lock. "Time to find out what's behind Door Number Two."

Melanie and Brandon watched as Ryan worked the screwdriver and eased open the middle drawer. Simultaneously, they all made noises of disappointment. The drawer appeared to be filled with . . . *trash.*

"Garbage?" Melanie asked.

"Well, now at least we've learned the guy has a serious Milky Way habit," Ryan said, reaching in and pulling out a candy wrapper and tossing it over his shoulder. He pulled the drawer out wholesale and got ready to turn it upside down and dump the contents into the wastebasket next to the desk.

"Wait!" Melanie commanded. "What are you doing? Lay everything out on the desk and go through it carefully."

"Ma'am, I can assure you that habitual methamphetamine users, if they eat at all, eat primarily candy
and ice cream. This is exactly what it looks like—a
bunch of grubby old garbage left over from his binges,
with junkie cooties on every last piece."

"Agent, when you're on the stand getting cross-
examined by defense counsel about the manner in
which you conducted this search, do you plan to testify
that you picked up a pile of potentially valuable evidence
and threw it in the trash without looking at it because
you were afraid of a few junkie cooties?" she asked.

Ryan stopped what he was doing and gazed at her.
"No, ma'am."

"Then inspect each item, please. You're wearing
rubber gloves, anyway."

"Yes, ma'am."

Ryan dumped the pile of trash out onto on the desk
blotter. As Brandon began picking carefully through
candy wrappers and crumpled Cheetos bags, examining each one, Ryan bent down to replace the drawer.
He stopped in midflight.

"What? Do you see something?" Melanie asked.

Ryan fitted the drawer back in place, then reached
in and removed a plastic baggie that had been Scotch-
taped way at the back. The baggie had been invisible
under all the trash.

"Okay, you were right," Ryan said, grinning at Melanie sheepishly. "But I have a good excuse. This is way more finesse than you'd ever see from a crankhead in Milwaukee. They're all too wrecked to think about hiding evidence."

"Life in the big city. Even the junkies outclass Ryan," Brandon said.

"Blow me, Mills," Ryan said.

"Yo, keep it polite, dude. Ladies present."

"Let me see that." Melanie held out her hand, her voice husky with excitement. She took the baggie and raised it up to the light. The small white rectangle inside was crusted with dried blood, but not so much that Melanie couldn't make out Suzanne Shepard's smiling face in the lower left-hand corner.

"What is it?" Ryan asked.

"The victim's driver's license. It was taken from her wallet by the Butcher as a sort of grisly souvenir. Gentlemen, everybody who said three respectable doctors would never lie was mistaken. We've discovered evidence proving that Benedict Welch murdered Suzanne Shepard. He *is* the Central Park Butcher."

FORTY FOUR

But when Melanie called Mark Sonschein to crow about her new evidence, he delivered some deflating news. Mark and Dan O'Reilly had been at the hospital showing photographs to David Harris, and they'd showed him the mug shot of Benedict Welch taken earlier that day.

"Please," Melanie said, squeezing her eyes shut, "don't tell me Harris clears Welch. I have such powerful evidence on the guy now. I can't go back to square one, I just can't."

"Harris doesn't actually *clear* him," Mark said. "What he says is less definitive than that. You see, Harris never got a good look at the Butcher's face. During the Suzanne Shepard murder, the Butcher wore night-vision goggles. And when Harris was kidnapped, the Butcher was sitting in the front seat of a limo with a tinted-glass barrier between them."

"So what's the problem, then?" Melanie demanded.

"He says the hair is wrong."

"The hair? Give me a freaking break."

"Look, I know you want this to be over, but we take the evidence as we find it, Melanie. That's what we do."

She sighed. "What *about* the hair?"

"Welch has this longish, very yellow hair. It's obviously dyed, right? Harris says the Butcher was blond, also. But he was staring at the back of his head on the whole limo ride, and he's very clear that the Butcher has close-cropped, naturally dark blond hair. Virtually a crew cut. And a big, thick neck. Welch is tall but he's not robust. The descriptions don't match."

"We're talking about a witness who only saw the Butcher from behind! And through tinted glass. That's meaningless."

"Would you be arguing that if Harris thought Welch *did* look like the Butcher?" Mark asked.

"Easy for you to say. He's not after you," Melanie muttered.

"I'm very cognizant of the threat to you, Melanie. That's what makes me want to be sure that we've got the right man. I'm not saying Harris's information is definitive, or that we should cut Welch loose. But I think it raises serious questions."

"There's a simple way to settle this," Melanie said, "and if I hadn't been so busy with these search warrants, I would have seen to it by now. We need to have Welch's DNA tested."

The problem was, the only way Melanie knew to get FBI technicians to show up when and where she needed them was to have Dan O'Reilly place the call. Dan was third-generation New York City law enforcement, a local boy. In New York, where circles were smaller than outsiders could possibly imagine, being from a family on the job counted for a huge amount. Cops had their own churches, their own rec leagues and Catholic schools—hell, their own entire suburbs. Dan was savvier than his true-blue, no-nonsense persona would suggest; and when it came to using his connections and pulling strings, he had no rival.

But if she'd wanted to talk to him, she would have returned his phone calls.

"Mark, is Dan O'Reilly still with you?" she asked.

"No, he went back to his office."

"You should call him and have him get the technicians over to the MCC to swab Welch's cheek."

"You do that. I've got a conference call in five minutes on another matter, and then I've got to get to my mother-in-law's house for supper. If I'm late—well, let's just say it won't be pretty."

What could she do? Mark outranked her. Besides, she couldn't very well tell him that she wasn't speaking to her case agent because they'd had a lovers' quarrel. How would that play in the front office when promotions got decided?

"Okay," she said, and hung up.

Melanie was standing with her thumb poised over her cell phone, having trouble making herself dial Dan's number, when Deputy Marshal Pete Terrozzi poked his head into Welch's office.

"Ready to go?" he asked. "I saw those two FBI agents hauling evidence out to the car. I got worried about you alone in here."

"I'm fine. We're supposed to meet up with them at Welch's apartment to execute the next warrant, but I need to make a phone call first."

"No sweat," Terrozzi said, and plopped into one of the leather club chairs.

"I need privacy," Melanie said.

"I have a security clearance, you know," he said, sounding miffed.

"Of course. I trust you completely, Pete. It's just— well, you wouldn't want to be called in to testify just because you'd overheard something about my investigation, would you? You could end up waiting around for hours."

"Okay, good point. I'll hang tight in the waiting room for a little bit." And he left, closing the door behind him.

Somehow the threat of Pete Terrozzi coming back in, which he surely would do sooner or later, forced Melanie's hand. She found herself dialing, and then holding her breath as Dan's cell phone rang. He picked up on the first ring.

"Hey!"

The eagerness in Dan's voice made Melanie wish desperately that last night had never happened. If only she could trust him without reservations, love him without doubts, like she had yesterday. She couldn't bear to think those feelings were gone.

"Hey," she replied, feeling battered, her voice flat.

"I'm so glad you called. I was getting worried that you'd never talk to me again." He laughed nervously.

"I'm calling about the case. I need you to do something."

"Oh." She could hear his voice tighten up.

"Here's what I need."

"Melanie," he broke out, "can't we make this up? All that happened was Diane calling to tell me her father died."

"That's hardly the only thing that happened! Either you're being deliberately obtuse or you really don't get it, and I'm not sure which is worse."

"Enough with the below-the-belt comments there," he said.

"I'm not upset because Diane called to say her father died. You were seeing her without telling me! Maybe you've forgotten. My father abandoned me when he left my mother for another woman. My husband cheated on me when I was pregnant. Do you have any idea what alarm bells your behavior sets off, with my history? So take the consequences. Tell me the whole truth. Apologize. Tell me how you're going to fix this. Don't act like *I'm* the one hurting *you.*"

"You *are* hurting me. I know all about your husband cheating, okay? I know about your father, too. I was there in Puerto Rico when you went to see him. I saw your face when you came out of that house. We've both had our heartaches, but that's got jack to do with you and me. I've treated you right, yet I get no credit. You're suspicious over nothing."

"Seeing your ex-wife behind my back is not nothing," she said.

"Behind your back? That's bullshit, Melanie. It's two days since I first saw Diane. Days where you and

I were crazy busy and never alone for a second. I didn't have a chance to tell you."

"You were too busy to tell me you were seeing your ex-wife?" Melanie asked incredulously. "That's baloney."

"If you think I'd go back to Diane after how she treated me, you don't know the first thing about me," he insisted.

Of course, deep down, that was what Melanie feared most. She knew his past had great power over him. But she wouldn't let herself utter that terrible thought aloud.

"We can't talk about this now," she said instead. "There's too much going on, and this conversation is making me too upset."

But he wouldn't let go. "You think I've been calling up Diane crying in my beer over old times? Is that what you think?"

"We should just let this drop, Dan," she said.

"I barely even talked to her. The dinner lasted thirty minutes tops, and it was all about her old man. Seriously. I had a burger and she had a tuna-fish sandwich. Melanie, please, there's no reason to flip out."

"If this is such a nothing thing, why is her number in your phone? How many times did you talk to her?"

"Not a lot."

"How many?"

"What am I, Mark Fuhrman on the stand with the bloody glove now? I don't like being cross-examined. Either you trust me or you don't."

"How can I possibly trust you after what happened? And when you won't answer a direct question? Do you think I'm a fool? When you put somebody's number in your phone, it means you talk to them a lot. Everybody knows that, and now you just proved it to me."

"I got a ton of stuff in my phone. Some snitch who called me three weeks ago with a bogus tip. The pizza place on the corner. Diane's number's in there, too, but it doesn't *mean* anything. There is nothing going on between us. End of story."

"This is a woman you've been in love with since childhood who broke your heart. I'm supposed to believe she's the equivalent of a pizza place?"

"You've been in this job too long. You've lost the ability to trust. That makes me sad."

"It's what you did that's sad. Even with my history, I managed to put my faith in you. And what did you do? You withheld information from me that you had every reason to believe I would want to know. I don't trust you anymore, and I don't know if I ever will, and it's your own fault."

Dan fell silent. Melanie's heart was pounding after her speech. She wanted to hang up on him. She wished she weren't in the middle of an investigation. She would go somewhere dark and quiet and cry really hard, then go to sleep for a long, long time.

"I got to confess, I'm surprised," Dan was saying. "I'm surprised this made such a big impact. It was really nothing. But I'm starting to see how upset you are over it. I'm finally getting that through my thick skull."

She said nothing.

"What do you want me to do?" Dan asked. "I have to see her, at least for a while, around this funeral stuff. Do you want me to tell you when I see Diane, like you do when you see your husband?"

"He's my ex-husband."

"Your ex?"

"That would be nice," she said bitterly. *It would have nice to begin with!*

"I'm not used to having somebody looking over my shoulder. But maybe I could, if that would make you feel better."

She didn't answer. They fell silent. Melanie closed her eyes and felt them stinging. She knew if she backed down now, and told him she was sorry for making such a fuss, and said please, please, indulge my insecurity, they could patch things up. That's what Dan wanted, but she couldn't give it to him. Not now. Not without more of an apology. She was like a crab that had been poked with a stick—closed up tight within her shell, unable to open herself to him. If she held back, she risked pushing him into his ex-wife's arms. So be it. If Dan went back to Diane, then it was meant to be.

"As I stand here, I'm not sure what would make me feel better, but certainly not the half-assed response I'm getting from you," Melanie said in a dead tone.

"Ah, crap, I don't know then," Dan said.

Melanie heard silence on her phone. She looked at the screen. It said CALL ENDED. He'd hung up. She felt like hurling the phone against the wall. Instead, she remembered her responsibilities—to her job, to her life—and forced herself to hit redial. Listening to the rings, she felt strange, like time had stopped, like she was watching herself from a distance.

"What?" Dan snapped.

Melanie took a deep breath and focused on the here and now. "I need you to arrange a DNA test for Benedict Welch."

FORTY FIVE

Benedict Welch's apartment was situated in a premier Fifth Avenue building and boasted treetop views of Central Park from every window. The living room was brimming with sofas and wing chairs and ottomans and benches, all pricey-looking, all done in shades of white that contrasted dramatically with the enormous black grand piano. The overall effect was beautiful and luxurious, if cold. It certainly didn't look like the lair of a psychotic killer, but Melanie told herself not to be taken in by appearances. People were so twisted these days. Once the rich and the powerful were done amassing their material wealth, they sometimes found themselves bored, with time on their hands, looking for the next thrill. If Welch had turned to darker pastimes to keep himself amused, would that really be so shocking? She'd seen it before.

By the time Melanie reached the apartment, the agents were nearly done searching, and Welch's wife, Gloria, was splayed out on a Biedermeier settee staring into the far distance with the eyes of a woman on heavy meds. She didn't fit the stereotype of a killer's wife, if there was such a thing, and yet she wasn't wrong for the part, either. She wore a bloodred dinner suit that made a gash against the white upholstery and petted a tiny Chihuahua as serenely as if she'd be heading out any minute to her regular table at Le Bernardin. Melanie envied Mrs. Welch her pharmaceutical calm. She could've used a sedative herself right then, but unfortunately she needed full command of her faculties to make sense of what Agents Waterman and Mills had discovered in the apartment. They'd struck pay dirt in the form of Suzanne Shepard's investigative file—the one Miles Ortiz had lifted from Suzanne's apartment at Welch's behest. Welch had kept it. Melanie was so anxious to get her hands on the contents that she couldn't wait for the agents to make copies. She snapped on rubber gloves, sat down at a lacquered table beneath a curving Art Nouveau chandelier, and dug in, determined to find some connection to the man of the house, whom she had locked up in the MCC.

The manila folder was marked with Benedict Welch's name in Suzanne Shepard's handwriting. Melanie opened it with a racing heart. Inside, she found copies of the newspaper articles Miles had described in his proffer session.

Thirteen years earlier, in Los Angeles, a man named Edward Allen Harvey had been convicted of the murder of a woman named Cheryl Driscoll and sentenced to fifteen to life. Cheryl had been twenty-four when she died, a wannabe actress earning her living on the seedy fringes of the sex industry, dancing at a strip club called Playground and landing the occasional part in a porno film. The microfilmed copy of the black-and-white newspaper reprint of Cheryl's high-school-yearbook photo from South Bend, Indiana, was grainy and blurred but still conveyed her megawatt smile and beautiful wide-set eyes.

Cheryl had been missing for three days, Melanie read, when her body was discovered rolled up in a blanket in a remote state park north of Los Angeles. She'd been raped and slashed to death. The *L.A. Times* said that the autopsy confirmed seventeen separate stab wounds on her face, chest, neck, and arms. But her stomach was oddly untouched, except for the word SLUT cut into her flesh with a carving knife.

Melanie read that, and the bright white room faded momentarily to black. This old murder had to have been committed by the Butcher himself.

When her vision cleared, Melanie pulled herself together and continued reading. Scandalmonger or no, Suzanne Shepard had been one kick-ass investigative reporter, and she'd assembled a thick file on the Driscoll homicide. Melanie pored over articles on the pretrial hearings that spelled out the course of the investigation in detail. The homicide detectives' path to the convicted man, Edward Allen Harvey, had been a straight shot. The murder weapon was a ten-inch-long butcher knife with an acrylic handle found lying in a gully twenty feet from the victim's corpse, and it had fingerprints on it. The fingerprints matched ones already on file for Harvey, who had a rap sheet for other sex crimes. Homicide detectives showed Harvey's mug shot around at Playground and established that he was a regular customer, one who'd had a few run-ins with the bouncers for getting rough with the girls. Melanie paged through the file in vain looking for a picture of Harvey. Every paper that had run a photograph had gone with the gorgeous young victim instead, who naturally would have sold more copies at the newsstand.

Melanie found an article describing Harvey's arrest. He'd been working as a handyman for a company that managed a bunch of motellike apartment buildings in the San Fernando Valley. Homicide detectives had located him at work with no difficulty, which gave Melanie pause. Three days after a murder, and Harvey was going about his business? In Melanie's experience of killers, that wasn't normal behavior. Men who committed heinous crimes had the sense to run, or at least to hide. They made more of an effort to cover their tracks than Harvey had, anyway. Either Harvey was a complete psychopath, accustomed to killing and getting away with it, skilled at hiding in plain sight like BTK and others of that ilk. Or else he was innocent—which of course was what he'd claimed. Melanie skimmed through a number of articles in which Harvey's lawyer loudly trumpeted his innocence, promising an acquittal at trial. Buried at the bottom of one of them, she finally found the connection to Benedict Welch that she'd been looking for all along.

In her rush, she'd almost skipped right over it. The page trembling in her eager fingers, Melanie read about the alternative suspect whom Harvey's lawyer had offered up to the media. The lawyer claimed that the real killer was a second-rate plastic surgeon named Howard Vine. Harvey had met Vine at Playground, where they both hung out and ogled the girls. According to Harvey, Vine had bragged to him repeatedly about having sex with patients while they were under, and had let it slip that Cheryl Driscoll was a patient of his, one for whom he had sinister plans.

The investigative reporter covering the Driscoll case had followed up on the lawyer's claims and actually found evidence to back them up. There had indeed been a plastic surgeon named Howard Vine who had been practicing out of an office in a small strip mall, performing cosmetic procedures on young actresses and models who couldn't afford anyone better. At the time of the Driscoll murder, Vine's medical license was in the process of being revoked because of patient complaints combined with certain irregularities in his licensing application. Even more critical, it turned out that Cheryl Driscoll had indeed been a patient of Vine's, that she'd been reported missing the day after she was scheduled for a mole removal in Vine's office, and that Vine himself had skipped town shortly after her body was found.

Melanie had years' worth of practice listening to bogus claims of innocence. A large percentage of the guys she'd put away—even those who'd pleaded guilty—filed appeals and habeas corpus petitions trying to divert suspicion onto somebody other than themselves. And they were usually careful to pick straw men who were dead or beyond the reach of due process, since things got complicated if your "true killer" showed up in court to defend himself. The fact that the mysterious Howard Vine was in the wind gave him every appearance of being a figment of Edward Allen Harvey's imagination. Yet, despite her ingrained skepticism, Melanie thought the whole scenario had the ring of truth—or at least plausibility—about it.

But the jury hadn't agreed. They'd had trouble with the fact that Edward Allen Harvey's fingerprints were on the bloody knife. Okay, Melanie had to admit she had a little trouble with that herself. They deliberated for twenty-six minutes before returning a guilty verdict.

"Ma'am?"

Agent Ryan Waterman was standing over her with furrowed eyebrows.

"What is it?"

"It's pretty late. We've been done with the search for a while now. I was hoping to place that file into an evidence bag and get going."

She didn't want to give it to him. But he was only doing his job, ensuring a proper chain of custody.

"If you want it back, I need copies," she said.

"I can do that for you once we get back to headquarters. I have no way to make copies here."

"All right. Give me a minute to make some notes."

Melanie drew her notebook from her bag and reflected on what she'd just learned. Benedict Welch had ordered Miles Ortiz to steal a file from Suzanne Shepard's apartment. Shortly thereafter, Suzanne Shepard had been brutally murdered. The file turned out to contain articles about a murder with an MO virtually identical to the Shepard murder committed over a decade earlier. In the earlier murder, a phony plastic surgeon had been implicated and had escaped justice. What did it all mean?

As if she didn't have enough on her plate. There was really only one way to get to the bottom of this mess, and that was to haul her butt out to California, track down Edward Allen Harvey in prison, and hear what he had to say.

FORTY SIX

A trip to California to interview Harvey was simply not possible at the moment. Monday morning dawned with the threat of rain and the promise of the Welch bail hearing, to be held before Melanie's least favorite judge. The Honorable Wilton Warner had the distinction of bouncing more good arrests on more inane technicalities than any other judge in the district. Melanie hated appearing before him on an average case. The thought of Warner holding Welch's fate in his hands—and by extension, Melanie's own—positively appalled her.

Terrozzi dropped her off early at the office so she could prepare. Melanie had passed a restless night, partly because she missed Maya, who was staying with Melanie's mom until further notice. Partly because Deputy Peter Terrozzi was sleeping on the living-room sofa—in his boxers, no less, which gave Melanie the heebie-jeebies. And partly because she was preoccupied with all the big, pressing questions in her life. But she'd risen with new steel in her backbone. She had no choice but to prevail and keep Welch locked up. Her own safety depended upon it. As to everything else—her career, Dan—well, she'd just have to look her problems in eye and overcome them.

As step one in her new regime, she left a message for Dan.

"Hey, it's Melanie," she said after the tone sounded. "This fight is weighing on me. I want to talk. I've been thinking that maybe I have some . . . trust issues. Maybe that explains why I reacted so strongly to you having dinner with Diane. I don't know if I can get past them or not, but I want to try. The Welch bail hearing is scheduled for nine and I'm not sure how long I'll be in court. But call me."

She paused, worrying that her words might not have sounded encouraging enough, or worse, might've come too late. Had he given up on her already? But she wasn't one for leaving mushy messages, or desperate ones. She depressed the button with her fingertip, disconnecting the call, and sat there feeling paralyzed, like she couldn't move on with her day. Luckily, the phone rang and jolted her back to life.

"Melanie Vargas."

"Hey, it's Pauline."

The caller ID indicated that Pauline was standing at the guard station near the elevator. "You're here?"

"You bet, baby doll. I brought you some kick-ass shit on your boy Benedict Welch just in time for the bail hearing. You're gonna wild out when you see it. Come get me. The guard's not here yet."

"Be right out."

Melanie opened the bulletproof door to find Pauline balancing a cardboard Starbucks tray precariously on top of a stack of files. Over skintight jeans, Pauline wore red cowboy boots.

"Welcome home!" Melanie said, grinning.

"I got you a latte and a banana muffin," Pauline said, gesturing toward the tray with her chin.

"Oh my God, I love you! Here, let me help."

Melanie took the tray and let Pauline slip by her through the door. A few minutes later, they were settled in Melanie's office wading through articles and photographs from a quarter century earlier.

"You were right on the money when you told me to investigate the real Benedict Welch," Pauline said. "I call him 'Dead Welch.' Like you said, Welch here in

New York didn't just pick this identity out of a hat. A doctor who died in Tulsa, Oklahoma, eleven years ago? He picked it for a reason."

"He had to have known him somehow," Melanie said.

"Exactly."

Pauline handed Melanie a group photo that, based on clothing and hairstyles, looked vintage late seventies, early eighties. It showed a bunch of boys of varying ages standing in rows as if for a class photo, with several sober-looking middle-aged men seated on chairs down in the front.

"This is a photo from the Marietta Welch Youth Residence taken the final year of its existence, which was 1981," Pauline explained. "The man in the front row with the blond hair and glasses is the real Benedict Welch, whose identity our suspect stole. The home was founded by Dead Welch's grandmother about fifty years earlier, and any search you do of the Welch name in Tulsa immediately brings up information about the home. Just so you understand what type of place we're talking about, it used to be called the Marietta Welch Home for Wayward Boys until they saw the light of political correctness and sanitized it."

"You said this picture is from the last year the home existed?" Melanie asked.

"Yes! The place burned to the ground about six months after this was taken. Arson. It was a huge scandal in Tulsa at the time. Four boys died, along with a psychiatrist named Howard Vine who was the director-in-residence. They said the—"

"*What?*"

"What?"

"The director's name was Howard Vine?"

"Yeah, so?"

"Pauline, Howard Vine was the name of a plastic surgeon in L.A. who skipped town after the murder of a stripper who had the word 'slut' carved into her stomach."

Pauline blinked. "Hit me with that again?"

"It's complicated, but the point is, Benedict Welch wasn't the first doctor from this boys' home whose identity our suspect stole, and I don't think Suzanne Shepard was the first woman he murdered, either. I have copies of all the paperwork from that old case. You should look at it."

Melanie's heart was racing with excitement. She held the group picture up so the morning light streaming through her window would fall directly on it.

"Our Benedict Welch has got to be in here, don't you think?" she asked urgently, scanning the rows of boys.

"Check out Mophead, middle row, third from the left. He looks promising to me."

Melanie squinted. "That's him! Younger and with dark hair, but it's him."

"You knew that yellow hair was fake, didn't you? That kid's name is Cory Nash, and he's one of the ones who disappeared."

"Disappeared?"

"Yeah. I didn't get a chance to finish the story. So the bodies of Howard Vine and four of the boys were discovered after the fire, right?"

"But not Benedict—I mean, not Dead Welch?"

"No. The real Benedict Welch survived the fire. He died years later in a car accident. Anyway, the bodies were burned to a crisp, but the ME still had the bones to work with, and listen to this. One of the boys' bodies was missing limbs. One of his arms and part of a leg were chopped off. Guess where they were found?"

"Where?"

"In the basement, inside a metal trash can. And the rest of the body had scoring on the bones like from a cutting implement."

"He was stabbed to death and dismembered," Melanie said.

"Exactly. Well, more like somebody started dismembering him but gave up because it's, you know, a shitload of work. I've had guys tell me sawing through all those muscles and tendons is not easy."

"So the killer got too impatient to dispose of the remains that way, and he set the place on fire instead."

Pauline nodded. "That's what the cops thought, that the killer burned the building down to cover up the murder."

"But he was never caught?" Melanie asked.

"No. I was getting to that part. Remember now, these kids were no Eagle Scouts. They were a bunch of delinquents, in fact. When the dust settled, eight of them who should've been present and accounted for were plain gone, never to be heard from again, and the cops believed the killer was among them."

"They ran away?"

Pauline shrugged. "Probably. Or met with foul play and the cops never found out. Who knows."

"Cory Nash was among the missing?"

"Yes," Pauline said.

"And he stayed that way, until we just found him masquerading as a doctor for the second time. Pauline, now that we've got him locked up, we need to make all three murder charges stick. Suzanne Shepard and Cheryl Driscoll and the boy he cut up and put in the trash. We have to close out those cases. Please, tell me you have background on Cory Nash. Fingerprints? A rap sheet?"

"No, sweetie, I'm sorry. I couldn't get any of that stuff. All the records were lost when the place burned down."

"Ugh. How am I going to prove all this to the judge?"

Melanie's phone rang. "Hold on. Don't go anywhere," she said, grabbing it. "Melanie Vargas."

"Melanie? Julian Hay. I'm here at the courthouse. We got a problem."

"What is it?"

"Welch is going through some kind of psychosis caused by meth withdrawal. He just tried to kill himself. Judge wants you in court. *Now.*"

FORTY SEVEN

The second Melanie walked into the ceremonial courtroom, she heard a sound like the wailing of a cat coming from the direction of the holding cell out back. But the screams were not by any means the most frightening thing in the room. Magistrate Judge Wilton Warner had taken the bench. On a good day, Judge Warner made Melanie quake in her high heels. And today wasn't a good day.

"Ah, Miss Vargas, so kind of you to join us," he cried sarcastically, his voice cutting like a knife across the football-field-size courtroom. Then he leaned forward until the light bouncing off his half-glasses made him look like some vacant-eyed madman. *"Get up here this minute."*

Melanie strode down the center aisle, her cheeks burning with indignation. She knew what was coming.

Warner routinely took the view that all problems with cases were the result of intentional wrongdoing by the prosecution. One of these days, she feared, she would lose her temper and give it back to him good, which of course would only result in heavy sanctions against her and possible disbarment.

She banged through the low wooden gate that bounded the spectator gallery and took her place at the government's podium. Her shoulders were square and her eyes determined. Out of nowhere, Mark Sonschein and Detective Julian Hay materialized to stand beside her. She glanced at them gratefully.

"Steady as she goes," Mark whispered.

"I'm cool," she said softly.

But Warner hadn't gotten started yet.

"Miss Vargas, I am holding you personally responsible for the fact that a man is bleeding in my bull pen. What kind of slack, shiftless custody are you maintaining over these prisoners that allows them to get hold of razors and try to kill themselves?"

Melanie had zero to do with housing or transporting prisoners, and Judge Warner knew that.

"Your Honor, the government just learned of this situation, as did the court, and we are shocked and dismayed," she said, her voice firm and her shoulders unbowed. Which, of course, only annoyed him more.

"*Don't . . . give . . . me . . . that . . . nonsense!* Are you claiming you didn't know this prisoner had a drug problem?" Warner shouted, his face bright red.

All the things she wished she could say came pouring into Melanie's head with such force that she worried they would spill out of her mouth. Who has a substance-abuse problem in this courtroom, red face? When they say "sober as a judge," they don't mean you! Luckily, Julian kept her grounded.

"I told the guards at MCC last night he had dependency," he said to Melanie under his breath.

"Your Honor, the Bureau of Prisons was made aware of the defendant's drug use. Many defendants have drug problems—"

"And meth usually ain't this bad," Julian whispered.

"—and I'm informed that methamphetamine withdrawal is not normally expected to lead to such severe—"

"No excuses!" the judge shouted. "I don't care what you knew or what you thought. You obviously didn't do anything! And you call yourselves public servants. If it were up to me, I'd fire every last one of you. Now either you fix this situation immediately, or I'm ordering this prisoner released without a hearing."

"Judge, you can't do that! He's potentially responsible for three homicides—"

"I can do whatever I damn well please."

"Judge, we respectfully request—"

"If you want him remanded, Miss Vargas, you get back in that bull pen and fix this problem. Now! Do I make myself clear?"

Her eyes went wide. "Yes, Judge."

Did he expect her to save Welch's life? Melanie wasn't squeamish, but neither did she have any medical expertise. She gave Mark a baffled look.

"I'm coming with you," he said, and turned to follow her. Judge Warner didn't stop him.

"What does he think *I* can do?" Melanie whispered.

"He's just grandstanding."

The "bull pen" was the holding cell adjacent to the courtroom where incarcerated prisoners awaited their court appearances. Melanie had rarely been inside one. She knew them primarily by sound: the clanging doors that meant a prisoner had been brought up in the secure elevator, the flushing toilet that meant he was ready to come out and face the music. What unnerved her now was not the sight of the bull pen, but the sight of Benedict Welch—or Cory Nash, as she now knew him to be—writhing on the floor, whimpering and sweating, his yellow hair matted and his blue prison jumpsuit stained with several coin-size droplets of blood. Suddenly he let out an inhuman howl, a sound so terrible that Melanie shrank back, fearing that he'd been mortally wounded. She didn't want him to die. At least, not before she convicted him at trial.

The cell door was wide open, and a number of uniformed men crowded around the prone figure. To Melanie's great relief, she saw that at least two of them were EMTs, not guards. She angled her way in and grabbed the arm of the nearest EMT, an enormously tall guy with red hair in a ponytail, who was holding a roll of bandages and watching his colleague attend to Welch.

"I'm the prosecutor. Will he make it?" she asked.

"Oh yeah, sure. This ain't nothin'. Shallow cuts on both wrists. Didn't go deep enough to even nick a vein."

"Does he need to go to the hospital?"

"Not for his hands. Carlos is taping the cuts now. He'll be fine to do his court appearance—physically, I mean. Only thing is, with meth withdrawal cases, we normally take 'em over to Bellevue for a psych eval, unless you'd prefer to have the prison shrink do that."

"I have to ask the judge what he wants to do. Do you know how the prisoner got the knife?"

"Oh, it wasn't a knife. It was just a little bitty nail he picked up off the street when he pretended to trip while being transported. He hid it in his shoe. Hold on, I'll show you."

He passed her a plastic bag containing a small nail encrusted with both rust and blood. "Small" was too generous a word—it was minuscule.

"Suicide by tetanus is about all that'll do for you. He knew it, too," the EMT said.

"So you don't believe this was a serious attempt?" she asked.

"He's a drama queen. We see a lot of this when people get arrested. He wants a bed in a nice rehab program instead of at Otisville."

"Not gonna happen if I have anything to say about it," Melanie said.

Several of the guards helped Welch to his feet. He caught sight of Melanie. His eyes without his contact lenses in were dark brown instead of violet, with a crazy glint that hadn't been there yesterday. He looked . . . unhinged. The transformation from suave Upper East Side society doctor to strung-out junkie was startling.

"Are you happy, you bitch? Is this what you wanted?" Welch cried.

Two guards instantly grabbed him by the arms. He screwed up his lips and sent a gob of spit hurling in Melanie's direction. It splattered on the floor a foot short of her. Mark Sonschein grabbed her arm and pulled her forcibly from the bull pen as the guards wrestled Welch to a sitting position on the floor.

"You think we can arraign him like this?" she asked Mark. Melanie was shaking but her voice was steady. She was damned if this lowlife would make her flinch.

One of the EMTs was now administering a sedative.

"Frankly," Mark said, "I think you ought to go out there and ask to have the prisoner sent to Bellevue for evaluation. At least then he'll be on a locked ward. With Warner on the bench, you never know, he might release the guy otherwise. Especially given the Brady material."

Melanie looked at Mark sharply. Brady material was exculpatory evidence that prosecutors were required to hand over to the defense prior to court proceedings.

"*What* Brady material?" she asked suspiciously.

Mark gaped at her. "You know."

"No. I don't."

"The fact that your one eyewitness states that your suspect doesn't look like the killer. And you don't have DNA results back yet, so there's nothing to contradict that."

"Nothing except the victim's missing driver's license in his desk!" Melanie exclaimed.

"I agree that's good evidence. But you know Warner. He'll want Welch's fingerprints on it before it's worth anything to him."

"The killer wore gloves."

"Nothing we can do about that. We're still required to disclose Harris's failure to identify Welch from the photograph."

"Mark, what kind of stickler are you? Harris only saw the Butcher from behind."

"What kind of aggressive hothead are you?"

"One with a psychotic killer stalking her. If you tell Warner that, we'll lose. He'll cut Welch loose."

"That's exactly what makes it Brady material. Maybe you should recuse yourself from prosecuting this case, Melanie. Because I know my ethical obligations, and if you don't disclose this information, I will."

"Ahem."

Melanie and Mark both whirled. Judge Warner's deputy clerk, Gabriel Colón, who was a good courthouse buddy of Melanie's, stood in the doorway, having cleared his throat theatrically to get their attention. Or to get them to stop blabbing their secrets in front of him.

"Defense counsel just showed up," Gabriel said. "Judge wants you front and center."

"Thanks, Gabe," Melanie said.

As she passed by him on her way back to the courtroom, Gabriel winked at her. "My lips are sealed, *mami*," he whispered.

The fact was, it was very important to Melanie to be an ethical prosecutor. She honestly thought Mark Sonschein was being overly legalistic in his interpretation of the evidence. Surely, if a witness hadn't gotten a good look at a suspect, his failure to recognize him in a photograph was not exculpatory Brady material. If she'd had time to do legal research, Melanie was confident she could have found dozens of cases supporting her view. But she didn't have time.

She waited in front of the bench. All the stars had lined up against Melanie this morning, because Donald Kerr, the prominent and respected defense attorney representing Welch, was good friends with Judge Warner. Melanie stood in silence while the judge and the defense lawyer gossiped about some charitable board they served on together.

After a few minutes, Welch was brought out from the bull pen. The sedative had been quick acting. He looked meek and glazed and pathetic in his blood-stained prison blues. Welch's wife, Gloria, sat in the front row of the spectator benches clad in a demure black suit. Mrs. Welch gasped when she saw him, and began weeping copiously and loudly.

Gabriel Colón called the case, and the judge began by demanding a report on the defendant's suicide attempt.

Melanie repeated exactly what the EMS technician had told her about the self-inflicted and minor nature of the injury. When Judge Warner wasn't satisfied, Melanie got the tall, red-haired guy to come out and testify about it in person. Any other judge would have recognized the suicide attempt as the blatant ploy it was, but with Warner, it was an error on the prosecution's part, and it put Melanie on the defensive. Donald Kerr saw that and exploited it for everything it was worth.

"Your Honor, Mrs. Welch is seated in the front row," Kerr said in his impressive baritone. "She is distraught at her husband's condition, as you can imagine. She has called in the best professionals in the field to address this extremely regrettable case of a man of medicine falling victim to addiction. We see it more and more. The stresses of the medical profession—"

Melanie just couldn't stomach that pretentious garbage given what she knew about the defendant.

"Your Honor, this man isn't even a doctor, and his name isn't Benedict Welch," she interrupted.

All hell broke loose. Melanie did her best to present the evidence concerning Welch's false identity, but somehow she just ended up getting accused of sandbagging the defense by not disclosing her argument ahead of time. She trotted out Detective Hay to testify about the methamphetamine bust, and Donald Kerr

turned that into a case of a hardened drug dealer—
Miles Ortiz—entrapping a reputable man by taking
advantage of his substance-abuse problem. Finally,
Melanie pulled out her ace in the hole: the very real
possibility, the likelihood even, that Welch was the
killer that the press was calling the Butcher. The
bloody driver's license found in Welch's desk. The
e-mail sent from his office. The fact that he'd ordered
the burglary of Suzanne Shepard's apartment. But
standing up before the judge, with the deputy chief of
the Criminal Division looking over her shoulder and a
court reporter taking down her every word, Melanie
couldn't allow herself to put her own safety before her
sworn duty. She disclosed David Harris's statement
that, from behind, Welch didn't resemble the man
who'd kidnapped him.

And she lost.

FORTY EIGHT

Disheartened and anxious, Melanie trudged back to her office to find Detective Pauline Estrada still there, on the telephone, with a worried look on her face.

"I'm on endless hold," Pauline announced, "but have I got news for you."

"I've got news, too. *Bad* news. We lost the bail hearing."

"You're kidding."

"Nope. The judge let Welch out on home confinement. He has to wear an ankle bracelet. That's the thing that Martha Stewart bragged on national television that she knew how to take off."

"Don't get upset."

"Don't get upset? Pauline, if I'm lucky, when he breaks out of his apartment, a little bell will sound in an office somewhere, so that when they fish my body out of the East River, some bureaucrat will go, 'Oh, that's what that noise was.' "

"Not that this is going to make you feel any better," Pauline said, "but Welch isn't the only guy you should be worrying about."

"Why do you say that?"

"While you were gone, a couple of agents stopped by to deliver copies of a file from your search yesterday," Pauline said.

"Agents Waterman and Mills?"

"Sounds right. Anyway, I was sitting here with nothing better to do, and I knew the file was about Welch, so I sneaked a peek. Hope that was okay."

"An extra pair of eyes in a case like this is a blessing, Pauline. What'd you find out?" Melanie asked.

"Nothing you wouldn't have found yourself the second you read my file on the Tulsa boys'-home arson. The man convicted for the Cheryl Driscoll murder, do you remember his name?"

"Sure. Edward Allen Harvey. I was thinking I should fly out to California and interview him. Ha, in all my spare time."

Pauline pointed at the telephone she held against his ear. "I'm on hold with Pelican Bay right now."

"Pelican Bay?"

"The maximum security facility in Northern California where Harvey was doing a fifteen-to-life bid."

"Was?" Melanie asked, with a sinking feeling.

"Harvey was released four weeks ago. Fifteen years doesn't equal fifteen years when you subtract out good time and so forth."

"Where is he now?"

"That's what I'm trying to find out. They're supposed to know. He was convicted of a sex crime. Second-degree murder and sexual assault. That means he was required to register as a sex offender and give notice of his address."

"Did he?"

Pauline shrugged and gestured hopelessly at the phone.

"Why am I getting a bad feeling about this?" Melanie asked.

"Because you have good instincts," Pauline said. "The second I saw Harvey's name, I made the connection. Edward Allen Harvey was one of the delinquents who absconded after the arson at the boys' home. The news accounts said that he was the biggest trouble-maker in the place, too, the one they suspected of killing the boy and setting the fire."

"Harvey had two rape convictions before he was ever arrested on the Driscoll murder," Melanie said. "And we have signature mutilations in the two murders. Carving a nasty word on the victim's stomach is a highly unusual move. We're looking at the same killer. Or *killers.* I knew that as soon as I read about the Driscoll case. The only difference is, I was thinking it was Welch. But maybe it was Welch and Harvey together."

Pauline held up her finger and sat up straighter in her chair. "Here we go! Yes, hello, I'm still here . . . Huh, really? . . . What do you normally do in a case like that?. . . . I see. Well, pardon my French, but that sucks."

Pauline fell silent while the person on the other end of the line spoke at some length. She took a few notes. At one point, Melanie caught her eye, and Pauline shook her head and made a disappointed face. Finally, she hung up.

"Well?" Melanie asked.

"In the wind. They don't have the first fricking clue where he is. But here's something interesting. You know who visited Harvey in jail the weekend before he was released?" Pauline asked.

"Who?'

"Suzanne Shepard. She must have tracked down the Driscoll case somehow, and come to the same conclusion you did, that Welch was in on it. So she went all the way to California to interview Harvey."

"All she accomplished was attracting their attention. She dug her own grave." Melanie picked up the group photo from the boys' home, which had been lying on her desk. "Which one is Harvey?" she asked.

"Top row, far left."

Melanie looked at the boy in the picture, who was big and blond and moon-faced, and the hair all over her body stood on end. "I've seen him before!" she said.

Pauline gasped. "Oh my God! Where?"

Melanie smacked herself on the forehead. "Shit. I don't know, I don't know." She shook her head. "I just don't know."

FORTY NINE

With two potential killers after her, Melanie suddenly found herself much happier to have Pete Terrozzi's company. She decided not to make a move without his protection, and when she learned that Terrozzi's ex-partner was currently assigned to the home-confinement monitoring division of the United States Marshal's Service, she actually hugged the diminutive deputy. Terrozzi made a couple of phone calls, and pretty soon he'd put Melanie on the line with the guy who was personally handling the Welch case. That deputy, whose name was Curtis Jones, had just come back from Welch's apartment, where he'd fitted and tested Welch's ankle bracelet and the portable tracking unit that went along with it. Not only did the thing work, Jones reported, but it was one of the newfangled bracelets that utilized GPS technology. Light-years ahead of the old models that merely sounded an alarm when the defendant broke confinement. If Welch left his apartment, not only would Jones call Melanie immediately, but he'd be able to inform her of every move that Welch made.

Melanie was relieved to have this inside connection. She just didn't expect to take advantage of it so soon.

Half an hour later, she was sitting in the sixth floor war room digging through the boxes from Target News that Assistant D.A. Janice Marsh had never finished searching. If Suzanne Shepard had interviewed Edward Allen Harvey mere weeks before her murder, Melanie reasoned, maybe there was a chance she'd kept in touch with him. Maybe she'd written down a phone number or an address that could lead them straight to Harvey. Melanie was deeply engrossed in Suzanne's datebook when the war-room phone rang.

"Melanie Vargas."

"Curtis Jones here."

"Hey, Curtis. What's up?" she asked nonchalantly.

"Benedict Welch is on the move. I've got him heading south on Seventh Avenue at a pretty good rate of speed."

It took Melanie a moment to grasp what Curtis was saying. "You mean . . . he left his apartment?"

"Yeah, why do you think I'm calling?"

"I'm shocked. I didn't think he'd actually do it."

"Well, he did. Do you want to know where he's going or not?"

"Yes, of course I do. Let me put you on speaker. Deputy Terrozzi is here."

Terrozzi, who'd been leaning back in a chair reading the sports section, tossed his paper aside.

"Like I said," Jones continued, "I got the man heading south on Seventh, doing around thirty, uh, wait a minute, closer to twenty. Uh, he slowed down. I think he hit traffic. He just crossed Forty-ninth Street. He's picking up speed. Now he stopped. He must've hit a light."

"Are you calling in the FBI?" Melanie asked.

"Not a chance. Prisoner's in U.S. Marshal's custody once he's remanded," Jones said.

"This is our collar," Terrozzi agreed.

"I'll go myself, but I'm waiting for some backup," Jones said. "We're short-staffed today."

"How long will that be?" Melanie asked anxiously.

"Not long. Fifteen, twenty minutes. But don't worry, we won't lose him. We got him on the GPS."

Fifteen or twenty minutes was far too long in Melanie's view. "We have reason to believe this man is the Central Park Butcher," she reminded Jones. "You

should get him back in pocket immediately. Think of the consequences if he kills again after escaping from home confinement."

"That *could* be a problem," Jones admitted. "Reflect badly on the U.S. Marshal's Service."

Melanie glared at Terrozzi pointedly. "Deputy Terrozzi can back you up," she said.

"Yeah, no problem. Curtis, I'll come meet you," Terrozzi said.

"He's still stopped. I got him at the same location for the past few minutes. I don't think it's a stoplight. Too long."

They waited until the blip on Jones's computer screen had remained stationary for nearly ten minutes, then agreed that Welch had landed at his destination and would probably be staying there for a while. Melanie wrote down the address.

"I know the spot," Terrozzi said. "I can almost guarantee you this is LaserMania."

"What's that?" Melanie asked.

"It's an arcade and laser tag place right off Times Square," Terrozzi replied

"Oh yeah," Jones said, "a real gangbanger hangout, right?"

"Affirmative. They got shootings in there a lot. You see it in the papers."

"What's laser tag?" Melanie asked.

"It's awesome," Terrozzi said. "You go into this dark room with all your buddies and shoot each other with laser guns."

"Does it hurt?"

Terrozzi snorted with laughter. "Does it hurt! Of course not. You wear these special vests. You shoot each other on the vest, and the hit registers on this digital scorekeeper gizmo. That's how you know who lives and who dies. The team with the most kills after ten minutes wins."

"Why would Welch be going to some laser tag arcade?" Melanie asked.

Terrozzi shrugged. "It's a fun place if you like to shoot people."

"But to break home confinement to do it? That makes no sense. The judge will be forced to remand him now." Melanie stood up. "I guess there's only one way to find out what he's up to. Let's go."

They drove to Times Square. Curtis Jones planned to meet them there with a couple of other deputy U.S. marshals. As they hit Times Square, Melanie leaned sideways to appreciate some of the crazy neon signs, tall as skyscrapers and bright as the sun. This place was a party for the eyes. It was full of glitzy office buildings and well-dressed yuppies now, but still with those Vegas-style lights stretching as far as she could see.

The arcade was on a side street. Terrozzi pulled halfway up on the sidewalk right in front of it and turned off the engine, sticking his police placard in the window. Just as Melanie was about to get out of the car, he stopped her.

"You're staying here," Terrozzi said.

"What? No way."

"If I'd been thinking straight, I wouldn't've let you come this far. You can't go inside. I know this place. Trust me, it's a fricking zoo. Full of people. Dark. Loud noises from all the video games. It's too dangerous, with the killer inside."

"You're supposed to be my protection detail, Pete. You stick to me like glue, remember? You can't leave me here undefended."

Terrozzi reached into a storage compartment between the two front seats and pulled out her Beretta. "Take this. You're not undefended now. I'm going in to find this guy Welch. When Curtis gets here, you show him where to go. You know how to work the radio?"

She looked at it. It was just like the one in Julian Hay's Navigator. "Yes."

"Okay, good. So call somebody if you have a problem, okay? And *don't* follow me inside or I'm gonna have to go up the chain on you. There's nothing I hate more than reporting protectees to their supervisors, but I do it if I'm forced to."

"I won't," she said. "Really. I appreciate everything you're doing for me."

Terrozzi smiled. "Thank you. That's nice to hear."

As Terrozzi disappeared in the direction of the arcade, Melanie put her gun in her handbag and resigned herself to a long, boring wait.

FIFTY

It was a thick summer afternoon in New York City, nearly ninety degrees, and the car heated up quickly. Terrozzi had turned off the engine and taken the keys, and in his rush, hadn't thought to open the windows. Melanie opened her door to let some air in. Sitting parked halfway up on the sidewalk with a police placard in the window and the passenger door wide open, she felt too conspicuous. Not just conspicuous, but nervous. Out in the open. Without protection. The side street hummed with traffic. Blazing sunlight beat down on car windows, so she couldn't see the drivers of the passing vehicles. Melanie told herself not to worry. Welch couldn't hurt her. He was inside, with a federal marshal after him.

Of course, the marshal *was* Pete Terrozzi, not the sharpest knife in the drawer. Curtis Jones and the others from the U.S. Marshal's Service hadn't shown up yet. She pulled her bag onto her lap, keeping one hand on the gun.

Her phone rang, and Melanie jumped.

"Hello?"

"Hey. It's Dan."

"Where have you been?"

"Working. Listen, I got your message. You're absolutely right. I want to talk, too. But that's not why I'm calling."

"Where are you?" she asked. With everything that was going on, she'd nearly forgotten about their fight. She'd forgive him on the spot if he'd come here and protect her. She'd feel a hell of a lot safer with Dan watching out for her than with Pete Terrozzi.

"I'm in Queens," Dan said. "I've been trying to get a lead on this guy Edward Allen Harvey."

"Who told you about Harvey?"

"CODIS told me."

"What?"

"We got the DNA results back. You didn't hear?"

"No."

"The sample taken from under Suzanne's fingernails matched to one Edward Allen Harvey, released four weeks ago from Pelican Bay in California. So I pulled his mug shot, and guess what?"

"What?" Melanie grasped the gun tighter. Her nerves were tingling. If Harvey was the Butcher, what did that mean for Melanie, sitting out here in Terrozzi's car with the door open?

"We already had a picture of him in line at the post office," Dan said. "Big, inbred-looking guy with blond hair and little piggy eyes, remember?"

"I do remember." That must be why, when Pauline Estrada had shown Melanie a picture of Harvey as a teenager, she hadn't quite recognized him. She'd seen the picture from the post office, but in that shot, he'd been twenty-five years older.

"Harvey mailed the box of dog shit to Suzanne Shepard," Dan said. "Harvey's our Butcher. I tracked him to this flophouse in Flushing. I'm in his room right now. He's not here, but it's a goddamn treasure trove. I found a laptop computer with e-mails on it that he sent to Welch."

"Do they prove Harvey and Welch were in on the Suzanne Shepard murder together?" Melanie asked.

"No," Dan said firmly. "From everything I've seen, Harvey acted alone."

"That can't be right," Melanie insisted. "We found Suzanne Shepard's missing driver's license in Welch's desk. And Welch was the one e-mailing me, remember? The tech squad traced the last e-mail to his office."

"*Harvey* e-mailed you from Welch's office. And Harvey planted the driver's license. He's trying to frame Welch. To get back at him for walking on the Cheryl Driscoll murder. Judging by these e-mails, they've known each other for a lot of years and pulled a lot of sick shit together. Welch sedated Cheryl Driscoll and handed her over to Harvey. Then he watched while Harvey raped and murdered her. It pissed Harvey off to no end that he did time for that crime and Welch didn't. He says Welch is gonna pay for covering up his role in that one."

"So where is Harvey now?" Melanie asked. She scanned the crowded street nervously. The man who wanted to torture and kill her *wasn't* inside LaserMania. He was at large. He could be anywhere. He could be right here on this very block.

"Harvey's gone," Dan said. "The night-vision goggles are gone, too, but the stun gun is here, along with rope and handcuffs and a bunch of other tools of his trade. And something else . . . I don't know if I should tell you." He paused. "Your protection detail is with you, right?"

"What did you find, Dan?"

"I don't want to upset you. Listen, put the guy on the phone."

"What guy?"

"Your deputy marshal."

"He's not here. He's inside the laser tag place, looking for Welch."

"Inside where?"

"LaserMania. In Times Square. Welch broke confinement, and we came to look for him."

"I don't like that place. It attracts scumbags in droves."

"Don't worry. I've been waiting outside in the car. Terrozzi went in without me."

"That doesn't make me happy, either, sweetheart. Welch isn't the Butcher. Harvey is. You're in danger just sitting there. Call your marshal right away and have him come out and get you."

"Okay."

"Do it now."

"I will. But, Dan, what did you *find*? You have to tell me."

"Polaroids. Of you. He's been following you."

"We knew that." She tried to sound calm, but her heart thudded sickeningly.

"You call that marshal right this second, understand?"

"Yes."

"I'm coming over there myself, but I'm out in Queens. It could take a while. You hang up and make that call."

"I will. I'm doing it right this second."

FIFTY ONE

As soon as she broke the connection to Dan, Melanie felt vulnerable, and very alone. With trembling fingers, she dialed Pete Terrozzi's cell phone. It rang once and rolled over to voice mail. She hung up and dialed again, breathing faster. Same result. Had Terrozzi turned his phone off? Was it getting no reception?

Melanie got out of the car and slammed the door. She had no choice but to go inside and find him. LaserMania's enormous neon sign boasted a half-naked woman with big boobs in thigh-high boots shooting what appeared to be a machine gun. Gold coins spurted from the gun in a steady stream, forming an arrow that pointed directly at the entrance. She ran for it, nervous about being exposed on the street, hoping to find protection inside. A bunch of guys with fade hair-cuts and gang tattoos hung around the door. They eyed Melanie with cool indifference and moved aside so she could pass. The panic in her face was nothing to them. They'd seen women running like that before.

Inside the door, a black rubber staircase led straight down for several flights, the walls and ceiling sur-rounding it painted a dead black. After the bright sun-shine and vivid neon outside, Melanie could barely see. She plunged down, praying not to fall. In the basement arcade, light blazed everywhere, assaulting her vision. Video-game pods and slot machines flashed like fire-crackers, making carnival noises and spitting out long strands of yellow tickets. The games had ten-foot-high TV screens, and guns and wands bristling from them. A hip-hop kid whirled around, pointing a silver pistol at her, and Melanie jumped.

"I could have shot you!" she shouted. He saw the Beretta in her hand and his eyes widened.

She put her gun away. It was more of a danger than a help in here. There were kids around. She pulled out her phone to try Terrozzi again. But she was deep un-derground, in a subbasement. There was no reception. That's why he hadn't answered.

The place was jammed. Groups of men and boys clus-tered around every machine, a weird mix of gangbangers and private school kids in blazers and ties. Between the low ceiling, the soaring machines, and the pulsating crowd, Melanie couldn't see more than a few feet in any direction. A wild clanging of bells and buzzers rang out all around her, making it impossible to hear any sound originating more than a foot or two away. How would she ever find her people in this chaos? She walked forward as calmly as she could manage, looking into each face she passed. But in the lurid, smoky light, all the players melded together into a swirling mob. After a few minutes, she came to a driving game dominated by a life-size replica of a Harley-Davidson, and realized that she'd passed it once before. She must have made a wrong turn. The space was so confusing and mazelike, and each part of it looked so much like the next. She was disoriented, with no sense of which direction she should walk to get back to the entrance. Full-fledged panic set in, and Melanie started to run. She immediately body-slammed into a guy in a wife-beater and baggy jeans who must've weighed at least three hundred pounds.

"Watch it!"

"Sorry!" Melanie cried.

Something caught her attention out of the corner of her eye. Finally! She'd recognize that dark head stubble anywhere. Pete Terrozzi was sitting in a chair in front of a game called Wild Wild West, his back to her. What the hell was he doing playing some cowboy shoot-'em-up thing at a time like this? But as Melanie approached, she realized with a horrible sinking in her stomach that something was very wrong. Terrozzi wasn't playing. He sat utterly still, his body at an odd angle, the screen before him flashing INSERT TOKENS NOW.

Melanie came equal with the back of the machine and rounded it. She gasped as she saw the staring eyes and the slick purple blood oozing down the front of Terrozzi's light blue dress shirt. All around her, people shouted and laughed and argued, not even aware that a man sat here with his life snuffed out, a man she'd known. Pete Terrozzi had been knifed to death mere inches from them and they hadn't even noticed, let alone helped. Had Welch killed him to avoid arrest? But why? Riveted by the horrific sight of Terrozzi's dead body, Melanie was having trouble thinking clearly. What could this mean? Was Welch the Butcher after all?

She needed to get help. Melanie turned around, looking for signs, but nothing was marked. She couldn't tell where the exits were, or which direction she'd come from. She turned back toward Terrozzi, and then she saw him.

Edward Harvey was a big man, and he stood out in
the crowd. He was heading for her slowly, taking his
time, a sadistic smile spreading across his moon face.
He was holding something up. He was showing her
something, displaying it to her. It was a small black
gym bag. He unzipped it, reached inside. Was he going
to shoot her? Her gun, her gun, she made herself reach
for her gun. But her eyes were riveted on that gym bag.
As she watched in mute horror, he pulled something
out, and it wasn't a weapon. Melanie opened her mouth
to scream, but she was too stunned to make a sound.
Harvey held up a man's foot and the lower part of a
leg. Bloody. The shoe still on. With a black contraption
around the ankle. Welch's GPS tracking bracelet, still
attached to his ankle, which was no longer attached to
Welch's body. Harvey had Welch's foot. And he was
laughing.

Benedict Welch, Cory Nash, whatever his name
was—he'd never been here at all. This whole thing was
a trap, and they'd walked right into it.

Melanie didn't know where the exit was, so she just
turned in the opposite direction and ran, pulling out
her gun as she went. The entrance to the laser tag
room was ten feet away, marked by a flashing sign. A
bunch of prep school kids milled around the doorway,

laughing and pummeling one another as they strapped on big Day-Glo-orange vests with blinking red lights on them. She blitzed right past them. Inside, the room was pitch dark, suffused with the eerie purple glow of a black light. It felt like a black hole in outer space. All around her, she saw the outlines of bodies moving stealthily, carrying big laser guns. There must have been ten or fifteen people in the room, but she couldn't see their faces.

She lowered her gun. It would be unsafe to fire in here. She'd be sure of nothing except hitting the wrong person, a kid probably. Nearby, somebody was breathing heavily through his mouth. Next to him, Melanie heard muffled giggles. The room was purposely filled with objects ideal for hiding behind—half walls and pylons and strangely shaped plastic constructs, most taller than her head, all glowing in eerie colors. Right beside her, a burst of red laser suddenly spurted from somebody's gun, and Melanie screamed.

"Awesome! I killed Porter," somebody shouted.

"Who screamed?"

"You did, you pansy."

Melanie retreated behind a big pylon and peeked out, her breath coming hard and fast. In the blackness, all she saw were the vests. When they got hit with a laser, their digital displays lit up red and showed the score. But the players' heads and arms, the color of their hair or clothing, and everything else about them faded to a weird empty black. Melanie realized that Harvey would not be wearing a vest. Why would he? He wasn't here to play. If his clothes were dark, he'd fade into nothingness, become completely invisible. In the heat of the chase, she'd run in here, and now he had her cornered. She needed to get by him, get out, go to the front desk, call the police. Have them surround the place and turn on all the lights.

Melanie steeled herself and stepped out from behind her pylon. She could see the door across the room, lit up and glowing. She headed for it, moving carefully, trying to reach out with her senses and feel where the people were. She was making good progress. She was feeling confident that she'd get there. It was so dark in here. If she couldn't see him, he wouldn't be able to see her, either.

But wait—the night-vision goggles. Dan had said they weren't in the apartment.

The next second, somebody tall and broad stepped out in front of her, and she stopped short.

"You're smaller than I thought. I like that," a voice said. A man's voice, low, guttural, slow, and cruel, with the remnant of an Oklahoma twang. Then he laughed. "Lotta good your little friend did you. Fucking twerp.

Who'd you think you were dealing with? You underes-
timated me, you bitch. I'm gonna do you right in here.
By the time they find you, I'll be halfway to Canada."

Melanie backed away, opening her mouth to scream,
but she wasn't fast enough. He punched her hard in the
stomach. *No mercy, he has no mercy,* she thought, flying backward through the air. *Mercy is for the weak;
who said that?* She heard her own cry as if from far
away. Then she was flat on her back on the carpet, no
air in her lungs. She struggled to a sitting position,
tasting something foul in her mouth, her insides feeling
like they'd been split open. Her gun had been knocked
from her hands. She felt around on the floor and found
it. The air above her went black as he bent over her.
She saw a purple glint of neon on metal. He had a knife
in his hand. Melanie pulled the trigger. He grunted in
pain and stumbled backward.

"You shot me!" he said, in disbelief.

He might be able to talk, and she thought he was
still standing, but she could tell by the movement of
the dark shape above her that she'd hit him bad enough
to stagger him.

"What was that? Did you hear that?" a boy's voice
said.

Some of the kids in the room had heard the shot.
Their movements became panicky. Melanie could feel

the air moving as they circulated all around her. She was losing her nerve. How could she fire again in this crowded place? She was a mother. She couldn't risk hurting somebody's child.

"Call the police!" she shouted. "There's a man in here with a *real* gun."

She leaped to her feet, and on the way up she felt a whoosh of air and saw the shine of a metal-toed boot as it came sailing toward her head. Her hands flew out instinctively to deflect the blow, but something hit her from behind instead. Something heavy and soft with flailing limbs. A boy, a teenager, had been running and had tripped over her. They both went down hard. She struggled to get out from under him. A scream reverberated in the darkness, but it wasn't her own. Whoever he was, he'd taken the kick instead.

"Aagh! I think my leg's broken!" the boy cried out.

"Chris? Where are you?"

"Make them stop the game!"

In the darkness and amid the cries of pain, Melanie could tell Harvey was on his feet and preparing for his next attack. She made out his arm as it raised up in a perfect arc. She saw the glint of a long, curving blade. In an instant, it would plunge, aiming for her but perhaps striking the boy on top of her instead. In a savage burst of strength, Melanie shoved the moaning kid in one direction with all her might and threw her body in the other. They rolled apart just as the knife came down.

"Aaagh!" Harvey shouted as he thrust downward.

Momentum took him, and he catapulted to the ground. From his grunts, she could tell he was in pain. Where had her bullet hit him? Why didn't he just die? Melanie got to her knees and aimed her gun, finger on the trigger. But from right beside Harvey, she heard the teen crying in fear. It was just too dark. If she fired, she could end up killing an innocent boy instead.

"Stay down! I've got a gun on you!" she yelled.

She could sense, but not see, Harvey moving.

"Stay down, I said."

In the darkness, he laughed, and the sound came from directly behind her. She whirled around. Where was he? How had he moved without her knowing?

"You can't see me, but I can see you," he whispered, so close she could almost feel his breath.

Melanie squeezed the trigger, and the gun kicked in her hand. Suddenly the room's emergency lights flashed on. She looked up to see a man wearing night-vision goggles brandishing a knife in one hand and clutching his stomach with the other. He must've thought she wouldn't fire, but she'd hit him good this time. She couldn't believe he was still standing. She got ready to fire again. But the next second, the side of his head exploded, spattering blood over her, as the sound of a single, far more powerful gunshot rang out, and Edward Allen Harvey collapsed to the floor.

FIFTY TWO

Melanie spent the next couple of days curled up in bed, not sleeping, haunted by the memory of Pete Terrozzi's vacant stare and Edward Harvey's hot blood spraying over her. Dan came by, but she wasn't ready to see him. Not today. He sent a message through Melanie's mother that Edward Allen Harvey was dead, shot by the police Dan had called in for her. That news brought Melanie great relief. He'd've gotten a life sentence, but even then, Melanie would have spent the rest of her days worrying that he'd escape somehow and come after her again. This way, she could be certain Harvey would never harm anyone. Cory Nash, aka Benedict Welch, had been found stabbed to death in his apartment, his right foot severed above the ankle. Melanie would carry around forever the horrific image of Harvey coming for her with the foot in his hand.

Charlie Shepard left Melanie a tearful voice mail thanking her for getting the man who'd killed his mother. Melanie believed that justice had been served, but it would be an overstatement to say she was happy about it. Seeing even a bloodthirsty killer die before your eyes was a terrible thing.

Dan brought her beautiful flowers, which her mother put in a vase beside her bed.

"You should give that boy another chance," Carol said. "I can see in his eyes that he loves you."

On Friday, Melanie got dressed and dragged herself to work. Peter Terrozzi's funeral was scheduled for late that afternoon, and she intended to be there. She'd stop by the office first and go through her in-box.

Melanie was considering the idea of resigning and getting a normal job. Apparently, others had anticipated this possibility. Fifteen minutes after she arrived, Mark Sonschein and Susan Charlton marched into her office.

"At least you didn't bring coffee," Melanie joked weakly, gesturing at the four cups sitting on her desk, already provided by concerned colleagues. She loved that about this office. Starbucks was the standard gift in moments of crisis, a latte left with no attribution and no thanks expected. She did have one note with a name signed to it, one that made her particularly happy. A card from Joe Williams, apologizing for blaming her for his father's political downfall, and asking if they could have lunch to set things straight.

"You'll want all that caffeine when you see what we brought," Susan said, smiling, her cheeks pink with the glow of good health.

Mark placed a thick black three-ring binder on the desk in front of her.

"What's this?" Melanie asked.

"Your supervisor's manual," he said. "I hope you read fast. In case you didn't know, you've been acting deputy chief of Major Crimes for three days now."

Melanie laughed, which made her ribs hurt where Harvey had punched her. "Oh, my! I hope I didn't authorize anything I shouldn't have."

"Nope, only good arrests and reasonable plea bargains," Mark said. "And keep up the hard work, because I see a bright future ahead of you."

"Thanks, guys. Really, I'm honored. This is something I've always wanted. But it comes at a terrible time. I'm not sure I'm up for it, after everything that happened."

"See, what did I tell you?" Mark said to Susan with mock indignation. "The girl won't give up the glory. I spend my days stuck in endless meetings on the Clyde

Williams leak, and she gets to go out and play cops and robbers. But when I ask her to share the burden of a desk job, she refuses."

"Mel goes for the gusto," Susan said.

"So be honest," Mark said in a more serious tone. "Have you drafted your resignation letter yet?"

"I've been thinking about it."

"I can't say I blame you. From everything I heard, you went through some awful stuff on Monday. And Susan tells me you've had a stressful year on a personal level, too."

"The big D," Melanie said.

"Divorce. That's huge. I must say, you have an admirable work ethic in light of it all," Mark said.

"Thanks."

"If anybody should stay in the fight, it's you," Mark said. "You're the whole package. You have the brains, you have the guts, you have the charisma in court. Do you know how few people in this office I can say that about? Susan, maybe. But not myself, certainly, and not many others. We live in dangerous times. We need talented people like you in this job."

"That was a beautiful speech, Sonschein," Susan said. "My favorite part was where you admit you don't have the right stuff."

"He's modest," Melanie said with a smile.

"I'm a bulldog in court, but I'm not likable," Mark said.

"*I* certainly don't like you," Susan said, her eyes merry.

"But, Vargas, seriously, what would do if you left the office?" Mark asked. "Criminal defense? I don't see it. You're no turncoat."

"Never. Corporate, maybe," Melanie said.

"Corporate work," Susan said, making a face. "Ugh, shoot me. Books and papers. No cops. No bad guys. You never see the inside of a courtroom. My idea of a good document is a scrap of paper in a guy's pocket that says *Flaco, fifty kilos.* No accountants' records for me. No thank you."

In her heart of hearts, Melanie felt exactly the same way. Even after what had happened, maybe especially after, she loved her job with a passion. A passion so powerful she'd hardly ever felt it for a person. Maya, yes . . . And Dan. The job was intensely difficult, but deep down, she'd rather have her life be interesting than easy.

"The job really takes it toll," she said aloud.

"Sure, of course, we all know that, and something needs to be done to relieve the pressure on you," Mark said. He pulled a piece of paper from his breast pocket and smoothed it open. "I took the liberty of ordering a statement of your accrued leave. Do you realize you have five use-or-lose days? Add weekends on both ends and you could get away for nine. I would strongly urge you to take a vacation before making any big decisions about your future. We'll cover for you here."

"I really appreciate the concern, but—"

"We think very highly of you, Melanie," Mark interrupted. "I personally think very highly of you. Bernadette has never backed you the way she should. She doesn't watch out for her subordinates. She'd rather have people under her thumb than create potential rivals by helping them succeed. And I can promise you Bernadette won't feel any more generous toward you once she learns Shekeya Jenkins is getting promoted and that you were one of three prosecutors who recommended her."

"That's great news. Shekeya will make a fine paralegal," Melanie said.

"Great news for Shekeya, not for Bernadette. But don't you worry about a thing. I'm in your corner from now on. I'll protect you. I'll also make things happen for you. You have my word."

"That goes double for me," Susan said. "I told you how I felt last week. This ain't no song and dance, Mel.

Mark and I are behind you in a big way, and we count for a lot in this office. Stick around, fight the good fight with us. We'll accomplish great things."

"So what do you say?" Mark asked.

Melanie looked into their faces and saw people she could trust. They were not without their complications, these two, but they were honest and committed, and genuine public servants. They were colleagues to spend a career with.

"I'm grateful. More than that, I'm touched. And I promise to give your proposal the serious consideration it deserves."

FIFTY THREE

Dan drove Melanie to Peter Terrozzi's funeral. When she cried, he put his arm around her, and she leaned into him, grateful for the comfort of his strong presence. It was Dan's second funeral in two days, since he'd attended Seamus Fields's the day before. Melanie appreciated his coming, especially because he hadn't known Terrozzi.

Afterward, Dan asked if she was hungry. For the first time in days, she had an appetite, and he took her to a romantic little Italian place in Brooklyn with tablecloths and candles. They ordered a bottle of Chianti and talked about work for a while. After the second glass of wine, Dan took Melanie's hand.

"You and me have some other things to talk about," he said, holding her gaze with those baby blues.

"I know," she said, sighing. "We should talk."

Dan laughed. "Here I am, the strong and silent type begging to talk, and Miss Bare Your Soul here acts like I'm asking her to get a tooth drilled."

"It's just, we were having such a nice dinner."

"And you're worried this will ruin it? What could we have to say that would be so bad?" Dan asked.

"A lot of things. What's going on with you and Diane? Why have you never introduced me to your parents? What's in our future? All those questions seem hard to me. But sitting with you in this restaurant, looking at your face, hearing your voice, that feels good."

"Live for the moment," he said.

"Yeah, sort of."

"Normally, I'd be all for that. But I almost lost you the other day. Standing outside LaserMania when the SWAT guys went in, when I couldn't find you? It hit me, I'm dependent on you. Couldn't get along without you in my life. I'm a guy who hates to be dependent on anything, but here I am dependent on Melanie Vargas."

"You make it sound like some disease."

"It's not a disease," Dan said. "It's love. I love you."

"I love you, too," she said, as if it were the most natural thing in the world.

"Looking back on it, the fight we had was bound to happen," Dan said. "People hit those bumps in the road when they start getting serious, sweetheart. You freaked out. I freaked out. Totally normal."

"I was worried that you still had feelings for Diane," Melanie said.

"You were right to be upset. Not because I have feelings for her, but because the way I behaved was wrong. Having dinner with Diane meant nothing, swear to God, but I should never have done it without talking to you first. Not with your history. I've been cheated on, and I've been left. I should have known better, and I apologize."

"Thank you," Melanie said, her eyes misting up for a second. She couldn't have asked for a sweeter apology. "But—I have to ask. You *don't* still have feelings for her, do you?"

"I won't lie. Diane looms large in my past. But what do I actually feel for her now? Nostalgia, maybe. Regret. Anger. Any lust? No, I can honestly say I'm over her for good. Love? Never. Love is only for you." He squeezed her fingers.

"But then, why didn't you tell me? I want to understand, so I can feel confident that it won't happen again."

"Let me explain something. This relationship we've got, it's new for me. I'm still learning. The example my parents set growing up wasn't something you'd want to imitate. My old man worked himself bitter. He'd come home late and retreat to the den with his bottle. As for my mother, after P.J. died—he was her favorite—she didn't have any use for the rest of us. She spent all her time in church. I never saw them talk, let alone show any affection for each other. That's what I knew when I married Diane. And Diane—she was a cop's daughter. I could disappear for days at a time working a case, and she'd never ask where I was. If she got pissed about how much I was gone, she'd go sleep with some other guy instead of yelling at me. I'm not saying that's good, but it's what I was used to. I've never been much for talking, or for having a woman looking over my shoulder, and that's why I got upset when you questioned me about Diane. I thought, hey, this chick is fencing me in. I have my pride. But that lasted about as long as it took to realize I'd hurt you. Then I felt like shit, and all I wanted was for us to make up. You've changed me, see, and I think I could change more. I think I could even get good at talking. Anyway, I have no choice."

"Why not?"

"You know me. I'm a homebody at heart. I imagine being married. Having kids, taking care of the yard. Sharing the couch and watching a little TV on a Saturday night. That what I want. Now that I've been with you, I'm ruined for anybody else. You're it. So I guess I'm gonna have to keep on talking."

"And you're okay with that?" Melanie asked.

He grinned. "Strange, but I am. I'm actually having fun right now."

"Me, too," Melanie said.

"Satisfied?" Dan asked.

"Yes. This was good, and I feel like we're done for now. I don't need to know what happens in the end."

"Oh, I can tell you how it ends," Dan said. "You really want to know?"

Melanie took a sip of wine. "Nah. Too serious for a Friday night. I'm on a campaign to lighten up and relax."

"How's this for now? You and me sitting by a pool, sipping piña coladas."

"Mmm, sounds good. You know, Mark Sonschein told me to take a vacation."

"And he's the big boss. Count me in," Dan said.

"There's only one problem. I can't leave Maya for that long."

"Who said anything about leaving her? You know where I've always wanted to go my whole life, but never had the chance?"

"Where?" Melanie asked.

"Disney. What do you say we take cutie, hit the Magic Kingdom in the morning. Then do the pool and the drinks with umbrellas in 'em in the afternoon."

"That would be great. Sounds expensive, though."

"What the hell, sweetheart. I've got a Visa card, and I'm not afraid to use it."